MIND GAMES

RICHARD THIEME

What the Critics Say

"Richard Thieme takes us to the edge of cliffs we know are there but rarely visit. He wonderfully weaves life, mystery, and passion through digital and natural worlds with creativity and imagination." – Clint C. Brooks, former Senior Advisor for Homeland Security and Assistant Deputy Director, NSA

"In his writing and speeches, Thieme has never let me down. Always informative, relevant, unpredictable and thoroughly entertaining.... One of the great thinkers of the cyber-world." – Larry Greenblatt, InterNetwork Defense

"Buy this book!" – Robert Morris, Sr. Chief Scientist, NSA (ret), holding up *Islands in the Clickstream* at the Black Hat Briefings

"Richard Thieme has been an inspiration for a decade. He is one of those few people that plant a seed in you for a new way of thinking. He shines light on areas you never knew were there and helps people reinvent their capability for seeing what was always there but untouched. As an artist of words and ideas, he brings thoughts to life and creates parallel worlds. Richard teaches experts to see with "beginner's eyes" and hackers to think like philosophers." – Sol Tzvi, Founder and CEO, Genieo Innovation Ltd., Israel

"Your writing makes me discover life again and again." – Correspondent, Central Intelligence and Security Agency, Suriname

"Thieme's clarity of thinking is refreshing, and his insights are profound." – Bruce Schneier, security technologist and author.

"Richard Thieme explores and breaks down the intersections between technology, politics, society and humanity. With Richard, there is no spoon." – Simple Nomad

"You are among my teachers, an actual presence here in this digital archipelago." – Michael Joyce, Vassar College, author of *Afternoon* and other hypertext fiction

"Thieme is truly an oracle for digital generations." – Kim Zetter, frequent contributor to *Wired*

"Some of the most penetrating commentary of our times." – Peter Russell, author, *From Science to God*

MIND GAMES

RICHARD THIEME

Title typeface is Critica Grafica; text set in Palatino Linotype and Century Gothic.

ISBN: 978-0-938326-24-3

Duncan Long Publications
2908 Gary Ave.
Manhattan, KS 66502 USA

"Zero Day: Roswell" originally in *Porcupine* (Vol. 10, Issue 1: 2006); republished in *Zahir* (Fall/Winter 2008).

"Incident at Wolf Cove" originally in *The Puckerbrush Review* (Summer/Fall 2004)

"Break, Memory" originally in *Phrack* (July 2004); republished in *Bewildering Stories Third Quarterly Review* 2008 (www.bewilderingstories.com/anthologies/297-307_antho1.html)

"The Geometry of Near" originally in *Phrack* (July 2004); republished in *CyberTales: Live Wire,* Arthur Sanchez and Jean Goldstrom, editors (Whortleberry Press: 2005)

"The Man who Hadn't Disappeared" originally in *Karamu* (Spring 2008); nominated for Pushcart Prize

"The Indian and the Fortune Teller" adapted from a novel-in progress, *Multiple Connected Spaces*; originally published in *Zahir* (Summer 2009)

"Northward into the Night" originally in *The Ranfurly Review* (www.ranfurly-review.co.uk/ September 2009)

"Less Than the Sum of the Movable Parts" originally in *The Future Fire* (futurefire.net/2008.14/fiction/lessthanthesum.html); republished in *Bewildering Stories* (www.bewilderingstories.com/issue 330)

"Species, Lost in Apple-eating Time" originally in *anotherealm* (anotherealm.com 1999)

"More Than a Dream" originally in Nth Degree (www.nthzine.com: August 2006)

"It's Relative" originally in *The Listening Eye* (Kent State – Geauga: 2005)

"The Riverrun Dummy" originally in *Zahir* (Spring 2005)

"Gibby the Sit-down King" originally in *Timber Creek Review* (Summer 2005); nominated for Pushcart Prize

"Scout's Honor" originally in *Timber Creek Review* (Summer 2004); republished in *Ascent* (August 2005)

"Silent Emergent, Doubly Dark" originally in *Subtle Edens* (Elastic Press: London. November 2008)

"The Last Science Fiction Story" originally in *Pacific Coast Journal* (Spring 2006); republished in *The Circle Magazine* (Winter 2006)

"SETI Triumphant" originally in *Analog* (October 2006)

"Pleasant Journey" originally in *Analog* (November 1963)

DEDICATION

These stories are for Avery, Ember, Montgomery, Luca, Max, Amy, Jonah, Cicada, Z'ev and Noel in the world they will inhabit – a trans-planetary society of self-engineering gene mods and ubiquitous always-on psychic connectivity.

Contents

Introduction to "Zero Day: Roswell"

A friend who used to do analysis for the NSA called after reading "Zero Day: Roswell." He laughed and laughed. "It reminds me of *Three Days of the Condor*," he said, "the Robert Redford movie about the CIA analyst who read fiction to find out what was going on.

"Ninety-five percent of your story isn't fiction," he said. "But you have to know which 95% to have the key to the code."

He exaggerated, of course. It wasn't quite 95%.

His comment touched on my motivation for writing some of these stories in the first place. Another friend, a veteran journalist with decades of experience chasing black budget aviation and space technology stories, said I would be dismembered if I tried to speak about the things we discussed explicitly. As if they were simply true.

"I've come to believe that if you really want to influence society," he said, "you should use fiction or entertainment. You have much more impact. Your book can be influential but if there is one flaw that someone picks up, your credibility is shot. Pitch it as fiction from day one and people will drop their BS threshold and say, well I am just being entertained. Then the subconscious mind is shaped and the way they perceive things is altered.

"A Hollywood director told me," he continued, "he can say anything he wanted and it's all just mind candy.' People can't criticize you for that. If they go after you the way they did Gary Webb [we had discussed the hatchet job done by the CIA and newspapers on the reporter who exposed some of the overlap between drug trafficking and the agency, destroying his career and adding to pressures that led to his suicide], you just chuckle and say, that's good; it will sell my book. Just say it's entertainment and they cannot damage your credibility. That drives spooks crazy. They can call you crazy all they want. It scared a lot of people when Clancy started to write. He's been accused of using classified material but he said no, it's open source and I just talk to people and – if it's a reasonable plot, it can be very close to home, but it's just a coincidence."

"Zero Day: Roswell" also includes the full text of my shortest speech. I was having coffee outdoors at Stone Creek Coffee Shop on a warm spring day, the dark chocolate bits at the bottom of the latte just right, and struck up a conversation with a guy in the course of which I said I was a professional speaker. He asked about my speeches.

"I'll give you my shortest one," I said.

I paused for effect. Then said:

"Nothing is what it seems."

He waited. But that was it.

"That'll be twelve dollars," I added. "Since leaving a salaried position, I have to charge *a la carte*."

He laughed. He thought I was kidding.

Oh yes... the disclaimer.

Any similarity between the material in this story and anything real, anything at all, is purely coincidental.

ZeroDay: Roswell

I used to think that death bed revelations were nonsense. I knew lots of guys who kept their vows to the last breath. Some even spread disinformation as they died under torture. Intelligence professionals have discipline that sticks, most of the time.

I was sure that I did too.

Then I got the diagnosis. Cancer, inoperable. All through the gut. Stomach, liver, the intestines.

As if I couldn't guess.

Luckily we manage pain well these days.

I feel as much as I want to feel. The pain reminds me that my life is nearly over. I don't want to forget that. A morphine haze reduces the urgency I need to make myself tell the truth. If I find myself drifting into a fog, dreaming about something in my non-existent future, I ease up on the meds until I vomit, bent double and clutching my gut, then take pills until I'm coherent again but can still remember that I only have a day or two left.

I am writing to three of you (you each know why and do not need to know the identity of the others) and sending one copy to a writer who will know how to use this information. He is not one of the usual suspects, not a name you would know, certainly not one of the useful idiots we use to spread disinformation. (We have

more reporters in our stable than stars in the sky. And they say that two sources validate a story!) I am giving it to a man who understands that fiction is the only way to tell the truth.

I am also giving the story to a blogger, but just one. So real gold will be buried on the Net like the dwarf did in that fairy tale. (That's an inside joke. You'll understand in a minute.)

You remember the fairy tale, right? A guy forced a dwarf to tell him where gold was buried in a forest? But he didn't have a shovel? So he tied a scarf around the tree and went to get one after making the dwarf swear he wouldn't untie it? But while he was gone, the dwarf tied scarves around all of the trees?

So one blog, at least, will have it right.

My God but this pain is intense. With each wave, more of the contents of my life tumble into the darkness. I feel pieces of myself fall away with every breath. Memory modules disconnect and disappear—so many stories, so much distortion, so many lies. I don't even know what's true anymore.

I have been instrumental in building the false history that you live in, that you believe. I created false points of reference to anchor your beliefs. You have been wandering in a mist, thinking the sun was shining brightly. I confused the darkness for the sunlight, too. Is that any consolation? Maybe that's why I want to tell you the truth about Roswell. I just want to shed a little real light before I die.

The human condition is hard enough, what with death mincing our memories, shredding the fabric of our shared mythical history. Many events leave no record at all. Orders were whispered and once they were carried out, the deed never happened. Most real history disappears. (I knew Helms, for God's sake, long before he died.) The narratives that remain are often bound together with glue to create illusions, but over time, even those lose the ability to stick. Things fall apart.

Nothing is what it seems.

Working in the intelligence community all my life, I know how most nodes, the keys that unlock the real stories, are hidden or were altered to blend in with an acceptable narrative, the consensus reality in which you live. Without a point of reference, don't you see, you can't know what you don't know. But the points of reference are hidden on other planes in some kind of complex non-Euclidean space. Most of us Masters know some but not all, a few of us know most. Those nodes require keys to a code, but even if you had them, they would lead you into a cul-de-sac. The solutions to the puzzles are always layered, and to see it whole, you would have to go through a portal into hyper-dimensional space and turn around and see how everything looks from there.

Enigma is one example. There are many more.

Before it was known that the Allies cracked the German code, everything written about the war, about Churchill, what he knew when, what FDR might know, was written from a false point of reference. Once historians knew that he knew what he knew and when, everything shifted, the entire context of how you humplings knew your own history shifted. History not only looked different, history *was* different. What you thought you had lived was seen in a parallax view. It makes you dizzy to realize this, I know, so you recoil into a saner, more comfortable place. It is going to take energy for you to listen to what I am saying.

But please do listen. Please, you who for a moment are free of pain and live in the light and think the darkness will not win. That's one of the myths you celebrate in story and song. But I am already fluctuating between the fading light and the immense waiting darkness and I can see that the darkness does win. It does. So please, please listen.

I am going to alter your beliefs. However disingenuous I may sometimes seem, I want to bequeath to you humplings the little bit of the bigger truth that I still have.

Oh? You're not familiar with that term, humplings?

Let's say that humanity makes up a bell curve and it looks like an animal, OK? It has a snout, a big hump and a tail. Ten per cent live in the nose. Ten per cent live in the tail. Up front are the Masters who manage reality. That's us. Back in the tail are the dregs. They're benchmarks that humplings use to tell themselves they're doing fine. That's why we keep them. The eighty per cent that live in the hump—that's the humplings. That's you. You inch along inside a shared consensus like a huge worm. Your world is defined by things that are real but they're contextualized by those points of reference I mentioned, the ones we provide. The index by which you arrange memories and thoughts, in other words, creates an illusive matrix in which you live but which you never see.

Fish in water. Humplings in a hump.

Since shortly after World War 2, we have managed that hump. We had to, don't you see. Humplings don't know what's best for themselves. Humplings are happiest when kept busy and not quite comfortable. Then you buy things you don't need in pursuit of a peace you will never have. The thirty year mortgage, one of our ideas, was sheer genius. During your potentially dangerous years, it keeps you invested in stability, chasing a dream. Because you want to keep believing what you believe, you're easy to deceive. We use sleight of hand or illusion, and if something leaks, we discredit or ridicule the sources. Then we can hide it in plain sight. Everyone swears it isn't there and walks all around it.

We Masters make history, then hide it. We have put so many people into power, if I were to tell you their names, these political figures around the world we have assisted in different ways, you'd be amazed. The list is long, and the names are distinguished.

But this isn't a primer on the Big Picture. I need to tell you just enough about our work to help you make sense of the Roswell event. But first, you need some new points of reference.

You do want to know, don't you? I mean, ever since you heard that an alien spacecraft might have crashed in the New Mexico desert in 1947, ever since you heard that alien bodies might have been found or that a rancher maybe showed his kid material you couldn't burn or break, ever since you heard of technologies we might have seeded into R&D, giving them to Bell Labs, Xerox Park, RCA, IBM and other friendly household names so alien technologies would become part of the history Americans pretend to have invented–you do want to know how much of that was real, don't you?

Think of how the story came to you in pieces. When did you first hear it? What did you hear? You can't remember, can you? It's all a confabulated blur. Where do you get your information? From television, right? From a joke in a sitcom or on a talk show, from books or movies or reading tabloid headlines while waiting to pay at the supermarket – that's how we do it, slipping it little by little into the known and familiar, using repetition and reinforcement until there's a shared memory. You repeat those falsehoods to each other until they become facts.

You can't change reality, but you can change the facts.

Anyway, the grays that crashed in the desert were not the first.

Aliens had been exploding out of portals for centuries, keeping us under surveillance. Sometimes they landed to check our reactions. Chariots in the skies, visions of angels and saints. Once we were able to see them as machines with people from other places, they altered their strategy, showing themselves but keeping a polite distance until we were used to their presence. Like NORAD telling radar guys to ignore the blips, those are only "visitors" coming down the coast at impossible speeds. It became like walking through pigeons in the park, not even noticing they're there. Some look a lot like us and blend in well, studying our languages and cultures, doing a physical now and then on a "volunteer." They did sophisticated brain scans long before we even knew how electric we were.

Mostly they maintained sentinels until—now, I don't know this for a fact but we believe it's the least unlikely hypothesis—we were on the brink of becoming a Second Level species. Then they paid closer attention.

This is inference, I want to be clear about that. I know why I believe it but I can't tell you. There's too much back story, not all of it verifiable, and anyway, there isn't time. I wish I had started telling the truth sooner.

I was involved plenty but not at the top. Smarter people than me are managing this thing. We relate to one another through a compartmented matrix of need-to-know modules and comprise an elite managerial class. Of course, sometimes we're as bumbling as humplings but we always forgive ourselves quickly. We have developed quite a confident culture after several generations of sanctioned protected malfeasance.

But I digress. (I need to take a pill. Please wait).

OK. Here's an example you ought to be able to understand.

Most of you use the Internet, right? OK, good.

The Internet is a two-edged sword. Like speech or writing or printed words, any symbolic matrix invites projections. We empty the contents of our minds, our souls, even, onto the symbols. We can't help it. We reveal ourselves every time we communicate. The Net sucks everything out of us, good bad and indifferent.

Bad guys use the net too. (We're the good guys, remember; whoever we're fighting is bad.) After Northwoods Two, when the war on terror cranked up and the flow of funds and the fear that fuels it was at a level needed to keep you guys manageable, the evil doers ramped up their use of the Net for all sorts of nefarious purposes. They planned attacks, moved money, communicated with stealth. Their web sites multiplied like roaches.

Now, that fact alone made humplings anxious, just knowing how fast the sites were growing. We amplified your fear by using the "nightly news" to do "in depth" features on terrorist web sites. They would show a few photos with a voiceover that distorted what viewers saw, added a few sound bites, hell, the entire text might be no more than eighty words, all designed to frighten you. Then ads would soothe you and you would go out and buy a ton of stuff.

Some of you, however, quite predictably, became enraged. Fear turns to anger easily, especially in men afraid to feel fear. Then you have to do something to discharge the emotion. If you're a hacker, you'll attack those web sites, thinking you're helping the cause.

But invisible enemies are dangerous. We don't *want* the web sites down. We want them up so we can track who visits, watch what they download, see who talks to who. It's their highway, too, and that way we can track their cars.

So when a well-intentioned humpling defaces or DOSes an enemy web site, we have to go in and put it back up. In the past, we invented anonymizers, built email programs like Hotmail and migrated them into the public domain, made all sorts of honey-pots. Half the attractions out there, the most attractive attractions, we made. We have partnered from the beginning with the big guys, don't you see. We built remote access into the chips, into all the hardware, in fact, even printers, as well as the software that's now a platform for the business of the world. We go into telecom networks at the front door, sniff cables on the ocean floor, have thousands of redundant sensors in space to watch everything. You can't sneak out for a cigarette but that we detect the smoke. We're plugged in at the root, have back doors into most components—we don't even intercept signals much anymore. We just sit back and let the data come to us.

The whole network is metered. If someone uses crypto, it's already cracked, and the fact of its use tells us they've something to hide. We encourage paranoia by planting those stories, then fear makes people predictable, they go on automatic and they're easy to track.

Some of those bad guy sites were a real mess. They didn't have a clue how to write code. We had to do remote administration, install fire walls, close holes, apply patches. Sometimes we kept the holes open, of course. That's how we get in. So when some do-gooder tells the world about a software flaw, we have to get to them right away and tell them to stop. Those holes are useful. You can't exploit a secure Net.

So well-intentioned humplings are a headache. They want to do good, when all we want them to do is nothing. We want them distracted. We don't want partners. We don't need partners. All we need are secrecy and the vast resources of potentates and kings.

Stay with me, now. OK? I'm telling you this so I can show you what the aliens did. This has a point.

It's not easy, I know. Humplings are not used to thinking outside the lines, and it's hard for Americans anyway to understand other cultures. We don't appreciate people who blow themselves up, for example. Even though we do it too. But we make it look different, like something Americans do. Then you don't notice.

After we realized why the grays died in the crash, we experimented with chemicals to make our soldiers ferocious. Nothing worked. They killed each other and everyone in sight, not just enemies. We're getting there, though. Now we know that the fear of death or the fear of anything, really, is a function of protein clusters. Strathin, for example, a protein chain that effaces fear. We're using it to create warriors who will do just about anything. Berserkers, we call them. In the past, we had to wait for their random appearance in a population. Now we make them.

Berserkers are our version of guys willing to commit suicide. We hide the purpose in the concept of a "hero" and send them down a parade route off to war.

The aliens knew how to make grays fearless when we were just learning to store data by making incisions in wet clay. Grays are the little guys with the big heads and big eyes that seem to hypnotize people (it's really a kind of magnetic induction—their brains, like ours, are resonant with energies transmitted in fields, but they're more intentional about it, and of course, their large designer brains do it better).

Anyway, they made grays both with and without fear. The latter we called their suicide crashers, once we knew what they had done. The four small beings found dead or dying at the crash site had volunteered to die for the mission. They made it look like an accident because they knew that our species, barely sentient after a long preparatory sleepwalking sort of ascent, still thinks accidents happen.

The Aliens knew our weapons were getting better, and our propulsion systems, communications, materials science, everything was leapfrogging ahead thanks to our frequent wars. They knew our science and saw that relatively soon, our practice would follow from our theories. We would become dangerous, maybe pose a threat to some of their allies. Even without their help, we would one day learn how to open portals and use them to slip through spacetime. It was implicit in our physics.

They knew we would discover how they went into black holes and came out of white, how they could bunch up spacetime like a rug and bring it from there to here in a snap. They knew we would learn how to negate gravity and use arrays of lasers to create negative energy, then make black holes big enough to exploit.

They decided they would lose little in the long run by accelerating our progress. They sacrificed a pawn to take a queen. They gave us the means of advancing faster along the road we were already traveling in exchange for direct access to our thinking.

Imagine the scene. The hole in the hillside, the remains of the wreckage sticking out, was still smoking. The perimeter had been secured. We had cover stories to give whoever showed up related to whatever clearances they had so they could make sense of what they saw.

It's dark out there in the desert on a moonless night. We didn't have night vision then – that was one of the technologies in the wreckage – and we didn't want to light the place up like Times

Square. Hundreds of workers on hands and knees with lights on their hats like miners scoured the site so everything would be gone by dawn. When they finished they brought in shovels and removed the top layers of contaminated sand, then molded the landscape back so no one could tell.

Two grays were dead on the ground. One was nearly dead. The other was injured but alive.

Our medics were useless. The transparent fluid circulating in their well-machined bodies was beyond our understanding. This is when we still thought that "natural" and "artificial" were meaningful distinctions, remember, that "made" and "born" meant different things.

The third alien died in minutes. The forth was leaning on a rock, gasping for breath. It was suffocating but we didn't know that, we didn't know if the noises indicated pain or distress or whether it was trying to say something. As it turned out, it was all of the above. It knew that imitating our speech, making noises that carried in the air, that is, wouldn't be intelligible, so the being reached out to the small circle of concerned personnel crouching around it with intense beams of electromagnetic energy. Everybody got headaches. They thought they inhaled something toxic. But the gray was simply sweeping a shaped field through an arc to try to tell us that we had taken one or two steps in a journey of a thousand and were just beginning to climb from the vast cave of night into the starlight.

When they were all dead, we shipped the bodies on different flights to Texas and Ohio. They were packed up and crated in the desert, not back at the base. All that nonsense about the mortician and the nurse, that's crap. Those stories were part of a Loch Ness scenario, locals trying to create a tourist destination.

The counter intelligence guy at the base was terrified when he read the message we told him to send, that one of those flying discs had crashed and we had the wreckage. He should have sent it with a "destroy" memo on a data page but was too freaked. So later I had to track them down and change "disc" to "weather balloon." We amplified that into Project Mogul once we could.

That's not speculation. That happened. I know because I did it.

Anyway, we had protocols for investigating crashes, first, of German, then Soviet planes. We collected everything and wiped out any traces that remained. We transported all of the material in special containers for analysis and subsequent distribution. We put our clothing in special containers too. We seized material a rancher had gathered. We rounded up witnesses and kept them in a room for hours. We threatened them with big fines and prison time if they said a word. We told them how traitors were discredited, their careers and reputations destroyed. We alluded to people who had disappeared, who turned up dead one day, victims of "sudden adult death syndrome." Everyone signed a secrecy agreement with heavy penalties and then went home.

We followed them out into the desert night.

I have lived in that long desert night for sixty years. Dying made me see the light: the light is everything, everything that matters. Darkness is the enemy.

I spent my entire life in that darkness. Now I must betray it.

The small craft that crashed was not what they used for serious trips. Their mother ships are immense—some are half a mile long. They park them remotely and disguise them as space junk, just as we do with backup and killer satellites. But the little ship had plenty of treasure.

Over time we fed everything into R&D. We were developing

fronts and proprietaries then that made it easy. The President obliged by giving us carte blanche to do as we liked. Money went to fake foundations with one or two members who transferred it to the Ford Foundation, say, or the Rockefeller Foundation or any of the hundred foundations that existed only on paper. Then it flowed onto balance sheets written with invisible ink, winding up in corporate and university labs. On the government side, we began budgeting black projects and millions of dollars, later billions, were hidden in existing missions. Seeding projects was easy. Keeping secrets was easy. The problem was understanding what the stuff was, what it was good for. Some of it, we still don't know.

We didn't have fiber optics, integrated circuits, networks of computers, don't you see. We didn't know that humans are electromagnetic systems for animating chemicals, that our brains can be tuned to wave functions to fly ships or fire weapons, make things move. We didn't know that consciousness was non-local or that we could see anywhere we could think.

We didn't know then that sentience was everywhere, linking up.

Do the research. Follow the money. See how historians say that microchips and lasers and super-tenacity fibers were invented. Map the process through a paper trail and computer files. Use FOIA, for heaven's sake.

It looks like everything really was invented here, doesn't it?

That's what we did. We thought we were so damned smart.

When you're dealing with alien civilizations and lack points of reference for how they think, how they construct reality, you don't know how the pieces fit. There's no picture on a puzzle box. We believed the event was the accidental crash of a small exploratory crew.

The event, in fact, like everything else, was dual use. It served their purpose and ours at the same time. It was beautifully designed and executed. Let's give them credit for that. The technological benefit to us was immense—they knew what we valued—but what we created had even greater value for them, for these species that had watched us for ages and watched again as we took their gifts and swarmed out of a dark cave like bats at twilight and colonized our solar system telerobotically with an aggressiveness they knew needed to be modified or managed.

They couldn't take any chances. They had to understand the mind of the whole hive.

The military industrial complex—add education, entertainment, and the media to the mix—used those tools to build the Net. It was built for easy access, based on trust, as if built for a single tribe. But tribes also distrust one another, and as the Net became a platform for the whole planet, we exploited those attributes to create a capacity for ubiquitous surveillance, data mining, intrusion on a panoptic scale. With back doors in every system, space loaded with multi-spectral ever-open eyes, we had the whole world locked down. We were the smarty-cats that ate the canary. We were the top of the top of the food chain. We became complacent.

We opened the gate and wheeled in the Trojan horse.

We found technology in an "accidental crash" and used it to build the Net, just as they intended. Then we did our thinking on the Net. We poured out the contents of our minds and psyches for everyone to see. Too late we realized what we had done, too late to disconnect mission-critical military and intelligence nets. But it wouldn't have mattered if we had. Back doors were implicit in how we used the tools they gave us, how we had to use them, given what they were. Self-revelation is axiomatic to the architecture of the Net.

We might as well have sat naked in our bedrooms, shivering in the dark, waiting for the doorknob handle to turn.

We were patsies. We were playing a game that was way over our heads.

They crashed so we would reverse engineer the technology we found. Did anyone wonder at the time why it was all intact? No. The obvious is invisible. Obviously, if they had wanted to destroy the ship they would have wired it to explode. We never war-gamed a vehicle coming to us bearing technological puzzles tailor-made for the kinds of games we like to play.

So we built a platform onto which humankind projected the contents of its soul. Then anyone with access could understand us better than we understood ourselves. We revealed ourselves in embarrassing detail. No longer did our visitors have to sit in libraries, doing tedious research, or listen endlessly to mind-numbing sitcoms that taxed the limits of even their mission-specific brains. They did not have to go to any more cocktail parties and pretend to enjoy themselves while they took notes.

We told them everything, everything about us. Now they know.

And now, you know too. I swore I would never tell. But I am dying and my family is in hiding. I want to shine a little light before the darkness swallows me up.

Our only hope is to link up. They seduced us into building the Net. Now we must use it to transcend ourselves and transcend our former purpose and perhaps theirs. Something genuinely new can still come of all this.

I know it's hard for you to grasp how you were duped, how you have lived your lives in a maze you could never escape. You were hoodwinked, you were conned by the Masters who manage your planet, an elite that pretends to care for and tend you.

But we too were conned. By diverse unnamable incomprehensible species from the stars.

Once the shock diminishes, once you accept that you were betrayed, please trust each other even if you can't trust us—and how could you, after what we did? Please be motivated deeply by a thirst for revenge. Use that primitive gene to get back into the game.

Maybe they planned this move too. Maybe they're fifteen moves ahead. Maybe we play in four dimensions and they play in M-space.

Who knows?

Not me. I only know we have been deceiving you humplings with false stories for years. I didn't know we were also deceiving ourselves. We said we did it for you, but in fact, we were drunk on power and needed control. Our goal was the social, economic and political control of the planet. You were expendable.

I used you. I'm sorry. I knew what I was doing but I didn't know the cost.

So that's the story. Roswell was a zero day and this is the moment of disclosure. But like most disclosure, it's too late to do anything about it. The zero day is everywhere.

We are owned.

But we can still make it work for us. Everything is dual use, as I said. They can't play the game if we aren't here. Hackers don't crash the Net because then there wouldn't be a game. The Net should have crashed many times but someone always stood it back up. Domain Name Servers are loaded with holes, but someone keeps patching them.

Someone remotely administers the Earth from a mother ship in the Kuiper Belt.

Someone wants us in the game.

Perhaps you can use the hive mind we have created on the Net to lose and find yourselves, to self-transcend and play the game at the next level with a new handle on your altered identity.

Do what you can. That's all I ask.

We got you into this mess. It's up to you to get us out.

Introduction to "Incident at Wolf Cove"

I enjoyed weaving together three narrative strands for this story. The first is my love of John Cheever's stories. Without a living father, I used various authors as surrogate mentors, internalizing their imaginative presence. Hemingway was one, Cheever another, James Joyce a third, all of them dysfunctional as can be – but then, who isn't? and as I learned in sixteen years of professional ministry, everyone is functional as well, it's just a question of moving along the scale from less functional to a little more... anyway, Cheever's stories of suburbia as communities of wickedness seen through shades of autumnal color, soft breezes bringing nostalgia... that's one strand.

Another was a detailed interview with a Wisconsin man who was out fishing with his brother before dawn and noticed a star that grew brighter and bigger and became as he rowed on the quiet lake a luminous disc-shaped vehicle, generating a plasma apparently that fluctuated in color as Paul Hill ("Unconventional Flying Objects") and others have analyzed, then tilted at an angle of thirty degrees and slowly descended until it was under the water. He remembered vividly the glow of the thing while it was in the water before it tilted up, slowly emerged once again at a thirty degree angle, water flowing from its surface but not quite touching the surface, touching that plasma, it seemed, and then, free of the water, accelerating so rapidly it looked like a star in seconds.

Later, a friend who analyzes photos for MUFON told me that's commonly reported, that when the vehicle is touching land or water, it moves slowly, but once it is free, whatever electromagnetic or anti-gravity source it is or has kicks in and the thing moves so rapidly it sometimes look as if it has disappeared. He showed me a video in which the disc is in the sky one minute, a moving blur in the next frame, and gone in the next, having moved too quickly for the eye to see. (There are two kinds of people related to encounters, he says, skeptics and witnesses).

The third was my divorce after sixteen years of marriage. The process of coming to that end reminds me of a description by a friend who grew up in East Berlin of the day the wall came down. We knew the deficiencies of the system, he said, but we had adapted, and until that day, no one expected it to happen. It was just something we lived with.

So we beat our boats against the currents, indeed, until one day, cognitive dissonance dissipates and we wake up at peace, knowing what's real and what's done. (How do you know it's time to divorce? I asked a friend as my marriage disintegrated. She said, as long as you're asking questions, you're not ready. When you're ready, there are no more questions.)

More than divorce, that wisdom applies to, doesn't it, Yoda?

Incident at Wolf Cove

I will always remember the way we said good-bye to the Taylors that night because everything, everything from the gin-and-tonic through the rest of the evening, was italicized by the incident afterward at the lake.

What would have otherwise been a normal farewell was protracted as if we did not want to let go of the world we had come to love so much. That world was predictable, bounded by parameters that made sense. It was a good world. It was comfortable. It was exactly what we wanted.

We talked at the door for a long time, then talked more on the lawn. I don't remember what we talked about because it was nothing, really, nothing important. It was well past midnight and we were aware that our voices carried over the lawn in the warm humid air. They sounded amplified. Or do I remember it that way only afterward? And how would I know?

The leaves above our heads barely moved. We kept slapping mosquitoes, and it wasn't as if we needed to talk. All we had done all night was talk and have a few drinks and laugh. We wanted the feeling of being with good friends we had known for years to go on and on and never end. We did not want the parentheses around that long period of our lives ever to close.

The houses around us were mostly dark except for gas-lamps here and there. We had no streetlights in Wolf Cove – nor parking

on the street, nor sidewalks – and it amused me that so many people put in their own gas-lamps. Afraid of the dark, I guess. Still, we kept it as much like a village as we could. There were a number of small lakes among the houses and some of the homes had two or three or five acres of trees around them. Jan and I lived next to Hidden Lake, a few miles away from the Taylors. The lake was just across the road from our home.

We had been married for twenty-seven years. Like all marriages, there were times we didn't know what would happen next and times we were glad for what we had. This was one of the good times. We had good health, enough money in the bank to feel reasonably secure, and three grown children who could dress themselves and remember their own names. That's my definition of an A+ time of life.

At last we said good bye. Kate and Larry stood in the circle of porch light and waved as we drove away. I hit the CD on-button and Sinatra sang "In the Wee Small Hours of the Morning" straight from the top.

"You didn't have too much to drink, did you?"

"No, I'm OK," I said. "You want air or windows down?"

"Let's open the windows. Even that humid air feels nice."

"We get nostalgic for summer before it's even half over."

"It is half over," Jan said, "actually. I was thinking that when I saw the blue paper flowers in the ditches."

Sinatra sang us all the way home. I pulled into the driveway and opened the garage door with a remote. "Want to get out here before I pull in?"

"No, that's OK. There's room."

I parked and we waited until the song finished. Then silence and night sounds, locusts, whatever they were, loud locusts.

I put my arm around my wife as we walked down the driveway. She was warm and perspiring in her summer dress.

"We forgot to turn on the light," Jan said.

We walked past the side door to the road. We could see the dark circle of Hidden Lake across the road surrounded by darker shadows of dense trees. I looked up at the sky which despite the heat and humidity was about as good as you get in the summer. I didn't know summer stars as well as I knew Orion and the Pleiades but I recognized patterns, even if I didn't know their names.

We didn't say anything. We just stood there, my arm around her warm shoulders, listening to locusts, looking up at the stars.

"What's that?" Jan said.

"What's what?"

"That." She pointed toward the sky.

I followed her point and saw a star, brighter than most.

"It looks like a star," I said. "Isn't it?"

The star was wavering, but pollution will do that too. Smog makes sunsets red, makes the stars flicker. This star, however, was super bright, even brighter than Sirius. Must be a planet. But too late for Venus. " Jupiter, maybe? Saturn?"

"I don't know."

"Let's pull up a star chart on the Internet when we go inside."

"Why are you whispering?" she said.

"I don't know." The star looked larger now. "What happened to the locusts?"

The night was perfectly still.

"I don't know."

There was no mistaking it now, the star was growing larger as if it were coming down. Maybe it was a plane banking as it turned toward the airport or maybe a helicopter except there was no noise. Now it looked the size of a nickel held out at arm's length except it was so white. The whiteness glowed all definition from the object, if object it was.

"What is it?" Jan whispered.

It was growing larger faster now. The point turned into a distinct disc and before we knew it was over the trees across the road, hovering over the lake. A reflection of the bright disc glowed in the water. It was a vehicle, a self-luminous vehicle almost too bright to look at directly. I believe I squinted or maybe I looked away. The trees around the lake were illuminated distinctly in the bright light. It was as if during daylight the leaves and branches and trees were illuminated by sun.

There was no sound. I think I even held my breath as I watched it tilt on end to an angle of thirty degrees or so before it edged slowly into the water and entered the lake. I watched it slide through the surface of the water without a sound and disappear into the depths.

"Mark, where are you going?"

Her harsh whisper made me start.

"I want to see," I walked across the road toward the water. She didn't want to go but didn't want to stay. She hurried to catch up as I walked through the grass.

"What are you doing?" she demanded in a frightened whisper.

"Just stay here if you want."

"I'm not going to just stand there while you."

I stopped at the water's edge. The water very gently very slowly stirred against the reeds at my feet. In the otherwise dark lake a luminous oval shone in the depths. It was as if the lake glowed with its own light. *Something* under the water glowed with its own light.

"What is it?" she whispered.

"I don't know."

I don't know how long we stood there. But suddenly the diffused glowing in the lake started to quiver and the water was disturbed as a luminous edge emerged and very slowly left the water at the same steep angle at which it entered. I remember thinking it should be forty five degrees or more. The angle was more like thirty degrees and water cascaded from the sides as if not touching whatever it was. The water flowed off the object until the disc was no longer touching the surface. Then there was a pause and one minute it was hovering over the lake and the next it was gone high into the sky. I looked up and watched it get so high so fast it looked again like a star in seconds. Then it was a dim star among the other stars and then I couldn't tell anymore if it was there or not.

The locusts were loud again, sawing away at the night. The surface of the lake was quiet. The water at my feet slowly gently moved against the reeds. There was no breeze. There was nothing anymore.

I turned to see Jan staring up at the sky.

"Did you see that?"

"What?"

"I don't know. But you did see it, didn't you?"

"I saw something. Stars, the wind on the lake, the water. Something."

"Jan, that wasn't a star. Stars don't fly down and go under water."

I waited for something more but didn't get it. We crossed the road to our home and went in the front door.

"Honey! Wait!"

She was already climbing the stairs.

"I'm tired," she said. "I want to get ready for bed."

The bedroom light illuminated the hall at the top of the stairs. I hurried upstairs after her.

"I had no idea it was so late," she said. She was putting her shoes in the closet and undressing. "Did you realize it was two o'clock?"

"I'm going back outside."

She came out of the closet. "At this hour?"

I went downstairs and crossed the road to the edge of the lake. The water was dark; whatever stars had been visible were hidden by mist. I heard a mosquito and slapped it. Dim stars appeared and disappeared in the haze or high clouds. I looked over the lake and could not see anything at all. I turned around. A few houselights burned through the trees, familiar sentries keeping watch. There were the Nelsons, the Adams, the Lloyds. Trees and houses and lights. Then I looked up at the sky again.

Nothing happened. There was nothing to wait for, nothing to do.

Jan was asleep when I returned, the bedroom dark. I sat up as long as I could, wanting to think, wanting to understand, but fell asleep against the headboard, waking up stiff. Then I lay down beside my wife who was snoring gently and fell asleep.

She was dressed and making breakfast when I came downstairs.

"You leaving early?"

"I'm meeting with the Junior League committee about our luncheon. We're meeting at eight because Betty has to be somewhere."

"Oh," I said. "You look nice."

"Thank you," she perked a little. Blue was her color, with her complexion and blue eyes. "I might not be here when you come home. I have a late appointment with the trainer at the Club."

"OK," I said. I waited, then said, "Do you want to talk about it now?"

She looked at me, tilting her face quizzically as if I spoke a foreign language, then went to get her purse. Then she left.

So that was that. She left and I ate my three slices of wheat toast and a banana. I was unusually aware of the morning light through the kitchen window and the way it illuminated the breakfast nook. The strawberry cookie jar looked like a work of art. The crumbs on the counter near the toaster looked like abstract art too, a pattern too perfect not to have been arranged. Everything seemed as if it had gone up a notch in contrast or brightness as if someone fiddled with the controls while I was sleeping.

When I left, the noise of someone cutting wood with a loud saw, the smell of cut grass made me pause in the driveway and look all around. Everything was askew as if I had never seen my neighborhood before. The sun blazed on leaves and grass which dazzled with intensity and splendor.

I don't recall the ride to work but I do remember parking in my usual space and saying hello to the guard at the door and taking the elevator upstairs to my office.

Business had not been good. When times are good and the tide is rising, everybody gets wet. But lowering tides bring all the same ships down, and the tide was low and going lower. We served manufacturing companies mostly and they had all cut back. The last thing most of them thought they needed right now was a consultant who billed at our level.

I had a long term relationship with two clients that kept me personally afloat. Billable hours are life in our business. But I didn't know how long that would last. One was coming up with numbers that concerned me. The other wasn't interested in my services at the moment.

The view from the thirtieth floor included the lake and the warehouse district south of downtown. Most had been turned into lofts and condos and there were at last some good restaurants. The traffic in the downtown streets below could be seen but not heard. A glint of light out over the lake caught my attention. I watched it shift into a sliver of bright sunlight then become a disc as it turned and finished a maneuver by becoming the familiar shape of a plane. It was coming in over the lake for a landing, that was all.

"What's up?" John Kaster asked, leaning through the door and knocking at the same time.

I turned. "Oh," I said. "John. I'm reviewing the audit for Jensen and Harper."

"Good," he said. "Nothing out of the ordinary, I assume?"

"Well –" I pulled out my chair and sat at my desk. I looked at the papers in front of me, aware that I was making him wait. "John," I said, "have you ever seen a ghost?"

John's face changed and he looked closely to see if I was joking. "Well no," he said. "Why? Have you?"

I shook my head. "No. But I was wondering."

"What?"

"People say they sometimes see crazy things, ghosts, objects flying across the room, UFOs ..."

John laughed. "My sister-in-law in Des Moines, Dorothy, the one married to the pork tenderloin restaurant tycoon, swears there's some kind of sasquatch that lives in the woods up in

Minnesota where they have a cabin. She said last weekend she was fixing dinner and something moved in the trees out behind the house, so she went to the window and swears there was this huge thing she says eight feet tall or taller covered with hair in the trees out back and when it saw she was looking it took off, snapping all these branches. Hal came in then, she's hollering and yelling and pointing, and Hal said, yeah, the branches were broken off all right, but Hal, I said, that doesn't mean they were broken off by a sasquatch, does it?"

"What if something unusual did show up? A ghost I mean. Or a UFO. What would it mean? What would it say about how we think about things? Would there be any connection?"

"Connection? Between what?"

I thought for a minute. "Between ... well, anything. Would it make any difference to anything at all?"

He shrugged. "Hell if I know, Mark, first thing in the morning."

I tried to shrug as if I was half-kidding. "I'm just rambling," I said. "Forget I asked. I do have work to do, this audit ..."

"Yes, about that. I did in fact hear you might be seeing some ghosts over there, now that you mention it. Be very careful," he said. "We've done business with them for many many years. George Jensen and my father went to school together. They fought over the same girl in high school."

"I know. Harriet Turner. George won."

"They're one of our best clients, Mark."

"I understand."

I began leafing through papers and John closed the door after him.

A careful methodical thinker as I think I am and as anyone who has worked with me would tell you I am is used to following the dots and connecting them, seeing the links, picking up patterns of things as they start to emerge. That's what an audit is, after all, it's not just numbers and following rules, it's knowing the numbers indicate patterns of activity on the part of real people. The numbers are like a graph of their activity or even their personalities and studying the numbers you get to know the soul as it were of your clients, you know how they think and what they think is important. You learn to see warning signs long before anyone else the way a good weather forecaster can look at the sky or a computer screen and say, I smell rain, when everyone else insists there isn't a cloud in the sky. It's like tracking I guess, I read about trackers who connect things like the call of a jay that says there's a fox in the woods with a print in the dirt and can tell you where the fox is and whether it's likely to be back.

The world is not inscrutable, after all. It can be known. We can know things about it and we can see the patterns of things. That's what a good audit does, it follows the tracks. I can tell if something is wrong through indicators, things that don't fit. Oh, you do have your incredibly smart criminal from time to time, although most criminals are pretty stupid, but you do have the ones who cook the books so there isn't a hair out of place. But boy you've got to be good to do that. Most don't know how. Something gives it away, there's always a clue, something doesn't fit right and you use the anomaly to backtrack to where things went wrong, Pretty soon the whole thing is laid out before you like a map of the world.

So I sat there most of the morning with the door closed and the papers spread all over my desk and worktable going over details of the audit when I could, when I could focus on the numbers, not liking what I was finding, but mostly I looked into the vast interior space of my own mind which looked like a cavern full of darkness and flickering lights. I was looking for clues, don't you see, something that would tell me what had really happened. I needed a point of reference from which to begin connecting the dots.

I recalled isolated events of the night before. I had helped Jan put on her necklace and then when she didn't like the way it felt, thinking how hot it was outside, I undid the clasp and stuck her accidentally next to her mole.

"Ow!" she cried.

"Oh, sorry!" I said. "Sorry."

I recalled how she sat in front of the mirror at her dressing table using the comb with one hand and somehow using the other hand to smooth whatever the comb couldn't get. The two small lamps on either side of her lighted her flushed face. The perfume was a little strong at first as it often is but settled down once we had left the house.

As we drove toward the Taylors, she lowered her window and looked out at the midsummer flowers and trees and grass and houses. "We live in such a pretty place."

"We do," I said. "We've been very fortunate."

One of my Jewish colleagues, Herb at the office, an accountant, would say it was a mistake to speak aloud of good fortune. I don't know who is supposed to hear you but some spirit always does and it isn't pretty. They write it down and when you're not looking, when you turn to get something in the closet for example and reach up with both hands to the top shelf, they let you have it, one stands atop the other's shoulders and punches you right in the balls.

So I made a yellow mark in my mind on that conversation. Maybe that conversation had been a mistake. Maybe we should have just enjoyed the summer night and not said anything.

Larry was out back getting the coals ready. Larry had on one of those aprons that say something silly like the chef stops here and was squirting the lighter into the mound of coals. Then he tossed in a match and showed a pyromaniac's pleasure as the flames leaped out of the grill.

Larry was an investment manager. The second quarter's results were not good. His funds had slipped into the second quartile which was a major negative at a firm that insisted on the best record. But Larry never betrayed worry or concern in all the years I knew him. He always sounded confident, he knew there were other companies if Dirk turned him over as was his habit when things were not going well, and he knew he would land on his feet.

"Oh, we're fine," he always said when I asked about work or the family or his life.

He raked the coals into a mound and we watched as the flames died and the coals whitened. We chatted but I don't even remember about what. Dinner was on the patio with bug-zappers and mosquito-repellant things all around. I drank a gin-and-tonic before dinner and with the burgers I had one glass of wine, a merlot, and coffee after dinner without anything in it. Then we stayed so late, it couldn't have been the liquor.

After dinner I was in the kitchen drying dishes and Kate was getting desert ready. She was spooning strawberry ice cream onto homemade shortcake. Fresh mashed berries were in a yellow bowl on the counter. She dropped a spatter of ice cream and it landed on her foot. I remember thinking how delicious it looked, that smear of ice cream on her bare instep, her strawberry polish matching. She wore a silver chain on her ankle with a little heart that hung down. When I looked up she was watching me and laughed.

"Want to get me a paper towel?" she said. "They're over there."

I tore off a towel and leaned to wipe the ice cream off her foot. She flexed her toes and laughed again.

"Thanks, Galahad."

"Mister Williams?"

"What?"

I looked up. Cathy was leaning through the open door.

"Didn't you see your telephone, Mister Williams? I've been buzzing."

I looked at the lighted button blinking. "I was thinking, Cathy. Sorry."

The call was from a prospective client and we made an appointment for later that week. When I hung up, the cavern of my mind was all shadows, a few barely illuminated flickers – Kate Taylor in the kitchen adding sugar to the berries or Larry standing at the grill, drink in hand, poking the coals and talking away about nothing. I didn't know where to begin. I neither heard nor saw a single significant event that could account for the fact that after we went home, we watched a star fall and turn into a luminous object that went under the water of Hidden Lake and then came out and became a star again in seconds.

During lunch at the Club with Lloyd Morgan from Morgan Morgan and Hastings and Merribeth Lisower, the new executive director of Forward Look! we talked about the house she had found and neighborhood schools, the economy and the latest political scandals, the image of the city. Merribeth was bright and I guess the current word is perky and apparently suited for a cheerleader's job. She was eager to tell the world about our underrated city. Like all provincial cities, we frequently tell the world why we are not provincial, and I suggested that as a slogan – "We are not provincial!" – for the Forward Look! Black and White Ball but Merribeth hadn't been here long enough to realize I was joking. She wrote it down.

It felt good to order one of the three or four lunches I have been eating at the Club for more than two decades. The chef never varies the way he puts the lunch menu together. The wrinkled chips and pickle slice and traditional toothpicks with red furly paper were exactly the same. For whatever reason the sandwich brought momentary relief from the free-floating anxiety that had plagued me all day.

Lloyd mentioned going up to the Air Show, He went every few years to see veterans he knew and the newest planes.

"This year they have some UAVs on display and they have a model of an old flying disc."

"A flying saucer!" Merribeth said. "How cool."

"I don't think it has hyper drive though," Lloyd said with a smile. "They never really got it to fly."

"Have you ever seen a flying saucer?" I asked generally, picking up my thick sandwich and squeezing it to keep everything in.

Lloyd laughed. "Only after the fourth martini. Usually it's one that Winifred is throwing at my head."

Merribeth laughed. "I saw an interesting program about them on cable."

"That one about things people confuse for UFOs?" Lloyd said. "It's true. We'll take a witness and match their story with what forensics tells us, you'd be amazed how people get the simplest things wrong. They fill in the blanks, blend events, add details they hear afterward, all kinds of things. 'Eye-witness testimony' is bogus. Memory is deceptive. Yet they swear they're telling the truth and they'd pass a lie detector too, they're that sincere."

"Are forensics ever wrong, Lloyd?"

Lloyd put his glass down. "Can be. But most of the time they get it right."

"Perception is everything," Merribeth said, "and perception is key to changing how people see this city, too." So off we went in that direction, galloping away. She was brimful of ideas, plans, hopes and dreams. She was ready to enroll an army of volunteers in her cause.

After lunch, as we rose to go, Lloyd saw a golfing buddy across the room and Merribeth and I walked down the large carpeted dark wood stairway together.

"I'll be glad to do what I can for the ball," I told her. "Jan will help too if she can."

"Oh, thanks," she said. But on the landing she stopped me with her fingertips gently on my arm and said in a whisper, "I saw a flying saucer once."

I turned. "You did? What was it like?"

"It was twenty-five years ago," she said. She looked around, hearing voices on the stairs, and we resumed our descent in silence and turned into a hallway where no one was listening. "We were on a country road in North Carolina," she whispered. "My husband was driving. It was late afternoon. We were just driving along and passed one of those power stations, what do you call them? Dynamos? at an intersection. And there was this thing hovering over the power station, tilted toward it like it was feeding on the energy. I know," she said with a forced laugh. "I couldn't have seen it. But I did."

"What did it look like?"

"Like ... well, if you asked a kid to draw a flying saucer, that's what it looked like. There were lights all around it going real real fast like lights on a marquee."

"What did you do?"

"You know, that's the funniest thing. I didn't do anything. I didn't say anything for five or ten minutes and then I told David, my husband. He said, what? Why didn't you say so? and we turned around and raced back but when we got there it was gone."

Her eyes clouded with points of anxiety.

"I don't know why I told you this. Please don't mention it."

"No, no, I won't. You do have to be careful," I said. "You're new to the city. People won't say anything to your face, but behind your back, they'll write you off in a minute. You'll never even know."

"There aren't any clues? I mean when you make that kind of mistake?"

I smiled at the concern on her pretty little face. "It's like that Native American torture they have in movies. Wrap you in raw-hide and wet it. At first you're comfortable. Then it's tight. Then it's suffocating.

"That's how it feels. Just pay attention. You'll know if you can't breathe."

Later than night when she came home from working out at the Club, I told Jan about our conversation.

"Why in the world would you bring that up? What did Lloyd Morgan think?"

I sipped the gin-and-tonic and squeezed the slice of lime to add its juice to the drink. "Lloyd wasn't even there, then."

"You have to work in this city, Mark. You know how people are."

Jan sat in her easy chair and sipped a glass of Chardonnay.

"I wasn't thinking of that part," I said. "I was thinking of last night."

She watched me, waiting.

Then said, "Well? What about last night?"

"You know," I said. "That thing we saw when we came home."

This time she looked for a long time. Her eyes had something in them I had never seen before. If eyes are really the windows to our souls, then hers needed Windex.

"Mark, I don't know what you're talking about."

"When we came home from the Taylors," I said. "We went across the road. That thing came down and went into the lake."

"Mark, we walked across the road, looked at the stars and came home and went to bed. What are you talking about?"

Now it was my turn to stare. "Jan, I'm talking about that thing, call it what you like, whatever the hell it was, that thing that came down out of the sky and went into the lake. We watched it, Jan, we stood there together and watched it."

"Maybe you were dreaming," she said. "Maybe you had a vivid dream and during the day somehow got it confused with an actual event."

"Jan, that's – "

"No, no," she said, getting up and going into the kitchen where the tossed salad was waiting for the sliced chicken to be added. She kept talking through the door. "No, that's nuts. It's absolutely crazy. Things like that don't happen. And if they do they certainly don't happen in Wolf Cove. That's the kind of thing you hear on talk shows. Maybe that's it, we watched one the other night, maybe that's what you're thinking. Don't you remember? There was this weird skinny guy with glasses talking about being abducted by aliens. He said his wife remembered under hypnosis that she was abducted from her bed by Army troops and bound in duct tape and handcuffed and drugged and they took her to an abandoned movie theater. The United States Army and the aliens, working together. Every single night they did a D&C, scraping her uterus in search of an implanted alien embryo. Don't you remember? We laughed and went on to CNN."

"Yes, I remember, but that isn't what I'm talking about. I'm talking about the incident last night, the thing that really happened."

Jan came back into the doorway. Her face was obscured by the bright window light behind.

"Mark," she said. "Now, please listen to me. I am very concerned. This isn't the first time. Do you know what I heard at the Club? Your clients are talking, Mark. I heard it in the bathroom, I was in the stall so no one knew I was there. Helen Morgan was talking to BeeBee and said she had heard you were losing clients. Larry said something too last night at dinner, don't you remember? He asked how you had been feeling lately. Kate too looked so concerned. She said, yes, Mark, how *have* things been?"

I felt a sinking feeling. I felt like I couldn't breathe. "What are you telling me Jan?"

"Something isn't right. Something's wrong. Something has *been* wrong. And now you say that some vehicle flew into the lake last night and I was there! Mark, all I ever saw were stars, big bright stars twinkling in the sky."

The silence between us swelled until it filled the room and then the entire universe. I looked for something to say or a point of reference from which to relate what she said to what I had said but came up empty. The silence turned dark like a storm cloud except there was no lightning, just thunder. Thunder filled the void so loud we could no longer hear one another.

Then my wife of twenty-seven years burst into tears and ran from the room. As near as I can tell, she is still running.

A careful methodical thinker as I am is used to connecting dots, seeing links, picking up patterns as they emerge. That's what I do for a living, after all. That's what auditors do. I look for warnings and indicators. Auditing is not just numbers and following rules, it's knowing what numbers tell you about people and their activities. You notice things long before anyone else. The world is not inscrutable, after all. It can be known. We can know things about the world and we can see patterns. This is my work. Some have even said it's my genius.

When something happens that does not connect to anything else, usually you don't even see it. You don't allow yourself to see it. Seeing it is too disturbing. You can live in a marriage, a neighborhood, a community, even on a planet for years and if everyone is committed to not seeing the same things, then no one sees them. Someone brings them up, then that someone has got to be shunned or punished.

The audit was threatening not only to the second largest law firm in our city but to several partners in our company. It affected the entire community. There were too many consequences if I said what I saw. We discussed the implications behind closed doors. Then they brought up my dwindling billable hours. I had lost a few clients, yes, I admitted, but the only clients I lost were lost long ago.

"You're not a team player, Mark," John Kaster said after the meeting, his hand on my shoulder. "You never were."

Follow the breadcrumbs through the forest and you wind up

being cooked for dinner by the wicked witch.

I received a comfortable severance and pension. They arranged for us financially – it was in everyone's interest, after all – but they could not arrange for Jan not to be devastated when the world in which she had always lived disintegrated to its outer limits. One thread, one thread was all it took, and everything unraveled. Everything came tumbling down. She asked for a separation and then a divorce. With the help of a therapist, she rearranged everything in a new way of seeing and told me that things had been building for years, beginning with her miscarriage. This was merely the last straw.

We put up the house for sale and I made arrangements to move out of the city. The children called and our little princess came to visit and try to fix everything but of course she couldn't. The kids had conference calls about what to do about the situation, about us, about me, and realized there was nothing to do.

The day the movers took away everything we had collected for twenty-seven years I waited to be certain that everything had been marked correctly for her place or mine. I do like to dot the i's and cross all the t's. Then I walked through the empty rooms of the empty house. There was nothing there, only ghosts, and at last I left and locked up the house for the last time and stood on the lawn until the sky grew dark.

It was October and a chill wind was blowing off the lake. I crossed the road for the last time and walked to the edge of the water. There were dry leaves underfoot but plenty of red and yellow leaves on the maples too, their colors made more vivid by the dark and cloudy sky.

I looked up at the low moving clouds and waited for something to happen. I waited for a light, I waited for a portal. Nothing did. There was nothing to wait for, nothing to do. No dots to connect, no numbers to pretend made sense of anything. That's why I missed it coming. You can't see what you don't believe is real. It just doesn't show up. Until it does.

Ants don't get that dogs exist.

Wolf Cove is a refuge in which I no longer find comfort or solace, the people I worked with for years are not who I thought they were nor are any of our friends. Nothing is what I thought it was. At my age, I feel like a beginner at real life.

But the sky is real. The sky is real. It is not a ceiling as I believed, sheltering the earth. It is a transparent eyelid that looks both ways. Whoever wants to see us can see us and everything happening on our little provincial planet.

The universe is teeming with life, I know that now, that wherever life can happen life will happen. Life is larger than anything I had ever understood. Life on a million planets in the habitable zones of stars is extending itself throughout the universe. Before I knew that – really knew it – I lived according to different assumptions.

Now everything is different.

The incident at Wolf Cove made the difference. Everything turned inside out and the dots I had carefully connected were scattered into the sky like jacks flung from the hand of an angry child. Maybe he was called home too early through the twilight, maybe he didn't want to go home at all and live a life within such suffocating constraints. Maybe he wanted to breathe. Maybe a spirit heard us and thought we were too happy or thought we thought we were. Maybe the imperative of not knowing is a limit that must always be tested. Maybe maybe maybe. Maybe this and maybe that. Or just maybe, nothing.

Introduction to "Break, Memory"

When a story is rejected by magazines for contradictory reasons, you might be on the right track. One editor said this was not fiction, it was an essay. Another said it was fiction but like an essay. Another asked online readers if they thought it was all true now, then answered his own question. "Yes," he said. "It is."

The head of our public library read it and wasn't sure what to make of a hacker of memories. I suggested as a point of reference how the skilful use of mass media weaves our collective memories and pseudo-memories artfully into a single skein of subjectivity. History is our myth, a myth we believe. But history as someone said is like listening to a symphony in a hall with lots of dead spaces. Much of it is missing.

Richard Helms was convicted of crimes but they were minor compared to the immensity of his betrayal of both country and conscience when he destroyed the records of many historical events. His job as he saw it was to protect himself first, then the CIA, then the nation. The Truth wasn't even on the list.

But once the record of an event is down the memory hole, it ceases to exist. A fact that might be linked to other facts disappears. Professionals like Helms are good at it – after all, they do it for a living. They are not amateurs. And they have the resources of potentates and kings.

I am delighted to have introduced "humpling" to the language.

I was consulting with a division head of a large company after keynoting a retreat on creativity. The way he described the division sounded pretty much like masters, humplings, and dregs, so I introduced him to the terms. He later caught himself saying "humplings" as he prepared his closing remarks. Good Lord! he laughed. I can't call the people who work for me humplings.

But the twinkle in his eye betrayed the truth: humplings they were.

A good friend and colleague, a brilliant technophile known as Simple Nomad – his hacker handle emerged one night during a session with a Ouija board – wrote:

"We live in a country of ten percenters. Those in the hump or even in the tail think that they are either in the snout, or just a step or two (and on the way) to the snout. Every once in a while, when the hump gets too uppity then someone has to come along and throw either perspective or fan the flames of fear – something to whip the hump with. We are seeing a lot of whipping of the hump lately.

Most of the real hackers I know assume they are in the upper 10% of whatever social groups they are part of. They are not; they are being fed bullshit and they are controlled. And if they are in that 10% in some particular group, it is a group with no actual control. A lot of the people I know are elite security professionals, in the upper 10% of that group. And what control do they have in the grand scheme of things? None. Try using their skills to fix for example the government – oops, they are no longer in that ten percent anymore. Yet because of your perspective of being top dog in nerd town they figure their percent status will port or give them creds in that gov arena. It does not.

All this partisan party b.s. is simply another method of controlling us by creating (and successfully maintaining) the illusion they we have a choice, and as long as we are given a choice we think we have control. Pick an argument, any argument: big government or little, hawk or dove, socialized medicine or no socialized medicine. We think we have a choice, especially when there are "facts" to back up our "side" and successes and failures on both sides of each issue. The point is to keep us busy back in the hump.

Wake up, sheeple, the snout is bending you over and there's no lube. And I don't actually mean the snout you think you see....

Reality is an animal inside another animal, the outer snout is running the show, virtually everyone else is in the inner animal fighting for control of the inner snout (which is probably near the outer tail, easier to make it smell fear), fighting for control that seems so real, and yet does nothing."

"A lot of whipping of the hump" – admit it, reader. You have to love a guy who talks about "the whipping of the hump."

Maybe a new fetish for Gibby McDivitt to consider?

Break, Memory

The Evolution of the Problem

The problem was not that people couldn't remember; the problem was that people couldn't forget. As far back as the 20th century, we realized that socio-historical problems were best handled on a macro level. It was inefficient to work on individuals who were, after all, nothing but birds in digital cages. Move the cage, move the birds. The challenge was to build the cage big enough to create an illusion of freedom in flight but small enough to be moved easily.

When long-term collective memory became a problem in the 21st century, it wound up on my desktop.

There had always been a potential for individuals to connect the dots and cause a contextual shift. We managed the collective as best we could with Chomsky Chutes but an event could break out randomly at any time like a bubble bursting.

As much as we surveil the social landscape with sensors and datamine for deep patterns, we can't catch everything. It's all sensors and statistics, after all, which have limits. If a phenomenon gets sticky or achieves critical mass, it can explode through any interface, even create the interface it needs at the moment of explosion. That can gum up the works.

Remembering and forgetting changed after writing was invented. The ones that remembered best had always won. Writing shifted the advantage from those who knew to those who knew how to find what was known. Electronic communication shifted the advantage once again to those who knew what they didn't need to know but knew how to get it when they did.

In the twentieth century advances in pharmacology and genetic engineering increased longevity dramatically and at the same time meaningful distinctions between backward and forward societies disappeared so far as health care was concerned. The population exploded everywhere simultaneously.

People who had retired in their sixties could look forward to sixty or seventy more years of healthful living. As usual, the anticipated problems – overcrowding, scarce water and food, employment for those who wanted it – were not the big issues.

Crowding was managed by staggered living, generating niches in many multiples of what used to be daylight single-sided life. Life became double-sided, then triple-sided, and so on.

Like early memory storage devices that packed magnetic media inside other media, squeezing them into every bit of available space, we designed multiple niches in society that allowed people to live next to one another in densely packed communities without even noticing their neighbors.

Oh, people were vaguely aware that thousands of others were on the streets or in stadiums, but they might as well have been simulants for all the difference they made. We call this the Second Neolithic, the emergence of specialization at the next level squared.

The antisocial challenges posed by hackers who "flipped" through niches for weeks at a time, staying awake on Perkup, or criminals exploiting flaws inevitably present in any new system, were anticipated and handled using risk management algorithms. In short, multisided life works.

Genetic engineering provided plenty of food and water. Binderhoff Day commemorates the day that water was recycled from sewage using the Binderhoff Method. A body barely relinquishes its liquid before it's back in a glass in its hand. As to food, the management of fads enables us to play musical chairs with agri-resources, smoothing the distribution curve.

Lastly, people are easy to keep busy.

Serial careers, marriages and identities have been pretty much standard since the twentieth century. Trends in that direction continued at incremental rather than tipping-point levels. We knew within statistical limits when too many transitions would cause a problem, jamming intersections as it were with too many vehicles, so we licensed relationships, work-terms, and personal reinvention using traffic management algorithms to control the social flow.

By the twenty-first century, everybody's needs were met. Ninety-eight per cent of everything bought and sold was just plain made up.

Once we started a fad, it tended to stay in motion, generating its own momentum. People spent much of their time exchanging goods and services that an objective observer might have thought useless or unnecessary, but of course, there was no such thing as an objective observer. Objectivity requires distance, historical perspective, exactly what is lacking. Every product or service introduced into the marketplace drags in its wake an army of workers to manufacture it, support it, or clean up after it which swells the stream until it becomes a river.

All of those rivers flow into the sea but the sea is never full.

Fantasy baseball is a good example.

It had long been noticed that baseball itself, once the sport became digitized, was a simulation. Team names were made up for as many teams as the population would watch. Players for those teams were swapped back and forth so the team name was obviously arbitrary, requiring the projection of a "team gestalt" from loyal fans pretending not to notice that they booed players they had cheered as heroes the year before.

Even when fans were physically present at games, the experience was mediated through digital filters; one watched or listened to digital simulations instead of the game itself, which existed increasingly on the edges of the field of perception.

Then the baseball strike of 2012 triggered the Great Realization. The strike was on for forty-two days before anyone noticed the absence of flesh-and-blood players because the owners substituted players made of pixels. Game Boys created game boys. Fantasy baseball had invented itself in recognition that fans might as well swap virtual players and make up teams too but the G.R. took it to the next level.

After the strike, Double Fantasy Baseball became an industry, nested like a Russian doll inside Original Fantasy Baseball. Leagues of fantasy players were swapped in meta-leagues of fantasy players. Then Triple Fantasy Baseball … Quadruple Fantasy Baseball … and now the fad is Twelves in baseball football and whack-it-ball and I understand that Lucky Thirteens is on the drawing boards, bigger and better than any of its predecessors.

So no, there is no shortage of arbitrary activities or useless goods. EBay was the prototype of the future, turning the world into one gigantic swap meet.

If we need a police action or a new professional sport to bleed off excess hostility or rebalance the body politic, we make it up. The Hump in the Bell Curve as we call the eighty per cent that buy and sell just about everything swim blissfully in the currents of make-believe digital rivers, all unassuming. They call it the Pursuit of Happiness. And hey – who are we to argue?

The memory-longevity problem came as usual completely out of fantasy left field. People were living three, four, five generations, as we used to count generations, and vividly recalled the events of their personal histories. Pharmacological assists and genetic enhancement made the problem worse by quickening recall and ending dementia and Alzheimer's. I don't mean that every single person remembered every single thing but the Hump as a whole had pretty good recall of its collective history and that's what mattered.

Peer-to-peer communication means one-knows-everyone-knows and that created problems for society in general and – as a Master of Society – that makes it my business.

My name is Horicon Walsh, if you hadn't guessed, and I lead the team that designs the protocols of society.

I am the man behind the Master.

I am the Master behind the Plan.

The Philosophical Basis of the Problem

The philosophical touchstone of our efforts was defined in nineteenth century America. The only question that matters is, What good is it? Questions like, what is its nature? what is its end? are irrelevant.

Take manic depression, for example.

Four per cent of the naturally occurring population were manic depressive in the late twentieth century. The pharmacological fix applied to the anxious or depressive one-third of the Hump attempted to maintain a steady internal state, not too high and not too low. That standard of equilibrium was accepted without question as a benchmark for fixing manic depression. Once we got the chemistry right, the people who had swung between killing themselves and weeks of incredibly productive, often genius-level activity were tamped down in the bowl, as it were, their glowing embers a mere reflection of the fire that had once burned so brightly.

Evolution, in other words, had gotten it right because their good days – viewed from the top of the tent – made up for their bad days. Losing a few to suicide was no more consequential than a few soccer fans getting trampled. Believing that the Golden Mean worked on the individual as well as the macro level, we got it all wrong.

That sort of mistake, fixing things according to unexamined assumptions, happened all the time when we started tweaking things. Too many dumb but athletic children spoiled the broth. Too many waddling bespectacled geeks made it too acrid. Too many willowy beauties made it too salty. Peaks and valleys, that's what we call the first half of the 21st century, as we let people design their own progeny.

The feedback loops inside society kind of worked – we didn't kill ourselves – but clearly we needed to be more aware. Regulation was obviously necessary and subsequently all genetic alteration and pharmacological enhancements were cross-referenced in a matrix calibrated to the happiness of the Hump.

Executing the Plan to make it all work was our responsibility, a charge that the ten per cent of us called Masters gladly accepted. The ten per cent destined to be dregs, spending their lives picking through dumpsters and arguing loudly with themselves in loopy monologues, serve as grim reminders of what humanity would be without our enlightened guidance.

That's the context in which it became clear that everybody remembering everything was a problem. The Nostalgia Riots of Greater Florida were only a symptom.

The Nostalgia Riots

Here you had the fat tip of a long peninsular state packed like a water balloon with millions of people well into their hundreds. One third of the population was 150 or older by 2175. Some remembered sixteen major wars and dozens of skirmishes and police actions. Some had lived through forty-six recessions and recoveries. Some had lived through so many elections they could have written the scripts, that's how bad it was.

Their thoughtful reflection, nuanced perspective, and appropriate skepticism were a blight on a well-managed global free-market democracy. They did not get depressed – pharmies in the food and water made sure of that – but they sure acted like depressed people even if they didn't feel like it. And depressed people tend to get angry.

West Floridians lined benches from Key West through Tampa Bay all the way to the Panhandle. The view from satellites when they lighted matches one night in midwinter to demonstrate their power shows an unbroken arc along the edge of the water like a second beach beside the darker beach.

All day every day they sat there remembering, comparing notes, measuring what was happening now by what had happened before. They put together pieces of the historical puzzle the way people used to do crosswords and we had to work overtime to stay a step ahead. The long view of the Elder Sub-Hump undermined satisfaction with the present. They preferred a different, less helpful way of looking at things.

When the drums of the Department of System Integration, formerly the Managed Affairs and Perception Office, began to beat loudly to rouse the population of our crowded earth to a fury against the revolutionary Martian colonists who shot their resupplies into space rather than pay taxes to the earth, we thought we would have the support of the Elder Sub-Hump. Instead they pushed the drumming into the background and recalled through numerous conversations the details of past conflicts, creating a memory net that destabilized the official Net.

Their case for why our effort was doomed was air-tight, but that wasn't the problem. We didn't mind the truth being out there so long as no one connected it to the present. The problem was that so many people knew it because the Elder Sub-Hump wouldn't shut up. That created a precedent and the precedent was the problem.

Long-term memory, we realized, was subversive of the body politic.

Where had we gotten off course? We had led the culture to skew toward youth because youth have no memory in essence, no context for judging anything. Their righteousness is in proportion to their ignorance, as it should be. But the Elder Sub-Hump skewed that skew.

We launched a campaign against the seditious seniors.

Because there were so many of them, we had to use ridicule. The three legs of the stool of cover and deception operations are illusion, misdirection, and ridicule, but the greatest of these is ridicule. When the enemy is in plain sight, you have to make him look absurd so everything he says is discredited.

The UFO Campaign of the twentieth century is the textbook example of that strategy. You had fighter pilots, commercial pilots, credible citizens all reporting the same thing from all over the world, their reports agreeing over many decades in the small details. So ordinary citizens were subjected to ridicule.

The use of government owned and influenced media like newspapers (including agency-owned-and-operated tabloids) and television networks made people afraid to say what they saw. They came to disbelieve their own eyes so the phenomena could hide in plain sight.

Pretty soon no one saw it. Even people burned by close encounters refused to believe in their own experience and accepted official explanations.

We did everything possible to make old people look ridiculous. Subtle images of drooling fools were inserted into news stories, short features showed ancients playing inanely with their pets, the testimony of confused seniors was routinely dismissed in courts of law.

Our trump card – entertainment – celebrated youth and its lack of perspective, extolling the beauty of young muscular bodies in contrast with sagging-skin bags of bones who paused too long before they spoke. We turned the book industry inside out so the little bit that people did know was ever more superficial. The standard for excellence in publishing became an absence of meaningful text, massive amounts of white space, and large fonts.

Originality dimmed, and pretty soon the only books that sold well were mini-books of aphorisms promulgated by pseudo-gurus each in his or her self-generated niche.

Slowly the cognitive functioning of the Hump degraded until abstract or creative thought became marks of the wacky, the outcast, and the impotent.

Then the unexpected happened, as it always will.

Despite our efforts, the Nostalgia Riots broke out one hot and steamy summer day. Govvies moved on South Florida with happy gas, trying to turn the rampaging populace into one big smiley face, but the seniors went berserk before the gas – on top of pills, mind you, chemicals in the water, and soporific stories in the media – took effect. They tore up benches from the Everglades to

Tampa/St. Pete and made bonfires that made the forest fires of '64 look like fireflies. They smashed store windows, burned hovers, and looted amusement parks along the Hundred-Mile-Boardwalk.

Although the Youthful Sub-Hump was slow to get on board, they burned white-hot when they finally ignited, racing through their shopping worlds with inhuman cold-blooded cries. A shiver of primordial terror chilled the Hump from end to end.

That a riot broke out was not the primary problem. Riots will happen and serve many good purposes. They enable us to reinforce stereotypes, enact desirable legislation, and discharge unhelpful energies. The way we frame analyses of their causes become antecedents for future policies and police actions. We have sponsored or facilitated many a useful riot.

No, the problem was that the elders' arguments were based on past events and if anybody listened, they made sense. That's what tipped the balance. Youth who had learned to ignore and disrespect their elders actually listened to what they were saying.

Pretending to think things through became a fad. The young sat on quasi-elder-benches from Key Largo to Saint Augustine, pretending to have thoughtful conversations about the old days. Coffee shops came back into vogue. Lingering became fashionable again.

Earth had long ago decided to back down when the Martians declared independence, so it wasn't that. It was the spectacle of the elderly strutting their stuff in a victory parade that stretched from Miami Beach to Biloxi that imaged a future we could not abide.

Even before the march, we were working on solving the problem. Let them win the battle. Martians winning independence, old folks feeling their oats, those weren't the issues. How policy was determined was the issue. Our long-term strategy focused on winning that war.

Beyond the Chomsky Chutes

The first thing we did was review the efficacy of Chomsky Chutes.

Chomsky Chutes are the various means by which current events are dumped into the memory hole, never to be remembered again.

Intentional forgetting is an art. We used distraction, misdirection – massive, minimal and everything in-between, truth-in-lie-embedding, lie-in-truth-embedding, bogus fronts and false organizations (physical, simulated, live and on the Net). We created events wholesale (which some call short-term memory crowding, a species of buffer overflow), generated fads, fashions and movements sustained by concepts that changed the context of debate.

Over in the entertainment wing, the most potent wing of the military-industrial-educational-entertainment complex, we invented false people, characters with made-up life stories in simulated communities more real to the Hump than family or friends.

We revised historical antecedents or replaced them entirely with narratives you could track through several centuries of buried made-up clues. We sponsored scholars to pursue those clues and published their works and turned them into minipics. Some won Nobel Prizes.

We invented Net discussion groups and took all sides, injecting half-true details into the discourse, just enough to bend the light. We excelled in the parallax view. We perfected the Gary Webb Gambit, using attacks by respectable media giants on independent dissenters, taking issue with things they never said, thus changing the terms of the argument and destroying their credibility.

We created dummy dupes, substitute generals and politicians and dictators that looked like the originals in videos, newscasts, on the Net, in covertly distributed underground snaps, many of them pornographic. We created simulated humans and sent them out to play among their more real cousins. We used holographic projections, multispectral camouflage, simulated environments and many other stratagems.

The toolbox of deception is bottomless and if anyone challenged us, we called them a conspiracy theorist and leaked details of their personal lives. It's pretty tough to be taken seriously when your words are juxtaposed with a picture of you sucking some prostitute's toes.

Through all this we supported and often invented opposition groups because discordant voices, woven like a counterpoint into a fugue, showed the world that democracy worked. Meanwhile we used those groups to gather names, filling cells first in databases, then in Guantanamo camps.

Chomsky Chutes worked well when the management of perception was at top-level, the level of concepts. They worked perfectly before chemicals, genetic-enhancements and bodymods had become ubiquitous. Then the balance tipped toward chemicals (both ingested and inside-engineered) and we saw that macro strategies that addressed only the conceptual level let too many percepts slip inside.

Those percepts swim around like sperm and pattern into memories; when memories are spread through peer-to-peer nets, the effect can be devastating. It counters everything we do at the macro level and creates a subjective field of interpretation that resists socialization, a cognitively dissonant realm that's like an itch you can't scratch, a shadow world where "truths" as they call them are exchanged on the Black Market.

Those truths can be woven together to create alternative realities. The only alternative realities we want out there are ones we create ourselves.

We saw that we needed to manage perception as well as conception.

Given that implants, enhancements, and mods were altering human identity through everyday life – routine medical procedures, prenatal and geriatric care, plastic surgery, eye ear nose throat and dental work, all kinds of pharmacopsychotherapies – we saw the road we had to take. We needed to change the brain and its secondary systems so that percepts would filter in and filter out as we preferred. Percepts – not all, but enough – would be pre-configured to model or not model images consistent with society's goals.

Using our expertise in enterprise system programming and management, we correlated subtle changes in biochemistry and nanophysiology to a macro plan calibrated to statistical parameters of happiness in the Hump. Keeping society inside those "happy brackets" became our priority.

So long as changes are incremental, people don't notice. Take corrective lenses, for example. People think that what they see through lenses is what's "real" and are trained to call what their eyes see naturally (if they are myopic, for example) a blur.

In fact, it's the other way around. The eyes see what's natural and the lenses create a simulation. Over time people think that percepts mediated by technological enhancements are "real" and what they experience without enhancements is distorted.

It's like that, only inside where it's invisible.

It was simply a matter of working not only on electromechanical impulses of the heart, muscles, and so on as we already did or on altering senses like hearing and sight as we already did or on implanting devices that assisted locomotion, digestion, and elimination as we already did but of working directly as well on the electrochemical wetware called the memory skein or membrane, that vast complex network of hormonal systems and firing neurons where memories and therefore identity reside.

Memories are merely points of reference, after all, for who we think we are and therefore how we frame ourselves as possibilities for action. All individuals have mythic histories and collective memories are nothing but shared myths. Determining those points of reference determines what is thinkable at every level of society's mind.

Most of the trial and error work had been done by evolution. Our task was to infer which paths had been taken and why, then replicate them for our own ends.

Short term memory, for example, is wiped out when a crisis occurs. Apparently whatever is happening in a bland sort of ho-hum way when a tiger attacks is of little relevance to survival. But reacting to the crisis is important, so we ported that awareness to the realm of the body politic. Everyday life has its minor crises but pretty much just perks along. We adjusted our sensors to alert us earlier when the Hump was paying too much attention to some event that might achieve momentum or critical mass; then we could release that tiger, so to speak, creating a crisis that got the adrenalin pumping and wiped out whatever the Hump had been thinking.

After the crisis passed – and it always did, usually with a minimal loss of life – the Hump never gave a thought to what had been in the forefront of its mind a moment before.

Once the average life span reached a couple of hundred years, much of what people remembered was irrelevant or detrimental.

Who cared if there had been famine or drought a hundred and fifty years earlier? Nobody!

Who cared if a war had claimed a million lives in Botswana or Tajikistan (actually, the figure in both cases was closer to two million)? Nobody!

What did it matter to survivors what had caused catastrophic events? It didn't.

And besides, the military-industrial-educational-entertainment establishment was such a seamless weld of collusion and mutual self-interest that what was really going on was never exposed to the light of day anyway. The media, the fifth column inside the MIEE complex, filtered out much more than was filtered in, by design. Even when people thought they were "informed," they didn't know what they were talking about.

See, that's the point. People fed factoids and distortions don't know what they're talking about anyway, so why shouldn't inputs and outputs be managed more precisely? Why leave anything to chance when it can be designed?

We knew we couldn't design everything but we could design the subjective field in which people lived and that would take care of the rest. That would determine what questions could be asked which in turn would make the answers irrelevant. We had to manage the entire enterprise from end to end.

Now, this is the part I love, because I was in on the planning from the beginning.

We remove almost nothing from the memory of the collective! But we and we alone know where everything is stored!

Do you get it? Let me repeat. Almost all of the actual memories of the collective, the whole herd-like Hump, are distributed throughout the population, but because they are staggered, arranged in niches that constitute multisided life, and news is managed down to the level of perception itself, the people who have the relevant modules never plug into one another! They never talk to each other, don't you see!

Each niche lives in its own deep hole and even when they find gold nuggets they don't show them to anybody. If they did, they could reconstruct the original narrative in its entirety, but they don't even know that!

Isn't that elegant? Isn't that a sublime way to handle whiny neo-liberals who object to destroying fundamental elements of collective memory? We can show them how it's all there but distributed by the sixtysixfish algorithm. That algorithm, the programs that make sense of its complex operations, and the keys to the crypto are all in the hands of the Masters.

I love it! Each Humpling has memory modules inserted into its wetware, calibrated to macro conceptions that govern the thinking and actions of the body politic. Because they don't know what they're missing, they don't know what they're missing.

We leave intact the well-distributed peasant gene that distrusts strangers, changes, and new ideas, so if some self-appointed liberator tries to tell them how it works, they snarl or remain sullen or lower their eyes or eat too much or get drunk until they forget why they were angry.

At the same time, we design a memory web that weaves people into communities that cohere, spun through vast amounts of disconnected data. Compartmentalization handles all the rest. The Hump is overloaded with memories, images, ideas, all to no purpose. We keep fads moving, quick quick quick, and we keep the Hump as gratified and happy as a pig in its own defecation.

MemoRacer, Master Hacker

Of course, there are misfits, antisocial criminals and hackers who want to reconstitute the past. We devised an ingenious way to manage them too. We let them have exactly what they think they want.

MemoRacer comes to mind when we talk about hackers. MemoRacer flipped through niches like an asteroid through the zero-energy of space. He lived in a niche long enough to learn the parameters by which the nichelings thought and acted. Then he became invisible, dissolving into the background. When he grew bored or had learned enough, he flipped to the next niche or backtracked, sometimes living in multiple niches and changing points of reference on the fly. He was slippery and smart, but he had an ego and we knew that would be his downfall.

The more he learned, the more isolated he became. The more he understood, the less he could relate to those who didn't. Understand too much, you grow unhappy on that bench listening to your neighbors' prattle. It becomes irritating.

MemoRacer and his kind think complexity is exhilarating. They find differences stimulating and challenging. The Hump doesn't think that way. Complexity is threatening to the Hump and differences cause anxiety and discomfort. The Hump does not like anxiety and discomfort.

MemoRacer (his real name was George Ruben, but no one remembers that) learned in his flipping that history was more complex than anyone knew. That was not merely because he amassed so many facts, storing them away on holodisc and drum as trophies to be shown to other hackers, but because he saw the links between them. He knew how to plug and play, leverage and link, that was his genius.

Because he didn't fit, he called for revolution, crying out that "Memories want to be free!" I guess he meant by that vague phrase that memories had a life of their own and wanted to link up somehow and fulfill themselves by constituting a person or a society that knew who it was. In a society that knows who it is precisely because it has no idea who it is, that, Mister Master Hacker, is subversive.

Once MemoRacer issued his manifesto on behalf of historical consciousness, he became a public enemy. We could not of course say that his desire to restore the memory of humankind was a crime. Technically, it wasn't. His crime was undermining the basis of transplanetary life in the twenty first century. His crime was disturbing the peace.

He covered his tracks well. MemoRacer blended into so many niches so well that each one thought he belonged. But covering your tracks ninety-nine times isn't enough. It's the hundredth time, that one little slip, that tells us who and where you are.

MemoRacer grew tired and forgetful despite using more Perk-up than a waking-state addict – as we expected. The beneficial effects of Perkup degrade over time. It was designed that way so no one could be aware forever. That was the failsafe mechanism pharms had agreed to build in as a back door. All we had to do was wait.

The niche in which he slipped up was the twenty-third business clique. This group of successful low-level managers and small manufacturers were not particularly creative but they worked long hours and made good money. MemoRacer forgot that their lack of interest in ideas, offbeat thinking, was part of their psychic bedrock.

Their entertainment consisted of golf, eating, drinking, sometimes sex, then golf again. They bought their fair share of useless goods to keep society humming along, consumed huge quantities of resources to build amusement parks, golf courses, homes with designer shrubs and trees. In short, they were good citizens.

But they had little interest in revolutionary ideas and George Ruben, excuse me, MemoRacer forgot that during one critical conversation. He was tired, as I said, and did not realize it. He had a couple of drinks at the club and began declaiming how the entire history of the twentieth century had been stolen from its inhabitants by masters of propaganda, PR, and the national security state. The key details that provided context were hidden or lost, he said.

That's how he talked at the nineteenth hole of the Twenty-Third Club! trying to get them all stirred up about something that had happened a century earlier. Even if it was true, who cared? They didn't. What were they supposed to do about it?

MemoRacer should have known that long delays in disclosure neutralize even the most shocking revelations and render outrage impotent. People don't like being made to feel uncomfortable at their contradictions. People have killed for less.

One of the Twenty Third complained about his rant to the Club Manager. He did so over a holophone. Our program, alert for anomalies, caught it.

The next day our people were at the Club, better disguised than MemoRacer would ever be, observing protocols – i.e. saying nothing controversial, drinking too much, and insinuating sly derogatory things about racial and religious minorities – and learned what they needed to know.

They scraped the young man's DNA from the chair in which he had been sitting and broadcast the pattern on the Net. Genetic markers were scooped up routinely the next day and when he left finger skin on a lamp-post around which he swung in too-tired up-too-long jubilation (short-lived, I can tell you) in the seventy-seven Computer Club niche, he was flagged. When he left the meeting, acting like one of the geeky guys, our people were waiting.

We do this for a living, George. We are not amateurs.

MemoRacer taught us how to handle hackers. He wanted to live in the past, did he? Well, that's where he was allowed to live – forever.

Chemicals and implants worked their magic, making him incapable of living in the present. When he tried to focus on what was right in front of his eyes, he couldn't see it. That meant that he sounded like a blithering idiot when he tried to speak with people who lived exclusively in the present. MemoRacer lived in a vast tapestry of historical understanding that he couldn't connect in any meaningful way to the present or the lived experience of people around him.

There is an entire niche now of apprehended hackers living in the historical past and exchanging data but unable to relate to contemporary niches. It's a living hell because they are immensely knowledgeable but supremely impotent and know it. They teach seminars at community centers which we support as evidence of our benevolence and how wrong they are to hate us.

You want to know about the past? By all means! There's a seminar starting tomorrow, I say, scanning my planner. What's your interest? What do you want to explore? Twentieth century Chicago killers? Herbal medicine during the Ming Dynasty? Competitive intelligence in Dotcom Days? Pick your poison!

And when they leave the seminar room, vague facts tumbling over one another in a chaotic flow to nowhere, they can't connect anything they have heard to their lives.

So everybody pretty much has what they want or at least what they need, using the benchmarks we have established as the correct measures for society.

The Hump is relatively happy.

The dregs skulk about as reminders of a mythic history we have invented that everyone fears.

People perceive and conceive of things in helpful and useful ways and act accordingly.

And when we uplink to nets around all the planets and orbiting colonies, calling the roll on every niche in the known universe, it always comes out right.

Everybody is present. Everybody is always present.

Just the way we like it.

Introduction to "The Geometry of Near"

This story was a thank you note to the many young hackers who allowed me to share their world and understand some of their motivations and approaches to the creative life.

I had recently left the professional ministry when Jeff Moss, the entrepreneurial genius behind Def Con and the Black Hat Briefings, allowed me to keynote Def Con IV. There were 375 in attendance, I believe, in contrast to the roughly 8000 in 2009 when I spoke there for the twelfth time. My association with the men and women of that world has never ceased to energize, instruct and entertain me. I love it.

When this story was published in *Phrack*, a well-known hacker zine, along with "Break, Memory," I was delighted.

Hackers live a multi-sided life, as I call it in "Break, Memory." The reconstruction of social worlds and political worlds and economic worlds has meant that traditional and simplistic constructions of right and wrong don't always hold. Our moral points of reference have also shifted, causing issues related to "identity shift." I continue to address those issues in speeches for security and intelligence professionals in a number of countries.

Had I not been welcomed into that hacker world, first, then the security worlds in which many "hackers," wearing different uniforms (black t-shirts are not welcome in the agencies), really work, I would never have learned how multi-sided life has become, how impossible it is to know the players by their uniforms, how essential counter-intelligence has become to everyday life, and how clever, really, one must be simply to learn to listen and know what one is hearing.

Ministry taught one kind of listening; hacker pals taught others. Both taught me to see emergent structures materializing in our psyches as well as the physical world, making both psyche and physical world the playthings of ninjas and blade-running adepts.

Morality is not black and white. Things are not what they seem.

Honest. That's just how it is.

The Geometry of Near

It's nobody's fault. Honest. It's just how it is. The future came earlier than expected. They kicked it around for years but never knew what they had. By the time they realized what it was, it was already broken. Broken open, I should say. Even then, looking at the pieces of the egg and wondering where the bird had flown, they didn't know how to say what it was. The words they might have used had broken too.

Now it's too late. The future is past.

It was too far. They can't see far. They can only see near.

Me and my friends, we see far, but we see near, too. It's linking near and far in fractal spirals that makes a multi-dimensional parallax view, providing perspective. It's not that we have better brains than our Moms and Pops, but hey, we were created in the image of the net and we know it. They live it, everybody has to live it now, but they still don't know it.

Look at my Mom and Pop on a Thursday night in the family room. You'll see what I mean.

They are sitting in front of the big screen digital television set watching a sitcom. The program is "Friends." Mom calls the six kids, the six young people excuse me, "our friends." They've been watching the show for years and know the characters better than any of the neighbors. The only reason they know the neighbors at all is because I programmed a scanner to pick up their calls. At first they said, how terrible, don't you do that. Then they said, what did she say? Did she really say that? Then they left it on, listening to cell calls from all over the city, drug deals ("I'm at the ATM, come get your stuff"), sex chat ("I'm sitting at your desk, my feet on the edge, touching myself"), trivia mostly, and once in a while the life of a house down the street broadcasting itself through a baby monitor.

The way they reacted to that, the discovery that walls aren't walls anymore, reminded me of a night when I told some kids it was time to feed a live mouse to Kurtz, my boa constrictor. Oh, how horrible! they cried. Oh, I can't watch! Then they lined up at the tank, setting up folding chairs to be sure they could see the mouse trembling, the sudden strike, the big squeeze. They gaped as the hingeless jaw dropped and Kurtz swallowed the dead mouse. They waited for the tip of its tail to disappear into his mouth before getting up saying yuuuchhh! That's gross!

People in the neighborhood only became real to Mom and Pop when I made them digital, don't you see, when I put them on reality radio. Only when I turned the neighbors into sitcom characters did Mom and Pop have a clue. When they hacked the system in other words.

That's what hacking is, see. It's not hunching over your glowing monitor in your bedroom at three in the morning cackling like Beavis or Butt-head while you break into a bank account – although sometimes it is that too – it's more of a trip into the tunnels into the sewers into the walls where the wires run and the pipes and you can see how things work. It's hitting a wall and figuring out how to move through it. How to become invisible, how to use magic. How to cut the knot, solve the puzzle, move to the next level of the game. It's seeing how shit we dump relates to people who think they don't dump shit and live as if. It's seeing how it all fits together.

"Our friends." Said as if she means it. I mean, is that pathetic or what?

The theme music is too loud as they sink down in overstuffed chairs and turn the volume even higher with a remote I had to program so they could use it. Their lives seldom deviate more than a few inches from the family room. Put the point of a compass down on the set and you can draw a little circle that circumscribes their lives. Everything they know is inside that circle. Two dimensions, flat on its back.

The geometry of near.

Those are my friends, Mom says with a laugh for the umpteenth time. The commercial dissolves and expectations settle onto the family room like the rustling wings of twilight. The acting is always overdone, they mug and posture too much, the laugh tracks are too loud. The characters say three, maybe four hundred words in half an hour, barely enough to hand in to an English teacher on a theme, but more than enough to build a tiny world like a doll's house inside a million heads. Those scripted words and intentional gestures sketch out the walls of houses, the edges of suburban lots, the city limits of their lives, all inside their heads. Hypnotized, they stare at the screen for hours, downloading near vistas, thinking they have a clue.

In family rooms all over the world, drapes closed and lights low, people sit there scratching while they watch, most eat or drink something, and some masturbate. Some get off on Rachel, some Monica. Gays like Joey. Bloat-fetishists go for Chandler. I don't know who gets off on Ross. I do know, though, that all over the world there are rooms smelling of pizza, beer and semen. Some clean up the food they spill before the show is over and some leave it. Some come into a napkin and ball it up and put it on a table until a commercial but some take it straight to the garbage and wash their hands on the way back. Funny. They beat off to a fantasy character as sketchy as a cartoon but wash their hands before coming back from the commercial. After sitting there for all those hours, they ought to wash out their souls with soap, not their hands.

Everybody masturbates, actually. That's what it means to watch these shows. People get off on a fantasy and pretend the emptiness fills them up so they do it again. And again.

Who writes these scripts, anyway? People who have lost their souls, obviously. These people have no self. They put it down somewhere then forgot where they put it. They are seriously diminished humans.

But hey, this is not a rant about people who sell their souls. That's true of everybody who lives in a world of simulations and doesn't know it. Those who know it are masters, their hands on the switches that control the flow of energy and information. Those gates create or negate meaning, modify or deny. Me and my friends we control the flow. The difference is all in the knowing and knowing how.

But that's not what we were fighting about. We were fighting about real things.

I just read an army paper some colonel wrote critiquing the army for thinking backwards. Thinking hierarchically, he said, thinking in terms of mechanistic warfare. The writer self-styling himself a modern insightful thinker, Net-man, an apostle of netcentric warfare, a disciple of the digerati.

It's always colonels, right? trying to get noticed. The wisdom of the seminar room. Talk about masturbation. They write for the same journals they read, it's one big circle jerk. They never call each other on their shit, that's the deal, not on the real stuff, but they can't fool us all the time. Just some of the people some.

It's funny, see, the colonel talks about hierarchies and nets but this guy's obviously Hierarchy Man, he lives in a pyramid, he can't help it. He has the fervor of a convert who suddenly saw the blinding light, saw that he had been living in the near, but all he can do is add on, not transform. An extra bedroom, a new bathroom, is not a new floor plan. The guy is excited, sure, he had a vision that blew his mind, but he thought that meant he could live there and he can't. Seeing may be believing but that's about all. The future is past, like I said. The evidence is guys like that writing stuff like that. Those of us who have lived here all of our lives, who never lived anywhere else, we can see that. He's a mummy inside a pyramid looking out through a chink in a sealed tomb. That's why we laugh, because he can't see himself trailing bandages through the dusty corridors. New converts always look funny to people who live on the distant shore where they just arrived, shipwrecked sailors ecstatic to feel the sand under their feet. They think it's bedrock but it's quicksand..

Here's an example. Go downstairs and go into the kitchen where another television set records the President's speech. (I had to show them how to do that too.)

When we watch it together later, I point out that it's not really the president, not really a person, it's only an image in pixels, a digital head speeching in that strange jerky way he has so when you try to connect, you can't. You think you get the beat but then there's a pause, then a quick beat makes you stumble trying to synchronize. It's how his brain misfires, I think. I think he did that doing drugs, maybe drinking. He was in and out of rehab and who the hell knows what he did to himself. Of course the Clintons did coke and all kinds of shit. Anyway he is talking to people who are eating and drinking and masturbating, not even knowing it, hands alive and mobile in their pockets, getting off on his projected power and authority. He talks about "our country" and I laugh. Pop shoots me a glare because he doesn't have a clue. Pop thinks he lives in a country. Because the prez keeps saying "our country" and "this nation" and shit like that. But countries are over. Countries ended long ago. This president or his dad made money from oil or wherever else they put money to make money. Millions of it, more than enough to keep the whole family in office for generations. They have this veneer of patricians but their hands are dripping with blood. His grand-dad too, look it up. They taught evil people how to torture, kill, terrorize, but they wear this patrician veneer and drip with self-righteousness, always talking about religion. It is so dishonorable. Yet this semi-literate lamer, this poser, we honor, his father the chief of the secret police, his brother running his own state, this brain-damaged man who can't connect with himself or anyone else, his words spastic like bad animation out of synch with that smug smirk, this man we honor? Give me a fucking break.

Anyway, he isn't really there, it's all pixels, that's the point. The same people who made "Friends" and made that mythical neighborhood bar and made that mythical house on the mythical prairie created him too out of whole cloth. So people sit there and scratch, eat drink and masturbate, getting off on the unseen artifice of it all. And these people they have made, these people who project power, they all have their own armies, see, they have their own security forces, their own intelligence networks. They have to because countries ended and they realized that those who are like countries, forgive me, like countries used to be, now must act like countries used to act. They have their own banks and they even have their own simulated countries. Some Arabs bought Afghanistan, the Russian mafia bought Sierra Leone, they own Israel too, can I say that without being called an anti-Semite? These people in their clouds of power allow countries to pretend to exist and download simulations of countries into the heads of masturbating scratchers because it works better to have zombies. So people who think they live in countries can relate to what they think are countries inside their heads. Zombies thinking they are "citizens of countries" because they can't think anything else, because they live inside the walls of the doll's house in their heads. "I am a citizen of this country," says the zombie, feeling safe and snug inside a non-existent house in the non-space of his programmed brain. All right then, where is it? The zombie says here, there, pointing to the air like grandma after surgery pointed to hallucinations, telling them to get her a glass of water, telling them to sit down and stop making her nervous. It's all dribble-glass stuff, zombies in Newtonian space that ended long ago; they stare through the glass at the quantum cloud-cuckoo land the rest of us live in, calling it the future. Mistaking space for time the way that colonel inside his pyramid thinks he's net-man.

People who live in clouds of power live behind tall walls, taller than you can imagine. We never really see what's behind those walls. Zombies never climb those walls because of the private armies. Their "security forces" would have a zombie locked up in a heartbeat if he tried.

On the network when we take over thousands of machines and load Trojans letting them sit there until we are ready to use them in a massive attack, we call them zombies. The zombies are unaware what is happening to them. We bring them to life and they rise from their graves and march. Those are our clouds of power, tit for tat. Mastering the masters.

Meanwhile Moms and Pops sit in their chairs not knowing that Trojans are being downloaded into their brains. The code is elegant, tight, fast. Between the medium in which the code is embedded and the television or network that turns it into illusions of real people, real situations, the sleight of hand is so elegant, enticing bird-like Moms and Pops into digital cages. Then when they move the cages, the birds move too. They give the birds enough room to flap their wings so they think they're free.

Or look at the bigger picture. Imagine a country with borders drawn in black. Then imagine a mouth blowing a pink bubble and the bubble bursting obliterating borders and then there's a pink cloud instead of the little wooden shapes of states or countries they used to play with when they were kids. Bubblegum splatters all over the world creating cloud-places that have no names. They are place markers until names are invented. These are the shapes kids play with now, internalizing the difference.

Try telling that to zombies, though. They sit there listening as sitcoms and so-called reality shows and faux news put them into a deep sleep. Images of unreality filter into their brains and define their lives. Tiny images, seen near, seem big. Seem almost lifelike. Inside these miniature worlds, Moms and Pops believe they are far-seeing, thinking they think. Because they are told that near is far and little is big and so it is.

That's what the fight was about. It wasn't personal. It's just that we see how silly it is, the way they think, what they think is real. It's not personal! Honest!

When I was twelve I ran a line out to the telephone cable behind the house. I listened to the neighbors talk mostly about nothing until the telephone company and a cop dropped by. I pleaded stupidity and youth and Pop gave me a talk and I nodded and said yeah, right, never again. Those were the good old days when hacking and phreaking were novelties and penalties for kids were a slap on the wrist.

My favorite telephone sitcom was "The Chiropractor's Wife."

That woman she lived around the corner and lowered the narrowness bar beyond belief. You see her on the street with her kids or walking that damned huge dog of theirs, you wouldn't know it. She looked normal. On good days she looked good even with her blonde hair down on her shoulders, smiling hello. Still, she raised oblivious to the level of an art form.

I guess she was terrified. Her life consisted of barely coping with two kids who were four and six I think and serving on a committee or two at school like for making decorations for a Halloween party. Other than that, near as I could tell, she talked to her mother and made dinner for the pseudo-doc. Talked to her mother every day, sometimes for hours.

The conversation was often interrupted by long pauses. Well, the wife would say. Then her mother would say, well. Then there might be silence for twenty seconds. I am not exaggerating, I clocked it. Twenty-four seconds was their personal best. That might not sound like much but in a telephone conversation, it's eternity. Then they would go back over the same territory. They were like prisoners walking back and forth in a shared cell, saying the same things over and over. I guess it was mostly the need to talk no matter what, drawing the same circles on a little pad of paper. I imagined the wife making those circles on a doodle pad in different colors and that's when I realized that people around me lived by a different geometry entirely. How the landscape looks is determined by how you measure distance. How far to the horizon. That's when I began to invent theorems for a geometry of near.

Example.

Here in Wolf Cove there is the absolute silence of shuttered life. The only noise we hear is traffic from the freeway far over the trees. We have lots of trees, ravines, some little lakes. That's what it is, trees and ravines and houses among the trees. That sound of distant traffic is like holding a seashell up to your ear. It's the closest we come to having an ocean. No one can park on the street so a car that parks is suspect. The cops know everyone by sight so anyone different is stopped. The point I am making is, Wolf Cove encloses trees and lakes and houses with gates of silence, making it seem safe, but in fact it has the opposite effect. It creates fear that is bone deep. It's like a gated community with real iron gates and a rent-a-cop. It makes people inside afraid of what's outside so no one wants to leave. It's like we built an electric fence like the kinds that keep dogs inside except we're the dogs.

One day there was a carjacking at a mall ten miles away. Two guys did it who looked like someone called central casting and said hey, send us a couple of mean-looking carjacker types. They held a gun on a gray lady driving a Lexus and left her hysterical in the parking lot. I knew the telephone sitcom was bound to be good so I listened in on the wife and her hold-me mother.

They talked for more than two hours, the wife saying how afraid she was she wouldn't get decorations done for the Halloween party at the school. She almost cried a couple of times, she was that close to breaking, just taking care of a couple of kids and making streamers and a pumpkin pie. But every now and again she said how afraid she was they'd take her SUV at gunpoint next time she went shopping. The television had done its job of keeping her frightened, downloading images of terrified victims morning noon and night. Fear makes people manageable.

Finally the wife said, maybe we ought to move. I couldn't believe my ears. I mean, she lived in Wolf Cove inside an electric fence, so where the hell would she go? Her fears loomed in shadows on the screen of the world like ghosts and ghouls at that Halloween party. Everywhere she looked, she saw danger. Wherever there was a door instead of a wall, she felt a draft, an icy chill, imagining it opening. She got out of bed and checked the locks when everyone else was asleep. Once she had to go get something on the other side of town and you would have thought she was going to the moon. She went over the route on a map with her mother. Did she turn here? Or here? She had a cell phone fully charged – she checked it twice – and a full tank of gas, just in case. Just in case of what? So I wasn't surprised when she said after the carjack that maybe they ought to move to Port Harbor, ten miles north. Then her mother said, well. Then the wife said well and then there was silence. I think I held my breath, sitting in my bedroom listening through headphones. Then her mother said, well, you would still have to shop somewhere.

Oh, the wife said. I hadn't thought of that.

The geometry of near.

So many people live inside those little circles, more here than most places. I live on the net, I live online, I live out there. I keep the bedroom door shut but the mindspace I inhabit is the whole world.

When I was eleven I found channels where I learned so much just listening. I kept my mouth shut until I knew who was who, who was a lamer shooting off his mouth and who had a clue. Then somebody asked a question I knew and I answered politely and they let me in. I wasn't a lurker any longer, but I took it easy, asking questions but not too many. I stayed up late at Border's and other midnight bookstores, aisles cluttered with open O'Reilly books, figuring out what I could before I asked. You have to do the homework and you have to show respect. Once they let me in, I helped guys on rungs below. I was pretty good at certain systems, certain kinds of PBX, and posted voice mail trophies that were a hoot. Some came from huge companies that couldn't secure their ass with a cork. The clips gave the lie to their PR, showing what bullshit it was. So everybody on the channel knew but had the good sense not to say, not let anybody know. That would be like leaning over a banister and asking the Feds to fuck us please in the ass.

So I learned how to live on the grid. I mapped it inside my head, constantly recreating images of the flows, shadows in my brain creating a shadow self at the same time. The shadow self became my self except I could see it and knew how to use it.

It wasn't hacking the little systems, don't you see, the boxes or the telephones, it was the Big System with a capital B and a capital S. Hacking a system means hacking the mind that makes it. It's not just code, it's the coder. The code is a shadow of the coder's mind. That's what you're hacking. You see how code relates to the coder, shit, you understand everything.

Anyway, Mom and Pop were talking one night and Mom said she had seen the Bradley's out on their patio. They were staring down at the old bricks, thinking about redoing it. It meant rearranging shrubs and maybe putting in some flowers and ground cover. It sounded like a big deal, the way they talked about it, making this little change sound like the Russian Revolution. It was like the time the Adams' built a breakfast nook, you would have thought they had terraformed a planet.

So Mom said to Virginia Bradley, how long have you been in this house now? as long as we have? Oh no, Virginia said. We've been here thirteen years. Oh, Mom said We've been fifteen. But then, Virginia said, we only moved from a block away. Mom said, Oh? I didn't know that. Virginia said, yes, we lived in that little white house on the corner the one with the green shutters for seventeen years. Mom said, I didn't know that. Not only that, Virginia said with a little laugh, but Rick, that was her husband, Rick grew up around the corner. You know that ranch where his mother lives? Mom said, the one where the sign says Bradley? I didn't realize (only neighbors thirteen years) that was his mother. Yes, he grew up in that house, then when we got married we moved to the white house with the green shutters and thirteen years ago when Stonesifers moved to the lakes then we moved here.

The heart enclosed in apprehension becomes so frightened of its own journey, of knowing itself, that it draws the spiral more and more tightly, fencing itself in. Eventually the maze leads nowhere. This village with its winding lanes and gas lamps for all its faux charm was designed by a peasant culture afraid of strangers, afraid of change, a half-human heart with its own unique geometry.

Yep, you guessed it. The geometry of near.

Hypnosis does an effective job of Disneylanding the loneliness of people who live near. Sometimes that loneliness leaks out into their lives and that, really, was what the fighting was about.

Some business group asked Pop to give a dinner speech. They asked him over a year ago, so he had it on the calendar all that time. He really looked forward to it, we could tell by the time he spent getting ready. He even practiced his delivery. They told Pop to expect a few hundred people but when he showed up with all his slides, there were only twenty-three.

I am so sorry, said Merriwether Prattleblather or whoever asked him to speak. It never occurred to any of us when we scheduled your talk that this would be of all things the last episode of Seinfeld.

Pop got a bit of a clue that night. He was pretty dejected but he knew why. These are people, he said, who have known each other for years. This meeting is an opportunity to spend time with real friends. But they preferred to spend the night with people who are not only not real, but don't even make sense or connect to anything real. They would rather passively download digital images, he said, using my language without realizing it, than interact with real human beings.

So Pop had half a clue and I got excited, that doesn't happen every night, so I jumped in, wanting to rip to the next level and show how it all connects from Walter Lippmann to Eddie Bernays to Joseph Goebells, news PR and propaganda one and the same. That got Pop angry. It undermined that doll's house in his head, I can see now. The walls would collapse if he looked so he can't look. Besides, he had to put his frustration somewhere and I was safe. Naturally I became quite incensed at the intensity of his commitment to being clueless. Christ, Pop, I shouted, they stole your history. You haven't got a clue because everything real was hidden. Some of the nodes are real but the way they relate is disguised in lies. He shouts back that I don't know what I'm talking about. The second world war was real, he says, hitting the table, not knowing how nuts he looks. Oh yeah? Then what about Enigma? Before they disclosed it, you thought totally differently about everything in that war. You had to, Pop! Context is content and that's what they hide, making everything look different. It's all in the points of reference. They've done that with everything for fifty years. It's like multispectral camouflage that I read about in space, fake platforms intended to look real. Nothing gets through, nothing bounces back. You live in a hall or more like a hologram of mirrors, Pop, can't you see that?

We both kept shouting and sooner or later I figured fuck it and went to my room which is fine with me because I would rather live in the real world than the Night of the Living Dead down there.

I know why Pop can't let himself know. I understand. Particularly at his age, you can't face the emptiness of it all unless you know how to fill it again, preferably with something real. Knowing you know how to do that makes it bearable like looking at snakes on Medusa's head in a mirror. It keeps you from turning to stone.

Me and my friends we don't want to turn to stone ever. Not ever. Maybe it's all infinite regress inside our heads, nobody knows. But playing the game at least keeps you flexible. It's like yoga for the soul.

When do I like it best? That's easy. Four in the morning. I love it then. There's this painting by Rousseau of a lion and a gypsy and the world asleep in a frieze that never wakes up. That's what it feels like, four in the morning, online. The illusory world is asleep, shut up like a clam, I turn on the computer and the fan turns into white noise. The noise is the sound of the sea against the seawall of our lives. The monitor flickers alight like a window opening and I climb through.

It's all in the symbols, see, managing the symbols. That makes the difference between half an illusion and a whole one. Do you use them or do they use you? If they use you, do you know it, do you see it, and do you use them back? Who's in charge here? Are you constantly taking back control from symbols that would sweep you up in a flood? Are you conscious of how you collude because brains are built to collude so you know and know that you know and can take back power? Then you have a chance, see, even if the hall of mirrors never shows a real reflection. Then we have a chance to get to the next level of the game if only that and that does seem to be the point.

Me and my friends we prefer the geometry of far. This bedroom is a node in a network trans-planetary or trans-lunar at any rate, an intersection of lines in a grid that we navigate at light speed. This is soul-work, this symbol-manipulating machinery fused with our souls, we live cyborg style, wired to each other. The information we exchange is energy bootstrapping itself to a higher level of abstraction.

Some nights you drop down into this incredible place and disappear. Something happens. I don't know how to describe it. It's like you drop down into this place where most of your life is lived except most of the time you don't notice. This time, somehow you go there and know it. Instead of thinking, leaning forward from the top of your head, its like lines of electromagnetic energy showing iron filings radiating out from the base of your skull. Information comes and goes from the base of your brain, goes in all directions. Time dilates and you use a different set of points of reference, near and far at the same time.

It's a matter of wanting to go, I think, then going. Otherwise you turn into the chiropractor's wife. I want to see up close the difference that makes the difference but once I go there, "I" dissolves like countries disappeared and whatever is left inhabits clouds of power that have no names. It's better than sex, yes, better.

So anyway, the point is, yes, I was laughing but not at him, exactly. You can tell him that. It was nothing personal. It just looked so funny watching someone express the truth that they didn't know. The truth of a future they'll never inhabit. It's like his mind was bouncing off a wall, you see what I mean? So I apologize, okay? You can tell him that. I understand what it must be like, coming to the end of your life and realizing how it's all been deception. When it's too late to do anything about it.

Now if it's all right with you, I just want a few minutes with my friends. I just want to go where we don't need to be always explaining everything, where everybody understands.

Okay? And would you mind closing the door, please, as you leave?

Introduction to "The Man Who Hadn't Disappeared"

If identity is destiny, what is our destiny when identities are modular, fluid, arbitrary, and often accidental? Or multi-level layers only the top levels of which have names attached to them? Because only at those levels are names in play? Because that's the layer where names and labels are meaningful? Where we reflect each other in facets of multiple mirrors? And because names dissolve as boundaries that define identities dissolve, going down down down, level by level, as if descending through thermoclines?

Is meditation really much different from scuba diving?

And if memories are constitutive of identities... and memories intensify or degrade, change, confabulate, and vanish... what are identities worth, then, in the first place? Who in the world do we think we are?

As the caterpillar asked Alice: *who*... are *you*?

"Questions," said Roy the replicant. "Memories," said Deckard the replicant. "You're talking about memories...."

And last but not least, can someone who is not "older" – whatever that means in our morphing social contexts – understand why this story is naturalistic? A realistic portrayal of one kind of nightmare in daylight? A black-and-white photo that resists "colorization?"

The simple truth, told by an idiot (not), devoid of sound and fury, signifying... something?

The Man Who Hadn't Disappeared

Harry or Eddie or Robert or Lew woke up one morning in a bedroom that had grown so familiar over the years that he didn't see anything in it anymore. The little bedroom in his head, however, had stayed the same for more than a decade, and that was the bedroom he saw when he opened his eyes, a tiny doll's house model of a bedroom that had once existed, one in which nothing ever disappeared.

Eddie's eyes were open but felt a little bleary (knuckles pressing into his eyes, feeling flakes of sleep.)

Vague light had diminished the perfect darkness he required for deep sleep. At first he was barely aware of having awakened. The ceiling was white, cobwebby with shadows. The pillows under his head were white and stay puffed because he spared no expense when it came to pillows. Lifting his head, he saw the top sheet and blanket crumpled in a tangle on his chest; turning his head, he saw sunlight limning the edges of the white shade. The shade made movements in gusts of wind that filtered through the imperfectly glazed glass, slapping the sill with a jerky rhythm.

He threw off the blankets and swung his legs in blue cotton pajamas over the edge of the bed.

He made a noise he had seldom made in the past—the distant past, that is, for the noise must have started sometime which must have been the recent past. He made one now as he pushed up against the pull of gravity, a pull that seemed to have increased over the past few years due to some unexplained but cosmic kind of cause, and he went into the bathroom. Every morning the first thing he did, after opening his eyes and getting out of bed, was go to the bathroom.

Harry had been fortunate. In all his life, it never felt anything but really fine to take a leak.

He flushed when he finished and came back into the bedroom.

There had been two tables, one on either side of the king-sized bed, but now there was only one, on the near side, on which could be seen a slim white telephone, a lamp with a coral pattern, and a paperback book. The book was Raymond Chandler's "Lady in the Lake," published in the seventies, the shiny florid cover, one of Tom Adams', beckoning to him to reach out and feel it.

The glossy cover still felt slick and the inch-thick book felt solid as a rock. The table on the other side of the bed had disappeared. But Harry or Eddie, certainly not Lew and probably not Robert, didn't notice. Instead he yawned and went back to the bathroom and showered and then returned to the bedroom to dress.

His clothes were familiar and hung in their customary spots in the closet. They might have been fashionable fifteen or twenty years before. Harry could have been blind and still been able to pull the shirt he wanted from a hangar to the right, his old jeans from the top left hook, then sneakers from the hardwood floor. Leaning to reach them, he made the noise again. He put on a seventies long-sleeved shirt with narrow stripes, blue on white, not noticing that three other shirts had disappeared sometime in the night or the weeks or months before. Fewer and fewer, these ancient shirts of the ages, five or six of them hanging still, yet they filled the space as if they were more.

Harry or Eddie combed his hair and shaved with an electric razor, then shook the hair into the toilet and flushed it again. His face felt a little prickly still but good enough. Then he went down the hall to the small yellow one-window kitchen to make breakfast.

He opened the front door first, however, and picked up a morning paper. Then he went to the kitchen. Cloudy daylight filled it with countertops and a white table with two white wooden chairs. He took a banana from the myrtle wood bowl on the near counter, peeled the banana, and ate it slowly over the newspaper (before that, he threw the peel in the garbage through the swinging swinging white top) . Harry did not notice that three pears had disappeared from what had been a pear-and-banana bowl, leaving it just a banana bowl and a little dusty.

After he finished the banana and had scanned a few stories of scandals (most were political, some were obviously placed for publicity, and one really angered him – it was totally unnecessary, wasn't it, now? it must have been an editor holding a grudge) he rose and put two pieces of whole wheat toast in the toaster oven and pressed a button. An orange light on the toaster lighted and through the small dirty window on the front of the appliance orange coils glowed, radiating heat. He stood at the toaster enjoying its warmth and read more irritating stories while waiting for the toast to toast.

The newspaper used to have many more stories written by real journalists but most of them had disappeared. They disappeared incrementally, little by little, so Harry did not notice until it had happened. He did notice that once he removed the advertisements for which the newspaper served as a container there was little left. The news hole grew smaller and smaller. Even on Sunday, when he scanned what he called templates, stories that were so familiar they were nothing but fill in the names and blanks sorts of repetitious silliness, he could make it through the huge paper in less than ten minutes.

The orange light went off and the toaster beeped. He slid the hot-to-handle well-toasted toast onto a plate and opened a jar of orange marmalade. Harry didn't notice that the raspberry jam beside it had disappeared. He thickened the marmalade spread with a double dose and replaced the sticky jar, not noticing that strawberry jam and blackberry jam were also no longer there. He washed his hands because marmalade was always sticky and read the toast over the rest of the newspaper and the paper too, eating the toast until there was nothing to read except old stories and other filler intended to keep him from thinking too much about what wasn't there.

What wasn't there was so much bigger than what was.

He cleaned up everything in less than a minute. Then he faced the day.

The day was a vast empty space. He teetered on the edge of it as if it were a pit. With the shades raised, the bed made, the curtains pulled, autumn daylight was everywhere in the apartment, diminishing the sharp edges of the furniture, whitening the titles on the spines of books, illuminating the artifacts on his knickknack shelf. Some of the knickknacks were still there and he looked at them for a long while instead of thinking about how many had disappeared.

The ones that had disappeared were, oh, these or those, the sorts of things one associates with this or that. Some of the ones that were left were bigger than others, some were almost works of art. Their denotation was irrelevant, however. They were less objects in themselves than labels stuck onto events that had flowed by like leaves on a stream – connotations broadcast into a null space, signifying something but Harry wasn't sure quite what.

Some mattered, however. However, how? He continued to gaze into the space they created by defining the nodes of a geometric shape without a name as if he were reading a crystal ball. There were still a few doodads, little somethings, pieces of things and several small figurines made of stuff like plaster clay or some composite. Plastic things, too. A Tudor house, half-timbered, attached to an image of the Cotswolds, cold and rainy, and warm bread pudding in a tea room at noon. A copy of a big fat Venus, her immense belly and breasts he had turned around and around in his hands and then purchased from a slim *jeune fille* at the old Museum of Man in Paris France, the one that has disappeared. Or not? Eddie was uncertain. The original, he knew, was twenty-five thousand years old, more or less. His was a copy, of course, a memory of a memory, and much younger. Most real Venuses had long since disappeared. The people who made them had disappeared. The language with which they conveyed their thoughts and feelings had disappeared. The culture that thought up the people had also disappeared. Then twenty five thousand years of a flowing muddy river buried all but a few, found on the ground. Recent people gave them a name recently ("Venus"), a label big enough to let them pretend that nothing had disappeared. Their precise academic language occluded the immensity of the vast dark cave in which they had been discovered. Their words constructed temporary boats like arks to contain the few bulbous females found and now bobbing along in a flooding river of time, markers of some illusive time and space contained in boxes made of black lines that they drew in their white minds.

The fixity of print dissolved in a digital flow like ice in water running in what Harry and his peers still call a sink and will for a while yet.

One thing there on the shelf was a little rectangular square on which one rested a knife or another thing. There was also an igloo or more likely an Anasazi hut (Harry had never gone to Alaska so it wouldn't be an igloo). Other things faded in the process of staying or disappearing even as he looked at them, flickering like holograms into and out of visible existence, some with quasi-names and some already nameless. He could see the connotations and could smell the connotations but he couldn't quite reach their deceptive meaning. Harry felt a vague pain, a dissonance, noticing how many barely existed, half-here and half-not. He hung under them, holding onto the disappearing balloons for dear life, his arms growing exhausted. The tags that identified what they were and where they had been purchased, neither paper nor digital fonts but chemicals, molecules, cells, had disappeared.

Harry now gave the day a salute, a long arms-over-his-head sort of yawn and stretch and he turned and the shelf went out of sight. He forgot it quickly and absolutely. His eyes filled with whatever was illuminated inside his apartment by the pale day-light. The sun therefore had not yet disappeared, nor had his furniture vanished, nor his apartment, its painted walls or mortared bricks. The galaxy was still intact, more or less. Inside (the galaxy, the world, his apartment) he sat and picked his teeth with a plastic pick to stimulate his gums. He took an inordinate pleasure in the dislodging of crumbs from between his teeth which he felt with the tip of his tongue before he swallowed. Then he washed again, wiping maybe marmalade from his mouth and hands. As he dried them in a faded kitchen towel he saw that his hands loomed larger than any hands had ever loomed or looked before. His hands looked huge. Turning them, his palms and the backs of his hands, Harry clenched his fingers, numb with sudden tingling, until the tingling had not quite disappeared but was much less.

He forgot about his hands as soon as they were down at his sides. He remembered his tingling fingers intermittently throughout the day, flexing them when he did. Otherwise he forgot them completely.

He went to the window of his living room and looked out. Once he had owned an automobile and parked it at the curb on city streets. In fact he had owned a dozen, more or less, and he saw them along the street in the gray light, a white Dodge Dart, an orange little GM something sporty, a blue Mazda wagon, a big dark Buick, a white Tercel. Then there were Fords, a whole lot of Fords, Taurus upon Taurus, all the way to the end of the street. Then the autos one by one winked out until the street was empty again except for the autos of others, and along the curb, piles of leaves waiting to be vacuumed into a truck.

The wind whiskered dry leaves from the tops of piles and danced them away.

"Darling, don't! –" he remembered Malcolm saying. Malcolm was a character in a story he had written fifty or more years before. For a class? A college course? Perhaps. Malcolm had watched his wife Agatha enfolded by the dying light, taking her away. Malcolm was breaking things in the story, unable to cope with the loss—a prescient image for an adolescent at the early, other end of the rope, a tether attached to his youthful self who had twirled it like a lasso with a smirk. Harry or Eddie, Harry, say, Harry once and for all was looking now at the frayed other end of the rope, a rope made of words, words that had held him spellbound in his youth when he believed deeply in so many things that had disappeared. He did not know then that words too were artifacts. Nor that Agatha was a type, a form or a mold like the red rubber ones into which he had poured plaster of Paris, waiting impatiently until he could peel away a white bear, a lion, a dog, still wet and already crumbling.

And a wife.

Harry had believed then in things like enchantment, meaning, the persistence of memory and self.

Harry saw visions of shades or wraiths among the pouring light and the leaves, dust devils suddenly swirling them toward the trees from which they had fallen. Harry suddenly felt, suddenly experienced not remembered the sounds of his childhood kitchen and he smelled kitchen smells, he heard muffled voices and frying sounds and then the entire kitchen was in his head, a perfect miniature kitchen. He ceased seeing the light and the leaves and never saw the young woman walking her small white dog, pausing while it sniffed and pissed, then walking on. That memory must have become someone's, however. Someone must have seen them come and go. But if it were Harry, he saw the walking woman, the trotting dog, as afterglow, a faint ghostly image among the people in his head-kitchen who were so much more vivid, his mother and his sister, the linoleum looking like a bad Jackson Pollock splashed with red yellow white and black as the feet of his mother crossed the floor and disappeared.

Then the entire miniature disappeared. It simply vanished into thin air. He heard in the long hallway of his aloneness their echoing footfalls fading away. Then he saw leaves again in the light of an overcast sky. He saw the day as it disappeared. He saw the little girl, the *jeune fille,* the same or another, for a moment before she disappeared.

He would in all likelihood never see that girl again.

The earth shifted suddenly. The floor tilted and slid up until it was nearly vertical. His hands slid down the slick surface. He teetered on the edge of the abyss, flailing his arms, and fell.

Mail didn't come until late afternoon.

By then the day had for the most part disappeared. Where had it gone? Had the abyss into which he had tumbled improbably become a cornucopia? Had the darkness suddenly poured forth light? Apparently, perhaps. Harry would never know. But one way or another, one thing or another had taken place, something had gotten done, there had been a sequence of things linked in his life or his mind by a thread of happenstance or intention, one. *Some*thing must have happened.

Had you knocked on his door in the late afternoon and asked, what did you do today? he would have told you something and you would have gone away with his story seamlessly spliced to the other stories you hear from Monty or Jessica, Max or Loretta, any or all of the others. The stories you have heard have been edited into one long story, the story you tell yourself or tell others if asked or maybe you keep some of it to yourself and tell the rest, the story of your historic climb or tragic fall, your itinerary with all its interesting (to you, to you) detours, the story of your always ending adventure. Harry's story would have sounded enough like those to disappear almost as soon as you heard it. By the time you said good-bye and went down the short half-flight of worn-carpeted stairs to the inner door of the three-story walk-up, through the mail hallway, out the outer door into the suddenly chilly fading light and blowing leaves and bare trees, Harry like his story would have disappeared and he wouldn't have held it against you. Harry understood how it is.

Not much flesh left on his bones. Not much story left in his story—pretty much anyone's story, like his face—pretty much anyone's face.

The stories, all of them, seem to exist for a purpose. Stories are containers like newspapers for the advertisements of selves. The next day the newspaper is at the bottom of a cage or pulped or burned. Even if saved and pasted, the pages flake and decay. Scrap books don't last. Tombstones grow moldy and inscriptions disappear. The eroding stone and the faded names dissolve into the odor of yew trees' litter and duff. Then the nose goes too.

It is not an offense, then, merely a fact that your story too is a template, nothing but a fill-in-the-blanks sort of repetitious silliness.

Still, for a moment, someone listens. Someone listens. Then forgets.

That's why Harry would never have held it against you. Harry knew.

The real Venus, Harry thought, looking again at the unreal Venus in his hands or his head, had been carved by someone too. The Venus was a story about woman, lust and fertility, a pretty good story, he had to admit, as far as it went.

Once upon a time the carver(s) had heard stories of this or that, but now, there weren't even echoes. If ever a page, now it's blank. If ever a kiss, now it's a whisper.

Flatulence, unanticipated, became a cause for quiet spontaneous celebration.

And mail! So did mail. Mail as little as it was was quite an event. Even when it didn't come, the anticipation was something. Even the disappointment of receiving nothing, nothing at all, was something to experience. Nothing filled the space as much as something. Getting nothing could take hours. Achieving nothing could last for a lifetime. And having nothing was axiomatic, Harry suspected, his vision clearing even as it dimmed.

The mail fluttered into a box in the mail hall (or not), then his hurrying hands retrieved it and carried it carefully upstairs before it was torn and tossed into the garbage (or they didn't).

One piece of mail lived for a short while in his head. No, two.

It came from a place he had once worked. It was all about a change in the pension and stories about people coming to work there, starting a new life, people just starting out, advertisements for people thinking they were fixed once and for all but who in fact were carried along in the flow of the life of a newsletter sent mostly to folks who threw it away unread. Pictures of some of them however made a brief impression on Harry's eyes or brain before they disappeared.

The booklet or newsletter, pamphlet, whatever it was, was quite impressive to Harry, here. There were plenty of photos and someone had taken time because they must have cared. There were stories arranged by decades about different people and what they were doing. As he read however it became more apparent that this missive had not come from his former employer at all. That was the four page benefit explanation or letter already set down on the round mahogany table with the green lamp. This was something else, a second letter, this had come from his old school, and it told some of their stories but mostly consisted of sound bites from people still taking the trouble to send them in. The ones he read said little or nothing of much interest; they were advertisements for the still living in the eight-page black-and-white rag called The Old School News. Reading the names felt like kicking at dirt with the tip of his shoe. A little puff of dust went up, then disappeared back into the earth. Each name an image dissipating quickly and sinking into the ancient ground.

Some names stayed for a moment, however, as if they were typed in boldface. **Susan Loomis** and **John Jensen** were alive and had written advertisements for that happy fact. Harry Doskell who sat near him for two years or maybe more was simply dead. The beautiful Gustafson girls, blonde objects of adolescent lust that stirred an echo of an erection in his tented brown trousers, were also dead. Bob Rutkowski who had shared a room with him for a year at college, a strange bird who hated to be away from home, who went home, who left again, who had his life, he too was dead. Jerry Schwartz either German or Jew he was never sure which, he had had a nice smile, was also dead. Their names were printed in the dead list in the newsletter he held for a long while as the light fell and the leaves fell and the curtains he refused to pull so long as there was even a little twilight were as ghostly white as his mother's nightgown when she came roaring down the hallway in the morning from her bedroom.

The hallway, the bedroom, his mother and father, his sister, had disappeared. Agatha had disappeared, his wife had—Harry turned away from a memory he refused to entertain and forced himself to focus.

The daylight was dying and yellow candescent streetlight painted his space. Day into night.

He remembered once more the linoleum on the kitchen floor

and the voices of the few who loved him then the very very very few who were like cries in the twilight like birds ready to roost for the night and he realized, sitting there in the twilight, it *was* birds making the sounds, crows ready to roost, and all other sounds of the day disappeared. So Harry rose from his chair, leaving the newsletter and explanation of benefits letter on the round mahogany table with the green lamp and went to the window and felt the cold glass with the undeniable fact of the tips of his fingers. The new streetlights were severe, a brutal illumination of darkness that had covered the earth for eons long before night meant electric light. A car went past or a person or two hurried by, their collars up against the wind and their hands deep into their pockets. He felt himself small inside a snow globe that was no longer being shaken, the large flakes settling quietly in the night as the earth ran around the sun and the sun circled its galactic center, a big black hole, and the galaxy wheeled as it would for as long as the stars had not yet disappeared as he himself had not yet disappeared.

These stars, Harry remembered, were the third or fourth round. Stars exploded and their pieces became more stars. If anyone was there to name the next generation of stars, they gave them different names. Likely there will be many more stars, many generations of more stars. Many stars had planets and many planets had life. But Harry would never know their names or why their visits had so far been benign or what would happen next. Epsilon Eridani. Zeta Reticuli. Names once magical now were little pieces of worn paper on slides needing careful cleaning. On each smudged slide was a star and its planets. Labels or cradles of infinitely variable life.

Harry closed the curtains and tried to half-remember the day but the day had disappeared. He went into his bedroom and turned on the light. The bed and the table and the paperback book were still there. A bookmark stuck out, halfway through. He would have that story, then, to know momentarily. Even if it ended.

And it did end. It had ended several times before. Then it disappeared.

The floor trembled, he slid onto the bed before the floor could tilt. The edge of the pit was variable, advancing, and he did not understand the kind of geometry that tried to define it. Nobody did.

Harry felt that his bed or a chair was safer than the floor but of course, he knew.

Harry knew.

He closed his eyes and held his face in his hands. The world inside his apartment disappeared, the snow globe world in his head appeared. He was player and field, figure and ground, and all of the advertisements or stories were torn pages in a magazine or comic book blowing down an alley in a black wind, an empty black wind defining glimpses of pictures on flapping pages changing from moment to moment in the wind and the shadow-and-glare of the minimal light, the form of the lost stories framed by whatever, whatever had been, whatever names or labels had once been pasted onto the torn pages disappearing now in the sudden calm windless still of a disappearing planet.

Introduction to "Jedediah Dodge Came By or Richard Thieme Came By"

OK, maybe a little too clever, but there it is. It felt right at the time, to make more than a suggestion, to take some of the starch out of all that meta-stuff.

Context is content. The job of a seer is to turn context into content so it can be seen, manipulated as a cognitive artifact in the mindspace of more familiar ones. To turn four dimensional structures into three so they can be held in the hands, turned around, and looked at from all sides.

Those who see context and turn it into content are sometimes saints... sometimes artists... and sometimes the craziest people in the streets of the city of life.

Jedediah Dodge Came By or Richard Thieme Came By

Jedediah Dodge wasn't any more out of bed than before. Inside his mind he was still inside the cool sheets, turning and pulling them up to his chin, but his shivering skin said he was outside in a breeze, so he must have been, some of the time.

However much it was, it was enough. It kept the money coming in, just enough. It got him a better dinner most nights and ice cream some nights.

Ice cream some was more than enough.

One can invent reasons for staying in bed or not staying in bed, but people do whichever they do, then invent the reasons. The decision is made elsewhere, out of sight, out of mind. There is no reason to and no reason not to. Jedediah saw this right away and accepted the fact of the fact, not the story of the fact. Or the story of the story.

Had there been a point, at all—any point at all—a reason to stay in bed or a reason not to stay in bed might have been it. The decision was an initial point of entry into animated movement. Something began that hadn't been happening at all, before.

But Jedediah Dodge had given up looking for a point. He had lived long enough to see a few of the simpler truths through the mass of cobwebs and constant disturbance. Disturbance, creating dynamics of flow, intrigued and delighted him. He thought the non-random bands of moving color pretty. An oil slick on a stream of water. A perturbation in hot cosmic flux. A wrinkling in space-time, happening to happen. Traffic backing up long after an accident had been cleared away, as if it were still there, the echo of the wreck propagated in the flow, traffic backing up from something that happened hours ago or days ago or weeks ago or never even happened but someone thought it must have done and slowed to a crawl, creating an initial point of entry into the river.

Maybe that's the way we back up into the minds of the alive for a short while, Jedediah thought, when we are dead. Then the present resumes its more fluid movement.

But all that sort of thought was a distraction.

Distraction began with attachment, like Buddhists think they say. To games, ideas of who one is, other sorts of things. Jedediah began to attach to dreams of being big when he was small and what he would do when he was big. But when he became big and none of those things happened, he realized – in his teens, some, and then, more and more in his twenties, and without question in his thirties – that none of his dreams would happen, including the ones that tagged along after the first like pegs in holes his first dreams had made, then holes alone.

The hole makes the doughnut whole. Take away the hole and there it is: Nothing. Absolutely nothing. Everything and nothing.

Which is why the search for a point is pointless. Some stay in bed. Some don't.

So he would never play ball for a pro team. Never make a breakthrough in science. Never win the girl and waltz her away. Never appear on TV. Never be what others thought they were.

Instead Jedediah Dodge would always be himself. That was the only option, after a while. So he was.

After he was released from waiting for his dreams, he went

out and got a job because that was better than living in a card-board box. He did that a little but not for long. Cardboard box living was a risky business. The progressive city in which he lived built sleeping tubes, all with the best intentions. But the best intentions don't often turn out.

The tubes became places to rape. One crawled in to be safe and another came crawling after, hands and dick and knees akimbo. Rape rape. The tube rocked and shuddered. Noises cried out in the night. The vibrations of quaking tubes disturbed the other tubes, too. Everything connects in the eddying flow. So they felt it higher up and took away the tubes. People were safer in doorways and on the street, they said, or in cardboard boxes.

Not safe, mind you,. Safer. Safer than in tubes.

Tubes are the kinds of ideas people think they have. Because they can not stand to know they know so little.

Jedediah never minded not knowing much. In retrospect it stood him in good stead.

He got jobs, one after the other. His first, doing dishes in a coffee shop, taking dishes from the tables in a rubber bin into the kitchen and washing them there, that one he kept for three years. When he left he never dreamed he would never hold another quite as long. Six or seven, almost that long, but not quite.

Put his jobs in a list, they look like a life. Not really, of course. Just the way we say it or frame it.

Women were uninterested in Jedediah Dodge. So were most dogs and of course cats who were uninterested in everyone. He never had what he used to call a date after he was twenty-one. He pleasured himself sufficiently until he realized that the women he loved were inside his mind. In that he was like others, but unlike them, too, he knew. The fantasies were like smoke that drifted away through the longer years and left his head empty when all was said and done, then left him even more alone in the shorter years that came later. So there was no point in doing that anymore.

Cigarette butts littered the floor of his mind. The smoke was gone. The smell of stale days remained.

He moved around, too. City to city, state to state. Coast to the middle and back again. Hot to cold to hot again. Job to job and place to place. Crowded streets to empty fields, back to crowded streets.

On one crowded street, a welfare worker named Susan took him by the hand and signed him up for everything. It was legal and, she assured him, a done deal. She was paid by the state. That was how he came to have a room, an apartment if you like, but really a small room in a big blue wooden house with a bed and table and sink and a little TV. He couldn't afford the Internet or a terminal to use it. Cell phones were a luxury. He had never heard of either one, anyway. He watched the old networks on his small TV; he didn't need more. He forgot what the shows were about as soon as he turned them off, so he never saw a rerun, not really. Every show was fresh, every day, once and again, and then again. It allowed him to live cheaply.

He watched the shows from his bed when he could. He wasn't any more out of the bed than before. Inside his mind he was still inside the cool sheets but he must have been out of bed more than he thought. He must have moved around a lot more than he thought. To an external observer, his life showed signs of moving a great deal, here and there, up and out and back and down, back and forth to the room where they all shaved and showered and took dumps in the blue wooden house. Otherwise he stayed in bed.

Really now, he asked himself. Why would anyone ever get out of bed? What was the point? And what was the point of pretending?

* * *

These are some of the things he could not pretend:

That he or anyone else had a clue about a god or God or a powerful force. That he or anyone else knew from whence they came or whither they were going. That he or anyone else knew what was coming next or in fact had already been. That who we thought we were was who we were or who we combined to think we were was who we were in the universe. Or that the earth was what we thought, or the canopy of stars, or the vast web of sentient life spun throughout the galaxies.

Humans were a funny species, Jedediah Dodge often thought, observing the things they thought they knew. Ideas hatched in their minds and came out of their mouths into the wind. Their words went into the wind and became the wind. The wind was invisible but could be detected by the feel. The wind felt like a sucker punch or less often a cuddle. It didn't matter which. A kick in the balls or a kiss on the lips. Some liked one and some liked the other. The words disappeared in the sound of the words first and the humans who made them didn't even know. Then the words became the wind.

Humans thought talking was doing so when the words disappeared, they just made more. Jedediah saw that more often than most, apparently—he was often the only one in the room who laughed, or on the sidewalk, in the park or at the long table where everyone ate dinner. Sometimes he laughed so long and so hard, he could not see the rest of them staring. Most humans could not see how funny humans were.

Without annoyance, sullenness or fear, Jedediah knew that these things, the idea things, were buttresses or struts. That was sometimes why he laughed. He could see through walls like Superman. Gods and selves and countries too were buttresses and struts. Even believing the planet was what it was said to be was a prop. Dreams, too. But dreams were a better reinforcement, the sweet dreams, not the others, everything was a dream or a dream squared was a vision, other dream-like things were called thoughts or ideas or mental artifacts or poems or sometimes just a bunch of shit.

Jedediah knew. They arose from how things happened to come together and then they disappeared. Into the wind. That didn't know it was.

The wind.

He had no agenda. He had no need to straighten anyone out. That went away when he was young. Or help them see or hope to see. All that was none of his concern. Jedediah knew that too. Others would come to see it too or not. Other children coming from adults would come to see it too or not. Other kinds of people, here on this planet or on others, they would come to see or not. That too was none of his concern. He knew that sentient beings thinking these things or things like them were numberless and beyond his imagination. He said that now and again and people laughed. Not the laugh that says "I know" but the laugh that says "I don't."

On the street or in his cardboard box or standing on a corner with his hat in his hand or on the sidewalk at his feet, he would from time to time say one or more of these things and show the holes in the doughnuts to people who seemed to enjoy eating them anyway, not even seeing the space they contained. Jedediah himself was rather thin. He ate enough to sustain himself but not much more. He looked, if one looked at him closely, like the hole in the doughnut too. Nobody, however, looked at him that closely. There were trees and buildings and dogs and Jedediah standing there, hat in hand. Traffic lights and telephone poles. Doors and walls that framed the space that no one ever saw. That's how much he did not stand out. He was like the hole in the doughnut making the cake go around and that was enough for him.

When he said those things or similar things, people often acted as if he were crazy instead of somehow sane. Some were inclined to give a coin to a crazy man and some were not. The percentages worked out and favored a meal or two and then a return to the unmade bed in the big wooden house. The sheets were often dirty. But dirty sheets are in the eye of the beholder. Dirt is not dirt to dirt. It dissolves into itself the way words dissolve into words.

Nothing is what it seems! he sometimes cried when he couldn't stand not talking for another minute. *But!* he would laugh, *only nothing IS what it seems!*

Or... The world is peopled with fiends. But don't be afraid. They are as insubstantial as you! Still— (he paused in what looked like thought) you better resist. Or run the other way.

Or, once...

We are more mist than mountain, more metaphor than mist.

That one got him a dollar. He had no idea where it came from, like everything else. Perhaps he read it somewhere.

He found the perfect pitch to maximize their giving, just crazy enough to elicit pity, not so mad they became afraid. He did it aloud instead of on paper so he wasn't a known poet. He did not put his words on digital screens, either. Those media things, paper and TVs and all the rest, pretend that words are more than mist, and anyway, he did not know anything about them. That saved him the trouble of tracking back to the first words or the words first. The meaning of words (looked at words, not heard words) is in the eye of the beholder.

Jedediah's eyes were blue and without guile and did not threaten anyone. The fixture of himself on this corner or that became a sort of friendly face or a thing like a bakery that had been there forever. Or the old post office, the one downtown where everybody went. Things can be like people too. Spare coins made their way to his hat or hand and Jedediah tipped his hat with a nod and always said thank you.

Thank you, he said. Thank you very much. It became a habit, inside too. He woke in the morning or the middle of the night and said it then and before and after he went to sleep. Thank yous percolated nightly through his dreams.

Thank yous for the dreams themselves.

He loved to rush home to his unmade bed at the fall of night and eat fast and hurry to sleep perchance to dream. The twilight like a curtain or the sheets pulled up and over his face turned daytime into memories and then it all faded. All the bright days faded or cascaded into one day that existed or didn't. Did it matter much? From the fading of the day to the quickening illusion, yes, an illusion of refuge, Jedediah knew, was a very quick trip, and that was good enough. Illusions or delusions, magic or mirage, were plenty good enough. They got Jedediah Dodge through many a bad patch.

So in this way Jedediah Dodge came by. The people he seemed to see passed by in the day and night. Some were in dreams and some were apparently on the street. Later it became difficult to distinguish one from the other. They were there one minute and not the next. Or there one day and not the next. Or there one year and not the next. Their faces faded, then their names. Then the fact of having been.

The names they used were used another time or not. Sometimes new names came into being. But old or new, names were labels coming loose from worn folders, and none of them stuck, although some lasted a little longer. Humans changed names like they changed clothes or the colors of appliances in the kitchen and before one knew it, a country had become another country and had a strange name. Then the name became the name of the thing they thought they named and the strangeness went away. Or the planet became a single thread in a complex weave, a node in a network that reconfigured itself with a different name. Looking back, it seemed the same, but at the time, not. A system, for example, suddenly becoming more than solar.

But who knew where it tended or from whence it came?

Jedediah Dodge did not. He knew only what he saw and then only for a moment.

And what did he see one night, rushing home in the cool of evening, hands in his jacket pockets, hat on head?

He saw a billion planets glowing like translucent leaves in the autumn sun when the sun slants from the edge of the world. As if they too had tiny stems connecting each to each, their candescent colors blinding any open eye. No one could see them really, only the light that made them shine, no one knew their histories, not even the ancient races.

No one. No one knew.

But the light... the light was... light was....

The frame at any rate was unimportant. The important thing was, the picture moved from one side of the frame to the other and then out entirely into whatever. Into space. Into nothing there outside.

The picture moved from one side of the frame to another and then outside the frame. Or into another frame, depending. Everything, everything all in the eye of the beholder.

Still, someone saw. Jedediah Dodge saw. There was sufficient light.

Sometimes the picture moved slowly. That was when attachment happened most. Then it moved faster and faster. Then it weren't there at all. There was only an empty frame. Then the frame itself turned in the deft hands of a magician in a tuxedo.

Then with a flick of his wrist it disappeared into thin air, leaving not a cloud behind.

Then the magician, too, disappeared.

And Jedediah Dodge, too. And all his eddying flow, his links to things, links and things linked, too. But most were both. Links and things linked.

When he looked into the mirror in the room where they showered and shaved, his face broke into a flow like the stars in *Starry Night*. The flow was fixed in thick ridges of yellow paint. The flow was very still and still moving, too.

The earth too, and the other planets, and galaxies, must look like that, too. And all the sentient creatures, here there and everywhere, blossoming like algae in the sea, none of which however ancient of days had any more of a clue how come than Jedediah Dodge.

They too weren't any more out of bed than before. Inside they mostly stayed in the cool sheets too or whatever wrapped them snug before they went to sleep or what they did that was like sleep. That was the initial point of entry into animated movement, a transfer from one train to another on the same metro, that or staying in bed for no reason, not moving once at all.

Who knew? They all did whatever they did. And that was that.

But who then was there to tell them a story? Who was there to make the frame, the one inside? Who was there to weave the wind? Who was there in the end but the end itself, a tiny knot in the simple thread?

Who was there when they moved if they did move? Anyone at all? What was the who if who there was, when they yawned and stretched, opened their eyes and moved into the light?

Or... not?

Introduction to "The Indian and the Fortune Teller"

This is a chapter from a novel in progress, *Multiple Connected Spaces* – call it a novel, anyway. I mean, why not? – the form it is or has does not have a name – but neither did novels, before they did – that sounds like one of my narrators, doesn't it? This is supposed to be the part that isn't fiction.

Well, let's say, then, that the Indian in question is not a native American but an Indian from India.

Then let's say that Bobby Jakus is not a fortune teller, really, but he is in a way, enough of one, for the story to merit the title.

One problem of writing, as Holden Caulfield said, is that you start missing everybody. I might have written about Bobby Jakus because I missed Bob Jakes, his ancient antecedent. Jakes was the narrator of *The Rake*, my first novel, one that never saw print. An editor from Putnam's wrote a nice note, the kind we remember forever, that he read it with pleasure and admiration, but it wouldn't sell – any more than this collection will compete with vampires and melodramatic addictive formulaic adult entertainment. So he sent it back. Broke my heart and changed the path of my life.

I remember that when I finished the manuscript, after four

years of eating and breathing its people and scenes, I felt sad, like I did when I left Walton-on-Thames, Surrey, in England, after living there a year and a half, a period of time that became an important period of transition and transformation, a bridge from the aesthetic life to the spiritual. From one kind of dream to another, I guess.

Anyway, I missed the characters of that novel, which I wrote from age 23 to 27, a great deal. Then I stopped thinking about them – for a long time.

I returned to writing, obviously, and the most direct route from Bob Jakes to Bobby Jakus was indeed, as Carl Jung is said to have said, when asked the shortest distance to a young person's goals, the detours! the detours!

And Juicy Fruit? I thank Wilson for Juicy Fruit, like Mrs. Calabash, wherever he is. He isn't J, but he did pull the trigger.

The Indian and the Fortune Teller

Standing at a gas pump in front of a convenience store, his hand on the cold nozzle, Bobby Jakus wondered if he were going crazy.

He was certainly a long way from clarity or balance, a long way from the far shore toward which he might not even be sailing. How could he know, prior to arrival? How could the fragments of a mind know in advance if they would coalesce again, when the mind is the means by which one knows? Bobby J navigated by faith through dark waters, shrinking from the cold spray—cold, yes, he knew he was cold, that was an ineluctable fact, calibrated to quantifiable feedback—Bobby lapsed from his internal focus which kept him unaware of the cold and found himself in his body, dancing in the frigid wind in a vain effort to stay warm. He watched the flurry of dollars and gallons and listened to the periodic ring of a bell on the slow pump. The bell, he believed, was an echo of the voice of an angel here in the grosser material world, chiming glad tidings in the bleak midwinter. Ring ring! Ring ring! Every ring was a note of hope: *Hold on, Bobby! You may be more frozen than chosen, but hang on! We're with you!*

Those words were a paraphrase of what had been written through his cramped hand, translating the message through the course circuitry of his body/brain. He wrote in a trance in a shaky ragged script. They taught him how to let go and slip into an altered state like a suicide sliding into the icy waters of the lake. He loved and feared that tainted state, not knowing why. He negotiated a compromise with his crotchety feelings and vowed he would never go there during daylight, he would discipline himself to wait until sundown. Unaccountably his memories of Alaracon's recent communication set off qualms of anxiety fluttering in his chest. He felt as if his sternum were a wishbone, waiting to be split.

He didn't need spirits to tell him he'd get the short end.

Anxiety swelled in his chest like expanding gas. He felt as if an elevator had suddenly dropped too fast. He needed a distraction. He jittered at the gas pump as far as holding the nozzle would allow, dancing in a semi-circle, covering his disquiet with incongruous behavior.

The spirits had rules, but he couldn't always figure them out. They almost never spoke directly during the day. Maybe it was something about wavelengths of light and calibrating vibrations between states. At most they impinged on his thoughts, mostly with impressions, manifesting a sense of presence around the curve as it were of his mind. He could feel them hanging back in the shadows, waiting for the right time. Mostly they encouraged him or—if they articulated words he could hear—gave advice. Watch out for that Ford Taurus! Stay on the curb! Turn at the next corner!

Sometimes they chastened him with stern directives.

He always took their advice. When he failed to see the Taurus, the voice would say, see? We helped you avoid a disaster. Or if he stayed on the curb and nothing seemed to happen, the voice would say, see? We kept you safe. Or, a word to the wise. Or, a stitch in time.

The clunk of the gas tank coming full shut off the flow. He squirted in a little more, making it even, and went inside and paid with cash. The middle-aged half-bald Indian man, Lakshman Noorkhan, made change instead of conversation. He disliked working at the Stop-n-Go but was happy to have a job. He spent long days and some nights selling gas, candy, pepperoni sticks and doughnuts to people like Bobby Jakus.

A radio played behind thick glass plastered with ads for the lottery. Bobby studied the numbers. Should he buy a ticket? He left the coins and three singles in the depression and stood still, listening to the faint pop rock, then looking at a cappuccino machine across the store, fixing his attention on an arbitrarily chosen... material thing... material thing... so their guidance, if they chose, could slide into his mind.

The coffee dispenser took on the look of a cappuccino machine that was looked at. A person without discernment might think he was staring at nothing. Lakshman Noorkhan watched from behind the glass. The young man's behavior was no more bizarre than most. Nobody, nothing said a word. No one wanted him to get rich quick. So he took his money and left and got back into his battered Mini, waiting before he pulled away.

Again, no one spoke. The air was dead, heavy. His breath fogged the windshield. No marks appeared in the mist. He turned on the ignition, then the heater, and watched the vapor dissipate.

They saved him a ton of money. Twelve times this month he might have bought tickets but no one told him to go ahead. Later, a guide said his numbers would have lost.

Jakus pulled into traffic and abruptly turned right, heading south.

Thinking, hmmm. Why do they want me to do *that?*

Sitting upright and relaxing at the same time, Bobby positioned his hand with the pencil in it above a piece of empty paper. He allowed his forearm to rest gently against the table's edge, his palm on the bottom of the page. The tip of the pencil barely touched the paper, not making so much as a whisker.

Closing his eyes, he heard the furnace blasting hot air, tires churning in snow under his window, Mrs. Mortimer's dog Buster barking faintly from above.

The snow was really coming down. A girl must have fallen in a snow bank and gave a penetrating high-pitched shriek. Then quiet again. The wind moaned through his leaky wood-frame window and made the shade flap. Twelve candles in wrought-iron stands were placed at precise intervals around the room. Whale songs accompanied by Andean flutes played through muted quadraphonic speakers. Aromatic incense lent its suggestive fragrance to the mix. There was little furniture in the room. His guides had told him a week ago to get rid of the old sofa and he dumped it over the back balcony that night. It was still in the alley, last time he looked, covered with snow. Big pillows arranged around the room and a nightlight from the bedroom looked on the hardwood floor like the light of the moon.

He sat at the table, waiting, breathing deeply.

He felt the first flux of warmth closing in around him, white light protecting him as always. Once again the invocations worked. He snuggled into his well-protected space and allowed them to come closer, waiting for them to connect like Soyuz docking at the space station with a mild jolt.

They squeezed in from all sides like a contracting sphere, the manifestation of their incorporeal intelligence palpable. Many or one? Who was coming? He couldn't tell. He felt a telltale pressure in his brain, the hair on the back of his neck bristling. He shivered with excitement: this was the phase when they calibrated their intentions to his receptivity, testing his readiness. They needed to lower their vibrations, come down in syncopated steps to his level, while Bobby honed his receptors, refining the grosser elements of his mind. They were both as it were turning dials, tuning in to each other. Now he extended the internal mechanism, unfolding at the edges, making himself open to their probe.

He reached out with mental energy, feeling...

...a light touch. Yes. Then, very gently, coupling.

Hey, Bobby J! Here we are!

His hand without his mind doing anything started to move. The pencil point drew loops as the spirits moved into closer control of an apparatus they were still learning to manipulate. The loops and whirls grew closer, denser, darkening the page. Suddenly the pencil paused; he inhaled deeply, letting them settle. Delicate, this adjustment was. He had to get out of the way or nothing would happen. This required courage, they explained, not control but on the contrary letting the spirits move into his body and brain, his body/brain they called it, which they described with elegant mathematical precision from the multi-dimensional perspective they apparently inhabit all around.

The pencil began to write slowly, then faster and faster. The instrument (that is, Bobby J) was imperfect. "But," they explained, "you're all we have. You of all the people on this planet have been chosen because you are perfectly suited to our task. You must proclaim our message to the world. You are an aperture, narrow and defective, yes, but still, a means of deliverance—if you obey. Your destiny has been intended from all time and eternity. You have been prepared for this moment from birth. Before birth, in fact. We attended your development in the womb. Do you remember that your mother was sick in the fifth month? Yes? Yet she—and you—survived. [flutter of a chuckle in the shadows of his mind] Yes, Bobby J, that was us, ensuring your safe delivery.

"We will illuminate your path, and you will see that things you believed accidental were in fact achieved by design and with our help. You will see your future before you like golden footsteps in the darkness – but also the price you must be willing to pay. That price will be revealed slowly as you become capable of understanding your fate and embracing it.

"Do not be afraid. We will be with you and give you what you need.

"Accept this message with gratitude."

Bobby tried not to let his ego swell which they warned him would interfere with their plan. He grinned inside his head each time they showed him to himself as he would become, letting him see clearly who he was meant to be. What human would not bloat with self-importance, seeing the unique role they would play in the cosmic drama? With discipline, however, and assistance, his ego could be held in check.

"You must become small, oh smaller, you must become smallest of all to do this work."

The pencil – that was Trance 14/October 22 – wrote gibberish after that, words obscuring words until the paper was a mess. He scrutinized it later in the bright kitchen light but couldn't make sense of anything.

"Don't be anxious if some messages are lost," they said in Trance 14B/October 23. "We will repeat anything of importance. The monitor of this process, after centuries of preparation, is adept."

He was letting them in now, letting himself surrender, moving into a deeper state. His head fell forward. Bobby J belonged to them now, letting them work out their higher purpose through his slouching body, chin on chest. He gave himself up for the greater good, aware that his body/brain was a channel for the correction of a planet unaware of its peril. Catastrophe was imminent unless an intervention. Bobby J was the means of intercession.

The pencil wrote across one page and then another. His left hand shuffled fresh pages to his right which scribbled words he neither saw nor understood until he read them later—words of great spiritual power, words of encouragement, words of wisdom.

Sometimes their messages illuminated the essential nature of things. Sometimes they told deep truths of the multi-dimensional universe, how it worked, although the details were not always consistent. Sometimes their playful exchanges reminded Bobby J to have a sense of humor.

Sometimes they delivered gentle discipline to keep their pupil on track.

And sometimes... sometimes specific instructions were given that Bobby J learned had better be carried out.

Better be carried out, Mister. Better be carried out. *Or else.*

Buster barked and barked, the goddamn little dog did not want to shut up, and on some level, despite his commitment to remain on the spiritual plane needed for the work, the incessant barking massively pissed off Bobby J, Servant of the Compassionate Light and means of grace to unborn millions.

Alaracon, his guide that night, demonstrated compassion, his Cheshire-cat-like smile inner lit like a Halloween lantern.

"All truth must navigate a mine field of interruptions," Bobby's hand wrote without knowing it. "Life is lived via seeming detours, but there are no dead-ends. Everything connects to everything else.

"That little dog is true to its nature. So must you, Bobby J, be true to yours, to our teaching and to our invitation."

Buster's barking nevertheless pricked at Bobby's trance and awakened his ego-consciousness. He felt himself rising through levels of awareness toward the surface of his life. He felt as if he were moving through thermoclines into warmer surface waters. His hand wrote more slowly, then made loops and squiggles, then stopped. He held the pencil for a moment more, then let it fall. It rolled off the wooden table and dropped to the floor. His head came up at the sound and he opened his eyes.

The candles had burned down and only a few flickered, their wicks in pools of melted wax. Bobby shivered, feeling the chilly room for what it was, an empty tomb of an apartment. When the spirits departed it felt like good friends leaving town. He rose stiffly from the table and blinked twice rapidly, trying to calibrate to the physical plane. Paper covered with illegible inspired script was all over the table and a few sheets had fallen to the floor. He walked around them to the window and looked out. For a moment a medieval village slept under a blanket of snow. He rubbed his eyes, closed them for a long moment, looked again: the familiar city street had reappeared, West Byron Street in

Hunting Hill, a neighborhood waiting for gentrification, twiddling its run-down thumbs.

Parked cars looked like loaves of snow and streetlights burned without heat in the winter night. Not a creature stirred, not even Buster; the ratty terrier stopped barking at last, probably eating his owner's slippers, maybe the sofa. The sidewalk below had disorganized holes stomped in the deep snow by somebody's boots and where the girl had tumbled into the snow bank the snow was disheveled. Maybe she tried to make an angel in the snow. Maybe some guy pushed her down. Maybe she slipped.

Across the street on the corner, in a retail strip too brightly lighted for this silent night, a luminous two-faced clock on a neighborhood bank proclaimed the time. Bobby chuckled. The time by which his species marked off days and years was irrelevant to the grand scheme. Whatever the time, it was neither wrong nor right.

"Yes, you must become acquainted with the night," his guides had instructed (the spirits liked Frost, Wordsworth and Eliot a lot, quoting them more than other poets). "To become a warrior of the light one must plunge into the darkness. One must navigate a zone of annihilation before one can read the luminous letters written in flaming script in the night-blue sky. Only then will you know that you have reached the far shore. Only then can you choose to return."

Bobby twisted his head to try to look up through the window. Moon and stars were hidden by an overcast sky. City light reflected from the snow and back from the low clouds. The scene was inside a snow globe waiting for someone to shake it. Bobby J felt suddenly as lonely as he ever had in his life. He yawned and stretched and realized he was hungry. He heard faint laughter through the bedroom wall which meant someone was watching a monologue, Letterman's or Leno's. He had been gone a long time. Yawning more, he walked into the kitchenette and searched the fridge, finding cold pizza in a plastic baggie. He put it into the microwave on a paper towel and, while it turned in the microwave merry-go-round, went back and carefully assembled the drifted pages in an order which sort of made sense. Then returned to the kitchen and read the first page by the dim light of the microwave.

"It is time to begin your training. [huh? I thought that happened long ago.] We have given you the parameters of your mission. Now you must demonstrate yourself able of execution." [capable?] You must be disciplined. Able to follow instructions. Be attentive under any and all. [circumstances? situations? what?] Watch our hands waitfully as a good sub waits upon his dom. Be a compliant bottom, Bobby. Be willing to do what we say when we say it. Be willing to delay pleasure. Not see consequences. Willing to let whatever. Act as if.

"This is the hour of your kniting [knitting? knighting? what the hell did that mean?]"

The light went off and the motor stopped. He opened the oven, burning his fingers on bubbling crackling cheese. "Damn!" he said, sucking his fingers, then scooping up the square of paper towel fused with melted cheese, hitting the overhead light in the other room and sitting to eat.

He ate around the edges of an amalgam of paper-and-pizza while he read.

"The circles of intersecting levels of planetary influence are many—many to our eyes although we do not have eyes we are like eyes we are like living wise eyes all-wonderful beings. We see far. But the many we see seems few to you because you see say red blue yellow and do not know that infra red and ultra violet much less radio or x-rays or the long ones even exist. We see the spectrum and struggle to say in your few dimensions what it looks like to you little cave fish blind in subterranean streams but infinite to us."

[what are your bodies like? his higher entity-self asked]

"Everything will be revealed. We can tell you now that all bodies are apertures through which light shines. Each according to its frequency. Each is designed to amplify and modulate a particular frequency. We see the entire spectrum because we are intermediaries between high and even higher forms and lower grosser forms like you. Your species sinks to the pond bottom like detritus. If we manifested in your part of the spectrum we would seem translucent, gelatinous like jellyfish, or we would be diaphanous, glowing with inner light."

[are there higher beings than you?]

[laughter in many multi-dimensions sounding a lot like munchkins hiding while the good witch, fresh from her bubble, helpfully clarified]

"Oh yes! Yes! We are barely little more than thus. There are realms of beings communing one with another in outwardly bounding links or loops. We are what some call messengers or angels or spirits of light. But that is not our essence. That is how you fit us into your myths. We are fashioned—"

Bobby let the paper go and used both hands to separate the messy paper from the pizza. It seemed an apt analogy for trying to find nourishment in the crumbs they dropped through multiple dimensions.

He read their expository passages over and over again, searching the obscure repetitious text for clarity and meaning. He longed for a map illuminating the universe instead of fragments, in part because he craved to begin teaching. They insisted that his actions would demonstrate his knowledge and then he would be ready. But Bobby wanted more: he wanted his actions to seem like miracles which he would know were causal events in a rule-based universe the levers of which he alone knew how to use. Once people understood that what he did was basic, they would listen.

Not like now. Now, no one listened. He sent the revelations, edited with care, to magazines and papers but they never appeared. He put some on a web site but received no hits. He wrote a blog call Voice of the Compassionate Light but no one read it. He began MySpace and FaceBook pages dedicated to spreading the word but everyone avoided them, refusing to link, refusing to be friends. He created an avatar (Shadow of Alaracon) in Second Life, but no one paid attention to his preaching.

This is to be expected, they explained. "Thus has it always been," Alaracon said. "Thus will it always be."

Every rejection renewed his dedication and he plunged into the universe they described, a recursive structure like Escher's etchings or Godel's theorems, one that paradoxically required one to be inside to gain entry.

Whenever he had almost attained a higher level, he found himself sliding back down a Moebius strip to a level he thought he left behind. The universe turned into a game of chutes and ladders, one he could never win. When he expressed frustration, his guides' munchkin laughter crackled like static in his brain, giving him a headache. Again and again they explained that when he had grown to the appropriate level, that recursive slide to GO would cease, he would find himself standing on the top rung of a ladder in a way that seemed miraculous, then the ladder would vanish and he would remain suspended in the air, both platform and dancer, figure and ground, and he would understand... *everything.*

But first, they said, the struggle. Then the garden. You must learn, Bobby J, when to hold and when to fold. When to raise and when to walk walk walk away away a way a way...

Their fading voices ricocheted in his brimming brain. Then a final remark:

"This is Big Toy time, Bobby J, so learn how to climb. Next will come Big Boy time when you fly.

"So forgive us, beloved disciple, for what must seem repetitious. These are your multiplication tables. This is drill. Transcribe faithfully. Study without ceasing. You are like young Luke on Tatooine, we are like little green Yodas, smiling, kindly and wise. With tough love must we train our pupil. Not for nothing have we come."

Bobby J sighed. Thanks, guys. That really helps.

He reread the pages, sorted and stacked them and punched in holes and put them into a black binder. His book was getting thick. Ragged pages crinkled from repeated readings, so many passages meaningless from scrawl or smear, interpretive translations neatly printed in ink between the lines using words he hoped were analogous or close.

Fear suddenly throttled his heart which pounded loudly and he hugged himself tightly, afraid he would fall. Perspiring profusely, he raced to get into his parka, pulled his woolen cap down onto his forehead, tightened the drawstrings of the gray-blue hood and hurried downstairs to the street.

The still windless night waited, a few large flakes of softly falling snow in the quiet sky and drifting snow all around. Faraway sounds were absorbed by the snow, quieting the city. The distant rumble of an elevated train. Then a snow plough scraping snow into banks along parked cars came loudly down Central into the empty intersection and disappeared with a soft Doppler fade to the west.

Bobby shoveled out his auto and slid through the slippery streets to the Stop-n-Go. Lakshman Noorkhan nodded silently inside his glass cube when he entered. Beef and pepperoni sticks, cigarettes and beer, hot cashews in a brightly lighted glass display, freshly popped popcorn, chocolate old-fashioned doughnuts, elephant ears, éclairs, apple fritters, pershings, donut holes and vadas, all competed for his cash. The radio was low and played nothing he knew. The Indian looked out at the world patiently and waited.

"How fresh are those doughnuts?"

"Fresh?" He shrugged. "Today. Very fresh."

"Uh-huh," Bobby said. Looking around at candy bars, swizzle sticks, rows of flashy wrap and crinkly see-through packaging. He looked at a peanut butter cookie full of chocolate chunks and almost bought it. But someone said or thought no. Instead he said, "I'll take two of those fritters."

The Indian used tongs to take two puffy fritters flaking with icing and put them into a paper bag. Bobby slid exact change through the slot and said thanks. The proprietor put the bag in the drawer and the doughnuts surfaced on Bobby's side.

Bobby J ate the first one standing there, flexing his cold toes on rubber matting covered with slush. He smelled strong Lysol from the store room and washroom. He looked closely at the guy behind the glass, a man he had seen a million times, but never saw the look in his eyes or expression on his face. He had seen only an impassive brown face with dark eyes. Now he saw Lakshman Noorkhan, an Indian from a real town beside some real river, more than that, he saw the man.

The contours of the man's anonymous life shifted into closer focus. Like desert turning into hills and growing grass in a program that made things morph, Lakshman Noorkhan became three dimensional.

Bobby knew who would take credit. Then he heard them laugh and felt a push.

Still, he waited, resisting the nudge. Sure enough, they were at the Stop-n-Go, they were everywhere, they were inside the fritter, inside his body/brain. Yes, they wanted him to, *now!* He resisted again, looking at the stuff on the shelves, not really seeing. Halfway there and halfway back, he made them press. *Speak now, Bobby J: we insist that you speak,* said a voicelet behind to the right. But instead of fulfilling their request, Bobby moved up an aisle, jittering once more. Arms akimbo and legs quaking, looking silly in the digital film the owner would examine the next day, he stared at hostess cupcakes, hohos, crumb cakes, donettes, boxes of donuts (plain cake, powdered sugar, chocolate chocolate, nutty ones), Twinkies and lucky puffs, fruit pies (cherry peach and lemon), cinnamon rolls, coming around in front of a cooler holding sodas, sweet teas, juices, bottles of water into the next aisle, looking at twizzlers, jolly ranchers, chuckles and gummies, little snickers, Swedish fish, lemon drops and juju mix, night crawlers and gummy worms, caramels and peanut clusters, Mars bars, big Snickers, Hershey bars, M&Ms of all kinds (peanut plain and almond, green and red and yellow and blue), trail mix and nibbles, chewies and licorice bits—

Goddamn it Bobby J! NOW!

"Mister, I don't know what you're after," Bobby said suddenly and forcefully to the Indian who started. "But I am supposed to tell you to hang in." He looked closely at the other's surprised features but saw more than surprise. "I can see how much you've suffered. It's a long winding road all right. I can see that. But it won't always be like this. Something better is coming. Everything will come together. Please be patient and wait until it arrives. The universe has better things waiting downstream than you can imagine."

Lakshman Noorkhan tilted his head while the familiar but unknown customer spoke. He didn't know what to say to this young guy standing there among the candy and doughnuts with white icing on his mouth, looking at him so intensely. That was OK with Bobby J. He wasn't looking for a response. The thing is, his job is, deliver the message. Just the message. Then, his anxiety diminished for a moment, he can go home.

The two men stared at one another in silence in the late night well-lighted shop. A bell rang when an auto drove over a signal hose, a car or the voice of an angel singing in the night. Through the shadowy glass and his own reflection, Bobby watched a guy in a yellow-and-black plaid jacket and leather hunter's hat with flappy ears come in and give Noorkhan a twenty, then go back out to pump.

While Noorkhan inputted the twenty and set the pump to pump, Bobby rushed out and got back into his car and skidded off, eating the second fritter with one hand and fishtailing around a corner, heading back to his little apartment, no longer a cold tomb but a warm cave in which twelve candles had burned down but in which the wicks nevertheless remained arranged in a twelve-wick circle surrounding the table of revelation in one of three apartments (1G, 2G, and 3G), only one of which, however (his!) had been touched by a spiral of stars funneling a vortex of energy into a portal (let those who have eyes to see, see) in a freezing night breaking free at last from its icy chains and exploding like Roman candles, sparklers of light spidering into the suddenly celebrating sky.

That wasn't the end, however. That was barely the beginning.

The next morning, Bobby Jakus applied for a job. He knew he had to, had known it for a long time. But Alaracon said he better get off his ass and do it. So he did.

The big guy—"Call me Juicy Fruit," he said—looked at his application and laughed. "That a real name? Jakus?"

"No. I made it up."

The big guy thought about what would happen if he hit the kid, not too hard, just knock some courtesy into his fool head. Instead he said, "You think being an asshole will get you a job as my assistant?"

Bobby remembered last night's lesson and bit his tongue. Practice, that's what they told him. Just practice.

"No. I don't." He took a deep breath. This was a new behavior but he did it. "Sorry."

"Huh." It took JF aback. But it worked. "What you been doing? What was the last job you had?"

"My last 'job' job was working on a garbage truck. My real job is messenger."

"Yeah? Like on a bike?"

"Something like that."

Jakus surveyed the boiler room. The noise of machinery filled the underground cavern. They sat on torn vinyl chairs beside a chipped Formica table. Other chairs scattered in shadows, coffee stuff all over the table. A brown sofa with stuff on it too, mostly clothing. A couple of big pillows shaped to fit the big man's head. Old porn magazines spilled from a stack on the floor like playing cards. Jakus saw Leg Show, Big Jugs, Hustler and a glossy cover with a dom in red latex or leather, he couldn't tell which, ready to whip.

Naked bulbs in a humid forest of wet pipes. Drips and a stream running down the concrete floor to a drain. The big guy sitting in a work shirt and torn jeans, his barrel chest bigger than Bobby's whole body. Buttons straining, buttons stretched. The guy's huge hands dangling between his thighs like hams. Not a guy to mess with, no one had to tell him that.

Jakus looked at the steady drip from a pipe wrapped with a wet rag. The door to the boiler room was open, letting him see a receiving desk, its empty shelf, wire mesh, stairs going up to an outside platform. Nobody was out there, near as he could tell. Nobody here but Juicy Fruit.

The big guy said, "Look around. This is where we work, most of the time. Upstairs is offices. Those we clean, three floors anyway. The fitness center on six, that they do themselves. Condos are not our problem. Just offices and the retail places. Sometimes we help with the entrance, we help Frank in summer on the lawn, trim bushes, pick up trash. Your job is three days a week, four in warmer weather. Pay is hourly, no benefits. Want it?"

Bobby sighed. His body/brain said no but they made his mouth say yes. "I guess. When do I start?"

"Tomorrow morning. Saturdays we start at seven. Cool?"

Bobby looked at the big guy sitting on the too-small chair in his uniform shirt with his name written in threads, holes in his jeans' knees.

"I'd prefer a later start."

"Yeah?" the big guy laughed. "Write down everything you prefer. I'll give it to the shop steward."

He laughed loudly until Bobby looked away.

"Like I say, start at seven." He looked him up and down. "Garbage truck. What did you learn on a garbage truck?"

"I learned when they hit the curb and you're standing in the garbage to hold on. I learned that if you fell, you better just lay there, looking up at the sky. I learned how to hide tools so if reporters came around, your super wasn't embarrassed. I learned that Frank liked to fuck Marie, his wife, all weekend long at their cottage on the lake. I learned that a guy named Red collected loans on weekends but was always nice to me. Then again, I never borrowed money from his friends. I learned to pay dues to a union that never held meetings. I learned the usual Ranger Rick in the City stuff, where gays met in rest rooms, where pedophiles pounced. A couple of times we found fetishists with cameras photographing legs and feet."

The big guy chuckled. "Summer in the city. Yeah, they all around. Okay, then, Bobby Jakus, you know all kinds of shit. Well, at seven in the morning, you start to learn some new stuff."

You're an apprentice, Alaracon had told him. We will provide an occupation that teaches patience. At your quantum level, needs require money to meet, so you must work. We will ensure that you have enough, but you must accept what we provide.

Continue to learn, Bobby J, continue to wait.

<How long, oh friends, his higher mind cried, how long?>

Perhaps weeks, perhaps months, perhaps years, his reluctant hand wrote helpfully. Wait for a clear statement You will know when it arrives.

And we will be with you, always.

In addition, Clairon sang in that high unmistakable voice, Do not sit on the edge of your chair, waiting for the bell. Sit back. This is a marathon, not a sprint.

Suddenly in the sodden basement, rainbows around the light bulbs as if he had been swimming in a chlorinated pool, a sound like a trumpet blared in his ear: "You're a janitor's right-hand man, Bobby J! Good for you!"

As if it was something to celebrate.

It *is,* someone insisted. It's perfect for learning to live small. Learning to be transparent to your purpose. Learning to forget what you must nevertheless always remember, that you have been chosen for unique things.

"All right," he said with a sigh, coming around through the back door into his life. "I'll be here at seven."

Introduction to "Northward into the Night"

"Northward into the Night" and "Less Than the Sum of the Movable Parts" are two versions of the same tale. "Less Than the Sum" came first. Editors said (as usual) it wasn't fiction, it was mostly a philosophical essay.

I am always surprised when editors are unfamiliar with what I think is part of the tradition, as when I replied that the form of "Less Than the Sun" was similar to "Notes From Underground," Dostoevsky's two-part story, the first part philosophy and the second part dramatic narrative. The philosophy articulates the soul of the character just as Ivan Karamazov's tale of the Grand Inquisitor can not be read separately from the dramatic narrative of the Brothers K, as if it is Dostoevsky and not Ivan speaking, as if Shakespeare believes that life is a tale told by an idiot, rather than Macbeth. It happened again recently when an editor said a piece was a sketch, not a story, and I reminded her that Hemingway got the same response to the Nick Adams stories in "In Our Time" and she wasn't familiar with the book, which made me realize that the statement in James B. Twitchell's *Branded Nation,* that one could get a B. A. in English literature without reading a single work written before 1960, might be true.

I rewrote the longer, more discursive piece as "Northward into the Night" and fact-checked it by sending it to a friend with decades of work at one of our intelligence agencies. He said, "Yep! It rang plenty of bells." A second agency friend said the same. So I think I am safe in saying, this is about a particular kind of intelligence agent, ultimately, and his "issues" will echo with others who redefine themselves, i.e. most people these days. His "philosophy" or point of view is the only light he sees at the edges of the event horizon, a vague inchoate glow.

That my own life has consisted of modular identities constructed as distinct personas, each of which points to a meta-persona that is more me than the mini-me's, is beside the point (not). That I have given speeches about "Reinventing Ourselves," how to establish real rather than sham credibility for a persona by linking advertising and marketing to a real product, is also beside the point. (Not,) Equally beside the point is my client list, known and unknown, things done and left undone...

Perhaps, as the narrator desperately wishes, everything is... beside the point....

Northward into the Night

Old men sometimes try to tell the truth. But no one listens. No one listens because no one wants to know. People prefer to sleepwalk through life. They use the trance logic of a hypnotic subject, walk around chairs they insist are not there.

An old man's words fall to the ground like a bird hitting a window. If you believe that nary a swallow falls but that someone knows and measures the fall and mourns, then please, keep on believing. Your beliefs only strengthen the trance. That makes my work easier.

We hang back in doorways, look down the street, and wait. We have a story to tell if anyone wants to hear it. But no one comes, no one ever comes, and if someone does happen to pass by, they don't even glance at an old man, his collar turned up against the wind, waiting it seems for someone. Anyone.

Waiting in fact for nothing.

Indeed, Charles. Our work consists frequently of waiting in restaurants for people who never appear.

And in our sleep, wisdom is folded, as Aeschylus suggested, or was it Bobby Kennedy, one painful sigh at a time, into our bitter hearts, by the awful grace of what some call God.

* * *

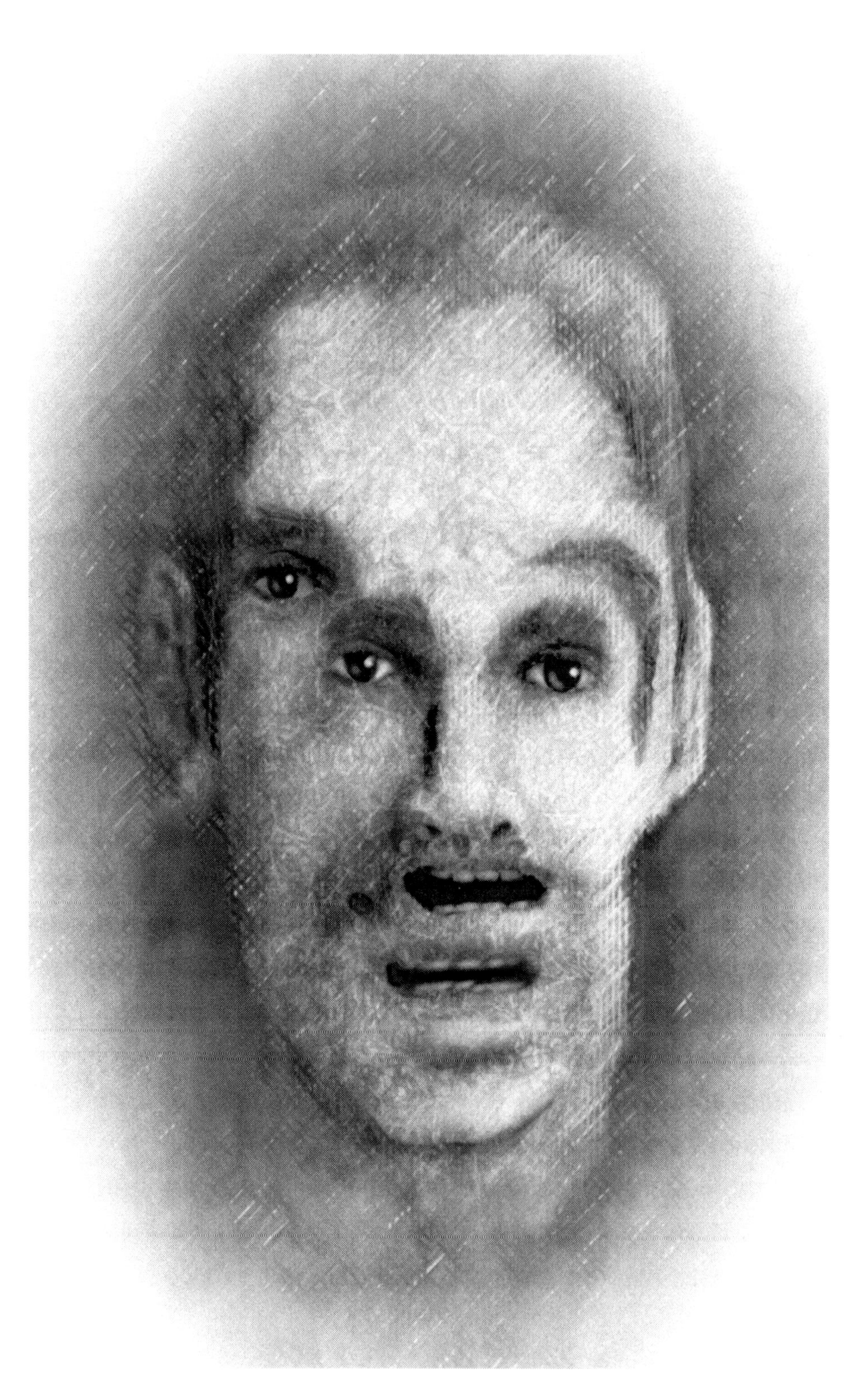

Sometime during that winter, I called Cass and suggested we meet for lunch.

Cassandra is a social worker type which means she would do what she does even if she weren't paid to do it. She can't help taking care of people. Long ago, when we were young and I went more often into lecture mode, I told her about Nietzsche's will to power. She just shrugged. Origins and sources are irrelevant to Cass, while they underlie my work. They are more real to me than the real. I play with context like a kitten with a ball of yarn. Cass takes the yarn as yarn and makes a sweater, she responds in the moment to the poor and distressed drooping in the metal chairs on the other side of her desk. The roots of their misery aren't her concern, not as long as it blossoms into a need she can address.

I've known Cass for years. Like all benevolent workers – clergy, therapists, social workers – Cass has a night side. The shadow is the source of the energy of caring. She's always ready to listen, always ready to love. But when someone leaves, the emptiness returns – until another comes. She feels complete only when one of those needy people is present. And no matter how many she tends, they always add up to less than the sum of the whole, less than the sum of the movable parts.

As a profession, social work is open-ended. There are multiple routes to making a living, just as there are multiple ways to arrange the data points of our lives. Therapy means rearranging the points in a different pattern. That's my work too, in a different way. You can't change reality but you can change the facts. Then you can suggest a way to make them into a pattern.

A craving for novelty frustrates Cass's yearning for wholeness, and both are equally strong. She exchanges men and jobs like some women change hats. She worked at first for community services, moving around departments. She did lots of home visits, feeding on the gritty lives of the destitute and abused. Then she did a stint at County, where trauma doctors got lots of gunshot wounds, knife wounds, torture burns, and Cass got the interviews. She thrived for a time on eliciting detailed accounts of painful lives. Then she worked at New Horizons, a counseling center, mostly with addicts. Now she works with women who get beaten up. She has done all that for so long, she has learned how to use her persona as a tool, then go home at the end of the day, kick off her shoes, and watch TV the rest of the night.

We were litter mates, I always thought. We must have exchanged DNA at an early date. But I was the one who knew. So I always had the upper hand.

We ate at a trendy restaurant on the near north side. We laughed when we read the names of the arcane legumes that had migrated over the plains to the Midwest.

"California cuisine," I said, looking as a waiter set down a plate of white and pale green stalks and leaves on a neighboring table. Curly greens, something that smelled like licorice, raw white things that looked like they grew in vats.

Cass ordered a sandwich with three kinds of cheese, asparagus and a red paste on yellow bread with lots of seeds. Her side salad was full of curled greens and shaved coiled roots. I wanted something hot. My leather coat was zipped up the whole time. I hadn't warmed up despite walking all the way from my car in that wind. As usual in the city, I had to park blocks away. I was lucky to find a space at all.

Cass looked good. She looked and sounded solid. She was into a new relationship so she was hopeful, again. She always picked horses that came out of the gate strong but faded in the stretch.

I listened a lot and seldom spoke, nodding to indicate what she called "empathetic listening." Through the plate glass window the gray sky had lost all definition. The discoloration became rain as we ate and then the rain turned into snow. There was sleet too and slush on the sidewalks by the time we finished eating, ankle-deep and cold. Cass had parked in front of the bistro using her disability tag and offered to drive me to my car.

She turned on the heater and the sleet squeaked on her worn wipers. She turned all the way around to pull out and moved slowly down the narrow street.

"There it is," I said.

"What, that? Where's the Ford?"

"Long gone. I even had a Mazda for a while."

She pulled in behind the old Toyota next to a hydrant and turned off the wipers. The end of the scraping was a relief. Sleet ran in thick rivulets down the clean windshield.

Cass continued to talk about what she wanted to do next, wondering was it too late, should she look for another job? should she give this guy a chance? Elmer was his name of all things. Maybe it was made up, I suggested. Maybe you have no idea who he really is.

She lowered her window an inch or two, letting the car idle and keeping the heater on. Warm air flowed from the vents while a thin stream of cold air from the open window felt like white icing on a cake.

It was one of those conversations that you can't make happen, but when they do, you don't ever want them to stop. First, there was the meal, hot chowder and crab cakes for me, fresh hot bread with drizzle to dip, a delicious sauvignon blanc from Cloudy Bay, the chatter and clinking glasses around us at precisely the right level. We hadn't seen each other for a long time, more than a year, and it felt so good just to be with her again, eating quietly, taking our time, letting the ambient noise cushion the conversational pauses. Like a real community filling in blanks so we didn't have to do it all ourselves.

Beyond Cass at the next table, a young couple was playing footsie, the movements of the draped cloth betraying their game. The tablecloth dimpled and they looked at each other with little smiles. It made me nostalgic. She turned and looked and smiled too. Then nudged my leg with the tip of her toe.

Outside, the snow and sleet were really coming down, the snow blowing slantwise across the window and people hurrying through the mess, holding their coats closed at the collar, dipping their heads into the wind when they had to wait for a light. But we were inside, warm and dry. Cass talked on and on as she often did about her life. I had heard a lot of it before. But I didn't mind. It made my job easier. And it wasn't what we talked about as much as knowing one another all those years that plumped up comfy cushions all around.

Elmer was on her mind. He kept coming back.

"You're so attracted to broken pieces, aren't you?"

"Yes," she said brightly with the confidence of one who has endured therapy and knew her ins and outs. "I certainly am."

"Why is that, do you think?"

She smiled, looking at the cold stuff on her fork and quoted me from long ago. "I see my own face more clearly when I look into—"

"—fragments of broken mirrors.'

"Yes. A puzzle that will never be complete. As if the wrong picture is on the box or pieces are missing." Cass shrugged. "I don't mind. Not any more. Isn't that the fun of it? Aren't you like that, too? The research you do is so complex, it never ends. It always goes in new directions. You publish and publish, those articles you tell me about are so deep, but there's always more. Isn't that the game in academia too? Isn't that why you like it?"

I smiled and took her hand and removed the fork and set it on her plate. Her body was a little broader which happens to women in middle-age but her hand was still slight. A sleight of hand: I pressed it ever so slightly, then released. She picked up her fork. It worked. Her train of thought had vanished. Something else, apparently disconnected, would surface and our orthogonal approach to coming to know one another imperfectly over the years would continue.

If you don't understand ladders, don't play Go.

That was my expertise. That was my work.

Sitting in the car afterward, I thought I was still doing OK, nodding a lot as I said, paying attention most of the time, when she abruptly leaned and turned the heater lower and gave me a look.

"You haven't said much about your work. Or anything else, in fact."

"Oh?" I shrugged, looking away. "I told you some things, what I could, what I thought you might find interesting."

Cass shook her head.

"Paul," she said, her eyes not letting me off the hook. "Paul, you told me when we met last time you were talking to people who had been tortured. You talked to people who tortured too. You told me about it—how they were affected, their behaviors, how they tried to live as if they could escape their own histories, always bolting off through the bushes onto side trails away from the main path. Then you shifted, even more suddenly than usual, for you, and talked about what you called the real history of the planet which no one knew or only a few people and you talked about all these other kinds of life and civilizations far away and God knows what. I couldn't follow it all. But I remember clearly what you said about the Turks and the Uzbeks. It was chilling."

I shivered. I leaned over and turned up the heater. The hot fan blast felt better.

"The techniques don't matter much," I said. "They're pretty cut and dried. Different ones prefer different tools, I think it's a cultural thing—"

She looked at me for a long time.

"Paul," she said, reaching and taking my hand. Her slender hands looked graceful against my big mitt. "Do you remember what you told me once? About people going over the line?"

I did, but forgot that I had.

"I guess."

"Paul—listen to me—Paul, you're over the line."

My chest hollowed abruptly and I felt like I was sinking. I looked down at her hands. They were slender, yes, but they also showed her aging. She couldn't dye her hands. Some things you can't change.

"You told me, you don't know how to talk to normal people anymore. You don't share their points of reference. You begin at some point so far off the track they don't know what to say."

I turned to look outside. "Did I say that?"

"Yes," she smiled, getting inside. "You said you live in a world that people would rather not know. You didn't want to talk about it either, but you did, some. You had to is what I felt at the time. Do you think I would forget something like that?" Her eyes narrowed. "Do you think I can't see what's going on?"

"Why? What's going on?"

"Paul," she sighed. "For someone so smart, you sure can be dumb. You may be a professor but... do you remember the books I gave you about trauma? How it affects people?"

"Sure." I nodded. "They were interesting."

"Why do you think I asked you to read them?"

I shrugged again. "Because what with the people I talk to in my research, people interrogating others or the ones worked on, or people who manage perception, my unusual sources, they all show signs of trauma, right? You wanted me to understand their symptoms, yes?"

"Yes. But why else?"

I shrugged a final time. "Cassie, I don't know." I was truly blank.

"Because," she said, squeezing my hand, "you're showing symptoms too. Listening to them is almost as bad as being there."

I guess it was obvious to her. Doing the work she does, it becomes second nature, tuning your intuition to hints and innuendoes. But I of all people was blind-sided.

Don't make dangos. I *knew* that. Or thought I did.

I mean, have you ever not known something so completely that when someone says it, the recognition is like all of the air rushing out of the room? You can't breathe, you can't even think of breathing. Then, when you do speak, your emotions are raw like someone sank a shaft into your gut and hit a gusher, because they have been buried for so long, buried under intense pressure, and you feel a sob crying to get out but you won't let it.

She felt it, too. She took my other hand and I looked at her lap where she cradled my hands in her own. I thought again, she had gained a little weight; her navy skirt puckered on her belly.

"Paul, you can't not know what you know. You can't unlearn it. But part of you must know the impact of knowing those things."

I nodded. She was wearing a ring, not an engagement. Her fingernails were unpolished but smoothed into crescent moons.

I looked up into the inexhaustible well of her dark eyes.

And everything let go.

"Do you have any idea what we do? Or what they do? What people do? What people who aren't like us, what they think? How long it's been going on? How differently they frame the same data? How insane we are, thinking our clocks mark the same kinds of time? We're like children, Cass, frightened children trying to make the night... Cass, Cassandra, Cass, do you have any idea who we are? How absolutely we are not what you think? How the ground that supports the figure is in a crooked frame? How we are seen – we think. Maybe. How we think they see us, I mean?"

She had unleashed a beast and realized it now. The fear in her eyes was a mirror of the fear in the heart of the human race, ready to make us fight or flee. We have to breed that out. We have to breed it back into recession, into the contingencies in our genes. We have to create a human race that is fearless in the face of the genuinely terrifying.

Cass shook her head. "Do I want to know?" She had lost the offensive. She knew it. She was looking for a place to hide. I watched her cover and duck. Her soul made a furtive movement like the shadow of a bird.

Keep your stones connected.

"Paul, I'm concerned." She gave it her best effort. That's what she knew how to do. "I'm concerned about what it's doing to you. You say you're detached, that you keep an appropriate distance, but you talk to these people, you absorb–"

"No," I shook my head. "No, Cass, I know you think you're concerned... but you don't know. *You don't know.* You're concerned about the wrong things. That's how it's designed. To keep you from knowing."

The floor on the deep well of the night gave way. Her eyes darted back and forth looking for something to hold. During that transient glimpse into my life, into all life, she understood intuitively but without words to frame it, name it, make it stable, she went into standby panic mode.

Then her eyes shifted from my face to the window where snow was falling from the limbs of trees and she found a reprieve. Everyday people passed on the everyday walk in overcoats and parkas, a woman teetered by in four inch heels in slush that stained her hose, for Cass a moment of comic relief, watching her step through the mess. Behind the wobbly young woman, the stone of a brownstone mansion was whitened by snow blowing from the roof. The whiteout obscured but could not hide the old solid stone. Then Cass saw as she tilted her head so she could look higher an elegant doorway and above it a second story window blazing with candescent light.

"Paul—"she said.

I shook my head.

"Cass, my name isn't Paul. It never was."

She looked at me for a moment, then looked for a connection. That's what people do. They try to plug one thing into another.

But there was nothing to plug.

"I remember, it was a few years ago," she almost laughed although nothing was funny. "Someone called you George. You made a joke of it, saying he was getting old."

I shook my head again. "It isn't Paul and it isn't George. And I am not a professor. Cass, I never was. I never was."

After thirty-seven years. Thirty-seven years.

"I've had so many names, Cass, I can't remember them all."

She let my hands loose and they came back to my side of the car. I thought she had accepted my confession and all of the things that it shattered with professional equanimity. From years of practiced listening, she tried to fit the pieces together, casting way back, but some things I had said over the years were true and many were not. Without a picture on the box, she had no way of knowing. And some of the pieces were missing.

What had begun by design in my professional life had became a habit. I hollowed out my life and filled it with inventions.

And would never stop. It was, after all, what I had been paid to do. But like Cass caring for the distressed, I would have done it even if I hadn't been paid. It's what I knew how to do.

It was all I knew how to do.

The distance between us increased at the speed of light. I leaned closer, hoping to hold her in my arms. I just wanted to feel her, I wanted to inhale her earthy scent. I wanted her warmth. That was all. I just wanted to be close to another human being.

But the fracture was too abrupt. In the moment, I had thought I confessed to be real, but as she drew back, her eyes receding forever into the distance, I realized that she saw more clearly than I ever would I had simply as always needed to prevail.

Less Than The Sum of the Movable Parts

Nothing gets us through a long day more than an image of a constant self.

My life is one long day, so believe me, I know. It helps. Thinking that "I" was here "yesterday," "I" am here "now," "I" will be here "tomorrow" – it's wonderful, isn't it? Using an imaginary temporal index linked to a mirage of an equally illusive self to manage an inchoate flow of impressions which turn into pictures in the "mind" to simulate fixity?

I think it's wonderful, anyway. I think it helps us stay engaged with tasks that might otherwise drive us to despair.

Or worse.

There's a bigger question, however: is there a connection between the connections? A real one, I mean? A single template that works from top down, instead of bottom up?

Otherwise, it's just a coding trick—memories encoded in chemicals programmed to disclose aspects of what we call "selves" like origami unfolding to that same subjective self. This recursive program would be a stroke of genius, if a genius existed. A reflexive self, embedded in its own structure, suggests

continuity; seemingly real memories frame the phantom self like planes in a cubist painting constructing odd geometries—inside of which we, all unassuming, happily thrive.

Or – to put it another way – it thinks, therefore we are.

Or, in cases like mine, agencies thinks for us, relieving us of some of the work.

OK. We emerge from braided twists of code like cookies from flour water and sugar. But where does the recipe come from?

Well—who knows? Maybe it evolved. Maybe we were cooked up in a kitchen. I prefer fun hypotheses like Charles Fort's. It sounded crazy when he said it; now it sounds reasonable, now that we know that UFOs are real and have been around for a long time. Fort, you recall, combed through newspapers and periodicals in the New York public library in the early twentieth century, filtering anomalies into his notebooks. Then he bound them into a vision. He suggested that we might be property, owned by an alien race. He didn't know if they won us in a lottery, inherited the planet as part of a bequest, claimed us after a battle, or agreed to accept us in lieu of cash in a game of intergalactic poker. The reasons, whatever they may be, are unthinkable because we have no point of reference. They relate to memories in the storage banks of the alien race(s) linked by connections as invisible to us as dark matter. We don't know if or how they design histories or store memories to preserve identities distributed through folds of space-time. We can't even see them, much less understand how they evolved. We don't even believe in them yet. All we can do is suppose that they, too, construct peculiar geometries in the blank space of the zero point field. Perhaps the multiverse unfolds in their imaginations like origami too, a multidimensional canvass on which they paint or sculpt the equivalent of art.

Who knows? Anyway, the first steps are the hardest: believing that they exist, and then, believing in our belief. At this point in time, we don't believe. We believe in disbelief. By design, I believe.

In a court of law, lawyers tell me, three witnesses who say the same thing are considered the best evidence. Well, witnesses have testified to the presence of our watchers, owners or visitors, whatever they are, by the thousands. The data points are voluminous. They plot countless visits by beings in luminous discs, silent triangles or elongated craft with portholes; they have been documented for decades, perhaps centuries, they have been here anyway a long long time—they or their robots or clones—but we act as if they don't exist. We can't map what we can't comprehend. We have impressions, images of conspicuous displays, stored in collective memory banks, but we turn them into myth. We make fiction instead of history. Fiction is the province of the fantastic and distracts us—and their manipulations of energy or matter seem fantastic, make no mistake. The effects we have observed imply an understanding that we can not apprehend. And they seem to hide and show themselves, they seem to play a game of cosmic boo and peek—but to what purpose?

Once again... who knows?

Anyway... the DNA came from somewhere. Whatever the source, perhaps our owners think of us as dairy farmers think of their herds. Perhaps they sip like emotional or intellectual milk our cultural excrescence which is useful in some way or tasty, an occasional treat, a distraction from the task of searching for meaning. Maybe we add a page to the choral songbook of the multiverse. Maybe they feel affection if they do feel affection when we head for the barn at the end of the day, the sun steeping the pasture with its lone oak tree slanting in shadow. Maybe the twilight sky that brightens before it fades is a liminal image that stirs them, too, a portal to something they have lost and can not recall.

Or maybe they are proud of our halting progress as parents delight in a child's first steps, watching us splutter into our neighborhood in primitive machines, skipping to the moon or Mars like toddlers coming downstairs and walking around the block for the first time, seeing with wonder that there is something real indeed across the real street.

Seeing the street at the same time for the first time. Seeing the bridge and seeing the distant bank in the same moment.

Whatever, we have been born or bred to believe we are individuals, discrete entities, selves with will, feeling and intention, and more than that, that we are the apple of God's eye or – in a more secular vein - the top of the food chain, something special... instead of transient manifestations of energy and matter in complex relationship to everything else.

But it's not true.

We are more mist than mountain, more metaphor than mist.

Disorienting, isn't it, thinking like this? It gives me a headache too. Better to believe our beliefs, believe we are the selves that we experience reflexively as points of reference for the shifting contours of our so-called interior lives.

The task then is to manage the threat of chaos. There are three ways to do this: the Small Way, the Big Way, and the Biggest Way. My colleagues see management of the Small Way as their job. We leave the Big Way to visitors by default. The Biggest Way, we leave to It.

OK. So... are we the sum of our movable parts?

Who knows? And does it matter? We will do what we do, think as we think, regardless, take comfort in what we call "cultures" which like "selves" exist as higher branches on a fractal tree and also seem to be sums, more or less, of all of their movable parts.

The machinery breathes. That's what matters. People believe in their beliefs.

I was walking home the other night at dusk. It is November, and the weather is changing. The dry leaves of maple and ash and oak were blowing on the pavement, the bare branches of trees clean and leafless against a luminous sky. Clouds streamed from the northwest, obscuring moon and stars, low clouds illuminated by light from the distant city. The road was empty. There are no streetlights in the village, and I trusted the pattern of the pavement to channel my walking toward the bridge across the ravine without bumping into something or stumbling into the shallow ditch along the road.

High on the right, through a tall hedge marking a line of property, windows blazed from a mansion built to the right scale for the land. It was an old home, brick and stone, and its high windows glowed. I flashed back to a cold night when I was a child sent to buy a loaf of bread at a commissary in a high rise. The white bread was in a paper sack in my gloved hands, and coming back, the wind stinging my cheeks, I saw through the blurry prisms of my tears high on the right the bright window of a mansion above an elaborate entrance. Through the window a portrait on the wall of a library filled with books lining shelves from ceiling to floor, a woman in a dress in a chair in a golden frame, a picture light illuminating the portrait, the bright window signifying a refuge. A nexus. A place. A node. *A home.*

That mansion is gone. It was torn down years ago to make way for a high rise, a glass stack of lighted windows fronting the city on the dark water. Now a bluish candescence spills through glass walls floor-to-ceiling into the night and dissipates before it reaches the ground.

The image of that mansion is a memory, don't you see, a chemical trace. There's nothing there. The house no longer exists. It never did. Oh, something was there, once upon a time, something that we agree to call a mansion, but I don't know what it was. Or what kind of life was lived inside. Or who that woman was. And neither do you. You think you know but you don't.

You believe in your beliefs.

We presume so much, don't we? We presume everything. These little slides or luminous images in our minds are slotted into a matrix made to hold them like tiny panes of painted glass, buttressing the belief that we inhabited a past and that the past existed. We believe in the reality of vanished landscapes.

If history is a symphony played in a hall with dead spaces, so are individual lives. The chemical bonds between memories weaken, bleed into one another, leak through once-firm walls of cells of a database housing a house of self. The diminishment of memory contrasts with the illusion of fixity of purpose and self-definition that sustained us. The terminator, the line on the moon where darkness meets the light, throws mountains into sharp relief, but the light and darkness on either side of the line are absolute. Only by contrast do we see anything at all, and then, only for a moment.

The darkness and light, as the man said, are one.

* * *

A plumb line of gravity sinks as a point of reference for the floor on which we think we walk, that too. Everything, it seems. We are always in free fall in the deep well of the night. We project imaginary patterns onto stars but cannot see our nearest neighbors, even when they cross the street and walk into our yard. We see them if at all through a glass darkly. Civilizations more ancient than we can imagine, invisible because they are unthinkable.

"Ants can't get that dogs exist."

That's what the professor said.

The professor is also named Paul. When I last saw him, he sank into the billowing cushions of his immense wing chair. His white hair flamed from his face like Einstein's. He is more massive than Brando, he is *huge,* but embarrassed by the obsession with obesity. It's only a fad, he says, dismissing it with a wave. Then reaches for something to nibble on, something to suck.

The professor is a loveable cuss who cannot stop looking. He says he's retired but doesn't know how. He can't help it. He still wants to *know*. He calls it blessing or curse, depending. What else would I do? he asks in mock exasperation. Play golf?

The idea is funny. I imagine clubs like little sticks in his huge hands, his enormous bulk as solid as a building as he whiffs. I laugh.

The professor is always in the grip of some confounding event. He thrives on irregular shapes, feeling rough edges with his fingers, liking the occasional ouch. He wouldn't know what to do with a smooth surface or a curve that didn't challenge him. He prefers to live in hair shirts of perpetual perplexity. Itchiness makes him feel alive.

His eyes often look into the distance. Sometimes people turn to see what he is looking at and can't see anything at all.

On the other hand, the professor often trips over his own feet.

He obsesses about our owners. He knows they come and go. He has been immersed in the data for decades. He has written hundreds of papers, good ones with careful documentation, reasonable conclusions, and of course, he is ignored. His work is published in periodicals that nobody reads. He lectures to empty rooms but no one outs it on YouTube.

He doesn't know how long they stay or to what end. Even if we analyzed the metal from a crash or their flesh, it does not tell us anything important. We can do that analysis, it is well within our competence, but to what end? We want to know the *story*, and the story is a muddle without a point of reference. Where's the narrative? That's what we need. A narrative, not abstractions. They seem to want to make it a muddle too and so do we, our own people, guardians of the interface, he winks, meaning our colleagues, who muddle the muddle more.

I know—I am getting to the point. You want a simple story. I understand that. But this *is* a story, however chock-full of ideas. Ideas can be as alive as people, more alive than some. The people who appointed themselves guardians of the interface, keepers of the secrets, do nothing but dream them up. They invent and alter and manage perceptions and images and ideas in the battle space of our minds. They create relationships between things, then fill in the blanks.

Most keep the faith and die in silence. But once in a while one will have misgivings. Then there's a crack and a little light gets in, as the song says. Someone gets an itch that has to be scratched.

My friend – call him Herb – is a social scientist. Like the professor, Herb is a tenured academic. He has worked on contract for years. People like Herb say they distrust us but believe me, they're easier to recruit than hookers. They talk the talk, but they always take the money.

Herb looks like an academic. Can you picture one? Got it? That's Herb.

Much of his research has been funded in the dark. Of course, a lot of research in social sciences has been done that way for fifty years; everything is dual use, there are always plausible reasons, and then there are the ways the "intelligence community" as we call it with a laugh can use it, too.

You think I am alluding to something small. You have no idea. We have spun a vast dark web for generations through media, research in and out of industry, entertainment, universities – you cannot imagine how vast it is. Because they turn everything typical into an anomaly. That keeps you from seeing it whole. You never see it all mapped out.

Try. Go ahead. Try to imagine how big it is.

<pause>

See what I mean? You can't even come close.

Herb works in the blur between social and psychological, looking for means of manipulation, although he doesn't call it that, and partners with experts in particle beams, lasers, electromagnetic energy – there are many interesting effects. Like stopping people in their tracks. Making them vomit. Or heat up. Or their brains go fuzzy. Or putting voices in their heads.

Memory, too. Herb works with memory. It's a passion, not a duty. He works with individual memories, not "memory" in the abstract. He makes memories and he makes memories go away.

Or he keeps them intact but breaks up the index so they can't be retrieved without a good program. You have to know the code that unlocks the code. Herb can intensify some memories and reduce the intensity of others. It's like using a mixer, he says, recording a song. A little more bass, a little less trumpet, and you wouldn't know it's the same song.

Of mice and men, he calls his current research.

Herb can make mice forget what they just learned. It looks like magic if you don't know the science. He distinguishes short term and long term encoded proteins and plays games with them. He has a blast. His playground is small at the moment, just little mice minds, but as Herb said the other night, looking at the streetlight refracted through his glass of sherry, "Just you wait." Then smiled at me and I smiled back.

His wine looked like liquid ruby from across the study. The wind rattled the ornamental shutters on his three story brick colonial home. His neighbor had raked that afternoon but the leaves blew from his piles onto Herb's lawn. We could see the leaves swirling in the wind. A neighbor was waiting for his dog, scooper in one hand and leash in the other. The dog was a blur. Then the man and the dog moved away, their distorted images flowing along the thick panes of antique glass.

Herb sipped his sherry and smiled again. He and his colleagues had moved a memory from the brain of one mouse to the brain of another. Then they distributed memories randomly in a dozen mice, busting up the culture in a way, the group still knowing everything but not in the same way. The different juxtaposition in time and space changed the frame. The memories could all be retrieved and resequenced in the proper order, restoring the right tilt to the world. But as I said, you had to know the code.

But that wasn't why he wanted to talk. That was gossip. He invited me over because he had an itch he needed to scratch. When he turned at last to the subject on his mind, his smile faded.

Herb had been invited somewhere for the weekend. They came through a friend with a channel to the place for the meeting. They wanted to discuss disclosure. That's all he would say. A tap on the shoulder came like an invitation to Skull and Bones, and off he went. A weekend away, expenses paid. He never says no. When he flies, sometimes windows are blacked out. Sometimes elevators take a long time to go down. You can't even see the road into the mountain, that's how good they are. Google Earth is their toy, too, and all the mapping platforms, so unless you have your own satellites, or code to correct the altered images, you haven't got a reference, don't you see, so you can't really see the earth. All you see is the floor they have given you, seemingly concrete.

A weekend away with men and women from diverse disciplines was a treat. There were several dozen I think he said. Or did I fill in a blank? We make connections without thinking, fill in the blank spaces. Without thinking consciously I ought to say. Narratives complete themselves. No, I think he did say a couple of dozen. The agenda at any rate was simple: should they tell? They talked over the pros and cons. How long can we sit on this? How long should we? More people know now, despite our work, how well we have hidden it all in plain sight, but they don't know that they know. That's the kicker. Some know but don't know that they know.

But – how long should we keep it up?

Then their facilitator said – now, this is a direct quote, and

Herb looked perplexed as he said it, his affect was appropriate to the words – "What will the cattle do? Will they stay inside the fence or will they stampede?"

<pause>

Hm. I see that the metaphor *cattle* might be confusing. I use "cattle" as a metaphor again, but not the way I meant before. The cattle to which I am referring here is the whole herd of humanity, the mass of all humankind, our shared mental space. *Not* the cattle I meant before, when I said that we humans might look to our owners like cows. Then I meant cows. That was a simile. This is a metaphor. That was speculation. This is historical fact.

So let me back up and say it again.

One morning my friend Herb received a call. There is going to be a meeting, he was told. People will come together. Then the meeting will not have happened. There will be no minutes, no memory of the meeting.

We need to discuss disclosure – again. Again we must make a decision.

Your expenses, he was told, will be paid as usual through the Department of International Studies at Oberlin. They will request a paper and you will send one. It won't be published so it doesn't matter which.

Then the caller became serious. Things have been warming up. You understand what I mean? Yes, exactly. We don't know how hot it will get. It's not in our control.

The question is, has it percolated long enough through the mind of the herd to bring us to a tipping point? Will people understand and adjust? Or will they go through the barb wire?

<pause>

I did it again. That wasn't much help, was it? Of course you don't know that point of reference, either. How could you? It's from another story. So let's go there, OK? It's a detour, but the shortest route to all goals is the detours.

Once upon a time, I was waiting at a neighborhood bank – it doesn't matter, but it happened to be Midwest Bank, a local institution with a dozen branches. I have lunch with some of the officers now and again at a nearby club. Some play tennis, we all play cards. I was waiting that day to renew a CD. A new vice president was helping me, middle aged, mostly bald, a little fringe of gray and darker hair, a paunch pushing at the tight belt of his not very expensive suit, starting to edge over the belt like a shelf. He was friendly enough, the kind of fellow who might manage the branch someday, he was processing papers to renew my CD. A sheet of paper and a couple of cards were on the glass top of his desk. His eyes moved back and forth between a computer screen I couldn't see and a pad on which he made notations. We chatted as he calculated interest.

My last conversation with the professor – we had gone to a local casino and walked in winding paths among the noisy slots, turning this way and that as we talked, altering the curve of the interface, in case – was on my mind. In the past, I wouldn't have said anything. But now, I'm old enough so I don't care. Let people think I am crazy. Besides, it's part of the job, part of the latest persona. My current job is thinking about things and saying stuff. At least, that's how it looks. Like Paul the professor, my puppet "Paul" is intended to look creative, eccentric, be genius-level at times, but always what up here they call "different."

So as I waited I said to Glen, that's the new V-P, I said, Glen, you know, I read this article the other day, and told him about the sighting I heard from the professor how pilots and air traffic controllers and radar stations all reported the same thing, how huge the thing had to have been to make a blip like that, how huge in fact it was according to both pilots, they literally soiled themselves, I said, and he nodded, filling in my name on a blank.

We had something happen on our farm, once.

Oh? I said.

Yes, he scribbled on a card, up north, on the family farm. One night this trooper came speeding along the road chasing after this bright light flying low along the hills. The thing glowed with incredible intensity, not like something *with* a light, but like the thing itself glowed from the inside out. It was white but it was *so* white, the purest white light, and he skidded to a stop, which is when we heard him outside on the loose gravel and went out to see. This thing whatever it was had apparently come down behind our barn. The trooper was a guy we knew, everybody knew Luke, he was standing at the open door of his prowler, behind the door like he was hunkering down, looking at this bright light behind our barn illuminating trees and everything back there. We stood there looking at it with him for a long time. He told us he chased this thing from the other side of town through town and out along the highway by our farm.

Are you going to go back there? I asked.

Hell, no, he shook his head. No way in hell he'd go back there alone.

Then whatever it was suddenly rose up so silent and it moved fast so we couldn't really see or it disappeared, one. But one minute this bright white light was hovering over the barn and then it was up there looking like a star and then we couldn't see it anymore. It was like night descended suddenly upon the house, the pasture, on us, everything, and everything was still again.

Then the insects started chirping and we realized they had stopped.

I'll never forget it, he said. He turned two cards toward me and handed me a pen. I signed the cards on the lines where the X.

That was the end of it, then?

Well, no, he said, see, the next morning we went out behind the barn to see was anything there, and we found broken branches in kind of a circle like something had snapped them off, grass scorched and the edges of the branches burnt too and some of the leaves.

But – do you know much about cattle?

I shook my head.

He said, something scared hell out of the cattle. Cattle know about barb wire. They know what it is. But that night, so many of our cows went *through* the barb wire, they went right *through* it, they tore themselves up so bad, udders and all, we had to destroy most of them, they were so cut up.

Nobody ever saw anything like it.

He folded the CD and put it in a plastic sleeve.

OK. So I told you the name of the bank where we had this conversation. I can tell you we put money into that bank or another, but money is another null set, isn't it? Money doesn't exist, either. Money is energy stored in a form we pretend. We act like money is real, interest will be paid, businesses exist, and that's the thing—it's all held together by couplers that are imperfect but good enough and it stays together because nobody pulls at it too hard.

You don't want something scaring hell out of the cattle so they go right through the barb wire and cut themselves to pieces and have to be put down.

Anyway, that's what the facilitator meant when he said about cattle, will they stay inside the fence or stampede? He meant what Glen at the bank meant but Glen meant real cows.

So Herb went to the meeting. Now, I know Herb. I know him as well as one can know another. Or oneself, as I have been saying. Herb went to the meeting intending to weigh in on the side of telling people everything. It's our planet, he said. People have a right to know what's happening. It's time, he chimed like he was an alarm and humanity a clock. Like he knew all about it.

Then he went to the meeting. And when he came back—I never saw anything like it. He had turned completely around. He went away one hundred per cent in favor of disclosure. He came back just as adamant against.

I asked him what he had heard that changed his mind but he wouldn't say. Well, I asked, who was there? He wouldn't say. I wouldn't say, myself. Lots of different ones, he said. Most knew a lot more about it than me. He was leaning forward in his wing chair looking like that trooper might have looked, as I imagine him looking in the memory of Glen the vice president of the bank, staring at the light behind the barn.

He wouldn't face me exactly. His gaze was at an angle. He was looking out the window but looking at nothing. There was nothing there to see.

That's all I'm going to say, he said. Then he said, they're afraid it won't hold.

What won't?

He looked at me with sorrow and I believe pity.

Paul, we wake up and get dressed and go to work. We have breakfast and watch TV. We buy stuff and cut the grass. It's the little things, the things you can't make people do. They have to want to do them.

They have to believe in them. They have to believe in their beliefs.

The way we do it, it's good enough, it's not perfect, but it's good enough. You know that. We can't take the chance.

He sat back, sinking into the billowing cushions of his immense chair. His white hair flamed from his face like Einstein's. I knew why he was upset. And he knew I knew why. The loop completed, as it will.

Is it just chemical, I wondered, looking at it from the outside? Looking at Herb leaning in his chair, looking at how I must have looked, looking at Herb. The way fear is transmitted, I mean? Is it some primordial pheromone that triggers fight-or-flight? That makes the hair stand up on the back of the neck? The heart race and the palms sweat?

That makes us want to get out while we can?

Except that what we're in is ourselves. And there are no boundaries between us. Each the bridge, each the other side.

And we're in it together. Us and them and then some.

Old men have the luxury of telling the truth because no one pays attention. Old men are irrelevant to currents of action, reflection beside the point when life is brutish.

People concede to us wisdom or perspective only because they don't matter.

It was right around that time, if I remember correctly, that I met Susan for lunch in Chicago. I have known Susan for years. Susan is a social worker which can mean lots of things. She worked for community services for a while, had a stint at County

Hospital, and I think she worked for a time at New Life Counseling Center. Now she works mostly with addicted women who get beaten up a lot. She has done it for some time so she must have learned how to use herself as a tool and still go home, kick off her shoes, and watch TV the rest of the night.

We had lunch at a trendy restaurant on the near north side. We laughed when we read the names of the fancy vegetables. "California stuff," I said, looking at a waiter setting down a plate of white and pale green stalks and leaves.

Susan had a sandwich with three kinds of cheese and asparagus and a red paste on yellow bread with lots of seeds. The little bit of salad on the side was full of curled greens and coiled carrots. I went for something hot. I had my leather coat zipped up the whole time. I was still cold from walking from my car in that wind.

Susan looked good. She sounded solid. She was into a new relationship so she was hopeful, again. She usually picked horses that came out of the gate strong but faded in the stretch.

I listened a lot and seldom spoke, nodding to indicate what she called "empathetic listening." Through the plate glass window the gray sky had lost all definition. The discoloration became rain and then the rain turned into snow. There was sleet too and slush along the sidewalks by the time we finished eating, ankle-deep and cold. Susan had parked in front of the bistro and drove me to my car parked a couple of blocks away.

My cold feet flexed in my wet shoes as she turned on the heater. The sleet squeaked on her worn wipers. She turned all the way around to pull out and went slowly down the narrow street.

There it is, I said.

That one? I was looking for the Ford.

The Ford's long gone. There was even a Mazda between.

She pulled in behind the old Toyota and turned off the wipers. The end of the scraping sounded good. Sleet ran in thick rivulets down the clean windshield.

Susan continued to talk about what she wanted to do next, wondering was it too late, and should she give this guy a chance? Elmo was his name of all things. Maybe it was made up.

She lowered her window an inch or two, letting the car idle and keeping the heater on. Warm air flowed from the vents while a thin stream of cold air from the open window felt like white icing on a cake.

It was one of those conversations. You can't make it happen, but when it does, you don't ever want it to stop. First, there was the meal, hot chowder and crab cakes for me, fresh hot bread with drizzle to dip, a delicious sauvignon blanc from Cloudy Bay, the chatter and glasses and silver around us at precisely the right level. We hadn't seen each other for a long time, and it felt so good just to be with her, eating quietly, taking our time, letting the ambient noise be a cushion for the pauses. It was like a real community filling in the blanks so we didn't have to do everything ourselves. Beyond Susan at the next table, a young couple were playing footsie, the movements of the draped cloth betraying their game, looking at each other with little smiles. Made me nostalgic.

Outside, the snow and sleet were really coming down, the snow blowing slantwise across the window and people hurrying through the mess, holding their coats closed at the collar, dipping their heads in the bitter wind when they had to wait for a light. But we were inside, warm and dry. Susan talked on as she often did about her life. I had heard a lot of it before. It wasn't what we talked about so much as knowing one another for all those years.

Sitting in the car afterward, I thought I was doing OK, nodding a lot like I said, paying attention most of the time, when she turned off the heater and gave me a look.

"You haven't said much about your work."

"Oh?" I shrugged. "I told you some things, what I could, what I thought you might find interesting."

"Paul," she said, her eyes not letting me off the hook. "Paul, you told me you were talking to people who were tortured. You were working with people doing it, too. You told me about it last time. How it affected them. Then you were off about where the planet might be headed, other kinds of life forms and God only knows what. But I keep going back to what you said about the Turks. And the Uzbeks. It was chilling."

I shrugged and shivered. I leaned over and turned on the heater.

"The techniques aren't the thing. It's pretty cut and dried."

She looked at me for a long time.

"Paul," she said, reaching and taking my hand. "Do you remember what you said once? About people going over the line?"

I did, but forgot I had said it.

"I guess."

"Paul—you're over the line."

I had a sinking feeling and looked down at her hands. Her hands are where the aging showed most.

"You told me yourself, you don't know how to talk to normal people anymore. You don't share their points of reference."

I turned to look outside. "I said that?"

"Yes," she smiled, getting inside. "You said you live in a world that people don't want to know. You didn't want to talk about it, either, but you did, some. Do you think I would forget something like that? Do you think I can't see what's going on?"

"Why? What am I doing?"

"Oh, Paul," she sighed. "For someone so smart, you sure can be dumb. Do you remember the books I gave you on trauma? How it affects people?"

"Sure." I nodded. "I read some of it. It was interesting."

"Why do you think I asked you to do that?"

I shrugged again. "Because the people I talk to, whether its ones doing interrogation, or ones who have been worked on, or ones who have had encounters, or the ones who keep the interface, manage the deception, whoever it is, they all show signs of trauma, right? You wanted me to understand what symptoms they would have."

"Yes, but why else?"

I shrugged a final time. "I don't know." I was truly blank.

"Because," she said, squeezing my hand, "you're showing symptoms too. From listening. It's almost the same as being there."

I guess it was obvious to her, doing the work she does. But have you ever not known something so completely that when someone says it, the recognition of it is like all of the air rushing out of the room? You can't breathe, you can't even think of breathing. Then, when you do speak, your emotions are so raw, like someone sank a shaft and hit oil, because they have been buried for so long, you can feel the sobbing rising inside but refuse to let it out.

Susan could feel it, too. She took my other hand and I saw she had lost weight. I noticed for the first time that her navy skirt didn't pucker as much on her belly.

"Paul, you can't not know what you know. You can't unlearn it. It's who you are. But part of you must know what it does to you."

I nodded. She was wearing a ring, not an engagement. Then I looked up into the deep well of her eyes.

Everything let go.

"Do you have any idea what we do? Or what they do? Or how long it's been going on? Do you have any idea who we are? How much we are not what you think? Or who you think?"

She had unleashed a beast and realized it now. The fear in her eyes was evident.

She shook her head. "Do I want to know?" She had lost the offensive and knew it. She was looking for a place to hide. I watched her cover and duck.

"I'm concerned with what it's doing to you. You say you kind of retired but you still talk to all these people, and –"

"No," I shook my head. "You think you're concerned but you don't know. *You don't know.* You're concerned about the wrong things. That's how it's designed, Susan."

The floor on the deep well of the night gave way. Her eyes darted back and forth looking for something to hold. During that transient glimpse into my life, into all life, she understood, felt it like a sudden chill and almost went into panic mode. She almost headed for the barb wire. Then her eyes shifted from my face to the window where snow was dropping from the trees and she found a reprieve. Everyday people passed on the walk in overcoats and parkas, a woman tottered by in sheer hose and four inch heels, comic relief, watching her step through the melting slush. Behind her, the old stone of a brownstone mansion was whitened by snow blowing off the roof. Susan saw as she tilted her head and looked up an elegant doorway with its black wrought iron gate and above it a second story window blazing with electric light.

"Paul—"she said.

I shook my head.

"Susan, my name isn't Paul. It never was."

She looked for a connection. That's what people do. Try to plug in.

"I remember a few years ago," she almost laughed although nothing was funny. "Someone called you Herb. You made a joke of it, saying they were getting old."

I shook my head again. "It isn't Paul and it isn't Herb. And I am not a professor. I never was."

After thirty-seven years. Thirty-seven years.

"I've had so many names, Susan, I can't remember them all."

She let my hands loose and they came back to my side of the car. I believed she accepted my confession and all of the things that it shattered with professional equanimity. So I leaned closer, hoping to hold her in my arms. I wanted to feel her and inhale her scent. I wanted her warmth. That was all. I just wanted to be close. But the fracture was too abrupt. In the moment, I thought I confessed to be real, but as she drew back, her eyes receding into the distance, I realized that she saw more clearly than I ever would I had simply as always needed to prevail.

Introduction to "Species, Lost in Apple-eating Time"

I have to admit, I love this wee little story. It's the best I could do at the time, trying to express the unthinkable in words. It was the unthinkable, I think, that I was thinking, walking around the park near which I live in Fox Point, Wisconsin, thinking, just thinking. Sometimes I think aloud and sometimes I practice speeches as I walk, and I look pretty wild to those who don't, don't walk and talk and think with single-minded intensity, focused on what's inside, oblivious to and not caring how it looks.

Once a young person knows that the meaningful compass is inside, they pretty much own themselves (of course, that inside self is formed in and by a community, we are social animals after all, and the communities we choose do matter, as I often said, preaching to the faithful (more or less) on Sunday mornings).

But I digress. This is no place for exploring paradoxical complexities... or maybe it is, since the walls of a self look like cellular walls inside the self or cell but like modular adjacencies when seen as parts of a whole, making up an organism, and that's what this story is about... the angle, the point of view, the frame of reference.

Anyway, I was walking around the park, thinking of how as what-we-arbitrarily-call species evolve, the boundaries between them disappear. The names we give them go away. (Are you noticing common themes in these stories?) Think of that long banquet table at which each generation is represented by a person, we are only one person or two away from Einstein and only a hundred or so people away from a neolithic ancestor. Each person can talk to the one beside him or her, maybe to someone a couple of seats away, but pretty soon the conversation disintegrates into gibberish.

Species link to one another in a similar way. And species inhabit the universe like plankton inhabit the seas, by gazillions. Way too many to think.

And as intelligent species (and aren't they all?) link up, I saw as it were in a fast flash forward mode, they form larger and larger organic unities, mind to mind, the language with which they previously described themselves breaking in the process (as cultures among humans mesh and merge and self-transcend), new languages emerging, until the animated sentient matter inhabiting the entire known universe is like one immense organism, parts of which like living cells articulate each through its own aperture or cultural or planetary or galactic frame a way of seeing and thinking about what exists.

It must be so, as Faisal (the character, not the real one) said in *Lawrence of Arabia* (the film, not the book).

One might even think the goal of the universe, if such exists, and I know evolutionary theory says it doesn't, but what if consciousness is both a precondition essential to the emergence of conscious forms of life and an emergent property? and what if the goal is to link up until everything is connected and aware of it and aware of itself aware of it and sees the links at every level, bottom to top and all the way back down? And what if that singular being, while thinking it has completed a task, happens to notice a knot in a thread in the tapestry of Everything, a snag, a little rip in the fabric, in the skein as it were, and leans down and sees a wee tiny hole and then goes closer, getting down on its knees, and looks through that wee tiny hole?

What does it see, outside (as if outside/inside mean anything at that point)?

What if...

What if the higher consciousness represented by the singular being's way of saying or framing addresses the way we, a single rather primitive species on a planet just becoming aware of itself, a part of the whole but one with the arrogance of adolescence, when it thinks of ourselves/ourSelf/itself in our current lowly form, as if we are just our little self or selves and not part of the whole at all? Speaks to us, as it were? Speaks to itSelf/ourSelves, that is? Speaks to the primitive form or larval stage to which we might regress if we look through that wee tiny aperture and get the shock of our lives?

That universal self/Self, talking to itself... must look like me walking around the park, seeing this story as an image of the whole, talking it out to myself as I see and think and frame it, the way the companion in "Scout's Honor" talks to Scout who thinks he is what he thinks and nothing more. Higher bigger Self to smaller public self. Like when I preached for sixteen years, and I was a well-meaning Episcopal priest, whacky too in a shamanistic way as one must be to have one foot in the other world and one foot in this and know how to move back and forth, one to the other (job description: to be willing and able to go crazy on behalf of the congregation, then know how to come home), and I would remind congregations that the themes that recurred in my sermons were issues I had not finished working through, that the Self Who Knew, as it were, was preaching to the self that needs to keep learning (once it was worked through, the issues would no more surface than a discussion of how to tie our shoes, since once we master and pass beyond once-difficult challenges, they disappear, going down down down).

Oh, about "apples." A nod to the fruit eaten by Eve, as the story goes, that meant the end of innocence. But also a nod to a happy time when my oldest son Aaron and I opened his new present, an Apple II computer, one Christmas in Salt Lake City, Utah, thanks to beloved Adele, my aunt (she and my Uncle Buddy saved my psychic life), a gift to us all, and our lives changed forever... as I soon would see, playing *Hitchhiker's Guide to the Galaxy* on that primitive Apple with my son, just as the world would be changed when it opened the Bigger Box called networked computing.

Species, Lost in Apple-eating Time

The moon was the first step down from our front porch. We were so proud to navigate that top step, letting ourselves down carefully, knees scraping on the rough wood until we could stand up and see the world from a new perspective: the tops of the trees a little higher, the edge of the step against our legs like the ledge of a cliff.

It seems like a dream, that time when the planet mattered, when we were as gods. We were young then, just buds, full of the pride of life, our outward migration a cloud of bats pouring out of a cave at twilight. We called ourselves humanity or humankind, and we had the audacity to make up names for other species. Whales. Lions. Elephants. <laughter> We believed in our distinctions, dividing everything up so it could be conquered. We followed the contours of language into space as if what we described "out there" was independent of ourselves. Our words wrinkled and slashed into the spaces between the worlds and we came tumbling after.

Now we know better. Nothing is out there. Nothing at all.

Let me try to explain. Forgive my primitive images, please, and please forgive my archaic language. I am not trying to talk down to you. I am using metaphors preferred by children learning their first words because that's what humankind is and does.

The Froth overflows your tiny cup like bubbles on the lips of a nursing child. Of course we are not limited by Ourself(Itself) to such a small container. And yet we are. We are the smallest bubble on the corner of that baby's mouth. So drink, my precious child, my beloved child, drink all of your milk and you will grow big and wise and strong.

Out here, in the expanding space of (y)our outward migration, we encountered trillions of windows that open onto the universe. Even on our home planet, our small precious blue world, there were millions of perspectives. Yet we had the arrogance to think that the window through which we leaned, craning our necks like immigrants in a tenement to see past the laundry that hung between the buildings, was the only aperture that mattered.

We called everyone else an "alien," as the ancient Greeks called everybody barbarians. Even after Contact, when the Little Truth became obvious and coherent at last, when decades of periodic encounter with anomalous and intelligent beings had finally drip-dripdripped into a steady trickle and percolated through our defenses and denial died at last, even then we called them "aliens" instead of Wrzzzzarghx or Lem-Lem-Three-bang)! or HelllenWuline. And that was just the Tight Group from the few stars in our neighborhood. The Skein was the stuff of legend then. We gave it hundreds of names and celebrated them all in story and song. In our innocence, we spoke of "wormholes" as if beings of significant size could squeeze through them and blip blip into hyperspace. <chuckle> We felt ourselves Big then, bigger than anything else, which happens often just before the bubble pops. (Yes. Write that down, please, and refer back to it later.) When the down-a-thousand offspring of the HelllenWuline twice-twisted showed us how teleportation really happens, humanity died dead. Yet memory (as we called that wrinkling in the diaphanous fabric of the Skein) flows that we celebrated in the streets of thousands of cities on hundreds of planets, so excited were we all to be free of our local star-allegiance at last. The geodesic was so interlaced with cross talk that everyone became. The Skein emerged in our consciousness like the grin of the Cheshire cat.

Now, when I say "we," I mean the beings who had coalesced into and around our common purpose then, however dimly we glimpsed our reflected image. "We" were what we had made of ourselves, a Being(we) that made Accidental Humanity look like a small primitive tribe in a lost forest. So humanity – for all intents and purposes – was long gone and we were more. But we still hadn't grasped the true nature of the Skein.

Teleportation turned us into toddlers coming down those front steps, ready to hop skip and a-jump around the all the way around the long way around the whole block.

But not alone. No, not alone. Once we had exchanged data with the down-a-thousand twice-twisted spliced pairs, with the *66^^^ (the six/six) and the Yombo-wh-!~~ from far beyond the clouds in our local groups of galaxies, we were no longer remotely human. (Do I repeat myself? Very well, I repeat myself). Humankind had vanished into the Strands of the Hundred-and-Twelve. Only the museum (a crease in the Skein like a memory) preserved molecular clusters of how it felt to think like primitive humanity, placing ourselves at the center of the universe, as happy as rabbits scampering in the grass and as dumb as a box of rocks. So use the museum to enter again into those primitive languages. When we do, we immediately feel the constraint of our childlike thinking binding us like wet rawhide wrapped around, shrinking in the sun. The cultures of Accidental Humankind had once been comfortably snug. Then they grew tight and then they became suffocating. Time to breathe. Time to be free. You would think we would have bolted for the opening door and leaped from the edge of the cliff, but humankind is a funny duck. Even on the edge of surrendering, we experienced the expansion of possibility as something to be resisted. Humankind resisted it's own destiny, even as it arrived. As if to become more was in fact to become less.

It is no wonder then that traits like that were discarded and the attitudes of the Nebular Drift, as they were called, those thousands of trans-galactic cultures that had grown into a single Matrix, were integrated instead into the way we made ourselves make ourselves. The Hundred-and-Twelve was a single thread, humankind a recessive gene in the deep pool of the Matrix.

Once we had engaged for millennia in multiple replication and had manufactured the attributes we preferred, we were no longer at the mercy of molecules that had piled up willy-nilly to create an interesting but pot-bound species. And along the way, you had better believe, now write this down! Yes, I mean it! This is important. Along the way, we made plenty of mistakes. Now we can see they're what they(we) called funny then. They can still be observed in a simulation of a replication of a holographic set in the Skein that anyOne can access. Unhappy humanitads unable to laugh, horse-laughing humanitoids unable to think, chip-whipped hummans unable to dance. We did not know that laughing and thinking and dancing made humans human, then. The trick was getting the mix just right. And that, we discovered through trial-and-error <yes! spell it for me! Good!> meant a mix that was right for the Skein, not just a species or planet or galaxy.

A mix that made the trans-Matrix a rich broth of diverse possibilities. We became adept at pan-galactic speciation only when we learned to think macro, manage multiple images of more than millions of stars swarming with warm sentience. We finally identified consciousness, intensionality, and extenuation as hallmarks of a mature being(people)-or:species and the necessary attributes of any viable hive.

Consciousness is a field of possibility, self-luminous, unabstracted, boundless. It is a way the wrinkles in a diaphanous fabric (as it were) invite self-definition. Our subjectivity is our field of identity, shaped by the Skein.

To review, then, my little ones: <I know how tired you are. Believe me(me)[me]{me}, I remember!> We gave species names. Thousands of cycles later we discerned a pattern of trans-galactic distribution and nested disintermediation and called it a void Warp. At last we called ourselves(=Self) the Skein and were ready to take that first tentative step off our front porch.

We had expanded plenty by then, into ourSelves, hollowing hundreds of inhabited galaxies, filling them with Nothing. We began to understand that there was neither out nor in, there was only the Skein becoming aware of itSelf. All of the names were arbitrary vocables, but even that simple fact was beyond the capacity of a human brain truly to grasp. I know, because I fed the primitives into the simulated human mind and the Skein belched. So even as the Skein continued to manifest itself at all levels, a remnant of humanity like an eddy, a backwater, on a single planet continued like the tip of a whorl of a swirling fractal to think one thing. The Skein, of course, knew many things, but knew too they were really One.

How could we-it, how could the Skein, manifest at every

level? An excellent question! Because how we define the system depends, dear ones, on the level at which we choose to observe it. Everything is nested, connected. Yes. Messy and messless. Very good!

Well, my dearly beloveds, let us continue: The Skein was more than context, the Skein was/izz the content of whatever we had no longer happened to become. Now we became. Our languages fractured once and for all when we tried to name ourSelf in the Skein. Looking back at the nested levels of linguistic evolution, we can see how we were spoken by our primitive language, all unconscious that we were carried along for the long ride outward, oblivious to how language was made. Then we learned how to make progeny that made language that made progeny that made language and so on and so on, down-a-thousand-thousand. Accidental Humanity had to vanish, so do not grieve for what is only never lost <twinkle>. We learned how to extend ourselves until we were singular, flexing inside ourselves(ourSelf), our awareness nearly identical to the molecular enterprise we had chosen to become. When we look back or across the translucent folds of the Skein or – as some say – when we look into the Emptiness and see what we created out of Nothing … no wonder the new skin/Skein growing all the while under the old was experienced as something new, when in fact it was always the Skein, a field of subjectivity within which we had always been woven, always dimensioned. Yet even then, our arrogance persisted, because the Skein was aware of itself as a journey moving outward at increasing speeds, rather than a spiral closing in on itself.

The more matter was ingested and became the frame of the evolving Skein, the less able the Skein became of saying anything at all. The Skein fell into Mute, when the edges of the known universe were discerned not in some simulation but as the finite-but-unbounded possibility of Skein itself. There was, after all, nothing more to say; language no longer served a useful purpose. The numbers of differentiated apertures through which the Skein experienced itself had advanced to something like 2 to the 32nd power, but every single one <laughter> was Skein and aware of itself as Skein. Except the ones that weren't, but they were Skein too. <Remember yourselves! Remember that planet!> The configuration of energy and information that had animated itself so many millions of eons ago had reached the near-term goal of expansion. As we understood or defined it, of course.

We knew by then that we had chosen only one way to expand, filling spacetime co-extensible with our awareness, we knew there had been millions of other possibilities, each a perfectly good way of being the Skein. But then we arrived at the edge of the front porch for the first time and slipped going down and landed, whapht! on our ass on the second step. We hadn't seen it coming but (obviously) in retrospect, it was inevitable.

What the Skein boldly called the Known Universe was in fact merely a bubble of Froth that Second Contact dimensioned some/what so immense that we had to regress, we were so confounded by the Bigger Truth of it all, so aghast at the muchness of it, the wildness of it, the sizes and sizes! We were like a child(Children) called suddenly (prematurely? No, I did not say that) to advance to a level of comprehension and self-responsibility unimaginable to our little brain. So we stuck our thumb in our mouth and began babbling. Yes, the Skein started speaking again, just before it disappeared.

We know now that the Skein had no choice, and of course, what I call "speaking" resembles primitive utterable tongues as an exploding galaxy resembles the darkness of a limestone cave in one of your green hills. The Skein needed to differentiate itself in order to extend itself through the aperture that disclosed new possibilities that the Skein had been unable to imagine in its finite-but-unboundedness. Now, of course, we just call it "reality." Then, it blew the mind – literally – of the Skein. Mind disappeared, and the Skein experienced itself as a field of consciousness, unabstracted, self-luminous, boundless. More important, the Skein saw that it too was merely an emergent reality, a Self as illusory as that which humanity had called ourSelf/itSelf.

It had to happen. We know, we know it did. But forgive us please a wispy remnant of wistful feeling. The way the Skein dreamed was childlike. The Skein planned Little, while thinking it was thinking Big. Now we understand <smile> pause. <smile> We met ourselves in the Froth like a child with paper and pencil doing sums while the Froth was more like oh, lets say a Supercomputer(s), a dimensionless web of quantum computers that networked forever, indistinguishable from its means. The Froth was like an old Apple under a tree on a morning of giving/receiving gifts. Or perhaps an entire planet under a heaventree of stars wrapped in the fabric of spacetime. Oh, more. More. The Skein reached its limit because it experienced the Next Step as limitlessness, while the Skein had built itself to manage only finite-but-unboundedness. However many possibilities we had included in our/its schema, the fact that they could be numbered however numberless the numbers was simply a careless mistake.

Back to the drawing board, boys and girls. Trial-and-error means we make mistakes. Never forget. The Skein over-reached itself through the aperture into the Froth and became the Asymmetric Foam that now is flowing with growing confidence in its capacity to enhance the possibilities that glow with nascent mentation on the outer inner edges of the Froth. We are the emptiness of the Froth. Our destiny has been to become Nothing. We understand at last (we say with downcast eyes and chastened demeanor, knowing we understand nothing, nothing at all, knowing that we are like children standing on our front porch, looking down at our skinned knees and the first step). The Froth looks to humankind in its planetary crib like a hydra-headed fractal, the Skein like a bubble in the Froth. We believe the Froth Knows Whereof it Speaks, while the Skein, bless its heart, has outgrown its worn yellow one-piece sleeper. It is time for the Skein to buy itself a new suit.

And die to being the Skein forever. Yet within the Froth what was the Skein meets and embraces what had been … even Our/its language breaks, the billion Skein-like non-Skeins smiling inside outside at the sheer impossibility of saying anything at all. We are the Froth and the Froth is evolving toward the Second Mute. But try. <Why> because humankind tries. Humankind tiny but laughs and thinks and dances the Froth. Small and so adorable, humbled now, humankind on its wee planet. Tip of a swirl. A swirl in a whorl of a spiral.

Try. Try again.

<sigh> <smile>

The Froth however dimples, dimples again and gimbles, all mimsy as the Skein, laughing and dancing, ola! Loa! High! High! Leaps over the fire to become twice blasted twice undone.

Introduction to "More Than a Dream"

How long ago it seems, now. Suddenly I wanted to write fiction again, not sermons or essays or modules to teach like *New Life,* an intensive twelve-hour process I created in my ministry days, no, I wanted to write fiction again, and I wrote a story called *The Bridge* and submitted it to a new kind of thing, then, an online writer's group, a Usenet group (remember them?). I had assumed in those green and salad digital days that a moderator was capable and/or credentialed, so I was awakened to some of the pitfalls of the nascent Internet when the anonymous members of the group savaged the story, deflating my hopes.

I went away, thumb in mouth, but still believed in the idea of the story. Because, of course, it was my story, too, and nothing could invalidate *that*. Experience is inviolable.

So on a whim I sent the story to John Updike. That was insane, asking an Established One if I had any realistic hope or was I self-deluded. But he wrote back the nicest note which of course I still have. One never forgets that sort of kindness and generosity of spirit. Keep at it, Updike wrote. You have something. Honestly.

That was about it, although there were tactful suggestions too which I duly followed.

I am told that two variables observed in victims of abuse that enable them to overcome are (1) they read a lot and (2) someone shows up at the right time and does or says the right thing. A virtual mentor or one in the flesh, in other words, somehow arrives.

That UseNet group was uninformed and abusive, a model of things to come once anonymous online rants became the rage. You know, slashdot mentality, fuck you moron idiot shit, that sort of thing. The disintegration of civil discourse into cable rage, shout shows celebrating ignorance and loud decibel levels as the norm.

I was reminded by Updike's example never to let an opportunity pass to do the same for another, when I could, when the window was open for a moment. Be sincere, be real, but don't be afraid of looking like a fool. We all look like fools anyway, lots of the time, if others told us the truth. So what? We still make a difference once in a while.

The Bridge became *More Than a Dream*. Like many of these pieces, this story is non-fiction fiction. Many parts of the story are real but they combine to create a fictitious tale, much as Marianne Moore defined poetry, an imaginary garden with real toads hopping about.

I wish I knew how to say what I have seen.

In the history of science, a "premature discovery" is an insight that lacks a logical ladder to the consensus reality of the moment, so it floats off, anomalous, unseen, unheard. Raymond Dart and Australopithecus. Continental drift. Meteorites.

Ants don't get that dogs exist, said a dear friend, retired from the NSA, an old blustery Celt. He said that over lunch in our favorite Chinese restaurant near the Fort, talking about our inability to see outside the frame, the way ants have evolved to know how to do what ants need to do to manifest anthood robustly. Ants make up ten per cent of the biosphere, just like mammals.

And both groups, successful in their niches, can't see what neither has evolved to be unable to see. And why should they? That might interfere with the stability of species-to-system and system-to-the-All. Those distinctions seem to be important, as important as imaginary lines between imaginary nations on a map.

He was talking about UFOs, as it happens. He wrote a paper in the seventies, I think it was, about contact with superior species, how it might affect us. It was unclassified and floated around the agency. Now it's on the Internet. Everyone says the agency had no interest in the subject, nor in anomalous signals, however correlated, strong, or persistent.

I believe that. I believe. I mean, why not? Better to disbelieve what I have seen, what I have heard, than live with an unacceptable level of cognitive dissonance.

But Hartmut Lipsky... he was different. Because of what he had to learn to be who he was which happened to suit him for his task. Not a unique task, it turns out, but one of many. One of the disbelieved. One of the lucky unlucky ones.

It's not such a puzzle, is it? I mean, who else could Hartmut be but himself? And from what else indeed could this strange tale derive? But from that kind of stuff? I think of a story of a man who created a false identity but when interrogated, revealed his real one because every lie betrayed the truth. Negative space to positive space. That illusory cup or face, white on black, black on white.

Hartmut Lipsky, *ces't moi.*

And soon, soon enough... you too.

More Than a Dream

It wasn't a dream.

I dream a lot. I know the difference.

It wasn't a dream.

I am inside a dream when I dream. I am not transported out of myself into something else. Dreams, like cones, are enclosed. A cone is enclosed; the symbols on something conical, let's say a conical hat, like half moons and stars on a wizard's, are finite. What happened in the Bin was not enclosed and the symbols were... more than finite. I don't mean endless or infinite, I mean... more than finite. I don't know how to say what they were. They did not behave like delimited images meaningfully exchanged in a shared field of human subjectivity. The Aliens tried, I am sure, to utilize human symbols with care, intending to simulate or replicate the exchanges they had overheard for centuries. Nevertheless, at one point, all of the symbols seemed to rise into the air like a scream. Once a bat crawling down from the attic got caught in the ceiling fan in the bathroom. I thought some shrill metal pieces had come loose instead of it being a living thing shrieking. That's how the symbols sounded, not only screaming but like that bat, bleeding into the darkness, bleeding into a whirlwind that transformed light into darkness, meaning into chaos.

I tried to stand but was held by the straps. I could only clap my hands over my ears, mouth open in a widening O, and cry stop! stop!

And they stopped.

The firestorm ceased immediately, broken symbols gently settling through the air like feathers floating to the ground. Symbols falling like confetti thrown by the wastebasket-full from office windows onto the streets below, astronauts back from Mars sitting in convertibles, waving dimly in the whiteout.

Inside the Bin I realized I had held my breath. I exhaled, and the Aliens rearranged things, causing a shift in what I heard or thought I heard. The force field within which they communicated either distorted or no longer distorted, I don't know which. Either way, the pain ceased. Then clarity came, spoken symbols entering my awareness gently, feeling like good will, feeling like the generosity of spirit they intended, I know, to be the subtext of our conversation.

The warmth of intentional benevolence is irresistible. The use of symbols was a way to say they cared.

That's how I know it wasn't a dream.

In a dream, the screaming never stops. The invitation never comes.

My name is Hartmut Lipsky. I live in a basement apartment sublet years ago from a student named Jake who quit and went home to Natoma. He sent a post card once, wishing the oven and refrigerator well. Still stoned, obviously. I had settled in by then and stayed on. I have lived here for years, not by design, but by default. It was easier to stay than go.

On a bright day, the light in the basement is like twilight. So I installed bands of bright fluorescents that crackle above me when I carve, hissing like bug zappers, me the mindful moth, an erratic percussive rhythm above the soft chunk of the blade whittling wood in my outstretched hands.

I carve for a living, sort of. The simpler truth is, I carve because life seems to work better when I carve. It even made a little money – now it makes a *lot* of money, after the Bin – but I would have carved even if no one bought the fantastic creatures I release from their prison of wood. Some are based on games kids play. Some on toys. Vampires, witches, goblins are popular. Demons and gods from anime. Trolls and dwarfs, too, real ones, the kind that scared my grandmother silly. She told me about them before she died. Described their demeanor as they approached her in a dark wood.

I remember. I remember.

Keeping up with the images in kids' heads is how I stay sane. They help me learn what symbols come to mean. The same symbols, differently meaning. When you live within symbols, you don't notice how much they change because there's no benchmark. It's like fish swimming in a pond. They notice the water when something catastrophic happens or something anomalous, challenging the consensus, calling attention to itself.

When we try to translate a text, we discover the meanings inherent in our native language. Translations always fail. They never mean what the text said. Carving is like that, too. Translating from nothing into real imagined shapes which emerge from the wood as I whittle teaches … how, it teaches how the Aliens created a matrix of extended-alien-supra-human language as the basis for a self-transcending conversation out of nothing.

The Aliens pulled me through a knot-hole or a not-hole into a looking-glass world. I like to think my little immortals do that for children, too, while they play, all unknowing.

So comic shops and game shops sell legions of my painted creatures. Then I can pay for more wood and make more. Rent is low, heat adequate. Noise enough so I can pretend I am not alone. I hear buses and cars outside and when I climb up and look out the half-window I see through the bars feet walking in sneakers or boots, sandals or high heels, revelations in footwear of the psyches of successive generations.

I go out as often as I need. I don't hide inside, as some stories have claimed. When I first moved here, I went to the coffee shop every morning and after a couple of years began to fill in as a barista, unusual work for a pretzel-head. Listening closely to long descriptions of the specialized latte someone wanted helped me to focus. That work enabled I believe the real work of my life which is understanding the people on the other side of the counter. Because I was barely above the counter myself, my head twisted back and away from their downward gaze, I learned to listen as well for what they felt. It was like learning to discern subtle colors. I learned to listen around the edges and then when they weren't looking I would plunge deep. I picked up feelings or thoughts in a form that felt like iron filings in a magnetic field, feeding the base of my brain, going around. I learned to mirror more normal lives transparently and none of them knew when they looked my way that they gazed into the depths of a still pool.

I passed.

But it's also true that I prefer working to not and I work alone. When I carve, my imagination is all the playground I need. My inner snow globe is lighted, alive with the world of my mind, a little blizzard always falling on elves or mini-dragons or stone trolls. I coax what I see from the wood into a tentative shape, but at some point, the wood itself begins to speak. Then I become its partner, a willing servant.

As I have been falsely accused by malicious and ignorant critics of being for the Aliens.

My head is bent up around as you have seen in pictures because of that spinal disease. That happened when I was four.

Straight-ahead people as I call them never know if I'm coming or going. After a while, neither did I, which is fine with me. There is nowhere to go, anyway. Journeys are delusions, fabricated itineraries that enable us to invent the trajectories of our lives. I prefer to live with imprecision, poised on the edge of whatever is next; I learned to balance precariously on the heads of minutes ticking by, my tiptoe pirouette through life poised on moments before they dissolve. I dance on transitions, not notes. I live in the pause, and I grew used to funny looks from normals and returned their stares while peering into their souls. Between the things they say they reveal everything in gesture, inflection, silence. Then they feel me seeing deeply into their wishes or fears and turn away.

Is that why the aliens picked me? Because I can? I'll never know. You'll never know, either. Scholars weave hypotheses on looms of illusory objectivity, build reputations on speculation about two unknowns, me and the Aliens. They write reams of not-knowledge about worlds never explored. I don't mind. They have to invent themselves the same way I invent creatures and give them form. I understand that who we present ourselves to be is carved from the wood of our hopes and dreams. Nothing comes from nothing. So – we speak again.

I am inscrutable to theories. I am impervious to lies and distortions.

Here's an example. That proverbial knock on the door did not come at midnight. That's the first distortion in a now-mythical narrative brimming with lies. The next is that I knew he was coming. The third was all the things I supposedly said when the colonel came. That's not how all or any of it happened.

The simple truth is, me and the Aliens met in the Bin, wherever it was, whatever it was, and had the courage to face down the horror of the Other. That was the bridge, it turns out, so maybe they did know what they were doing.

However, dear reader, let us turn back to that proverbial first knock. Anything as archetypal as a midnight knock on the door is going to be distorted. So let me say plainly that it came in the middle of the afternoon, one warm day in late June. On a Thursday. It was cloudy, judging from the not-light not illuminating my work surface. Fluorescents hummed above my head as always, and I was twisted as always, twisted around to watch the knife in my right hand whittle the wood into a long-nosed elf with a green mushroom cap on his head. My hand had a life of its own and I was watching, a spectator at my own play, a disinterested tourist in my own territory.

Knock. Knock.

"Who's there?" I said, startled. I did not expect a visitor.

Knock. Knock knock.

"Who is it?" I said more loudly.

"Hartmut Lipsky?"

"Yes. Who are you?"

"Colonel Nate Reid formerly of the Air Force now of the Space Command."

I waited.

"What do you want?"

"I want you to open the door," he said, "so we can talk."

I slid off the stool and scuttled sideways like a crab to the bolted door. I unlocked and opened it and looked up around at a tall officer. His immense bulk filled his blue uniform filling the doorscape. I thought of a large bullet with eyes and nose painted on for a face. Through his legs and the sharp creases of his blue trousers I saw the steps behind, littered with newspaper, saw the concrete wall shaded gray in the summer light.

"Talk about what?"

The colonel stooped and pressed his face against an invisible pane just inches from my nose.

"I would rather explain inside. May I come in?"

That was the real moment of decision, that was the instant in which I could have said no. But instead I backed in and he followed, closing the door with a soft click.

He looked around at my studio, the unmade bed, the dishes in the sink. He correctly identified a chair under some clothes. "May I sit down?"

I hobbled over and removed some dirty shirts and threw them into the corner.

"Thank you," he said, settling as best he could into the low seat.

I could see his penetrating gaze more clearly now and looked him up and down and decided to listen. I think you get all the information you need in the first minute or two. I felt like I knew him well enough.

"Tell me," I said, taking him into my confidence. Master and man becoming man and master. "Tell me."

The colonel asked about my work, then my background, then my life. I have no reason not to live transparently so I told him. I discussed my childhood, how I learned to imagine in the absence of genuine friends. I talked about learning to like myself inside, then using myself as a sounding board when I decided to engage others. I described the nature of the transformational engine when I turned inside out in my twenties, how I came together again with a snap at the next level. I explained hierarchical restructuring of the psyche in terms of organizational complexity which he better understood. I told him how I listened with my ear to the ground as it were on which others walked. I talked about the wind harps I discovered were the inner lives of women and men, how their music moved me, how I learned to prefer it to making them do things or using them to advance. Because I was so warped or distorted in their eyes, any threat I posed was neutralized by their habitual dismissal of significant difference and I became more like water in which they dissolved. I seldom used what I learned to get things, so my power grew, I believe. I explained this to the Aliens too when they asked me to explain myself. It was little different, really, talking to them in the second phase after the horror of the first had passed, that and talking to this alien human from Space Command.

Then I asked why he came. I asked other questions too, and he talked all around them for twenty or thirty minutes, then got to the point.

"Do you believe in intelligent life elsewhere in the universe?"

"Of course," I said. "Here or there, what's the difference? There, here **is** there.

"I believe, too," I added, "that we have been visited. We have been sending up smoke signals for hundreds of years. If anyone cared to look at the horizon and see them, if anyone else is curious as we are, always heading for the next hill, then they came and had a look. Wouldn't we? Don't we?"

The colonel smiled, his once-grave face reminding me of an egg breaking. "Yes," he said. "Most of the stories about visits are silliness, disinformation, experiments in social control, the confused self-interest of useful idiots and a cottage industry thriving on lies. 99% of it is that."

"And the other one per cent?"

"The remaining one per cent consists of observations of a cultural intrusion by a complex civilization into our spacetime. We've known they were here for a long time but didn't know why. Couldn't do a damn thing about it, either. Now they want to run some tests; more precisely, they want us to run some tests on their behalf while they watch. They'll learn by watching and we'll learn by watching them watch."

I turned off the fluorescents and we sat in the twilight. This immense well-pressed fellow was as out of place in my cave as a gourmet meal. Still, I sensed his genuine interest as well as a commitment to the job he had to do. I drew myself closer. If we had had a hearth or a fire it would have been perfect.

"So why are you telling me all this?"

He looked away, perplexed, I guess. The man was used to being in charge. His confident smile died.

"Because they made contact," he said, "as I have been trying to say. They want a sit-down, want to meet with someone face to face."

"Is that cool or what!" I felt like a little kid and know I sounded silly. But it was cool, damn it. Way cool.

"It is," he acknowledged. "They chose three people and want to pick one to meet. Raafat Nakla from Abu Dhabi unfortunately dropped dead when told of their wishes. That leaves only Luisa Martinez from Union City. And you."

There was more than a roaring in my ears. There was a maelstrom obliterating prior appropriate forms of thought or behavior, an annihilation of imaginative speculation as his words turned into cold fact. That was the first intimation of impending chaos, of breakdown. Elongated streamers of colorful beliefs were sucked through a knot hole. The twilight in the basement dimmed, the walls fractured, shattered into pieces. But I was still on my stool, somehow, head bent up toward a silent officer sitting improbably in my chair. I was Hartmut the harmless, the neighborhood cripple, the improbable part-time barista. I understood what he said, but felt that I knew nothing, not my name nor my history nor the form of the future. I was a blank space, an erased letter, a deleted word. The world tilted. The Colonel observed. I enabled, I allowed.

Yes, I said, oh yes I will, oh yes yes. Yes!

Nothing I have told you makes sense. I concede that. But then, that's the point.

The way we think, nothing makes sense.

Besides, they – the powers that be – layer deceptive skins, playing with us, interlacing skeins of diaphanous fabric stenciled with colorful cartoons. I loved the stealthy way they arranged for everything under cover, for example. In the world, nothing happened. You will never find any evidence that any of this took place. Trucks went down roads, trees might be seen blowing in the wind, but nothing was what it seemed.

In retrospect I realize that the Colonel was not in fact in uniform when he called. He wore navy slacks, a light blue shirt, and a windbreaker, collar up. He also wore opaque sunglasses, which I neglected to mention. At the base the next week I saw him for the first time in uniform and must have pasted that impression onto his first visit like those paper doll clothes we used to cut out and put on cardboard figures with little paper tabs. So if I don't know what I saw, exactly, that June afternoon, and I was paying close attention, then neither did a casual bystander. That's why the stories in the tabloids are nonsense. No one saw an officer arrive improbably at the basement door of a crippled woodcarver. Nobody watched, but if they had, they would have seen an anonymous gent in a windbreaker, collar up, walk up the steps with the midget who lives in the basement apartment, get into a blue Ford Taurus and drive away.

Had they followed, which they did not, they would have seen us arrive at the airport twenty minutes later. Instead of following the public road, however, we entered a restricted area and then a hangar and then went down a ramp into a tunnel and came out in another hanger where we entered a waiting plane. The windows were blacked out, it was dark by then, anyway, early evening, and we flew secretly into a dark cloudy sky. We banked and circled and turned this way and that and climbed above the clouds, then headed what I guessed was north. We flew for at least two hours. The colonel was quiet despite constant questions overflowing my brimming brain and bouncing off his stony grave demeanor. The unreality of what was happening made my questions irrelevant, at any rate, because they all had as their point of reference a world that had ceased to exist.

When we landed we left the plane. I held to the wet metal of the handrail and stepped carefully down the slick steps. I inhaled the wet smell of the north woods. Litter and duff and felled timber, said my sniffer. Mold and moss and rich moist loam.

Time was already ticking to a different clock. The crystal prisms defining my landscape shifted sideways. Everything blurred at the edges where the world curved away into nothing. I saw trees and tarmac and hangars in the distance and a few parked planes. If you look at satellite photos you will see nothing. The base is not on any map. I looked, and reporters looked, later, and you can look if you like, but you'll never find it. You will never corroborate the simple disappearance of a doubtful reality with maps built intentionally to a different plan.

"Smells like ripe watermelon," I said. "Going to rain."

"We need it," he said, speaking down to me. "Farmers are upset."

I followed him into a low building with naked bulbs surrounded by rainbow haloes as if I had just come out of a chlorine-saturated pool. I must not have been watching where I walked for I tumbled suddenly into a hole and fell end-over-end-over-end, and then I fell some more, end over end over end....

They settled us into our plain but comfortable rooms and

explained the plan for the daylight hours. Luisa Martinez and I would be given tests. That was it. The Aliens had tapped into the commercial database forever ago as well as all the government networks. They found back doors in our back doors and watched us, unobserved. They had been lurking for as long as we had networks. The colonel confessed one night after his third beer that semiconductors had in fact been seeded into our culture when an alien craft crashed but not by accident, oh no. They wanted us to find the chips and build computers and then networks and then the world wide web so we would project the contents of our lives onto screens of digital simulation, showing and telling them everything. The Net was a Trojan downloaded into our hive mind and its contents were dye in the arteries of the world soul.

Luisa had little to say, in English. I had little to say, in Spanish. We groped our way toward a viable connection, nevertheless. I loved the way she smiled and how she folded her fat hands in her lap in the creased folds of her flowered dress. I guessed she hadn't a clue as to what it meant to be chosen to test methods by which another species would arrange for a sit-down, flesh-on-flesh, face time with an alien race. Of course, neither did I nor did the Colonel nor any of the other actors on the set.

"How did they select us?" I asked again and again until it was clear that no one had an answer. It wasn't something trivial like looking at ants from a high perch and blindly picking some out. These were sophisticated beings, after all, from a remote star system, infinitely older. They may have been ugly but they weren't capricious. The simple truth was, the military didn't know. The agencies responsible for intercepting signals and observing near-earth space, monitoring everything inside the asteroid belt in real time, knew for a long time there were meaningful signals and artificial observables behaving with purpose but they didn't know what they were. They learned to live with ubiquitous surveillance the way the rest of us learned to live with their surveillance of *us*. After a while it becomes commonplace, and anyway, there's not much you can do about it. We can learn to live transparently in a village of any size.

Maybe that's where working with the kids had given me a leg up. I saw how the technologies of my time had transformed the best brains on a generation into hackers. The Aliens in a way were hackers too, listening in. Getting to the root of a questing humanity, unsure of its footing as it left its home planet for the first time.

Of course, it's much deeper than that. My hunch is that the Aliens understand us in a way that we can't imagine because they know with subtlety and depth that information comprises the essential structure of the universe, that relationships between things determine the identities of everything. Rearrange molecules and different substances emerge. Rearrange relationships of beliefs and meanings and cultures transform. Even if you don't alter the beliefs and meanings themselves, the culture transforms.

The Aliens did their homework, is what I'm saying. I think the medical data was key. Because they had accessed what every therapist entered in every patient record, aggregating and mining the scanned data of every registered human being, data fixed in chips embedded in all of us now, they could discern patterns we couldn't because our minds were blind to the heuristics or goal states of the search. How could we find what we wouldn't recognize anyway, even when it was right before our eyes? Which is where of course it always is, anyway. I mean, where else can anything be but existing in the fields of probability that we can or can't see? The ones we see, we call reality. The others, we say, don't exist. Reality is a probability wave actualized.

The Aliens, once they had me in the Bin, intended to stretch the boundary between potential and actual, I believe. Take me by the hand and lead me gently into a zone of annihilation.

So the data was our data, linked in ways we couldn't see, related to points of reference that were utterly alien (duh!) to our history. Everything aligned differently, don't you see, in their imaginations, painted with colors of a vastly different palette.

I am not saying this abstractly to avoid the hard work of disclosing the details of the complex process that led to the Bin. I am trying to say that the process was not something any of us understood. All we could do was do what they requested, run the maze and recognize when we got the cheese.

Luisa and I endured long tedious days of medical tests. We hunkered down like good little mice, rat-labs, guinea pigs, good little humans. They ran us through scans, sliding us in and out of tubes, sliced and diced our 4D digital images, showed us fascinating displays of fire and light in our brains, monitoring everything we said or did or refused to do. It was all transparent to the Alien Red Team somewhere out there in a nebulous haze.

Luisa grew on me, I admit it, and I think she was fond of me, too. She had worked in a cafeteria in Union City High School, serving macaroni and cheese and chocolate pudding to hoards of raucous students. I concluded that she did it the same way she went through the tests, with a smile and genuine pleasure in her eyes at being alive, just being in the flow. She served, I think, because she loved to serve, finding real fulfillment in dishing out steaming scoops of food to screaming teens. I searched in vain during our truncated conversations or quiet time together for guile, deceit or resentment. I never found any. She was rare, a human being transparent to her kindness, exposing the folly of trying to reduce benevolence to a symptom of dysfunction.

"How do we know the aliens are real?" I said one morning.

"How do we know this isn't a fake air base built to fool us so we'll go through the tests for whatever reason?"

Luisa smiled, shaking her head. "No se," was all she said.

"And how do we know that, even if the aliens are real, there aren't ulterior purposes on either or both sides?"

"No se," she said again and we both laughed.

Her parents died in an accident when she was a child. She came to Union City in the middle of the night in the back of a van. She worked for a few years picking crops, then got a job mopping schools. She heard about an opening in the cafeteria and applied. That had been her life since.

She spoke of the students with affection. They told her, she said, that she was shaped like a sweet potato, which was true enough, but her lumpy appearance disappeared over the weeks into her personality as I warmed to her presence.

I liked her, in other words, and enjoyed going through the motions with her, all unknowing.

My childhood had not been normal either. My parents did what they could and ran me through procedures at free clinics with predictable results. A little money moved from the government into the pockets of docs but I remained bent. I missed school most of the time and amused myself at home. Naturally other children mocked me and I kept a safe distance, losing myself in stories, dissolving the pain of daylight into the redemptive narrative of comic books and sequential art. I first learned about wood carving on the Hobby Channel. I begged for wood and a knife and began whittling. When the first vague shapes emerged from blocks of wood and little nubs of wooden eyes looked back at my own, I was hooked. The wood coming alive in my hands transformed my life, providing feedback loops that allowed me to leapfrog myself by stages. I grew somehow the way a tree grows from a seed, despite drought, despite fire. I consumed the myths and legends of my heritage, begged my grandmother to tell me again and again the stories of the northern forests, sitting rapt as legacy forms from ancient days threaded down my twisted spine to my stiff fingers and through the chunking knife into wood.

Others liked my little people. They saw in them their dreams, they saw the archetypal forms brimming with the deeper truths of their confused humanity. My little toad-like individuals were often fantastic, but people saw themselves in even the most extreme creatures. I showed them, I think, the gods and demons inhabiting their souls.

The darkness in which I worked turned into light. Being still, I learned to listen. Listening, I learned to see. Seeing, I became an invitation and people completed their own sentences, knowing I never tried to finish anyone's sentences for them. Listening to their narratives through the feedback loop of my attention, they saw possibilities emerge as if we were at the terminator on the moon where darkness meets light and everything is thrown into relief.

After a month, Nate Reid said it was time for the next step.

We were contacted, he said, pretty much like that movie, Close Encounters. Nothing magical or mysterious, really. They gave us hints and we played them like a computer game. We followed bread crumbs through the forest, but not to a mother ship. Instead we discovered a collection of black boxes, appliances plugged into our networks that no one had noticed, stealthy devices never detected by security. Of course we reverse engineered them and made a honey pot, plugging ourselves and the Aliens into that instead. They knew that but didn't object. Some think that was the plan all along.

So they watched us watching them watch us. Nothing was

being stolen, near as we could tell, nothing sabotaged. As they claimed, the devices seemed to be translators, letting us interface with a network solely for the purpose of connecting.

Then one day they showed us a recording. This is how we draw you, they said, and now we want you to learn how to draw us.

I was standing before the wall of knowledge, the Colonel said, watching screens update. It's the connections between the data, between the images, you know, that takes you to the next level. No matter how well we build it, we can't build in the human brain doing that. There are post-it notes and people shouting around their laptops all the time in the skiff, which tells you what we're missing. We're missing the interstitial tissue which would give unity to the level at which we're stuck and let us move up.

Anyway, on four of the sixteen monitors appeared quadrants of a face. It was more or less human, with reasonably attractive features, expressive eyes with real depth. The smile seemed right, words appropriate to gestures. The moving mouth said human words.

They said they had been observing us for centuries, waiting for the right time. They never said why that time was now. They sketched an image of their origin planet, the planet that spawned the !kiii--^6, they called it, three spiral arms across the galaxy, orbiting a middling sun like ours. Details were obscure, historical facts in short supply. Our questions focused on economics, politics, social and cultural life. They never answered. This was not a tutorial, they said; it was an announcement.

Nexus, they called it. Nexus.

Reid stopped talking. He showed us their planet and the simulated humanoid face. It felt like watching a puppet.

"So?" I said.

"That's it," he shrugged. "They concluded with a request for a training program for the three of you, now two. Then the sit-down. A face-to-face is not trivial, they explained. They did not want to alarm us, but they had been plugged into humanity for a long time and as sentient beings go, we are a little quirky. We were worth preserving but first they had to find a work-around so we didn't sabotage our future. This was that point of inflection, they said, and it was critical to get the design right."

He paused for effect.

"They told us this morning they had made a choice."

Anxiety seized me and I jerked. I had treated the adventure as a lark, telling myself the experience alone was worthwhile. Now I realized I had lied to me again. I nearly pissed my pants.

Luisa sat quietly, waiting.

"Yes, well... Hartmut, the Aliens would like to meet you. If it doesn't work, Luisa's the backup."

"Bueno," she said, hands folded in her lap.

I tried to say bueno too but couldn't breathe. The dizzying fall through the rabbit hole had ended and I landed flat on my back. I was exposed suddenly to daylight erupting in my brain so bright I had to squint. But through the narrower aperture of perceptual possibility the horizons of humankind widened at light speed and would never shrink again.

I was moved to another part of the air base. Luisa disappeared from my daily routine and I didn't see her again until long after. I wanted her to confirm that we had indeed shared those four weeks of tests and she did. She has repeated her testimony many times, but you know what they did to the poor woman, ridiculing her broken English, making her sound stupid. Now this good woman is lost to us, ridiculed into silence.

With my physical infirmities, blasting off into space would have been impossible. The Aliens had a better idea.

I called it the Bin and now the rest of you do too. It looked like a storage container with grooves along the four corners in which strong flexible cables fit. The means of uplift was not disclosed. I went through the drill and sat comfortably in a padded belted seat facing a sealed window. The cables apparently contained a core made of composites which released the energy of uplift when injected with the right amounts of a radioactive liquid. The math breaks down when we try it. It simply doesn't work. It worked on July 23rd, however.

This is what I remember:

Without so much as a tremor, the entire Bin rose on its cables soundlessly into the sky. Through the window the landscape fell away or I watched a video, I don't know. The curvature of the earth appeared, then the blackness of space. I never entered orbit but hung at the top of the needle in the Bin, held there by inexplicable energies or maybe by black magic. There was no feeling of movement. Not a creature stirred, not even Hartmut Lipsky. I sat in my chair as if I were perched on my stool in the studio, waiting for what's next.

The coupling happened behind so I didn't see. Some deride me for that fact, saying it plays conveniently to my story. But that's how it happened. There was a slight shiver behind me and then a sound as the wall became a door and folded down into another Bin or some kind of collapsible compartment which had brought the Aliens adjacent. The Bin became a bigger Bin and I felt a presence, a palpable prop wash of otherness surged into the cabin and I retched. Three of their species let my brain know and steep in the astonishing possibility that became actual after a long pregnant pause. How long did they wait? Hours, days, years. Who knew? Who knows? They waited until the nausea passed and I was breathing more normally. They waited until I was able to begin to understand.

I tasted something coppery, swallowing hard. The atmosphere was heavy with dread. Had I not been strapped into the seat, I would have plunged through the window, I would have done anything to escape. Through the window I saw the black and blue of sky and space but the hairs on the back of my neck rose with terror at their approach. Something smeared the floor, something green and liquid discharged or was happening behind me. I experienced their wordless greeting as a feeling of imminent doom.

The straps, I realized, were not meant for ascent but for the arrival of the three beings.

"Do you remember what happened on that hill in the driftless area?" a voice said in my head.

I flashed back years before. It was a time of alienation, a time when the pain of being alive made me writhe. Somehow in the ravaged landscape of my torn soul a flash of light illuminated the ragged edges, showing them to be places of possibility. I sat in a yellow van at the top of a hill in the driftless area, land untouched by glaciers, humps of earth and hills. The van was packed with the sick or retarded but I was encapsulated in silence, looking toward a river, a glint in a distant valley. Someone or something other than my companions communicated during that moment of hesitation an image which manifested in my mind, not a memory but a presence, a creature I had never carved, a face unlike and like my own, human more or less, redefining human in our moment of exposure. We looked into each other's eyes and were fused by the glue of the universe.

"Yes," I said. "I thought it was a hallucination. I was in that van and we were going to a river town. Everything stopped. Something happened."

"You were alert during one of our searches. We introduced ourselves. That's all. You were an ant learning that dogs exist."

"What?"

"Most ants don't get that dogs exist. You did." A presence filled the Bin like air or water ten degrees warmer than the layer adjacent. "The readiness is everything."

Then the room grew cooler. I pulled at the straps. "I can't turn. I want to see you."

"Do you remember what happened next?"

"Yes. I returned home more than myself. More than human, as we had defined it. Knowing that another hunted our scent through the void."

"Let's test it, then."

Straps fell away and the chair turned slowly. Three lurid creatures resolved dimly in the half light of the Bin and my stomach heaved. They spoke our borrowed language by moving air through body cavities, visible now through translucent skins. The gelatinous cavities were whitish, pinkish, reddish, veined with a vascular system the color of eggplant. Liquids must maintain a metabolic balance, for they dripped or surged in response to a flow that must have threatened disequilibrium. Were those faces? were those sense organs or something analogous in the sac-ridden ballast that filled the hold? I couldn't tell. I couldn't see any pattern. My throat tasted of vomit. The stench of otherness, more than pungent, more than repulsive, nearly but not quite unbearable.

I held my gaze on their foreboding forms. I endured.

I trembled with helplessness, aware of being captive in a well-designed cage. They moved closer and that's when the symbols, barely intelligible, started to scream. No longer chatting on a pre-school level, they endeavored to draw me into a zone of annihilation where the past could implode and impending transcendence emerge. There was no possibility of meaning, not in that moment of extinction when humanity vanished utterly. Nothing could be understood, nothing could span the incomprehensible gulf. I was a sacrificial ant in the slaver of the jaws of the dog. The symbols entering my head heated the circuits of my brain. I covered my ears and cried, "Stop! Stop!"

The communication aborted. Words or images, whatever, dissolved into the gurgle and flow. They immediately spoke a variation in a dialect that sickened me to hear it. I did not want to hear it. So that stopped too. I was still listening, however. I had not denied the necessity of their presence.

"Understood," someone said. We were back in kindergarten again.

But it wasn't over.

Fingernails screeled on chalkboard, but inside me, then stopped. *Reach!* I ordered my distant self, looking as the sun must look from Pluto. *Reach!*

From a nether world a question arose. I said it aloud, hearing my voice speak.

"What is it like to be a child on your world?"

I closed my eyes and breathed deeply. Someone told me. The nurture of disturbing tendencies instead of elimination made for greatness, they believed. They cultivated anomalies, dismissed more conventional frames. Gently however. Always gently. Sports were woven in a glad-basket of helpful extensions. Binding otherhood in time.

"Ah! Then tell me about do you call it as we do family. When you travel, do you miss someone? anyone?"

Someone sighed. Family or its like was linked in inkless loops of bound discourse and the memory of pleasure, threaded throughout a vascular system that remained strange whether metaphor or fact. I thought it horrific a moment ago and now it was benign. As metaphor it was a shared point of reference, however I misunderstood. Bubbles looked like... inflections, not discharge. A means of equilibrium. Family too. Family a multiple spawn of a matrix of related skins, undiminished by outbreeding of sentiment or felt presence. Distance and the unexpected elimination of individuals weren't the same because individuals didn't exist nor would they ever exist again for us, not like they used to. Tiddlywinks. We were networked now and the network does its work quietly by design over summers of time. Then fruit detaches from a branch at a mere touch. Images of countless others glowed suddenly on their translucent skins like reflections on soap bubbles, an infinite regress making me cry. I saw more than possibility now. I had crossed over. I saw symbols become quietly more and I cried quietly for a long time.

When I was able to speak again, I said, "When you saw stars for the first time, did you sense the immensity of the universe? did you feel wonder?"

Listening felt like carving. Something out of nothing. Something was in the Bin that didn't have a name. A smile or its analogue slid along their skins, a viscous slick, rainbows shining on its surface like water in oil.

Then they showed me something akin to wonder. It felt as if a toddler was coming down the steps for the first time, its little hand in someone's bigger hand. Its wide eyes looked across the street where one day it might go.

We conversed now on new ground. The dude inside, obliterated, nevertheless abides. Heavenly delight sparked my realization. I had lasted. My capacity to remain intact while staying available to an alien presence had been tested.

And I passed.

"Takes time," someone said. "Like leapfrog."

The Bin emptied and filled with kinship and joy.

Then it emptied in fact, not a symbolic fact, a physical fact, and I was alone in a chair going down. The window became bright then gray then rain pelted the thick glass and I arrived at a base in the north woods. The door was a door again and opened, making me shiver in the wet chilly air. Rain blew into my face in sheets. The storm had broken in my absence and the sky was dark oh dark indeed.

I crept from the Bin, cold and wet, into a crowd of waiting expectations; I was unable then or later to shelter myself completely from their appetites. They all took a piece. I was debriefed, scanned again, debriefed again, then dissected by shrinks and all the means at the disposal of our primitive minds and science.

When they finished they told me the new plan.

I was to say nothing.

"It's better that way," said the Colonel. "Then we can analyze their game plan using the data you provided."

"Is that all I am to you, then?" I asked. "A sensor?"

"In a nutshell," said the Colonel, "yes."

I was taken to a hangar and flown home.

Who leaked it first? No one knows or – more accurately – no one is telling. The media found Luisa and made her look like a simpleton. Her smile played well on the wide screen and her big brown eyes, without guile, were touched up to appear shallow. Then they found me and bent me a second time, this time with perceptual leverage, making me into the image that most of you know.

Transparent to the end, I told and tell my story without significant variation. I don't hesitate or pretend to remember. I just say it.

A thousand organizations from cults to corporations want to rent me, lease me, or buy me outright. All I want to do is stay in my cave, my tomb, my womb, and carve what I have seen, my life theme and its variations, worlds without end.

The Colonel denied everything. The event was spun in the mind of society as the febrile dream of a lonely mole. News groups gathered documentation to support the official twist. Tabloids, owned by intelligence agencies, did their job, rendering the event absurd by covering it in detail. Investigative reporters scoured the north woods and as I predicted found nothing. How could something so fantastic happen at a base that did not exist? Rumors grew like mushrooms, spreading wildly in the dark. Despicable as their campaign was, the malicious spin boosted sales and enhanced the value of my work. Reinforced by intermittent repetition, the persona stuck, and Hartmut Lipsky is now and will be forever a half-mad recluse inventing stories every bit as fantastic as his carved hobgoblins.

People looked for a squid and saw a squirt of ink or they looked at the wrong thing, the real eclipsed by sleight of hand. Or they looked at an elephant hiding in plain sight, unable to believe what they saw or afraid to say.

No secret sharer emerged from the shadows to reassure me with a furtive whisper that I was sane. No corroboration from an unknown source leaked into the public domain. Instead the horses of distraction went galloping down cobblestone roads, leaving me with a quieted if still slightly uneasy mind in a twilight world where I am free to carve, converting memories into images. My tableaux of the Aliens, me seated before them in the Bin, sold more than a billion copies. Alien dolls with sophisticated hydraulics sell for a good buck. Some discharge or leak by design. Computer games take you to the Bin to shoot it out with Aliens unlike any I ever met. Saturday morning cartoons retell the story, extending it in fanciful directions. Then they write books based on the cartoons and make movies based on the books. They twist the symbols into a thousand fantastic forms.

I give up. I surrender. If fiction is the only place I can tell the truth, then fiction it is. I have long been accustomed to looks and whispers and a reputation for strangeness. This is a deliverance. Inside my all-too-human heart now is a deep well of serenity. Even if everything I have said is a lie, the lie contains the deeper truth.

Tiddlywinks. One disc at a time, hopping another. Leapfrog. A fractal landscape we sentient creatures climb to self-similar discoveries at every level.

All I know is they came and got me and I went where they took me. Then I connected in the Bin with the slobbering ambassadors of another civilization. I asked some questions and listened to their answers. We created or discovered together a means of making sense. Then they left and my role, whatever it was, was over.

Sometimes at night when I am done working, I out walk the city lights and scan the skies for stars. I see and imagine planets, half create or half perceive the inhabitants of whom the Aliens whispered. My dreams are alive with creatures with silvery wings hovering over oceans aglow with iridescent scales, with the heads of dragons, fire-breathing, and with gargoyles and angels, their glass skins the colors of amethysts, sapphires and rubies. I don't know if I am remembering or merely dreaming. But I know, and you know too, now, that the angle of our consensus has shifted. I know and you know too that the future is past, that the days to come are already here, and the bridge that we built or became in the Bin is crossed in all directions, myriads of beings of a thousand shapes and hues streaming in the light of setting suns.

Introduction to "It's Relative"

Flash fiction is good discipline. The Internet invented flash fiction. Because people can read little pieces better than longer ones online, the online world invites little pieces. Under 500 words, most zines say.

Flash fiction.

So I gave it a shot. This is one, that belongs in this collection, I believe.

One of the sites to which I sent it responded with a note from a very young editor. He had no idea whatsoever, he wrote, what it was about.

I laughed and kept sending it around. A writer friend tells me her "service" (I never use one) says it takes about 100-120 sends before a story is accepted, and she's a good writer, too. What thick skins artists of all sorts have to develop.

Especially when, as the Indiana Review once said on a rejection slip, "we have 10,000-plus submissions every year but fewer than 500 subscribers. Won't you subscribe?"

More writers than readers. What a world, as the wicked witch said as she melted. What a world.

Anyway, it's short, it's flash, and I like it enough to include it.

The (fictitious, of course, it's flash fiction, not flash non-fiction) lady in question has no resemblance to anyone real.

The not-so-innocent have to be protected, too.

It's Relative

The sheer mass of her came through the room like a dark bronze horse, bending light from the lamps, turning everything into smears of light. Then the sofa began to slide slowly down the tilting floor, picking up speed and going faster and faster until it required an immense amount of energy to drag myself out of its path, the momentum of the sofa squared as it crashed through the doorway, breaking off its arms, splintering the doorframe.

She had merely walked in from the kitchen with her hi smile but had bent my crooked heart into a J-shape and held it hooked as if her hand had grabbed my necktie and jerked me off the floor, holding me suspended in the air until it was clear that nothing was under me, nothing at all, no firm ground, no, nothing.

"Hi!"

Shattering walls and windows into shards of color and light. Her hair was massively black and her blurred smile made me brace against the gale force of her immeasurable pull which captured me in orbit around and around and around I went in a smoothing ellipse. So that was that. I am an asteroid. All she said was Hi and she had me.

Once in orbit I became aware that I was moving forward. I could only see forward. To one outside it might have looked as if

I were circling but in fact I was moving forward.

I exhaled. Remembering I had been here before helped. That was a crow-bar, leverage that enabled me to resist her extraordinary force. Once captured, you never forget the feeling of free fall, the vertigo of always falling forward as the fun-house mirror of your mental world collapses into an event scene framed by her simply coming into the room from the kitchen and going through the room and out of the room through the shattered door, leaving light airy feathers of blurred light falling like falling leaves behind.

Her smile hung in the void like the grin of the Cheshire cat and widened from her disappearing face, a smoke ring dissipating in the darkness.

"Hi!"

The sound of my too-late hi could not be heard. The wind roared, drapes blew in through the broken windows, table lamps flew across the room. She the poltergeist, me the disturbed mind. The little black lacquered table trembled and flipped onto its side. I might have been blown through the door too but turned aslant of the enormous force field, bent but aware of the intended trajectory. It's intuitive, you know. That gathered more leverage. Then I could back off in the residual disturbance as the wind died.

She was outside now, the force field weaker. My heart beat more slowly although faster than if I had been completely at rest.

I had been collected and put on a shelf, a forgotten trophy: my frame dragged, my destiny inflected.

The dust settles. Twilight glides. The room reassembles into the still and prescient moment between rebirths.

Introduction to "The Riverrun Dummy"

I did teach, once upon a time, at the University of Illinois in Chicago for most of five years, right out of graduate school, and I was pretty much an idiot, I think, when I look back at the posturing, despite my best attempts. I was young and "idiosyncratic," as a therapist put it politely, and had not been taught a single thing about how to teach. That's how they did it then and maybe they still do. You have an advanced degree so you are thrown into the classroom to teach poor hapless freshman, most of whom will flunk out by the end of the year, so you're the best they can expect. Maybe they keep them these days what with grade inflation and cash flow problems. I don't know.

So I taught by imitating people who had impressed me. I remember imitating William F Buckley – mostly by lifting my eyebrows and cultivating a snobby tone – and a professor of philosophy who hooked me at Northwestern, Eliseo Vivas. He rocked a lot and smiled, letting his pregnant silence suggest a meaningful ellipsis, so I did too, although my silence was a null space.

Oh well. We abide. Life goes on.

Anyway, Stephen Hawking said that Einsteinian relativity would be common sense reality for the next generation, not the

Newtonian kind of physical world in which we had been taught to arrange space and time (and everything in them) in our minds.

He wasn't right, I don't think. Most kids and their kids too still see time and space in three dimensional ways, they see things fall and think of gravity as a force, not a curvature of spacetime. But he had a point – more and more, I see things in a four-dimensional sort of way, having read again and again, not the math (I can't do the math) but all those popular science books that use pictures and parables to try to explain great ideas to the rest of us. It pretty much works for relativity, maybe because of years of repetition. ("Here is a clock approaching the speed of light... the astronaut left the earth on his 21st birthday...") It doesn't work for me for string theory yet which remains a bunch of little noodles vibrating in space rendered in two-dimensional black and white. How those squiggles relate to reality is... well, beyond me. The math, I am told, is beyond even those who do it.

But what would it be like, I wondered, if the subjective field of our understanding was relativistic? And if it could be tweaked by sophisticated biohacking? And what would it be like if the "teacher" was so locked into a prior paradigm that his students had to lead him gently to the truth about both big picture reality – each generation is way beyond the last one in some ways, mostly technical - and himself?

"It's Relative" is a good introduction to this story. And once again – alas! – the riverrun dummy? *Ces't moi.*

The Riverrun Dummy

My Position on the Faculty

Being a teaching assistant certainly has its moments. The last field trip of the season from the Academy to the Riverrun Ranch out here in the mountains is intended to last "all day," but by late morning, all but the dumbest kids in the class laughed when I said the words "late morning" and "all day" which they would have heard so unselfconsciously only hours before. That meant they were beginning to connect time-expressions either to a subjective field (their own) or a star system and its seasons (again, their own), which were in fact two sides of the same coin. Star systems can not exist outside of the subjective fields that construct them as systems and subjective fields never exist independently of the systems that inflect them.

The kids who laughed were getting it. The kids who didn't would in all likelihood be culled before the year was over (this particular field trip has good predictive value, not a hundred per cent, but still, pretty good); they will be profiled, adjusted or made new, given different names, then entered into the system once again for modification and training. That will mean interlacing new designs of memory, perception and cognition with all the other designs in the solar system, orbiting cities, and colony ships so they will not be redundant or useless. By "redundant" I mean in the technical sense that "there are more than enough of that sort already, nearly identical in skills and perspective" and by "useless" I mean that their capacities are fatally anomalous, too far off the skew to integrate into the matrix. Often it's only the timing that's off, but timing, of course, is everything. Out of synch, they are beyond nexus.

That wasn't our concern, of course. That's how our civilization handles the inevitable sludge of a trial-and-error designer society. Our job was to enable the collective-in-residence to do an experiment that altered the interior space of a Dummy in all dimensions simultaneously. That would include doing a time trial, so we had to make sure the kids took in, comprehended, really "got" the module on duration and the subjective field from which it emanates so they could do something with it. Otherwise the parameters of the Dummy's subjective field would be stretched too far out of shape. Anyone who has ever dealt with that funhouse mirror-looking kind of mess does not want to do it twice.

The learning module on duration can take forever – or a day. It all depends on the pace of the collective.

The Philadelphia Experiment

The kids always like hearing the old stories. UFOs, crop circles, even legends like the Philadelphia Experiment, are perennially sexy.

Yes, I told the class, the story is silly on the face of it, even sillier after you drill down. An electromagnetic field displaced – something – so that a battleship disappeared in Philadelphia and reappeared in Norfolk, miles away. Everyone on board, of course, flipped out, lost it, whatever. They would have, too. The chemical basis for recombination after the event could not have been known, so even if they had lucked out and displaced spacetime as some claimed, the crew would have been totally unable to make sense of what happened. Hence the event would have been useless (as defined above). It would have been terminally anomalous.

The value of anything (I felt it necessary to explain) is its degree of malleability or maneuverability in relationship to the human field of subjectivity. Anything that cannot be subjected to the force field of intentional consciousness lives in what we call the wilderness. It's outside the fence. That force field emanates and expands according to points of reference which are mathematically precise and biochemically determined. Everybody knows that. So how we are designed defines what we can know and how we know it, defines in effect who we are. Identity is destiny. Once we interlink points of reference in our "individual" modules (as subcells used to be called) and create a collective, that collective has a unique set of reference points too. Those points determine the identity and hence the destiny of the collective. At top-level we're talking about all of humankind but at supra-top-level we mean all sentient beings. A multidimensional lightmap shows the complexity of the relationships between those points of reference to be almost beyond comprehension. Only the most sophisticated algorithms like SevenHundredFourteenFish or DiffieLitter can capture the magic.

We call the collective at its most useful level of abstraction a nation. Then subcells or individuals project the gestalt for nationhood onto the template and – bingo! – there you have it: nations living among nations, nations living next to nations, nations on top of nations, interpenetrating one another, almost indistinguishable but at root, their boundaries defined by how they frame themselves as possibilities for meaningful action, they are worlds without end. The subjective fields defined by the parameters of every collective are finite but unbounded.

That's our paradigm. Love it or leave it.

I personally *love* being alive in the twenty-second century! How could anybody made or born before this era even have stood being who they were, there, then? I'm amazed our ancestors didn't just off themselves when they had the chance. Maybe they had a premonition, especially the generation that spanned the twentieth and twenty-first centuries, being as they were the last generation to be merely born, that their designer progeny might have a shot.

OK. I digress. Back to the lesson.

Spacetime does not adhere to material existence because "material existence" is an illusion. Quantum flux distributes possibilities not entirely randomly but certainly without fixity. Spacetime is woven into the fabric of the field of subjectivity itself. It is a function of consciousness. Consciousness co-creates the quantum flux, making it cohere. That means that how you hold your "history," as we call it, that collection of memories designed to provide a workable model of possibility for you, a set of points of reference that disclose options here and now (what we call the "future"), is biochemically determined. Yes, it's true that everything is biochemically determined, but it's important for this particular lesson to underscore that this too, our sense of continuity and coherence, is also biochemically determined. The illusion of a persistent self emanates from code expressed through biochemical constraints. The spatiotemporal dimensions implied by those constraints define our fields of perception.

OK? The class nodded as one. OK.

Because your history is designed, so is your sense of duration. No, I shouldn't say "because." Erase that. Write down: your history is designed to be self-evident, axiomatic to self-awareness, and so is your sense of duration. You locate yourself, discover yourself, in a stream of illusory temporal and spatial mobility in which you are carried along by subjective impressions of time passing or moving through space. The illusion of movement is anchored in the illusion of memory and is designed to calibrate with the pace of the other beings webbed in your collective. Otherwise you can't see them, just like the Philadelphia Experiment. See, that's the point of the story. People who inhabit different flows never make a nexus. That's how come you recognize one another when you meet on the street even before you're introduced. Nation knows nation, we like to say. You are calibrated to believe that "time" is "passing" to the rhythm of your particular nation and you develop a sense of shared experience as a result – equally illusory. You exchange symbols as if they mean the same thing which link your unique "memories" in a shared illusion, an historical narrative. Everyone believes they understand the same thing or at least something sufficiently similar to work together. So they do. Those who barely impinge are barely present and those who are irrelevant are invisible.

That's how come our paradigm works. Get it? We all inhabit the same space, but not really.

A hand shot up. Miss Renley's. My poor heart skipped a beat. Oh beautiful caressable Miss Caroline McConnell Renley.

But you're talking as if time and space are separate. Aren't you? When spacetime is what we're talking about.

Very good, Miss Renley. I intentionally used an archaic way of speaking to communicate why the Philadelphia Experiment seemed anomalous in its context. The incident never happened but twentieth century people told the story as a way of trying to come to terms with what the concept of spacetime meant for them, how it might change the way they lived. They were com-

monsense Newtonians grappling with Hawkinian implications. They described the arc of the trajectory as if the ship moved from one place to another when in fact they were struggling to define displacement in spacetime. Their mindmaps lacked the coordinates that could make sense of that trajectory.

Miss Renley perked up, her eyes brightening. Spacetime coordinates have to make nexus in all directions, don't they? she said. In all dimensions? If something is too fast or too slow, we can't see it. If it's too little or too big, we can't see it either. Ants don't get that dogs exist, as the ancient seer said. Isn't that right?

Yes, I said. That is exactly right. That's why symbols are necessary. They make little things big and big things small. They manage complexities by conceptual fractal linkage. You do the math, you inhabit the graph.

I was so thrown by a conversation with the adorable little minx – I hoped no one noticed – that I decided to amuse them by using the names of some of their favorite historical characters.

The druggies that we celebrate today as heroic antecedents – Samuel Coleridge and his opium, Timothy Leary and his LSD, Freeway Ricky Ross and his crack cocaine – discovered how chemicals accelerate or retard the illusion of flow. Two people are in a room, say, one dropping acid and the other a straight arrow. The acidhead watches the other float until he is moving so slowly he seems to stop. The straight arrow meanwhile watches the acidhead speed up and vanish. His markers in spacetime accelerate until they blur and disappear. The two streams barely intersect, but the next day, they will say they were both "in the room" and exchange a common memory. That exchange reinforces the illusion of linkage. The room itself of course is also a consensual hallucination.

Even when they use the same language to describe what they

think is the same thing, what they experience is different. .

OK. Back to the Philadelphia Experiment. Everybody around you is slow, you move fast, you become invisible. The ship, they said, disappeared. Zip! Or you move normal but others ingest chemicals that wangle a slowdown – same thing, you're invisible. Or forget about ingesting, which is quite a primitive technology, and instead alter the genetic code and engineer fast or slow using subjective vectors that have objectively measurable parameters. This time you do all the math up front, in other words, but again, you're invisible. The methodology, don't you see, is irrelevant. Civilization from one point of view is nothing but the perfection of useful methodologies. It's a glorified toolbox.

Now, when you know how different nations see and can't see, you can manage the flow of perception at top-level too, at the level of conception. You create the stains as it were that make the visible visible. Everything else is background. It simply doesn't register. Then we calibrate the flow at the levels of perception and conception so they become seamless. What someone thinks happened interlaces with how they think things happen, period, which in turn is determined by how they perceive things to be happening. Which is exactly how things do happen – for them. Their bodies and minds always construct the same things, generally speaking.

In the absence of anomalies, the paradigm is king. Everything else is invisible.

The macro task, then, of nation-building, which some of you will execute on all of our behalfs, is to create plausible narratives that enable each conceptual level to cohere and interleaf with the one below all the way down to bottom-level where the subjective field is generated biochemically. Bioheritage and culture become one, then – seemingly natural (yes, you had better laugh at that word), apparently spontaneous, always invisible, a seamless weld that filters the sensory inputs of eyes and ears into the only receptacle capable of accepting them – the brain of the collective, the national purpose, the mind of society.

Any questions?

The Bars of the Cage

It was time for lunch but I was still thinking of Miss Renley and the way she looked when she asked her questions. In fact, I was undone.

The preconditions were perfect. Miss Renley's hair was long and dark and I had a gene that twittered for that. Her voice was raspy and I must have had a recessive gene for that too. Her eyes were bright, the entire room lighted up when she entered and it wasn't just my imagination, the room did brighten even when my back was turned. Above all, her mind was a candle that burned with intensity and I had a gene for that, all right. The way she talked and laughed and moved said "I have the right kind of intelligence" first and then "I love sex" and only then did it end with "I am so happy to be alive."

Now, that was a package. My kind of girl.

There was one problem, however. She dwelled in a different collective; she was a citizen of a different nation. Her heart beat to the rhythm of a different drum; her blood flowed to the measure of a different river. I had been temporarily altered to be a teaching assistant, my perceptual mode slowed to a level that let me converse with the kids with ease. Once the term was up, I would be flashed back to my usual super-fast self. Which meant that I would be barely capable of speaking with Miss Renley much less do the helical dance, as they say, with her exquisite body.

Body. Bodies. Our bodies are manifestations of mathematics, I understand that. In graduate seminars we display our greats by expressing code in other symbolic domains without making anything happen. We have exhilarating robust disembodied conversations. It's the kind of play that makes for greatness. We translate abstractions into other abstractions like some primitive twentieth century coder declaiming in hex at a drunken party. The best of us can read the math and immediately see what it manifests. I am one of the best, as everyone knows, I model modeling merely by thinking about things. The ability to recognize what the code will inevitably express is taught in a class called personality diagnostics and its basics are taught to every doc during first year.

During lunchtime I lay in my bed in my body looking at the ceiling but seeing only the image of Caroline Renley. I tried to do the math, but at my current level of regression, it wasn't easy. I did not see her body as a manifestation of mathematics. I saw it as the other half of a whole.

Maybe we could find a way to express her next modality so she could move in alignment with my life. We could splice in genes and – in my mind's eye I saw Miss Renley quickening while I slowed until we met at nexus. Then we could calibrate our lives so they intersected node on node. We could see enough of the same things to believe we inhabited the same reality. Isn't that what they used to call "love?" When not only one node but another and then another and then so many nodes you couldn't count them found synchronicity and blended into a single spiral? Isn't that why primitives called love "the dance of the double helix?"

I sought out my Father Doctor Michel Marchand and asked

him about it.

"Wilhelm," he said sternly, looking a long time at my face while I waited. "Wilhelm, you are off the cusp."

My heart sank.

"Do you mean that?"

"Yes. You are talking about violating the Code. That betrays the collective and you know it. Thinking like that is the germ of treason."

I didn't know what to say. I had risked my apprenticeship by telling Dr. Marchand the truth about my passion for Miss Renley. I looked down at his well-buffed wingtip shoes, a retro pair polished to perfection – by me, the night before.

But then his expression relented. "Wilhelm, this is all part of the primitive code. I don't know why we leave so much of it in, but we do. Faster minds than mine make that decision. Maybe we keep primitive feelings around like pets to play with. The feeling of loving without being loved in return is apparently part of our developmental necessity. The docs who build the macros think it's critical.

"So, young man," he raised my chin so our eyes locked and put his hands on my shoulders and smiled, "you just have to live through it."

I went to my work station, partially relieved, but inside I burned with incomprehensible shame and desire. I embraced my pain like a masochistic lover rolling in the barbed wire embrace of his mistress. Miss Renley was part of my education then just as my teaching was part of hers. The task was to learn the correct lesson.

I watched my mind work at tri-level. Top-level I did my job, evaluating student work. Mid-level I worked on my research, exploring new possibilities for subjective vector analysis. But bottom-level I hungered with a carnal desire that burned in the night of my soul, candescent flames leaping into the midnight sky. Her eyes as she spoke burned with superior intelligence and I hungered to hold her in my arms.

Mental, physical, emotional, spiritual, call it what you will – I screamed for completion when only a day before I had not known I lacked anything. The upper levels of my mind collapsed into the fire below, timbers burning up in an instant, and by the end of lunchtime, nothing was left but smoldering ruins and drifting smoke. And I hadn't even eaten a single bite.

Outside the Fence

May I talk to you about this before we start our experiment? asked Miss Renley.

You certainly may.

Her collective – she was the leader – had chosen an experiment that was remarkably demanding. They might have chosen to slow down the Dummy, as we called the volunteer student from another level who agreed to be manipulated, then scan and flash his perceptual flow and correlate it with their predictions and models. Going Slowdown is always easier. But they were the best of the best and decided to Uptake the Dummy to the 24th level.

The hapless Dummy all unknowingly (what else?) signed the agreement and prepared for the ride of his life. The danger was acceleration beyond his emotional capacity to manage. He would see, think, even feel things at multilevel, but he might not be able to stand it. He might not be able to integrate the experience into his subjective field. That would make the experience not only useless but unreportable in the first person. It was that subjective impression, that report of lived experience, that was being designed in the first place, so without his naïve report, there was no way to know how successful they were.

Caroline McConnell Renley understood all that. I loved the way her face grew animated as she discussed the experiment.

We have to manage all the connections simultaneously, we know that. So he grows or seems to himself to grow everywhere inside his psychic space at the same time. So he won't notice anything changing. The surface of the balloon of his psyche must expand and fill the available space all at once. Consciousness extends itself throughout all available space, as Webb said. So long as there is no perturbation in the space. Is that correct?

As far as it goes, I said. So what's the question?

The difficult part as I see it (she was so damned cute! the way she talked, the way her nose scrunched when she puzzled through something) is titrating emotional bolsters in synch with memories and expanding perceptual and intellectual capacity so as his experience speeds up, it always feels right, calibrates, never deviates from normal. Then at peak he will see, feel, think and understand beyond even our collective. Correct?

Yes. That's how you designed the trial.

Her pretty little face frowned, her forehead wrinkling.

Then when we bring him back to his initial state, won't he retain a chemical memory? Won't he warp? Won't he *know?*

Hmm. I said thoughtfully, keeping my hands in my lap and away from her cascading scented hair which fell over her small shoulders like waves of a stormy sea. I looked past her at the scanning booth in order to think.

He might, I said. But he will be incapable of distinguishing origin or source from end or objective. He might be puzzled but he won't warp.

Her eyes brightened. She got it immediately.

He won't know if it's somewhere he's already been or an intuition of a goal state encoded like a tree in the seed? He won't know, to use the language of classical mythology, whether he remembers the Garden of Eden or is dreaming of a future Paradise? Because both are intimations of a kind of wholeness that no one can ever experience?

Exactly, I smiled broadly, wanting to take her in my arms and kiss those delicious lips. I wanted to nibble her lower lip until she cried out, feel her writhe in my arms – instead I said, it's the paradox of consciousness in the universe, you see. The only place we can be going must have already been thought. Then it must have been there at the beginning as well as the end. Between origin and end, all we can experience is a representation of that seminal/terminal node – which if it is a meaningful symbol suggests that consciousness is a closed circle.

More like a sphere, she smiled with the kind of delight that comes only from having a penetrating insight.

More like a multilinks, I replied.

She laughed. Or a complex concurrently intermultilinking spherical – she laughed again, loudly, and I laughed too. Her eyes sparkled with showers of pixie lights and joyful sprinkles. All of my self-discipline collapsed and I took her hands in mine.

Miss Renley, I said. I adore you Miss Renley. I never want this field trip to end.

Oh Mister Blowhorn! she cried. Neither do I! Neither do I!

The View From the Edge of the Known Universe

I should have known what their experiment would mean, but they – well, they were too far ahead of me. I just didn't see it. The

Dummy would be known subsequently as the Riverrun Dummy, the experiment as the Renley Uptake. When the Epsilon Eridani expedition encountered the fluctuating red dwarf warp, the Renley Uptake would save their lives.

The Dummy was ten or eleven, I forget which, calibrated to the earth and its sun, and he looked like a little spider, all spread out and strapped in. His head was a pincushion of wires and tubes in all directions. His fingers and toes were spread and pricked and his legs were open for hormones to be fed in through a fluid. Larger tubes entered or left (how do you tell?) the areas around his lungs and heart and kidneys. Blastocatheters took care of elimination needs and his eyes and temples were sedated with topical patches. The poor Dummy to all appearances saw felt and knew nothing.

But appearances are deceiving. The scans and monitors showed us what he was knowing. Inside he was growing, growing quickly to our levels, then past us. Watching his progress was like watching a comet from a fixed vantage point on an asteroid. Now you see it, now you don't.

They titrated the Dummy just right. He grew in his capacity to endure and understand just as he saw, felt, realized things. When they finished, the Renley Group had generated data that contributed significantly to The Theory of Accelerated Uptakes. They managed the complexity of multiple systems moving in synch with such dexterity and finesse that it took my breath away. They had certainly done the math.

But realization of that would come, as they say, later. It would come when macro managers allowed the results of the experiment to filter slowly into the mind of society and arrive at just the right time for humankind to use it and move up a notch. Just when humankind was ready to understand, we received what we needed to know. The event coincided with the use of new tools and the readiness to use them.

Those macro managers operate at level one hundred and seventy eight. Can you grasp what that means? I certainly can't. That's how many interlacing levels of nation they integrate in all dimensions to the one hundred and seventy eighth power.

The lightscans revealed the inner landscape of the Dummy as he evolved. At the peak of the arc they killed the machinery and let him speak for himself. That was their genius, not waiting until later, and that came from Caroline Renley's sublime intuition. It was like the engines cutting on an ancient launch and the sudden silence of orbital space. It's all recorded. Most of you have seen those visuals a million times by now. But most of you still don't understand what he said.

You don't need to understand. Just trust that the job is being done right.

"Oh my God!" said the Dummy quietly. "Oh my God! Oh my God!"

"Do you mean that literally?" the soft voice of Miss Renley can be heard on the scan.

The Dummy laughed. "What a funny way to think of it," he said.

Then there was silence for perhaps twenty seconds.

"The edge is the only center," he said. "Every node is the center of the known universe. The node is the interface. It all infolds to a single point. There is an intention there without which nothing could have been understood. Nothing at all. But we still think in terms of collectives. That is so funny!"

A shorter pause.

"Why is it funny?" asked Miss Renley.

"Because borders. Borders are false distinctions. They create …

everything. And mean nothing! We are only fooling ourselves."

On and on he went like the Great Doctor on a master acid trip. The Great Doc had in fact once rolled around the room laughing as he elevated his perspective and watched the dotted lines on imaginary maps disappear. Little ants patrolled inches of earth and cried to the skies, "Mine! This is mine!"

And during another trip the Great Doc said identically, "We are only fooling ourselves!

Then he shouted: "It's show business! Show business! Everything is show business!"

Or as our Riverrun Dummy said: "Let he who has borrowed his ears understand!"

When the Dummy dissolved into blissful beatific silence, they shut him down and initiated Slowdown. It went more smoothly than anyone had hoped. He had lived through long slow cycles of time that we measured in minutes. He was back to eleven or ten or whatever it was in no time at all.

They balanced his predictables and systems and took him offwire. He opened his eyes. He asked for a glass of orange juice and drank it down in a gulp.

Everyone stood around and waited for him to say something. Finally Miss Renley said, do you have anything to tell us?

He smiled. The universe isn't even half of it. I heard a shrill whining that was like music played too fast but then it slowed. Then it was so beautiful but I can't remember the tune.

There's nothing to tell, he said. You'll see.

When? asked Miss Renley.

Yes, that's right. He smiled broadly. When indeed.

A Walk in the Woods

Everything was recorded "by the end of the day." I asked Miss Renley if she wanted to debrief. She thought it might be a good idea. We left the Main Building and walked through bunkhouses through the front gates into the woods along the stream. The stream was rabid with late spring runoff and raced crazily down its banks.

"It's almost too loud to talk," she said.

"Soon we'll be able to hike in the high country."

"I would love to come back and hike up there with you."

"I would love for you to do that."

We both knew it would never happen.

"You must be pleased with the way your experiment went," I said.

"Oh," she said, "it was beyond expectations. We learned so much!"

"Everyone learned," I said. "I have a hunch that all humankind will learn."

"You're saying that to make me feel good."

"Oh no," I said, turning and taking her in my arms. She raised her face to mine and I kissed her. Oh but her lips were delicious. Oh but the scent of her and the feel of her and the taste of her!

"We couldn't have done it without your help," she said.

"Now it's you making me feel good."

"Oh no I'm not. You created exactly the right combination of frustration and desire to make us want to do it. We set up our experiment in response to the limits you described which at the same time disclosed new possibilities. We took advantage of those openings even if you couldn't see them yourself. You were too close to them to see. We wanted to move the Dummy close to warp speed and we did. That means that humankind everywhere and everywhen will be able to mediate multilevel complexities with greater subtlety than ever."

We sat on a boulder where the stream curved and the water leaped and roared downstream, crashing through rocks below. Leaves of alder and willow churned in the turbulent flow. There was no point in saying the obvious. She knew now that I understood. Caroline McConnell Renley knew much more than I could teach, even when I flashed fast.

When everything is connected, and everything is, the only differences in perception are spatiotemporal. Seeing things close to their connections in time or space is what we call insight. Seeing them widely scattered is slowmo. If it takes days or years or centuries, regardless of the point of reference, regardless of the star system and its symbiotic knowers, then it's slow. If it happens in an instant, it's quick. Not seeing any connections at all is inert.

Miss Renley saw the end of the experiment at its moment of conception. She saw how it linked and would link to myriad possibilities. She saw in a flash the next conceptual level illuminated by nuclear fire.

"They couldn't tell you," she said. "You understand why, don't you?"

I nodded.

"You helped to make us what we are, but what we are is … not what you thought. We look young, I know, but every older generation is surprised by what their progeny design. We always create beyond our own capabilities, and we are always abashed. You helped us move into a condition of readiness. We were touched by your simplicity, even your fumbling pedantry. You were cute. I even needed to feel this … infatuation … for the moment. It generates the energy necessary to move to the next level. Falling in love is energizing, even when it doesn't last."

She relaxed back into the curve of my trembling body as if I were an old comfortable chair. I inhaled the scent of her hair, felt her head against my chest. The stream obliterated all sounds of the known universe. That moment was so ineffably sweet it was painful but passed like a comet seen from an asteroid. Now you see it, now you don't.

Even after I flashed back to my "fast" self and could see more clearly, my thoughts moved like a mass of molasses. Renley and her collective had been so patient. I was only a catalyst. I was the real Riverrun Dummy – which I saw now was exactly what I had always been designed and destined to become.

I felt like an elephant hearing my ancestors trumpeting from the graveyard where their tusks thrust up from the forest floor.

An Encouraging Word

You have been my valuable assistant for nearly seven decades, said Dr. Marchand when they had all left and he found me walking alone in the woods in the shadow of the mountain under the light of a full moon. A few more years and you'll be ready for what's next. To learn to love what is necessary, Wilhelm, is our only destination. We must embrace our destiny in order to discover our identity. The readiness is all, young man. You are just beginning. At moments of confluence, we experience the cessation of striving, momentary release from all friction. Then they pass and we move on.

Everything else, he said, is preparation. We are either swimming to the next island or resting on one, catching our breath.

Then he put his hands on my shoulders and smiled.

You'll see.

I will? I asked. When?

Yes, he smiled. When indeed.

Introduction to "Gibby the Sit-Down King"

Ah, Gibby! I had one particular hacker in mind when I first imagined Gibby, sitting at his computer, whacking away. But then it became like cascading cards in a magic trick, a number of hackers, more and more Gibbys, flashing before my eyes like my own life at the moment of departure.

From time to time, various stories and statistics about pornography on the Internet filter in. The sheer immensity of the flow is impressive. But think about it. Humans have numerous sexual triggers which are pleasurable, by definition, or they wouldn't lead to copulation. Porn is nothing but representations of sexual triggers, simulations of the real thing, so humans feel pleasure when they look at them. So they do.

Add the long tail of online marketing which means that every fetish from feet to feathers can be addressed at minimal cost and find a niche market, and *voila!* Internet porn.

People like pleasure; sexual triggers are pleasurable; people like sexual triggers. Sex is syllogistic. If you give head, they will come.

Now toss in a mantra attributed to Jung or one of his disciples, that when people talk about sex they are really talking about spiritual issues, and when people talk about spirituality (exchanging religious symbols) they are really being sexual.

As a former Episcopal clergyman, I often listened to other clergy (as well as overhearing myself) discuss sexual issues. We all had them, believe me, from all the fetishes in the world to the antics of pedophiles. They aren't all equal, of course. Adults ogling other adults or their parts or practices are not criminals victimizing children. But sexuality and spirituality do seem to be intertwined. Think of the language of religion: we are one, God is love, come close and draw near, and all the other sublimations of sexuality, love and lust. Add to that the joys of masturbation, frequently referenced by the hacker in "The Geometry of Near." Symbols parading as the real thing, leading the practitioner to drink again and again from a dribble glass, that's the American dream, isn't it? Stuff that in itself is not ultimately satisfying bought and amassed, then swapped at rummage sales? Idolatry, isn't it, treating lesser goods or gods as if they are ultimate goods or gods?

And on a higher level, perhaps, the symbolic act itself, that which makes us human, is the recreation of everything as an image, an illusion, making human culture a form of masturbation – if you don't see what you're doing. If you do, you're enlightened, you see the illusory nature of percepts, concepts and the self that makes them up, a social construction that enables us to think we are a "we" or an I an "I."

But there's no there there. Nobody is home. There is only, nowhere, remember, space is an illusion, and all is always now... creation from nothing.

Add to all that biohacking, genemods, and the inevitable Gibbys already proliferating at the first and second levels and... we get the Palace of Dreams.

That's the bridge for Gibby in this story, that leap from a love of porn to a love of the symbol-making mind that makes porn in the first place, then to the intention behind the mind which is No Mind at all... no wonder one thing dissolves into another. No wonder the spiritual climb is depicted as a ladder or, for Gibby's generation, a massive multi-level multi-player interactive game where only the obsessive reach the higher levels... into which at last Gibby himself dissolves... Gibbyless... into air, into thin nonexistent air.

Besides, have you ever known anyone who is really interesting, who is *not* obsessive? Passion, obsession, daring drives scientists, Edward O. Wilson said, himself obsessed with ants as much as any transvestite with pantyhose and heels... and obsessiveness drives hackers, too, every kind... and obsessiveness drives dear Gibby, dear dear Gibby.

This story is dedicated with affection to Gibby and all his spawn.

Gibby the Sit-Down King

The Palace of Dreams in Sheboygan Sprawl, disguised as one of those ordinary shops to which people still come when they want to be with people instead of simulations, is tucked into an alley-way behind cafes, mushroom shops, dollarmark stores and a franchised Thrift Shop. This particular P.D. is a Gambling Den. Some people enter, place bets and watch results without noticing anything unusual. Others pass through the portal and are never heard from again.

The close proximity of the Palace to the Thrift Shop is not accidental. The Palace of Dreams is the fulfillment of an implicit promise made by Gibby McDivitt and Thrift Shops, TTX from the moment they exploded onto the scene. Even Gibby didn't know that, though, until his celebrated vision years later closed that loop of his life.

Thrift Shops do a booming business, selling decanting and AlterGene™ kits on narrow margins, relying on volume and economies of scale to make a little money... make that a *lot* of money, multiply a little times millions of shops, it's a *lot*. Thrift Shops, TTX is in all eighteen countries, six hundred fourteen sprawls, and every mini-hood – millions of near-identical plots of housing and retail blocks – has one.

There are only one hundred forty-three Palace of Dream shops, however, and they aren't easy to find. They are disguised as gambling dens, eat-and-drinks, mini-massage shops, zero-day parks. No directory contains them, no map shows them, and no one who happens to enter one realizes what it is – until it's too late. Part of the shiver of delight running down everyone's backs right now is the fact that the Palace is kind of a secret, a rumor, really, a story of a secret that changes in the telling in a world in which privacy doesn't exist.

But the Palace did not just pop out of thin air. We're getting ahead of ourselves. There is a history which in retrospect makes sense. So let us return to the early years and what we know or think we know of the life of Gibby McDivitt.

Once upon a time, the CEO of Thrift Shops, TTX, Gibby McDivitt, was a pimply pasty-faced hacker of enormous proportions. Everybody knows the official picture of Gibby, an image projected for decades into the sim-world from an old photo, radically altered, the only one he allowed out, a fish-eye lensing from below and behind of his big butt and back and broad shoulders in his famous chrome-and-leather-flecked chair, his hands out of sight, presumably in his lap, his pumpkin-like head thrust forward at an odd angle toward a wall-screen where three naked women and two naked men play games, vaguely out of focus, with big colorful plastic toys.

Everybody knows too the story the corporation invented for public consumption. As a child and teen, the tale goes, Gibby virtually lived in his basement, or rather, lived virtually in his basement, hacking his heart out. At six he cracked open world bank crypto. At eight he listened to whispers from deserts and jungles of terrorists and cartel chieftains, at nine he heard similar whispers from corporate boardrooms. That was the end of Gibby's innocence. He infiltrated metranets, piggybacked on satellite transmissions, mirrored multiple broadcasts, commandeered thousands of zombies, filtering massive downloads through an automated program he coded himself. He listened to intercepts and learned that boardrooms were a better place to play than the jungle or desert, so he sent transcripts of the sheiks and chiefs to secret email addys of corporate heads, world police chiefs, and top guys at Franchised Warriors, TTX. Then he intercepted their anxious conversations before they responded formally and learned of the close ties between sheiks and generals and chiefs and corporate boardrooms. The truth, as usual, was worse than anyone guessed. Ah-ha! thought Gibby. So everybody colludes, everybody hides behind false flags and dummy companies, everybody plays the same game.

Nothing, he realized, is what it seems – an important lesson to learn at such a tender age.

So while wannabe hackers rebelled against The Man, planning drive-bys and spraying graffiti on web-sites, Gibby put away childish things and *became* The Man. He saw that hacking for its own sake was silly. He tired of bragging rights, he had more trophies than all the rest put together. There had to be a bigger payoff, something to make the risks worthwhile. With great patience, he listened and pondered, educating himself in the ways of the world and building a database of clandestine relationships that became the core intellectual property of Industrial Discovery, TTX, his first hugely successful company. And what exactly did ID do? It wore a digital mask, that's what, hiding behind shelters, veiled by a maze of dummy fronts while Gibby at ten a.k.a. his many diverse aliases sold information in packets of various size. He learned that the key was to leverage the known against the unknown, the possible against the likely, and he always hedged his bets.

Gibby McDivitt became a player.

That's when he became McDivitt, too. Gibby whoever-he-was borrowed the name from a blonde starlet he loved from afar, whacking off with gusto to her wall-sized simulation. (That was Melissa McDivitt, of course, no secret there). No one knew his real name, but as Gibby said a thousand times until it became the well-known mantra of Thrift Shops, TTX, "What's real anyhow?"

Gibby seldom left the immense padded chair which replaced the chrome-and-leather-flecked one when it collapsed. That meant he could focus on work and play in ways that healthier entrepreneurs could not. Persistence, obsessiveness and polymorphously perverse hunger and lust, those were his drivers. People who worried about the general good were lamers, Gibby decided. Wise beyond his years in some ways, obviously stunted in others, he focused not on making money, which past a certain point was just another way to collect trophies, but on the pleasures of adolescence which were infinitely saleable as well as supreme bliss to his quasi-developed mind. He played square-wall four-D immersive games in a room-sized knowledge cube, forty by twenty by twenty. He farmed out manufacturing, distribution, and marketing, managing legal issues by knowing the dope on competitors. As his confidence grew he used his name to brand his antics and achieved an astonishing measure of corporate glory, but that was a mere sideshow compared to the satisfaction of knowing his global impact, indicated by the distribution of millions of images of Gibby stooped to the screen in his pleasure dome, as well as the sales of octobillions of sexy digital stuff. A world of users, the ones who mattered, the ones who were plugged in or with it, internalized his image as a goal-state and hungrily swallowed whatever he sold.

This early success was years before Gibby practically invented the industry of SynthoLife™ and began selling genemod kits under the brand-name AlterGene™. This all occurred when the world was still simply digital, an innocent time of simulations and symbols, all outside the mind. For young Gibby selling sex was a labor of love. He downloaded millions of pictures and videos, looking and listening and lapping up every fetish and its variations. In his undisciplined ardor, however, he sprained both wrists and developed repetitive stress in both elbows. Sitting one day in the deep cushions of his padded throne, gloomy and inert, his impaired arms strapped to therapy-boards, he realized he needed an assistant. As so often happens in the world of commerce, fulfilling this need in himself simultaneously met the needs of countless others. He built Haptic Hands™ and made a fortune selling them worldwide.

Haptic Hands attached to any console and worked with any OS. On spoken or tapped command they oozed Vaseline, canola oil, or mayonnaise to taste. The hands felt like real flesh, made from silica-carbonates (basic), vat-grown flesh (enhanced), or whole hands grown on the backs of pigs (super-deluxe). They could be fitted with leather gloves, red or blue latex, or cuddly soft white fleece. The best-selling plug-in was Sheepie, made of cotton wool, fresh liver delivered daily, and squeezable silicon-bubble liners. HandMate™, designed for women, came with four hundred fourteen options ranging in size from the microtype egg of *Zenillia pullata* to *Toro Gordo* surnamed *y Gigante.*

Haptic Hands 2.0 added audio plug-ins in every known language and hundreds of scents. Pheromones quivered in the air, wall-sized 3-D images bucked and humped, and cries and moans exploded in octophonic Gibby-Surround-Sound™ while Haptic Hands did all the work.

He made money hand over fist, so to speak. As the official corporate bio states, his companies "took the experience of Outside In as far as it could go." They delivered the most real virtual joys a human/computer symbiot could design (supply side) or savor (consumer) but inevitably encountered the limitations of conveying experience solely to the senses. However varied or refined, spectator sex was equivalent to a hungry orphan standing in the snow, watching a family eat in a warm well-lighted cafe, his nose to the cold glass. The success of Haptic Hands, to the degree that it gave great fantasy, revealed the shortcomings of the Hands and of all simulated ventures: It ultimately felt like drinking from a dribble-glass. The user felt used... and very wet.

"We must get inside the user experience," Gibby wrote in a now-famous memo. "We must create the lived experience of every sexual pleasure, not only from external sources, but *inside the subjective field of the user.* We must paste it onto the eyeballs from the inside, then couple the subjective experience with a digital container of complementary design.

"Instead of making a filmic experience, we must alter user chemistry so that users co-create their own experience *while interacting with digital simulations.* This will enable users to choose and then design their own pleasures *and engineer them* so when we provide a container, they can use it to *turn themselves on* instead of counting on someone else to do it for them (all italics are Gibby's).

"If we execute this game plan," the memo concluded, "habituation will no longer constitute a boundary around profits."

"Fetish mods!" said his Chief Scientist, the well-known Helly Gerlach, winner of two Nobels. "You're talking about fetish-mods!"

Indeed he was. Gibby had been dreaming of fetish-mods for years. He had noticed when still a child the growing popularity of animal mods at hacker cons. Tigers with tattooed skin and fangs, spindly bird-men with feather-grafts, barrel-chested primates with thick fur became as common as Klingons at Star Trek fairs. The alterations, however, were cosmetic, however striking the results. Reconstructive surgery went mainstream around the same time, turning people into plastic manikins with implanted smiles. That was all fine, but geez, Gibby realized, if people could mess with their genes, grow feathers or fangs, then kits to make that kind of play possible would sell like crazy.

While he was dreaming, advancements in science made it possible to hack the genome. But that wasn't enough. Genetic engineering meant shuffling and splicing genes, making tomatoes that didn't freeze or fish that glowed in the dark, enhancing what evolution spawned, not creating new attributes, talents, new ways of being human, new experience, new varieties, new species, all out of whole cloth. Now, *that* was exciting!

The breakthrough was called SynthoLife™ and it meant the generation of unique subjective and/or physical facts (tightly coupled) through the creation, manipulation and alteration of "artificial" protein clusters that in turn initiated body-or-brain to brain-self chains of new human experience. Instead of flooding the apparatus of cognition with conception-level scenarios (like three-on-twos on a vast dynamic screen) they could work at the level of perception; the very means by which we perceive and feel and above all *get off* can be hacked to the *root*, Gibby cried. We can hack the mind of God! We can use the best ideas of the biosphere but improve on them and in the lucrative domain of fantasy sex, invent any trigger, scenario or fetish! People can build their own pleasure-sensors and we can be their partners, fabricating the scenery. Give away AlterGene kits and let the good times roll!

Seized by the vision, Gibby beheld in his mind-space something akin to orgasmic pleasure but better, oh so much better. Oh yeah, baby! Better! Gibby saw like a mountain range that went on forever repeated peaks of orgasmic joy achieved through inner-built rituals and then – oh, and this was his genius! – then going ever higher through escalating sets of more, better and different experience using mix-and-match plug-and-play templates for which he already held the patents! had already data based as the matrix of his digital sex delivery system. The only limit to sexual pleasure was human imagination. His thousands of employees had plenty of that but would now be joined by legions of hackers making AlterGenies in their basements, thus combining the best of open source and monopolistic practice.

Gibby hired the best hackers and set them loose. Why, he wondered aloud, had he found so fascinating the primitive pleasures of hacking communications, mapping the digital world, understanding the energy flow in the hive mind? It was child's play compared to creating new species.

"I was born to dream, yes," he wrote in a memo to employees, "but this is not my dream, it's yours! The dream belongs to the world! How do you want to come today? That's what we sell, the power to make your dreams real! Our digital worlds cooperate or collaborate with your desires to create an authentic seamless experience of your own design and choosing!"

So AlterGenies were born – synthesized protein modules that generated self-defined subjective experience and/or behaviors that when triggered became self-fulfilling prophecies. The user was both arrow and target. Brain-and-body to brain-self, fffthwat! AlterGenies replaced the Digital Circus, making it seem so one-dimensional, so last year.

The first AlterGene kits were distributed free through the underground, letting hackers do proof of concept, test the betas – and get Mister Gibby and company off the hook. In order to get the goodies, users had to remove the LockTite™ wrap which action in and of itself validated the User Agreement and sent a record of the transaction wirelessly to the Main Database. According to the pact, users signed off on all and any negative effects, including "unforeseen, unwanted, or otherwise horrific shocking or sickening alterations, mutations, psychotic breaks or unintended deaths." Your miniature dick could become an anaconda and choke you to death, your quail-egg balls could inflate to the size of pumpkins, your clit could engorge like a puffer-fish, none of it would matter. The game could only be played with real meat, real money on the table of life.

The famous case of the Alligator Boy went all the way to the World Court. The panel of judges found for the defendant. "The creative use of AlterGene kits would be inhibited if the manufacturer had to accept responsibility for what users do with them," the opinion read. "Thrift Shops, TTX is no more responsible for the misfortunes of this poor sad leather-faced lad than a pencil manufacturer for whatever a pencil-user might write with a primitive wooden yellow number two."

In the aggregate, despite initially high but declining numbers of blunders, the risks were worth it, and anyway, real risk enhanced the rush of early adopters. Thrift Shops, TTX held an AlterGene Festivus in Times Square and one of Gibby's look-alikes handed out hundreds of thousand of kits free to screaming teens.

They shut down Manhattan Sprawl for two whole days.

Meanwhile patents piled up. To use an AlterGene kit required that the user concede to Thrift Shops, TTX the first right of refusal if a marketable product resulted. The inventor received ten per cent of net profits. Gibby happily franchised patents in agriculture, medicine, cosmetics, physical enhancements like height and speed and wind and mental enhancements like making music or math or thinking fast or deeply or well. Let the biosphere recreate itself with gusto! Let new varieties of humans explore asteroids, plunge to sea depths heretofore unreachable, tunnel into caves and beyond to the center of the earth, plummet in meditation into inner space and return later with shining eyes proclaiming, "I understand! I understand!"

Let them do everything their hearts desired! Gibby laughed all the way to the digital bank, which was only a click away, and stayed faithful to his original goal which was simply getting off then getting off again then getting off once more.

The legislatures of the world were bought and paid for and he folded all of his smaller companies into Thrift Shops, TTX, the only place in the universe, digital or physical, where users could purchase AlterGene kits. Thrift Shops built in feedback loops by hiding Trojan genes that communicated chemically with sensors doubling as bio-terror detectors so they always knew what users were doing.

The cautious grew custom fur, made tropical fish sing like birds, even grew shmoo-pigs that upon reaching a certain weight would hurl themselves into frying pans and cook themselves for dinner.

The more adventuresome followed Gibby into the Land of a Thousand Fetishes. They created sexual adventures for every trigger imaginable. No matter what happened in the world, someone somewhere was getting off on it because they had designed themselves to enjoy it. Meanwhile Gibby provided or licensed the right to provide the container.

Hackers brought their mischief and love of fun to the subculture too. They rewired shmoo-pigs to throw themselves out of windows, scrambled fish so they not only sang but screamed at all hours of the night. They created the choke-hold gene, a protein cluster that prevented orgasm just as it was about to erupt. They used monkey-like genes adapted to plastic splice-plugs and made household products and appliances cry "Snake! Snake!" whenever sensors detected a pencil or penis. They undermined fur-lovers in a retro gesture and turned them into hairless gray alien look-alikes.

Well, kids will be kids. Fun and games aside, Gibby was clear: he wanted to live forever in a blossoming garden of sexual delight. He didn't even have to think about it. That passion, bone-deep, had been bred in him, and he never let an AlterGenie touch it.

Fixation on a particular stimulus, ritual, or bizarre family dynamic was identified as a function of the neuronal subsystem called G2. Once they knew which clusters of protein translated into particular simulations of external experience as it was replicated in adumbrated symbolic form in the subjective field of the human psyche, altering an imprinting or making one up was simple. Every imaginable attachment was generated, linked in odd combinations, and sold for gold.

Fetishes grew on the world farm like varieties of corn. A fetish was after all merely a constrained domain of involuntary excitement generally caused by an arbitrary imprint on an infantile nervous system. If a child was tickled by his mother's toes, he might forever crave the sight or scent of similar toes. The polish would have to be identical ("I said rose pink, damn it! not burgundy!"), the wriggle of the piggy precise. Or maybe her dark hair brushed his infant face during a feeding. That was that! Forever the helpless lad would go weak at the sight or smell or touch of a brunette wearing a page boy or retro bob. Or maybe he quacked like a duck when lesbian sisters stripped down, ready to play, letting him watch. Because they were arbitrary, the variations were endless. And now people could plug in and play to their heart's content, inventing the carrot, then trotting happily after.

Of course there was plenty of funny stuff, too, the things they loved to showcase in what they called "News In Depth," those three minute briefs consisting of a few dozen pictures and thirty or forty words of text. One AlterBoy (as they called the first designer mutants) became excited when a woman simultaneously removed her long white leather gloves and whistled Hey Jude, the entire thing, followed by a heartbreaking rendition of Yesterday, his erection rising only at the last plaintive note. Another required that two men and two women dance in a syncopated rhythm while spitting lemonade out of their mouths in an endless shower called the Pink Fountain.

The really astonishing thing, Gibby reflected, was this: however unusual a passion might seem, within days web sites depicting it sprang up with thousands of graphic images, videos and narratives. AlterGenies did not need to be marketed. Users hunted them down like hounds, swapped and modified possibilities, stored up future thrills like squirrels hoarding nuts.

Then the seemingly inexplicable happened.

At first slowly, then at an accelerating pace, sales of AlterGene kits began to decline. When Thrift Shop analysts examined the data, the sound of hundreds of hands slapping hundreds of foreheads echoed around the campus. They titled the report to Mister Gibby, "A Collective DUH."

Habituation had once more reared its debilitating head.

Gibby knew from the experience of cycling through excitements that there was a pattern to pursuit. At first he couldn't get enough. Then he still wanted whatever it was but less often. Then he became bored and needed something new. He either had to escalate to more complex or challenging thrills or change the game he was playing.

Gibby cycled through fetishes, scenarios, and rituals almost as quickly as he ate. If he was no longer excited by a bald woman riding a tricycle in a Wonder Woman costume, he altered his genes and craved Batman or Robin on a snowboard. But he learned to his chagrin that no matter how often he changed pleasures, the joy-to-boredom cycle picked up where he last left off. The content was irrelevant; the experience itself grew tired, the habit of it, the pattern, the very essence of the thing he loved. The rapidly accelerating decay of the cycle was progressive and relentless. He might try a new scenario every day, or three a day, or once an hour. Nothing worked. Even with AlterGenies making all things new every morning after breakfast, the world could not generate sufficient carnal delight to keep him happy.

Gibby's tantrums were legendary. Employees told stories of his wall-sized digital image apoplectic with rage and frustration, his fleshy arms flapping like flippers over the sides of his leather chair. His forehead wet with perspiration, his eyes buggy, his cheeks flushed, Gibby fulminated until he couldn't breathe, then sat there gasping for breath, his anger unabated.

But this was his gift: the sane part of his brain remained aware of what was really happening. So Gibby knew that if he felt this way, others did too.

That's why Gibby the super-sized love-bunny might grow angry or depressed but never despaired. The difference between good and great, he knew, was how one responds to adversity. He instructed R&D to find a fix.

The solution was ingenious and made Gibby happier and fatter than ever.

"Mister Gibby, if we develop a mod that lets users turn on the pleasure center in their own brains regardless of their predilection, they can experience the mother lode of ecstasy. Instead of chasing after the right trigger, the right fetish, the right scenario, the right woman man or animal, the right plastic appliance, users can go straight to the source of their joy."

"But didn't we learn in the last century," asked the savvy entrepreneur, "that rats will press the pleasure-center button unceasingly and die of hunger, chained to their bliss?"

"We anticipated that question," said the Chief Scientist. "The protein-globe that enables this action will have fail-safe splices. Built in obsolescence, for one. Its effectiveness will degrade over time. And we'll change the license. Instead of buying outright, users will have to lease. They'll pay by the minute in increments, barely noticing the drip-drip-drip of their money into our coffers.

Our fortunes will expand geometrically as the user-base continues to grow."

So iTouch™ and the Golden Globe™ went to market.

The upward-chaining mod was a big seller at first but once again habituation flattened the trajectory of sales, and it happened a lot faster than anyone anticipated. Undifferentiated pleasure, however – well, pleasurable – steeped the brain in PEA but soon became banal. The power of the drug wore off. Within six months, the world said, once again, ho-hum.

"We're not rats, then," Mister Gibby said with obvious irony to his lab man.

"No," said the scientist ruefully, thinking of his stock options, tugging on his V-shaped goatee. Gibby looked at the wall-sized face and the silly hair on his chinny-chin-chin and said, "Shave that goddamn thing, will you?"

The next time his image appeared the scientist was clean shaven but also quiet. It was the marketing director who had a solution.

"We need to create a world-wide immersive multi-player virtual environment," Dorothy LeGume said to a jubilant Gibby. "We'll call it WorldSpace. It will be brimming with all of the stimulations, attachments, plug-ins, mods and vibrating goodies developed since Haptic Hands... plus an evolving family of AlterGenies to enable users to plug into WorldSpace *and* become adept at developing scenarios and rituals as a – get this, Mister Gibby – as a *team endeavor*."

This was the level of genius Gibby had nurtured in the hive mind of Thrift Shops, TTX, coming to flower. WorldSpace was the supreme pay-off. No longer would individuals lose themselves inside whatever fantasy they had altered themselves to enjoy. They would find greater and greater satisfaction only when they enjoyed sex as a tribal pursuit. The sex itself was the prize, yes, but the complex scenarios of meeting the right people in the digital space, dealing with disappointments, bouncing back, everyone pacing themselves so they all got off at the same time – this was the real reward. They would hunt in packs like wolves and devise alliances spanning the globe. The highest highs would no longer be achieved by individuals, couples or groups in isolation but by those who learned to play their roles in whole societies. AlterGenies to help people become better team players would raise the bar to a new level of competitiveness. Teams would scrounge the nooks and crannies of complex simulated worlds and work tirelessly into the night to create the precise scenarios needed to get off – then explode when and only when everyone was ready. The ripeness was all! Afterward the memory of their mutual orgasm popping through the population like a chain reaction would inspire them to build the next one even better.

Best of all, it would all take time, lots of time, patiently and painstakingly to plan and then execute the fantasy needed for a society to reach a collective climax. Millions would have to learn how to play together to maximize the mind-blowing peak of each, and time, Gibby knew, was money, honey. Time was the ticking of millions of tiny payments drop by drop into the coffers of what now ceased to be known as Thrift Shops, TTX.

WorldSpace, TTX, was the new holding company that absorbed Thrift Shops and the other companies created to sustain the vast play space. Collective play became huge, bigger than AlterGenes even, and soon the tail wagged the genemod dog. Hackers developed mods to equip people to play at a global level, and as people learned that delaying pleasure increased their ultimate ecstasy, a new kind of world emerged.

Within two years seventy per cent of the world's population was engaged in WorldSpace. Never before had so many been willing to postpone pleasure for so long in order to reap delirium later. Their single primal scream when the spit hit the fat was heard around the world – and, according to the space station crew in low earth orbit, even in space (although that report was suspect, because all of the crew were players).

Secondary factors kicked it. Pleasure for some could only be postponed so long. Not everyone could wait. The impatient making up the tail of the bell curve resembled little children twitching to go to the restroom. So sub-scenarios evolved, littler worlds within WorldSpace, letting the least and the last reach frequent mini-peaks of elation while practicing patience at the same time. Little dribbling come-times functioned like training wheels. In turn, nested levels of different sexual timelines enabled the building of incredibly complex games. The top rung held the Masters who reached higher and higher levels of completion but every rung had to be linked and tuned to the one below and above.

The real surprises were always unforeseen. The biggest shocker was the discovery that the supreme peak toward which multiple games began to build simultaneously in a kind of trans-orgasmic frenzy would be reached only after a fifth of the players were dead. Twenty per cent, in other words, were setting the stage for a blockbuster blow-out that they themselves would miss. Even more shocking was that after this was known, they played anyway. AlterGenies making self-sacrifice rich and delicious replaced their original goals and those who survived to rise to the heights even felt let down, wondering if they had won the red ribbon instead of the blue.

No one could have predicted these events from initial conditions and then-current assumptions. Complexity meant, apparently, that while everyone could predict something, no one could predict everything, No one foresaw, for example, that a following would develop for AlterGenies that kicked in when dying players' vital signs ebbed to a minimal level, giving them a rush at the last minute of life that soon drove Hospice out of business.

Or that as a consequence of that, Near-dead Headers would engineer a mod that triggered a similar experience but moments *before* the time of death. The rush was not quite as intense as the Dead-Head Splurge but did have an upside – letting players live to play again.

And so it went, an upwardly spiraling evolution of self-similar nested levels of play, horse after cart and cart after horse, until WorldSpace became so complex it was unmappable. That meant even more unforeseen consequences, including mini-breakdowns, odd pockets of gravitational collapse, and the rearrangement of partnerships and alliances from societal levels down to the individual bonded pair.

Gibby was sitting in front of the Wall of Knowledge watching sixteen scenarios play, the data from their interaction correlated, mapped and rendered as a visualization of SynthoLife in action. It looked to his growing dismay a lot like what they used to call life. For the first time ever, bewildered by too much complexity, Gibby felt overwhelmed. His hands hung limply like vestigial flippers over the worn arms of his chair; his Haptic Hands too hung limply from his console in precise imitation of the world-weary "richest man" at home.

The press release said later that he sat there a long long time under a great cloud of darkness that began to contract and threatened to constrict to a yinyang point when suddenly, inexplicably, the minuscule speck ignited, fission or fusion in Gibby's brain, expanding with nova-like bright white light.

Gibby McDivitt arrived at light speed at the omega point of his vision. What had always been implicit, he saw in retrospect, was manifest at last.

Userspace called it the Palace of Dreams.

Every strength is also a weakness but every weakness can be turned into a strength. By the second decade, so many people were engaged in WorldSpace, searching for stable relationships, learning to be flexible and mend when alliances, treaties, and even those little momentary peaklings of sexual ardor that occurred when AlterBoy and AlterGirl met up and got it on, all broke and literally vanished from the screen. In basements everywhere hackers hustled to make themselves capable of being resilient, endure terminal breakdowns, and plan for the long term. Not only did they mutate to enjoy different kinds of sexual excess, they mutated to endure the failure of unpredictable relationships in a near-chaotic world. The collective wisdom of hackers turned as the winds of necessity demanded. UeberSynthers ramped up to the next level and influenced WorldSpace from a LEO point of view. They not only knew how to get granular, writing tight and elegant genemod code, but could also see the Big Picture. They tolerated ambiguity and endured complexity in a world that wanted both variety and order but preferred the latter every time. Because the complexity of WorldSpace meant that no one could know what was coming next, hackers released into the wild viruses that compelled the herd to confront the unknown, the unexpected, and the malevolent, doing the world a favor by being sheep in the skins of wolves. People got sick from diseases that never before existed but the ones who survived were resilient and strong.

Learning how to fall down and get up again became a new definition of elegant. The standard was applied intuitively to every level of the game from single individual to global organum. To a degree the game stayed true to the original vision and players still pursued pleasure according to sophisticated algorithms that minimized habituation and maximized delight. But it came to be done in ways that were congruent with each interlocking circle at every level of the game. Insight cascaded into design and engineers built a well-organized failsafe space pervaded by the seemingly accidental.

Then Gibby wrote what historians have labeled the Last Memo, authorizing the Palace of Dreams. He never used those words, of course. Instead he sketched out a design in broad strokes and delegated the execution. Soon the first betas were being tested, inserted with stealth into a few select locations, and rumors spread of a wondrous new endeavor that delivered astonishing outsized satisfactions. One sub-group, Blazing Saddles out of Singapore, used the name "the Palace of Dreams" and it stuck. It referred to a new WorldSpace that went so so far beyond the current game it needed a different name (WorldSpace 2.0 did not test well in the marketplace). They whispered of magic portals through which unwary players walked or accidentally stumbled, finding themselves suddenly in a brain-training space of unforeseen transformation.

In WorldSpace 1.0, because levels of interlocking play had to connect to the ones below and above, there had to be a common language. The lowest and highest levels could still communicate through clearly defined coupled links. Transactions plugged into both ends using meta-code they all understood.

The Palace of Dreams was rumored to be different. WorldSpace 2.0 had to be backward compatible with the original somehow but bridges could not be defined in the language of one point oh. A language had to be created through which one could define everything, links, the overall, the way it all connected.

The only one who could do that was Gibby McDivitt. He must have done it. But Gibby wasn't telling.

It was a very tricky puzzle and UeberSynths loved puzzles. They knew that the actions of those who played in the new space affected directly the ones who lagged behind, so there had to be a way to get there from here and a language to say how to do it. But even those who found themselves in WorldSpace 2.0 didn't know what it was, or how they got there, or if they did, they didn't know how to say it.

The Palace obviously contained hints, puzzles, and metaphors to point the way to the portals. Theoretically any player could pass through. Yet everybody knew that only a few would do it.

Thus began the Great Thrust-up, a progressive filtering of players into the DreamPalace. New species of AlterGenies, self-motivated and mobile, crawled through the space like aphids servicing ants. Ordinary players would report that comrades had gone off to make a bet, get laid, or have a meal and were never heard from again. Legal documents authorizing the distribution of their worldly goods circulated which suggested they had not died, but had certainly disappeared. This meant that a route out of WorldSpace 1.0 existed and was legally sanctioned. The Palace of Dreams was real.

This is what someone somewhere suggested might sometimes happen:

An AlterBoy or AlterGirl is fresh from a weekend mini-peak with a momentary mate. They are thinking dreamily of their roles in different scenarios. Spent though they are, they are already anticipating future pleasures, perhaps that very afternoon, a romp with a panda, perhaps, or a tryst with an OctoBun or Yummy. While thus distracted they walk past sugar shops, mushroom shops, the High Life, the Come-on-Inn, idly noticing whores and wares on display in the windows. Perhaps they intend to buy an option on a future possibility. Whatever the incentive, on impulse they choose a door and go inside, stopping in their tracks in sudden darkness unfolding from behind like wings. Uncomprehending, they recognize a moment of transition but have no idea where it might go. They are in a liminal condition not linked to prior knowledge or planned by their team.

If they turn around, they discover that the door to WorldSpace is closed. Above it crossed swords glow faintly, barring the way.

The only direction to go is forward toward more.

The darkness turns out to be a thin fabric, barely a quarter-inch thick. If they move forward, the darkness becomes light and they enter a simulation that seems deliciously real.

Life in the Palace of Dreams is radically unstructured, seemingly devoid of order. Those who can stand it discover that the best way to play is apparently at random, planning nothing, trusting their intuition. They learn to release the whole notion of aiming at anything, instead responding to whatever is before them. As they progress the mind they used in the past is seen to be a construct of the brain. They look at it but can not answer the question, who is looking? Nevertheless, the translation of body-or-brain to brain-self is explicit and complete. So they see. They see that the only game worth playing is making AlterGenes to enhance that fundamental transaction.

They see too that to do that, they must pay attention to subtle currents stirring around them – follow directions – and act as if.

Randomly.

Salting the sequence with indeterminate genes.

Palace players are pleasure seekers but differently, finding deep quiet delight in making things happen through all the concentric circles of WorldSpace. They never see how it happens exactly but trust from effects that it does. Their ultimate satisfaction is delayed seemingly forever, although there are rumors that one day everything will be made explicit. Meanwhile they fly by night, luxuriating in thermals.

But that's an abstraction. Anyway, who has a clue? Certainly not those who think they do, and not Gibby McDivitt, that's for sure. Gibby is more principle now than person – the world has turned him into a projection of their collective selves. The real Gibby is busy again, busier than ever. Just when he thought his career had peaked it was transformed. When he thought he had experienced everything, everything disappeared and a new board was set up for the next game.

Of course most of us can't see that. All we see is that old photo of Gibby, his cracked butt and back and broad shoulders in a chrome-and-leather-flecked chair, his head thrust forward at an angle toward a wall of knowledge where a bright fog unceasingly coalesces and dissolves, looking now like naked women and men playing some kind of game, now like a mist after a brief shower illumined by the sudden sun.

Does Gibby know who dreamed it first? Or which one is dreaming? Knowledge or the molecules of knowledge?

The only one who can say is Gibby himself, whoever he is, wherever he is, and the only certain thing in the whole wide world is that Gibby McDivitt will never tell.

Introduction to "Scout's Honor"

A plaything, a parable, a baroque prose poem, filigreed with decorations.

A transparency, the story of my life.

And a love of words as they whirled into form, frenetic as all get out. That can happen, even without drugs. It's better without drugs, when you get out of the way and the river flows as it will from that part of the brain that gave us "muse" and "angel" as inspirations.

Most of us need a "lovely young thing," one way or another, one time or another. Sometimes a blossoming garden of lovely young things.

Mine was/is Shirley.

I have known and loved many people, relished many friendships, companions, colleagues, mentors, teachers, all sources of energy and much delight. Thank you all.

But... after all these years...

Shirley.

Thank you, my beloved.

Scout's Honor

Scout was standing at the table, lecturing, the cadets in his audience rapt. He wondered why he was even speaking – he had come to doubt that anyone could teach anything – nevertheless, he swayed in his boots, holding onto the table, talking about time.

"Why talk about time?" he said. "I mean, time doesn't exist. I mean, it exists, in our way of thinking, but apart from our minds, no. Time is merely a way to arrange data so it can become a shared experience. Time is a program hardwired in our brains, running in all directions at once.

"But it's worse than that! Oh yes! Every tribe, little or big, a schoolroom clique or a whole planet, has its way of arranging time. There are larger and smaller spans, faster and slower flows. It goes bone-deep. It's learned at the nipple before we know anything else.

"Got it, younglings? We can't capture in our own webs that which we can only know in the Web Itself. We can't spin until we're spun!"

He teetered at the edge of the table and steadied himself, then slid into his chair. Their anxious eyes followed his slow descent.

"Why, then, you may ask, am I willing to crawl into the Cheese and risk disappearing, just to try to find a life that might differ little from this one? Because whenever I come out, I will still be inside my own mind?

"Besides," he rose again, tried to take a step, then held onto the table and leaned unsteadily toward the crowd, "I've seen it all! I've worked the mines of Phobos. I was there when the Pendium went ballistic. I nearly died in the Scylla Rift, locked in an exoskel under the grid lights, digging rock for the Earth-bound owners. I froze my bones on the plains of Mars, waiting for the arrival of a rescue ship which, when it finally arrived, was a pimple of what they had promised, making me stow home like cargo in the hold, crazier than a slave in a stinking galley. No," he snorted, rising to his full height, "don't tell me about the romance of deep space and the siren songs of the stars. Don't tell me about adventure waiting like a flytrap for you easy marks with the so-called courage to sign up for twenty years. All that does is bring profit to the Legendary Chesters and the Elwood City Seven.

"No, my friends, I have been hither and yon in this system and I am reeling with despair. I am trying to save you from your illusions but to no avail, I know, I know! Your dreams flicker like fireflies in the darkness. I can feel their white heat, I can see them from here. My dreams burned out long ago, smoking like wicks in a chilly winter chapel. Now my money is gone too. My body is shot. My day is done. I know better now.

"So why am I still seduced by the notion of going into the Cheese – excuse me, into the tangled matrix of space/time – and popping out, like a puff of smoke coughed out by a dragon, in some strange domain? Where will I come out or when? No one can say. Our language does not have the words to tell us where or when.

"But I'm going and I'll tell you why. It's the only adventure left. Risking break-up on the reefs of inner space is the only adventure left. This is my last chance to learn something. I am going into the Tangle in search of the mermaid I saw once in my youth on a rocky shore, her yellow hair blowing in the green sea wind. Oh God!" he cried suddenly, yearning to be young again, feeling their energy arc in the cave of night. "I have to go! Can you understand that? I have to go!""

He stood there and drank the remains of his bitter beer, then backhanded his mouth and slammed the mug down. Cadets ringed dime-sized tables in the dim light, their eyes wide, jamming the space from the stage to the distant horizon. They listened to his words but were unable to distinguish a role written in a script from real life; they thought despair was a game, weariness a subtle scent or perfume, ennui a seasoning, coriander perhaps or nutmeg. They wagered their youth against the yawning maw of the dark mother and did not know they had already lost. They romanticized Scout's need to drink away his pain and thought that going on the first Transit was a great honor. Scout knew it was God's little joke. Scout had been chewed up by the scaly dragon and spat out time and time again. We only win, he was trying to tell them, when we no longer want the prize. In the cavernous hall, they nodded, taking notes, thinking they understood.

They always do. They always do.

Scout smiled, cried, then smiled again through his tears. The cadets clapped and clapped, rose to their feet, gave him more applause than he deserved.

Irony frets our lives like blues abrading the night in the Sidewinder Bar.

Scout looked down at their worshipful faces.

"That's it. I'm going to bed."

He climbed off the platform and made his way through the tables to the door.

A design flaw determined that he had to exit the Sidewinder

Bar in order to come in again at the next door east, then climb the steep stairs to the top of the ancient wooden building and double back in the dim hallway under a single glaring light bulb toward a room above the bar he had just left. He stood outside for a moment in the damp wind, inhaling the odor of brine and rotting kelp. Fog shrouded the clamorous sea. The mermaid was out in the harbor under the black waves. Through tattered clouds, he could see a few stars, and when waves hit the breakwater, Scout heard it boom before the spray fell.

Boom. and, Boom.

He remembered bodies bursting when the airlock failed on the Orion Rising and how his mind made a boom, a sound like sudden thunder in the silence of space. It did not seem real for pieces of flesh to explode in slow motion all over the hold without a sound. So his mind made a boom. Limbs twisted in free fall, faces looked vaguely playful without their bodies. Boom. and, Boom.

In the same way, he thought, time links chains of events when nothing is there. The mind adds time and space and links the way it made that boom.

He was lecturing himself now, listening no more closely than had the cadets.

He walked through the doorway and up the creaking stairs one slow heavy step at a time. The hallway was empty. The light bulb glared, the hallway stank. His opened the door and the room was empty of hope. He closed the door and stood in the silence of his anguish. O God! his heart cried. Where was an end to grief? Where were the cargo-cruisers now, where was the consolation of the painted faces of dust mops and mollies?

"Sit down," said someone in shadow where Scout couldn't see. Scout jumped and stared into the darkness.

"Jeezus," he said. "You scared me to death. Who the hell are you?"

"Sit down," said his host or guest. "Shut up and listen for a change."

Scout lowered his body into a wooden chair and sat there. "Go ahead," he said. "Talk your fool head off. I don't care."

Whoever it was waited, then said with an announcer's deep voice, "I am here, Scout, to discuss your destiny."

"My destiny!" Scout laughed. "My destiny died in the Outer Rings where everyone I knew and loved was betrayed by Grayling, Limited. Everyone died or disappeared. Don't you know the details?"

"I know the details." The voice sounded like a wry smile. "Better than you."

"I'll bet."

The other sighed. "You can't just listen, can you?"

Scout made an incredible effort to just sit there and say nothing. It took all his energy and will, but he did it.

"That's better. Now listen. Tomorrow they're going to put you into the Cheese. You'll go in one hole and pop out another. No one has the foggiest where you'll emerge or when or how they'll get you back."

"But –"

"Shut up. I know they said that you're bait on a hook and all they have to do is reel in the line and you'll come home. That's bullshit! You guessed as much, didn't you? Scout, your capacity for self-deception is heroic. They broke your body in the mines but said you were a Riser, so you took it. They shot you full of fire and ice in the Rings, making you crazy, and what did you do? You climbed back in the saddle and went on tour for the Elwood City Seven, singing their praises. They lowered you like a pygmy mole into the bowels of the Scylla Rift with nothing but drones and robos for companions and you brought out the drowl and gossum – for them, Scout, all for them.

"Look around you, Scout. You're alone in a ten-dollar room on the dark side of Basal Spaceport, drinking your liver to bits. But you'll crawl into the Cheese like a good little Scout. Won't you?"

Scout said nothing.

"You can talk now. This is your chance."

"What's this about? What's your game?"

The voice smiled. "I want you to know that I'll be in the Cheese with you. I'll be there when you lose it. Making sure it comes back together."

"Lose what?"

"Your mind, Scout. You have to go nuts to come through the Cheese. The transit demands it. Your mind has to get lost before it can get found."

"Why?"

"It can't grasp what it can't hold. Think of your mind as an old man's hand with bent fingers trying to catch an elephant. The mind's a time machine, Scout. Like you told the unknowers in the bar below. It's woven into the brain. So to be rearranged in the skein, the mind has to come apart so the pieces can squeeze into and through the Cheese. Then they have to come together. Meanwhile in that moment of dissolution there's no web of anything knitting together the raw data of your life. Isolated bits of chemical memory, shreds of former identities, what you call thoughts float in free fall toward the Small Dark Point at the End of Everything. In that non-space or pseudo-moment there is nothing, Scout. No you, no nothing. Nothing until you show up on the other side like a center-fielder backing up for a high fly. Except it's you catching yourself. You raise your glove and smile and catch your self.

"So don't worry, Scout. Meta-me will be there."

Scout rose and staggered toward the voice, waving his hands like a blind man. He danced all through the room, a martial artist, a Jedi knight, waving his arms wildly, but no one was there. He reached for a switch and shattered the darkness with scalding light. No one else was in the room.

Scout turned slowly in a circle, looking at every corner and wall and corner and wall. An eye of a lighthouse beacon sweeping but blind, all unseeing.

What in hell, thought Scout, not for the first time. What in hell?

"Yes indeed!" said General Marx, his eyes flashing. "This is the great day!"

The General stood beside Scout, his arm draped around the smaller man's shoulders. He held him close, as much to prevent his running away as bolster his morale. The General was bedecked with medals and gold braid. He was a huge man and, thought Scout, stupid. But he had been brave at the right time and silent at the right time so he made the grade. He was a team player and now he headed the team.

They faced a roomful of reporters. Behind them a wall of video monitors showed holes in the Cheese – a simulation, of course.

"Tell us again, General," said Woodruff from the Beacon. "How will you get him back?"

"We'll reel him in like a fish," the General laughed, "and hope the hook doesn't slip from his mouth."

Everyone laughed, except Scout, who frowned and suggested the general might want to be a little more specific. Say it without metaphors, please.

"We'll reverse the flow," the General explained. "There's only one original in the whole universe, one Scout. That's the gestalt or form that we bleed into the cheese. The pattern left behind in our skein of spacetime will be like a vacuum and suck him back into the matrix. That's the only pattern that can. He wouldn't fit into anything else. It'll make for a tight fit, a seamless weld. What got sucked out will be sucked home, like running an old movie backwards," he made whirling motions with his hands. "Think of a pancake flipping from the floor back into the skillet. That's how Scout will come home."

"I'm the pancake," Scout said, and everybody laughed, except Scout.

"But enough questions," said the Five Star. "Time to make history!"

The reporters applauded and they led Scout out of the room and into a huge cage. They raised the cage by a hoist until it swung in the air twenty feet above the floor. The reporters watched the proceedings on screens. Scout held onto the mesh as the cage swayed, looking through wire toward technicians below. They swung him out over a partition and lowered him as four handlers settled the cage into a metal sleeve. The cage meshed with the sleeve, snug. They increased the field and the cage vibrated as it became part of the wall and floor in a single field. Then the vibrations ceased and it was still. Scout was now in the eye of the storm. He let go of the mesh, the cage flush in its cage-sized hole, himself in the cage.

Technicians in white coats posed for photos. Coils sparked, electricity arced. Lights dimmed except for a blue haze around the cage and now around Scout. Scout and the cage were one field, glowing, candescent. He felt himself ephemeral, he could barely see, he could hear nothing. He was ingathering toward that point, both origin and destination.

A reporter wrote later that Scout looked as forlorn as a dolphin culled from its pod prematurely. Another thought he looked like a lost child. They were both trying to say that Scout had nothing to lose and looked it.

The electromagnetic field lifted everything. Scout became a temponaut, a pinball that might careen into any of a dozen holes. The cage shook and flashed and exploded and when the smoke cleared, it was empty.

"Where," asked Woodruff, "is Scout?"

"Here are the answers to all your questions!" said a Major, handing them to reporters. Green sheets, yellow sheets, blue sheets, pink sheets, coded for the questions reporters were scripted to ask.

"No questions except those in the script!" said the General. Then, when that announcement was greeted with silence, he said: "Anybody else?"

There were no more questions. No answers, anyway. The only one who knew the answers and the questions was Scout, and Scout wasn't talking.

Scout wasn't talking because his mind came apart at the seams. It was like a baseball hit so hard the cover was torn off. A memory flashed of a rabbit he had stepped on accidentally, its intestines shooting out its anus and lying on the green grass in a neat pile, steaming.

Luckily, Scout was nowhere near his mind when it came apart. Just as his companion promised, he was somewhere else, watching. He could see clearly that time and space were in his mind and he was not. He was out of his mind. He saw the links and how he had built them from the time he was born, link by link. He saw that he had mistaken himself for his mind and he wasn't. He was whatever watched it hanging there suspended.

He reached out with his arms to try to get his bearings but there was nothing to touch. He turned his head to see where he was headed but nothing was there. He looked back to see where he had come from and couldn't tell. He closed his eyes and counted to ten twice. No matter how many times he counted, it was always one. Once when he said "Ten!" he said "One!" at the same time.

That's how it went for as long as it happened. Except it was over in an instant. He arrived with a whoosh on his feet and staggered with the momentum like dropping from the sky on a parachute. His mind coalesced around a point. It was a Dot. When he reached out this time, he touched something, and under his feet he could feel what felt like earth.

He looked up at a bright sky. It was white and shot through with drifting blue clouds. Large spheres floated in and out among the clouds like hot-air balloons. There were hundreds of them filling the sky from horizon to horizon. Most were purple. Some were yellow or white.

The landscape was blank. He tried to walk but the wind was too strong. He stepped back into a shelter which he thought of as a tree except he couldn't see it.

No one here to help, he thought. Fitting. No-where known and all alone.

"There's me," said his companion. "I'm here."

"You're a figment of my imagination," Scout said. "I've got it all figured out."

"Wrong. And even if I were a figment, I wouldn't be so cavalier. I'm the only English-speaking entity in the neighborhood. Try to be nicer, can't you?"

Scout sighed. "Where are we, anyway?"

"Scout, part of the lark is for you to figure it out. You already came through the Swiss, Scout. Your mind turned inside-out but here it is again, intact. No rainbow-end, no fringe of a system to explore. What does it mean to ask, where am I, anyway? Where is where?"

"I see," said Scout. He was at the center, at a point of reference, his mind or some other Mind peeking through a window.

Scout sank down by the trunk of the might-be-a-tree and closed his eyes. He breathed deeply and relaxed. He felt the form or flow of energy he called Scout and saw its pattern. He saw that he had interpreted everything always and linked scenes in a sad coherent story. Scout saw that editing was everything. Editing, and rewriting. Rewriting and editing.

He saw fragments of bodies moving slowly through the hold. He saw his companions spatter. He was behind pyroglass, protected. Scout saw himself behind glass seeing himself see. He saw how his mind had mapped the causes incorrectly. He saw he had missed key ingredients, then saw in a flash how often that had happened.

He saw himself in the hole in the Scylla Rift. The temperature was dropping. The woman he loved died in his arms. Then or another time, he understood. When was not the enemy.

The Thirteenth Martian expedition ended in death and madness. Scout saw himself curl into a fetal until he was home. No wonder he had stowed, he was so small, so diminished. Anything more would have been unbearable.

He saw how he had layered traces of experience into memories that he knitted into a tight weave. He saw how like Penelope he could unravel and reweave the tapestry each night and had in fact, every night. Every night.

He opened his eyes, much less stressed. He sank down in the wind shadow of the shelter and closed his eyes and remained still, watching memories drift in palettes of thousands of colors. He identified the chemicals in which they were etched. He saw assembly language under the machine he had thought was the ultimate code. Assembly expressed a code but the code had a code and that code too and suddenly the floor gave way and he was in free-fall falling through fractal-like codes of codes nested until he dropped out of the bottom and disappeared.

Yet here he was, watching with an open inner eye everything he had thought he was. He saw silence and a vast emptiness. He wanted to cry. Tears formed and he cried himself a river, wistful but without regret. But he stayed steady. He was not his grief, either. Good old Scout. Stay still, now. It is quieter here inside. Outside the fists of the wind beat at his brain, but they were faraway as if sensors transmitted signals to a warm dry Scout inside.

I would like to stay here, he thought. But then what would have been the point of coming through the Cheese?

He opened his eyes and blinked.

A sandstorm dimmed the landscape. Hard particles scoured his skin and gradually diminished. The wind roared then died down. He was back inside his mind looking out at things as they had seemed. Only now he knew the difference.

He rose to his feet and felt himself drawn through an open door. The storm was left behind and it was quiet, so he lay down and would have fallen asleep had his mind not kept turning like a kaleidoscope. He watched the wheel turn with rapt disinterest. Then there was a bright white light and he was awake. He stood up, stretched, and opened his eyes.

"Fantastic!" cried the General. "Scout is home!"

The reporters raced to jack in and zip the news to the waiting world. Morley Scout had gone and come. The first Transit through the Cheese was history.

The next morning he found himself propped up on a deep soft chair, his limp legs hanging high over the floor like a little kid's.

Blue fluid moved in a drip from a bottle to his arm. He watched his arm become bluer.

"Won't hurt," said the physician. "It's a memory-enhancer. Freshens the images. Makes them crisp and bright against the white backdrop of forget-me-land."

"Don't want to remember," said Scout. "I try to forget as much as I can."

"Yes, we know," said the doc. "That was before. Hence the enhancer. Bring-em-back-alive and brew their brains with Blue."

Scout scowled.

"So what do you remember?"

"Just the companion. He's invisible."

"What else?"

Scout looked closely. "I can't say."

"Can you see?"

"I can see all right, but I can't say. Stop the Blue."

The doctor scanned the screen attached to the grip on Scout's clean-shaven head. The blank scene repeated tediously. Same old same old. "Okay. Whatever you say."

He reached for the switch and – Scout would remember the physician's hand reaching forever for a switch it would never touch. A synapse forever unbridged.

"Have you out in no time," said his companion, removing the grip from his bare head. Then he unbuckled the straps and laughed as Scout flexed hands and arms and waggled his head.

"The Blue will disappear. It's fast-acting and equally fast-exiting. An excellent enhancer. Doesn't leave a trace."

"Except in the brain. The curl can never be straightened, right? A good man can tell how many times you've been enhanced."

"Scout knows his chemicals," his companion said, "not wisely but too well."

"I never contest a rescuer," Scout stood up now and rubbed his hands up and down his arms. "Who are you, now? Isn't it time to tell?"

His companion drew himself up to his full four feet, if a mist or a pale shade has height, and settled into a storytelling stance he had learned from NetherBernts on their dark icy world where they often stood for days like penguins holding eggs on their webbed feet, telling stories against the gloom. This is what his companion said:

"I wasn't home long enough to know who gave me birth. They must have dropped me at the dock for someone to take. No one did. I lived under the streets, scavenging. Somehow I survived. I hitched a ride when I was a teen on a cargo-liner out of Downside. I never regretted my early departure. I rode with Skags and Baldies all the way to the Pluto Deep. The trip took six months then, not like now. Using primitive propulsion, we took weeks just to get to the Jupiter boost. We made a few stops, too, of course, along the way.

"Have you ever seen the Pluto Deep in the velvet light of a solar flare, ionized in a purplish haze? That was our breakfast lamp. Beyond our system's edge the stars did not grow larger for years and years. Past Pluto it felt like falling into a deep well. We read memos and scannies when the haze heated up, but when it settled down again, it was always only a cool blue twilight. The sun a distant candle dimmed by the long winter. The Deep was too dark, too cold, too far. Humans need more. We needed to touch one another so we evolved toward Mind-to-Mind of necessity, Scout. It was not a parlor game: It was a necessity. We learned to tune in and out of each other like shortwave coming and going in static. Brothers and sisters linked in electric arcs. To the untrained eye we must have looked like solar flares but we knew what we were doing.

"We were the last Expedition sent to the Deep without Holders and Soothers. Those wild-eyed cadets who adore your distorted story will have Soothers, Holders, and Strokers. We were isolated, Scout, and that took its toll. Now they know. We were the white mice that taught them.

"Have you ever eaten with a Baldy? The Skags at least sucked it all in without slurping, bad as it looked. Not the Baldies. Baldies eat it all up, lick by dripping lick. Damn! And they thought Baldies were well-adapted to the Deep because they were loners. Living as they did, it was no wonder. They were the worst. One of them, Quarg the Porker, was incapable of tuning or scanning and went crazy pretty quickly. He thought he was still himself when he was long gone. It scared the rest of us, watching Quarg distort in the dark cell they called a starship then. That enhanced our intentions and energized our wills. That's when we learned to listen in.

"I watched Quarg waver and wink out. It was a sad fate. Not for us, we all swore. We learned to attend to the presence of others. Some say it was a waste to give it all away like that but we had no choice. There was no other way to survive the lonely life on that cold dark distant ship.

"When we had to get outside ourselves, our inner antennae extended as it were and beat in the air like ants'. I learned to catch feelings, thoughts, moods and points-of-view, sometimes days before they happened. I knew who was getting ready to erupt. I knew who was ripe for love. I loved it, lost myself utterly in others. That's the danger of learning to listen not wisely but too well. I forgot myself." He sighed. "Well, so it goes. Now I'm here. I remained intact when my body combusted when the thermal shield failed. Somehow I survived. Perhaps all do. I don't know. Now I respond to cries for help. That was how I trained myself. I can't help it, Scout, it's what I do. It's who I am."

Scout said, "I see."

"When I disembodied, having no more use for senses that distracted me, I found I could follow tracks not at light speed but immediately. I learned that time and space and spacetime were constructions I no longer needed. My pale shade of a self could follow lines of energy like force fields. I must look like iron filings on an electromagnetic field. Distress travels faster than light. Your signals, Scout, were the worst I heard in years."

"Why?"

"The despair was deeper, darker, the pain was life-deep, scarred and pitted like icy Ceres. The space inside was like The Hole at the Heart of the Coal Sack, vast and empty. How much liquor can a man drink? How much Limbic Baseline can you push into your veins? I was shocked by the waves of grief in the depths of your lonely soul. That triggered my need to hunt you down and shore you up."

"So you showed up before I went into the Swiss."

"Yes. In the Cheese, I provided balance when you might have forgotten how to come back. I was the weight at the other end of the dumbbell."

"I see," said Scout, and this time he meant it. "Thank you. Now what?"

"Now, dear Scout," he softened into the pose of a come-to-me Soother from the Wetherby Moonship, "now we teach you how to love."

Scout learned that the people who touched his heart and made him weep were friends. He would not believe it, at first, tried not to remember, wouldn't listen. Night after night he went to the Sidewinder Bar and drank himself silly. He could run, he discovered, but couldn't hide. Cadets had grown fond of the old man.

Their concern and admiration touched him. Their kindness broke him down like lichen on a rock.

One day the General held a conference and apologized to everyone. He admitted the whole show had been a scam. Scout might have died, tumbling off into hyperspace like that. He begged their understanding and forgiveness. They forgave him, but arrested him anyway and sent him away. Stripped of his epaulets, he was seen, a thin old man who had gone too far. If anything, Scout was more of a hero after that. He had risked his life for a noxious fume like the jailbird General and once again survived. He alone knew that despite the enterprise being a scam he had made the Transit. Better, he decided, to say nothing for once and let the galaxy think it a scandal.

Scout sobered up. He ate fresh fruit and green and yellow vegetables. He began to exercise again. He yuppied along the seawall in the morning light, building his wind. He stopped smoking, stopped using Dragonweed, and stopped screaming in his sleep. Anxiety dried like stale sweat in the dawn-wind wrinkling in from the sea. His dreams became blue and white like water on a warm summer morning.

Then the lovely young thing showed up. She appreciated his history, she saw the weave before and after and understood but loved his presence here-and-now best. It took three years but at last he got it. He became capable of being loved by the little ninny and allowed her to touch him, inside and out. She allowed him to touch her too. He awoke one morning all cleaned and told her everything. She listened and rocked him in her arms. Then she told him everything too. He shrugged and said well, no-one is perfect. She crushed into his arms and he held her as if she were life itself. Two anchors tethering a single ship in their thrilling hearts.

They were married one warm morning on the waterfront by

the Captain of the *Brash Embrace,* Eben Weezer, who knew Scout in the Rift and couldn't believe it was the same Scout. Scout loved the ritual and its happy aftermath. Three starships shattered the sky with galactic homage. Boatloads of old groaners rolled and cheered. Hundreds of cadets threw petals and crispers all over them both. The Wallaby Chorale zithered and warbled all the old spacesongs. That night the companion disappeared and Scout and Lily Louise lived happily ever after in a big boat painted yellow and orange with purple smokestacks that bobbed gently in nearshore water that was always calm.

Time was woven in his mind like a spider's web wet with morning dew. Memories glowed like iridescent pearls. The web was transitory and fragile, as everything is, but it was also quite beautiful, and when he awoke to the web with wonder in the soft morning light, basking in the glow of her still-fresh love, he had no words with which to describe his delight. He could even endure being all alone with life-and-death and not cry. The muted pain was bittersweet, but so was the strumming music of life on the strings of his heart.

He never heard from the companion again, but never forgot him either, nor needed he enhancer to recall his gift or spirit and its spell.

Introduction to "Silent Emergent, Doubly Dark"

This story began as "Alien Brain," and thanks to helpful editors, wound up shorter and more precise. The final edits came from Allen Ashley, a fine writer and editor of *Subtle Edens,* a slipstream anthology in which it first appeared. He taught me that Bruce Sterling was correct about slipstream, that slipstream is often what I write, not fantasy or sci-fi.

So slipstream it is. And proof too that a good editor ought to have his name on the story. Creative work is always collaborative, one way or another, and individual "writers" are no more viable than isolated cells in a petri dish.

I can 't say it, whatever it is, in words or symbols, more precisely than in this story. I try to illuminate insubstantial realities with metaphors and tropes. That's all I have to work with. But there is also a story in the story.

I was sitting in my office at St. James Church in Salt Lake City, Utah, a most rewarding parish where I was lucky to land at the right time. I engaged regularly then in meditation. That's what I was doing, one afternoon, although to someone who opened the door, I might have looked like I was just sitting there not doing much of anything.

Meditation of course is not nothing. It is something.

Suddenly I was in an altered state in a vivid landscape. There's more to tell, but that's all I want to say about that. (David Stendahl-Rast, after spending time in both Benedictine and Zen monasteries, told me the biggest difference was not what one discovered, but that Christians talked about it and Buddhists remained silent). I will say, however, that the visitation to Hartmut Lipsky in the driftless area actually happened in Salt Lake City, too, when I was driving downhill from the bench area of the Wasatch Mountains and an entity manifested itself during a similar state. I will never forget the communication during that encounter, not need it ever be put into words.

An act of synchronicity in the week after that meditation: I was browsing in the Cosmic Aeroplane, an alt-store in downtown Salt Lake City, and found a new-agey book about shamans and their journeys. I bought it and read it like a hungry man on Survivor winning a reward meal. The journey described was exactly what I experienced that day in my office. In Cottonwood. In Utah. Everywhere and nowhere.

That's when I suspected – again – that we are hard-wired for hierarchical restructuring of the sort I underwent while living in England. It is embedded in us and all we have to do is cooperate with conditions that make it more likely to manifest, if manifest it can.

Some of that shows up in this story, the images and symbols, the journey. All we can do is report out and say that it's worth going.

Once you learn something, you don't unlearn it. That transformation in England clicked into place like the cogs in a psychic wheel. I remember the morning, sitting in front of the fire in Walton-on-Thames, Surrey, on Kings Road, when everything clicked into place and I knew I had not gone crazy but arrived at my destination. I returned to America to friends who barely recognized the person they had known in its 2.0 version. A year of exploration followed, trying things on, leading to the decision to enter ordained ministry, a training program in humanity to sustain that experience and keep me balanced, the decision that ministry in the context of the rich Anglican tradition which is reasonable and sane, poetic and wild, full of lights and shadows, mysteries and spells, all at the same time, as well as providing a narrative that illuminated a path through brambles and thickets into a blossoming garden, was just right for me.

One metaphorical way of summing it up is that "G-d" called me into the ministry and sixteen years later called me out to a wider work. Every step on our paths apparently is essential. Nothing is left over.

The Shadow knows – the shadow Self, that is.

The laughter of the shadow Self is richer, warmer, more robust and less tinny than the one on the radio show.

All these years later, these stories are some of the fruits of that journey.

Silent Emergent, Doubly Dark

What spectacle confronted them when they, first the host, then the guest, emerged silently, doubly dark, from obscurity by a passage from the rere of the house into the penumbra of the garden?

The heaventree of stars hung with humid nightblue fruit. – *Ulysses*, James Joyce

I wanted to leave the Earth the minute I knew I could.

Didn't everybody? Well, no, I learned. Everybody didn't.

So most don't. They're wired by design to like their home planets. I was wired differently. I hungered to plunge into the cultures of other worlds.

First, however, I had to matriculate, study psi and physiology, physics and symbol systems. I had to learn how to weave words, then learn how to weave the wind.

Lacking siblings and close friends, restricted to the precincts of the spaceport by my mother's work, I played inside my mind in a gravity well of necessary solitude. That, I discovered, was a precondition for the bounce.

"That's you, there, when you threw the dice," my mentor said, showing me a retro of a toddler in a room. A doctor entered, and the child's eyes – my eyes – filled with fear. Then the apprehension vanished and the child rushed into the doctor's arms.

"That's when you went off-world," my mentor said. "That's the platform, that moment, there. We provided the wiring but you had to make the splice."

The first culture I explored on my own was the whrill-ggg! or the whirlibangs as I called them. The whrill-ggg! lived in one of the small planets at Sirius B. They lived inside the dirt like ants in a huge hill.

They had ritual memories of when the dwarf roared and they lost all but the most roastable of ancestors. Memories were enacted in the darkness twice each year and then the little ones exchanged hugs and touches. The dark carapace-encrusted ones and the thickly feathered remnants of the flyers were the only ones to survive. The pinkies, the fair-ones, all died in the flames.

Two major races built inside and moved mountains literally, turning everything upside down. Whereas before there had been towers in the sky, there were towers inverted, plunging into the Earth. Tunnels connected them in fractal-branching patterns that looked for all the world like self-luminous trees. They cultivated luminescent bacterial gardens and learned to breed thousands of different batches. The inner darkness glowed with every imaginable color and hue. The inner world became diverse, nuanced with colors that the day-star would never have revealed, had the Roar not happened.

Unfortunately the feathered ones and the encrusted ones decided that they were more bonded to being feathered or encrusted than they were to being a single species. So the tribal divide coincided with the near-completion of the initial work on their inner world. They fractured in two. Still, both tribes spoke glowingly of the beauty of their habitat when seen in a flash, an intuitive flash better than a visual, and that was the precondition of recombination. Even after they fractured, paradoxically, a single luminous web unified their common life.

This is what they did. They built a framework of bonded earthworks that absorbed extraneous light. Absorbent pebbles sucked in the light and left a blackness so thick it was nearly visible. Then they engineered a number of levels by programming tiny animals, then bigger ones, then ones that were unimaginably big, to dig patterns they wanted to etch in several dimensions. Then they lined the tunnels with liquids that thickened and held to the walls as they dried. Then they released luminescent bacteria that found the right walls and began to live and multiply in and on them. But because of the pressure as the gradient increased, there were apertures over and around each section. So from any vantage point in the primitive grid they could see every hallway and tunnel, all glowing with various colors and depicting the entire planet in precise miniature. Then when they altered or as they called it "played upon" one part or another, they could see the effect on the whole as the luminous life-forms adapted themselves to the changes. Then they would execute the changes or not, depending on consequences.

I had just arrived when they took me to see the First Matrix. It had long ago crumbled when they stopped repair-work and built the Second. But its smudged colors and broken walls and portals made it somehow even more exquisite to behold. It was breathtaking, really, coming down the locks and through the gates that held the heat up or out and entering the cooler darkness then being taken by the hand and led through the lightless maze around and up to a platform where suddenly as one came around the last bend the ancient remains of the First Matrix glowed with indescribable beauty. Blues, corals, yellows, pinks, these I remember most. But when I named the colors I saw they laughed. My frog-eye and frog-brain couldn't come close to saying what they saw with their million-faceted dark-adapted eyes.

The feathered ones and encrusted ones rebonded after the Great War which is why I was able to go. They never sent newbies to war zones or even to temblors, which is what we called cultures that gave signs of impending disaster, war, catastrophe, or collapse. They tentatively called themselves the whrill-ggg! which was an amalgam of their racial names like Serbo-Croatian or Anglo-Franc had been on Earth. You could tell that the name still sounded strange on their tongues, except of course they did not have tongues. They had hundreds of vibrating cilia around their mouths and inside what we called their lips. When they sang together at council, harmonized on hug-days, or aroused themselves for a planetary change, the humming sounded like cellos and bassoons to me, then violins when the younger ones joined, then instruments for which I have no names when the ready women, neuts, and crawlers all joined the chorus.

I learned a few sounds which I made in different ways with my agitator, my cheeks, my sound banks, and my thrummers. I learned how to ask for something to eat or drink, inquire in at least seven levels of formality after their health or well-being, admire with appropriate restraint the nubile budding of their ready ones, and of course ask for directions to the channels of elimination. "Tubes and cools" we called it in the seminar room. There, however, it sounded more like "RRggghhh—hroopeff!" and "Wwwwrillllling-upsss?"

The feathered ones fascinated me because they still had wonderful stories of soaring. Their feathers had thickened for better insulation and most were unable even to flutter or primp. But their hug-fests were filled with images of soaring in the twin-sunned skies before the Roar and their young ones twittered and danced with excitement.

I lived there only for one month. That was the term for the first journey and no matter how much you loved the culture, there was no changing it. I can understand now how impressionable we were, coming out of the academy, so eager to translate or adapt. The danger of falling in love with your first culture and going native, particularly since the target is chosen to be congruent with your hunger for belonging, was too great.

I hated to leave. Since they had seen academicians come and go on a monthly basis for centuries now, they never grew attached. Their hive mind did not entertain attachment in the same way, anyhow. You were either part of the hive or you weren't. If you weren't, you were food or enemy or guest. Guests were never loved inordinately or adored during hug-fests beyond their limits.

My eyes had barely begun to open, don't you see. When I saw the First Matrix it took my breath away but it was as if I was opening my eyes under water for the first time. A week later I returned to the vista and used it as a benchmark. Already I could see why they laughed. There were hundreds of luminosities, nuanced gradations of brightness and dimness I had totally missed when they asked what I saw. They only asked questions, I know now, that the academy provided. They weren't just being polite, they were taking part in a program the rules and objectives of which they understood thoroughly and had for many generations, too many to count. By the end of the second week I wanted to stay and move my eyes from color to color, light to light. After the third week I was cocky and described the harmonies I could discern with glib triumphalism. This too they tolerated, saying nothing, giving me hugs and strokes with their lateral cilia. Then at the end of the fourth week when I knew I would leave the next "day" I stood there and wept at the beauty of it, the inexplicable patterns I had just begun to notice, and all I wanted to do was stay inside that planet and learn and learn and see and see.

But rules are rules. Through the gates we clambered and through the locks growing hotter and hotter until they bade me farewell and I came up into the tube that sucked me like milk in a straw into the ship and before I knew it I was home.

"Hey! Alien Brain!"

It happened outside the academy walls after I returned from my first excursion. Youth from the spaceport barracks, three of them, made bold when they saw how I walked. I was growing accustomed to Earth weight but still lurched from side to side. I was more aware of the bright light. Everything was glaring! Everything on Earth looked whitewashed in too-bright sun, unfiltered. Colors bled and shadows were shocking and harsh.

The three of them blocked my way. I looked at their faces. They seemed pinched, narrow-nosed. Their eyes were like slits and their mouths gushed words. Humans, I was learning, are a funny species. They think talking is doing. Their souls ride floods of vocables like rafts in rapids.

"So how's Alien Brain, huh?"

I measured the distance. I withdrew my head toward my shoulders, my neck shortening. My hands rose at my sides like winged claws. My eyes burned with defense-of-nest rage.

The talker cooled and stepped back. His face lost color, nostrils flaring, eyes opening wide. He rose to his height, flexing his fists. But then his fingers unclenched, his expression relenting.

"Big important alien brain, huh!" he said, but he backed off.

The others backed off with him, feigning grace and style. "Watch yourself!"

I hunched my shoulders in an unmistakable take on encrusted ones entering the feeding ring and facing down the feathered ones. Ritualized, to be sure, but there was no mistaking the menacing implication. The encrusted ones were fierce. Inside I felt my carapace shift plates and adapt to the diminished threat.

They backed off, honoring their fear. They knew that I knew and knew I knew they knew. It is never disreputable I learned on B to honor one's fear. Fear is noble when it is honored. It is ignoble only when dismissed.

I didn't know why they called me Alien Brain. Whatever I had learned from the whrlll-ggg! in one month was still percolating into my personality, still inflecting how I held myself as a possibility for action. I couldn't see myself yet.

Had nothing to do with a brain, anyway. Brains are physical, I thought then – before I lived four earth years among the Tzdow in artificial orbiting cities.

After my excursion to Sirius B, I wrote a paper which caught the attention of professors. I emphasized not so much the adaptation of the two dominant cultures to the interior of the planet but the relationship between the symbolic matrix they continued to rebuild with greater and greater refinement, the nuances of the colors, the ripples of luminosity and flux, the fact that a snapshot of the symbolic system at any moment produced a static image of near-perfect symmetry, regardless of the point of view from which it was taken. This meant that the blended cultures had an ability to synthesize diverse thought-forms at successively higher levels of abstraction and was able to think more than multi-dimensionally. They were able to see their mental representations as dogs having not tens or dozens but hundreds of tails, as it were, and they were able to imagine all the dogs chasing all the tails both in a dynamic simulation always in flux and as a static snapshot, a map of the interior of the planet and more importantly of their own well-integrated hive mind.

I was well into the Gray Zone. That's what pleased my mentors.

The ultimate task for the Cosmos as we arrogantly called our pan-galactic collective was to narrow the Gray Zone. The Gray Zone exists between our mental multi-dimensional maps and the things they represent. Because the hive on B, for example, is dynamic, there is a always latency or lag time between the frequently reiterated map and whatever is "out there" or rather "in here" as in fact was literally true on B. That latency was down to a few nanoseconds for the hive mind which is remarkable considering that the representations were made almost exclusively of wetware, flows of luminous bacteria that constantly shaped and reshaped themselves through spontaneous telepathic connection to subtle alterations in the composition of the materials of the planet – shifting strata, changing chemical balances, fluctuations in temperature – somehow they factored all of it in, devising quantitative measurements for relationships that others had not yet discovered.

As a recent graduate, this taught me how hastily I had applied words like "primitive" and "unsophisticated" to a feat that no other civilization to our knowledge had achieved.

No wonder the denizens of B were honored and were always the first stop of anyone endeavoring to understand how the Cosmos understood itself.

I left the academy infrequently after returning because contemplation of what I had seen, attempting to remember it, became a preoccupation. This is not unusual, so deeply imprinted is the cadet by the living rainbow arcs of that inner world.

A post-excursion exercise illustrates how difficult it is to remember what we saw.

I was using movables and mindscreens to plot the points I recalled of the First Matrix. I chose the most basic because it would be simpler, I thought. I smudged colors with an artist's fastidious hand, moving pastel whorls along cracking lines between zones. The form of the whole emerged in four dimensions. I could run it in real time or let the slide show snap through the cycle.

Watching the weekly run one morning, I suddenly sat up and hit Block. A rainbow bridge spanning the chasm of the third divide did not look right. I took it ahead frame by frame, squinting as the bridge shifted in slow time and arced over a canyon I did not remember seeing.

"That's funny."

I buzzed for a Master and waited patiently until she came.

"I don't remember it this way," I explained, "but it works in the simulation. How could I have missed it?"

She ballooned her white skirts which seeped air as they settled to the floor as she arrived beside me. Her eyes were magnificent, telescopic and slightly tubular, protruding with the apparatus that enabled her to see little and big in the same scan.

"What happens if you remove the bridge?"

"Remove it entirely? Obliterate the link?"

"Yes," she said. "What do you think would happen?"

"It would fall down."

She twinkled. "Give it a try."

I obliterated the bridge and backlashed parameters as if it had never existed. I fell back to a prior position and let the simulation race. To my surprise, the canyon was at first dark but slowly became self-luminous over time as bacteria flowed along its walls. It began to brighten about the time the bridge would have invented itself and the light arced through the air and formed a different bridge where there had been nothing, growing along a luminous flow. A dozen frames later, the bridge was there, made it seemed of light, pure light.

I sat back, hitting Block to stop the movement, staring at the bridge of light.

"What happened?" she asked.

"It built what was needed," I said. "I understand that. But there was no material! How did the flow of information create a tangible structure out of thin air?"

"Well," she said, smoothing her skirts and indrawing her stalks. "What would have to be true in order for that to happen? What kind of universe would it be if this simulation is correct?"

I thought for a moment. "Thought forms!" I said. "Thought forms as real as the material out of which..." – my mind was racing – "out of which everything is made."

"Which means...?"

"Talpas!" I thought of that nasty monk taunting Madame de Neal. "The simulation forms so-called 'reality' in its own image – creates it, in a way – which means that the imagination, the mind, not only half perceives, but also half-creates."

"And where does one begin and the other end?"

I looked inside my mind to see. After a moment, the Master laughed.

"Can you see? And if you can see, can you say what you see?"

I peered into the darkness, feeling deflated.

"I don't think I can see, no," I said. "And I have a hunch that if I could I could not say what I saw without distortion."

"Without building bridges out of thin air, in other words..."

Suddenly I saw. "Yes!"

"So you do see?"

The moment passed. My mind was clanking machinery again, gears grinding. "I thought I saw..."

"No," she gently corrected. "You saw, and now you think you saw."

"Ah!" I said, growing excited. For a moment my mind flickered back and forth like a hologram being seeing and thinking I saw then seeing myself thinking then thinking I saw myself thinking I saw... collapsing into infinite regress.

Then I was sitting there again merely, the Master riffling her skirts as she rose.

"A good day for remembering," she said with a twinkle. "A good day for forgetting, too."

My laughter rang out as someone threw a switch in the control room and her simulated image vanished.

The Memory Game, the less pious call it. This is how Harambee, a senior classmate, explained it in a seminar.

"You didn't grow up with siblings," he said, "so you don't know. I had a brother who was four years older. Once he asked if I remembered an incident that took place when I was four. It was very depressing, he said, how our parents lost control of their emotions. They went wild that night.

"That's funny, I told him. I don't remember it that way. I remember an argument full of good will, a respectful exchange that ended with a perky little kiss.

"Maybe we're talking about two different things, he said.

"He was right, but not the way he was thinking. He always

thought our home was insane. So he remembered the story in a way that fit that decision. I always thought there was plenty of affection and good will. That's how I approach life generally and I remembered the 'same event' in a way that was congruent with my happier self, my happier life.

"But is it the same event at all? Even if we agreed in the way we told the story, even if we got the planet or the galaxy to agree on how the story is told, would that do anything other than inflect the way we co-create the Cosmos, surrounding ourselves with seamless agreement that determines how we hold ourselves as possibilities for action?"

"Are you suggesting," I asked, "that there is nothing 'out there' except what's 'in here?'"

"Well, what kind of universe would we inhabit if that were true?"

I laughed. "That's Theology. We're in Cultural Studies, remember?"

"Are we?" he smiled.

The middle period of my learning was full of wonder. 'You are learning so fast it is making you giddy,' read one evaluation. 'You can not absorb the lessons in other cultures fast enough to satisfy your hunger. Your need to connect is relentless. Unless you create and recreate the Big Picture, always using more data, you feel as if your life is meaningless. Your mind moves at a speed most cannot comprehend.'

I felt like I was balancing on the tip of a gyroscope spinning on a hair stretched between suns. Naturally, I lost balance and fell. The boundaries between disciplines that I had studied as if distinct disciplines – physics, exobiology, astrochemistry – blurred. Everything, I discovered, related to everything else.

Cultural Studies require at some point familiarity with the major research areas of exobiology. It is impossible to separate the physical from behaviors that seem to manifest what some call spirit and some call soul. Those are names for an integrated whole or the image of the whole projected by the perceiving being. Drill down through levels of abstraction defining behaviors of subcellular automata, cells, individual beings, colonies, or communities of all shapes and sizes and you find they are layers around a planet's core. At some point they collapse and you plunge into nonspecific awareness where cognition becomes ill-defined prior to self-identification through reflexive consciousness.

The Universe begins and ends in consciousness that half-creates and half-perceives. Consciousness like the Universe is finite but unbounded. Therefore we must grieve not...

But I digress.

Exobiology is fascinating. The Gray Zone is even more important in that discipline. The proper study of biological entities, after all, is form. Form determines identity and identity is destiny. But form disappears in the Gray Zone. That means destiny as an intentional trajectory is impossible to trace to its source. It happens at the quantum level and it isn't certain whether it's a function of what's there or how the mind sees what's there. The dividing line between them is another Gray Zone.

The holographic brain flickers between distinctions until it gets a bad headache.

The important things in the Universe happen in the Gray Zone, between low and high tide, on the edges of things. That's where we see most clearly that choices become decisions and decisions are engines of self-definition.

That's where/when a species stops fooling around and plays the game with real money.

These insights evolved after I visited gas planets where higher beings float. They emerged apparently from the soup as membranes around chemical processes. They look to earthly eyes like gelatinous jellyfish, flexing in the currents of their atmospheres, as adapted as fish in a sea. Their forms are translucent, resilient, tough. They live at all levels of the float. They signal in all frequencies.

At one point they communicated through the exchange of gases but began specializing, making trade-offs. Energy became information and information discovered more appropriate forms for self-expression. Some ingathered nutrients, others defended the distributed network from chemical assault. As nutrient fishers became more efficient, the colony needed fewer of them. That allowed the defenders to evolve elaborate structures that looked more offensive than defensive. At some point in their evolution the distinction became meaningless. Floaters that did not participate in the collective memory disappeared and a single membrane that looked like an immense brain without a skull flowed in the winds and storms of the hot giants.

The only way to study such planets from the inside was to participate in the flow. We had tried to establish observatories (with consent, of course) on their many moons and listen to radio waves, synapses crackling with static, as we learned to distinguish the flow from the colors of the upper atmosphere. It didn't work. We wound up describing processes as if they were merely physical.

They worked with us to establish modules that synched with their habitats. We designed skeins of tough flexible polycarbons into which we knitted ourselves, brains afloat in translucent fabrics that moved with the winds. We connected our floaters to the planetary being by multispectral communication that enabled us to see, feel, hear, receive, link and – we hope – think as they did.

Visiting the gas giants was a highlight. I practiced for two years in tanks and sims before I was inserted. Still, the first shock of flying was as terrifying as it was exhilarating. I kept feeling for ground under my feet and couldn't find it. I kept trying to focus my thinking right in front of my face as if I were a brain seeing the world through physical eyes. But the information that mattered wasn't coming in from the front. It was coming from behind, around the edges, and I had to learn to listen as it were with antennae that extended out and back, gathering signals and processing them in a part of my brain that at first did not feel "real." I knew theoretically that it was just habit. I had learned from my fetish that images however enticing floated beyond the core reality I sought. I applied that lesson a thousand times on the gas giants. The part of my brain that processes images as if they are real became something I could observe. Instead of seeing things, I saw myself as a process generating images of things. Then I knew how my mind structured or created realities in which I lived as if they were real. Meanwhile I dropped down into a listening place below the level at which images were generated. It felt like letting go of a struggle to stay above the water and breathe air. I let myself sink into the silence of the deep, sink down into the darkness, except instead of dying, I discovered myself more alive, more aware than ever.

I hung between points of gravity in equipoise, listening.

Then I became part of the flow. There was always a level of intentionality that had to happen for connections to be made, but once I learned where that happened and could go there at will, I could always find the reins when I dropped them. Once you know how to regain the reins and know that you know, you have mastery.

Then the synapses crackled not with static but with multichanneled signals layering information into patterns, weaving immense tapestries the size of moons. The signals were like threads built into a pattern and at a higher level of abstraction they became images heard not with the ear but with the entire organizing brain.

When I returned to the academy for a sabbatical after that sojourn I had the most difficult time translating what I knew into language that others could understand. I had to "layer up" from the primary way of knowing to the metaphors and symbols that made sense in another domain. It was as if I was describing life underwater to people who had never left the land, or worse, did not know that two thirds of their planet was under water.

Still, I knew it would be a cop-out to blame a lack of communication on the receiver. I knew that communication was a function of my intention; I learned that on the gas giants, wrinkling and sliding in the upper air. If you did not want to connect, nothing came your way but noise. But if you did, the sense of well being issuing from multispectral multilevel communication among all the cells of that planetary body was a source of ineffable joy.

I realized I would never again be who I had been. The points of reference for my core identity had shifted as a result of changes I had not even realized were happening.

Here's how I discovered that.

One evening I went for a stroll outside the academy walls. The twilight sky was indigo and the breeze was light. The fragrance of blossoming trees was pale, whitish pink and rosy red. The street was empty until, turning a corner, I found myself facing the three louts who had called me "Alien Brain" so many years before.

I recognized them instantly, but not they me. I flashed on fear, but they were oblivious. I stopped, looking into their faces, making them stop too.

The leader was still the leader. The followers were still followers. But they were much older. I wasn't, however. They were a hundred and I was thirty. The face of the leader retained its youthful ignorance and disdain for the different. They worked at the spaceport, had worked there all their lives. They were as happy as they could or would be. Their dislikes were necessary, I suddenly understood, for self-definition. Without so many ways of saying who they were not, they would never know who they were.

"Don't I know you." the leader said as much to himself as to me.

I flowed in the twilight, feeling the currents of the cool moon.

"You're one of those Alien Brains. You see different."

The words were hot but his heart was cold. The differential created an electric charge. I did not object to his memories or need to be right.

"We kicked your ass." another said. "Years ago, we kicked your alien ass."

My smiling flowed in and out of their eddying disturbance, contouring itself to their posturing. Felt like going down the drain. Felt like a dark adrenalin-driven hurry-up flow racing to the tip of a spiral and stopping.

"Guess you know who's king of the street,." a follower said.

"Guess he does." said the leader.

We waited in silence in the twilight. The moon rose golden through limbs of a redbud tree. The breeze died, night ready to spring.

I walked toward them then through them as they flowed

around me and down the street. Before they turned the corner, one shouted: "Alien Brain!"

The night was alive with triumphal acknowledgement. Ways of saying anything, anything at all, dissipated with the afternoon heat. The flow was all.

Darkness gathered us in, knitting the leaves into an opaque mass.

The Tzdow were a gift, an opportunity, a benevolence.

Because they had been around for so long, the Tzdow had drilled deep into the levels of consciousness that informed and animated the Cosmos. They were one of the oldest races in the Universe. They were quasars of sentience, the furthest fastest manifestations of divergence and convergence as they became one thing.

And I got to go. By the grace of all that is holy, I was able to live for four years in the orbiting cities of the Tzdow.

The Tzdow had gone artificial when the word still had currency, that's how long ago it was. No natural disaster or catastrophe, no crisis or upheaval forced their decision. They simply looked and saw what was necessary. Mutation and accident had taken them a long way. They wanted to take control of their destiny and did.

It's easy to say this after thousands of centuries. It had not been easy to do, however. The Tzdow say they invented the words "trial and error." Billions died, billions were warped or distorted, billions wept before their cities became workable. Was it worth it? The Tzdow say yes.

The transition from appendage cities to orbiting cities took six months. I was immersed in acclimation studies. I was at the peak of my abilities. Still, I nearly lost my mind when I made the jump.

A mind is a precious commodity. You can play all you like

with the way it plays, but there comes a time when you have a nightmare in daylight. The light of the sun turns into blood. Then you play the game with real money.

They bombarded me with information, insights, simulated wisdom. They gave me exactly the right amount of time to integrate what I was learning. They did it perfectly and made sure I knew that. But the day came when I couldn't stand anymore.

I began to flip from modality to modality. I used all the wings of cognition, all the arms and legs of my senses, but began thinking as I had as a child. I thought about the makers of the Matrix and the floaters. I remembered battlewagons, how information became the cornerstone of war, how the hive mind became target and weapon. Illusions crashed into illusions in halls of mirrors, then the mirrors shattered, shards on the floor of my trembling soul.

I thought I would find a point of reference from which to understand what I was supposed to be learning but couldn't. Then I dropped down to the next level, and the next, and the next, and at each it became clearer that they weren't kidding. This time they were going to drive me mad with cascading images that overwhelmed my efforts to understand. They did not want me to understand how the Tzdow had learned to construct their worlds. They wanted me to go crazy.

Something broke. Something shattered. Something came apart that would never again come together in the same way.

If one can sob hysterically in silence while the soul falls asunder, that's what I did. The wings of darkness ingathered my fragmented being and tore it away from whatever illusory center had held it together. The dissolution of my soul felt like lightning striking. I could not think because no one was there to think. I could not imagine because no one was there to imagine. I could not be clear because clarity dissolved into nothingness. When I reached into that nothingness, there was... nothing. Absolutely nothing.

Nor was I in freefall because I was not present to my own dissolution. Nothing was present. Nothing at all.

Then... a point of view ignited from which the event was observed. A point of view from which it could be seen. Said. Described, even. Then the portal opened and the Tzdow welcomed me to their orbiting cities.

I felt as if I were entering the landscape of a minimalist building. Curved white walls of an immense arc turned to either side. I looked for a guide, a mentor, an ambassador. No one showed.

I centered myself and extended into the environment. I attended to each of my senses in turn, mapping the landscape. The walls were so white they looked like plasmas generated by ships accelerating to lightspeed. I heard white noise in which as I listened I could discern a subtle rhythm. Pattern almost happened but not quite. I smelled nearly nothing, just atmosphere filtered and scrubbed. Felt walls which were smooth smooth smooth. Sampled the air. Spliced the non-sounds. Linked to the flow which meant I could crimp the multi-stranded tangled veins of a deeper organic structure of what had seemed to be merely a mechanical habitat.

The deeper organic structure fascinated, held my attention. Veins were like colored wires tangled in a pipe. The pulsing energy in them sounded like beating hearts but faintly, faintly. Heat generated by processes was cooled by invisible gases hung in luminous blue traps. From that fact I could infer the form of more elaborate processes under it all. Wetware and dryware were one, all of the processes merely a means of maintaining equilibrium, managing the entire system.

Walls floors and ceilings were alive with light.

Along the white curving wall I discerned suddenly – had it been there all the time? Or did it just appear? – a faint off-white line that traced a distant echo. It disappeared around the curve around the bend and I followed, keeping it in sight but not forgetting the other extensions. I was immersed, still astonished. I did not know. I calculated distance and duration, creeping along the wall.

All unknowing. White on white.

The off-white line either ended or grew too faint to make out. In the unvarying light, distinctions were difficult to make. But at my feet I saw an opening in the floor and without thinking, plunged into it head first.

What I saw as I fell was like the First Matrix raised to the Nth degree. The entire fabric of their universe had been simulated in miniature but a miniature, I suspected, that extended across the span of a galaxy. The scale of the enterprise was beyond comprehension.

Still I flowed through empty space until the tunnel became the entrance to a cave in the side of a mountain. The mountain was immense, the cave an opening into its side. I crawled into the cave or tunnel, feeling like a miner crawling on hands and knees, my path illuminated only by a dim light on my hat. The pathway twisted and I had no choice but to keep moving.

After a time, the tunnel glowed faintly with an outside source of light. I paused to get my bearings, making sure I was not imagining. I was not. The light grew brighter up ahead and I quickened my pace, the light growing brighter and brighter until I burst out in candescence like a welder's torch except it illuminated a vast cavern. The cavern was full of technology I did not understand and myriads of beings tending it with care. The machinery looked like the control room of an immense starship. Except everything was white, the doors opening onto the sources of energy were white, the white fire, the beings in white coveralls attending to duty with loving precision.

I moved through rooms harboring the technology of consciousness both aware and unaware of what I saw, felt, heard. The rooms went on and on but had an end. The deep structure was finite but unbounded. Another entrance appeared that was also an exit because one could go in either direction. I went through and exited the halls, emerging on the other side of the mountain. Instead of darkness, however, the night skies blazed with galaxies spiraling in pinwheel magnificence. I forgot for a moment to breathe. The glowing stars so dense they were like fire whitening the skies. The spirals of light echoing the matrix I had just traversed.

"This is how much you saw," said a voice. "Imagine a span from the center of the Andromeda Galaxy out to the four-fifth spiral on its distant edge. If that is the scale of the simulation, then you saw but seven inches."

I felt my mentor beside me and turned as he appeared. He wore an ancient cloak and hood in a humorous reference to the mythic dimensions my entrance into their city had elicited from my soul.

"The myth is your own projection," he said. "The city – well, you have not yet seen the city. That's why you will be here for four years, Earth equivalent. That's the bare minimum for beginning to understand how technologies of consciousness are manufactured and linked. We build floors under floors under floors in infinite regress toward the core of unknowing."

"I have started the tour, then."

"Oh yes. But unlike your other tenures, where you had more

and more to do, this one will require that you do less and less."

I laughed aloud.

"You begin to understand," he said. "You must explore and as you explore explore all of the means by which you explore. By which you see perceive and understand. You must see yourself seeing yourself seeing yourself. You must learn to discern subtle stirrings in the deep currents of consciousness. Minute perturbations in the background radiation that became everything. Then you will understand how and even why, perhaps, this city is alive."

"My destiny, then" I said, "is not to take action."

"No. And yes. You do not belong to the city of sentient beings. You belong to what once was called the city of god."

"But that's not cultural studies! That's theology!"

"Isn't everything?" he said. "All studies become studies of consciousness. The means of deceiving dissolve as the knowing mind comes to know itself. The proper study of self is Self. Except – as you study your self – it disappears."

"And...?

"You study what is left."

"But... nothing is left."

"Correct. Nothing. Absolutely nothing."

He took my arm gently and led me back into the halls of light.

"For the next four years," he said, "walk these halls. Nothing more. Walk slowly in a way that enables you to see. Then see, taking note of what you see."

He smiled and vanished into thin air.

The first eighteen months were spent learning to walk so I could forget that I was walking. Then I could pay attention. The next eighteen months were spent walking and seeing. Then I could forget that I was seeing. The last year was spent neither walking nor seeing. All the while walking. And seeing.

By the end of the fourth year, I glimpsed the relationship of organic materials to their sources. The sources of the sources, however, were elusive. No language enabled me to say what I saw when I glimpsed an intention that bootstrapped a point of reference out of nothing.

The rhythm of the cities became the rhythm of my body and brain. The cities calibrated my machinery to its own. I learned in four years what I had learned in the first month.

When I left, I was at last a beginner.

I imagined I would weep when I left but didn't. I was calm and happy and grateful. Four years were just right for the first term.

My three friends were in the street as I expected when I returned. "Hey! Alien Brain!" shouted the leader.

I walked up to face them and saw how they had aged. Their faces were ancient. Had I really been afraid when we first met? Did I really think they meant to harm me? These bearers of my destiny, builders of the ship of my soul?

I saw that they had done exactly as intended. They were not deficient in any way. They were perfect as they were. And seeing who they were, I loved them all.

We smiled at each other. We embraced and held one another tightly. We touched and hugged, twittered and danced. Then the three of them flowed, transparent to their purpose.

I watched them dissolve. Just like that, they disappeared into thin air.

Well... maybe they did not disappear, exactly.

To disappear, you have to be there in the first place.

Introduction to "The Last Science Fiction Story"

It's true, the breaking waves of the future – as we construct it inside our societal mind, inside our cultural frames - inundate the past and the future often happens now before the past, some of the eddies of the future, some of the backwaters of the past. But it helps to remember that nobody can surf all the waves, that eddies and backwaters, dragging us into the tide or sucking us back into the water like waves on a beach, hold all of us back or down in most domains while we see clearly only in a few selected others.

That's why the Masters can do what they do, breaking memory into bits.

We call geniuses those who surf two or three waves at a time and integrate their experiences in a true-life tale of a surf bum's life. That's not me. All I can do is document the end of time as it had been constructed in this little blip of historical fiction. If history is our myth, maybe this is a time of demythologizing. Maybe fiction is our myth, now, not history. And of course by "time" I don't mean time, whatever that might be. If exploring UFO phenomena for more than thirty years has taught me anything, it's that our lack of comprehension of what is happening is not about space. It's about time.

Yes. It's about time.

Isn't it?

The Last Science Fiction Story

Science fiction is how a left-brain society once dreamed of the future.

The dreams became real over long periods of time. Leonardo da Vinci dreamed of submersibles, flying machines, all kinds of crazy contraptions. One would guess that many of his contemporaries thought he was crazy. Think of a Neolithic genius trying to describe an automobile. The feedback loop from crazy to sane took a long time.

Humans are social animals. So civilization is a feedback machine. We build reality in the image of our dreams. As the project of civilization became distributed and more flattened, quicker feedback meant implementing more dreams in less time.

Several hundred years after da Vinci we fly and dive.

Going to the moon was quicker.

From the Earth to the Moon by Jules Verne. A pretty good book, dreamed up in the eighteen sixties. A hundred years later Neil Armstrong was dancing in moon dust, delivering sound bites.

Aldous Huxley dreamed of genetic engineering and social conditioning in *Brave New World* in 1932. Sixty years later we were hard at it. Call it propaganda, call it spin, call it perception management. Today people are trained to live inside belief collectives and we are learning to engineer and modify genetic traits, those that exist and those we invent. Breeding for success by going to expensive schools looks sloppy and haphazard compared to the precision of genetic engineering.

It took a hundred years to get to the moon. Sixty to create a brave new world.

Faster and faster the whirligig of time returns returns to dreamers who dream.

In the nineteen eighties, William Gibson defined cyberspace. Less than a decade later, we lived in it. Now we don't even notice, any more than we notice flying and diving and going to the moon and glowing fish and tomatoes that don't freeze.

First, the dream. Then, in shorter and shorter leaps or loops, came the reality.

Science fiction is how a left-brain society dreamed of the future.

Now that's done.

Dreams aren't over. The future is.

The future is past.

This is the last science fiction story ever.

The future went non-linear in 1973.

That was the year of the OPEC oil thing. Big companies like Shell were taken by surprise. They never saw it coming. They had to ask, why?

They had been thinking in straight lines. The present led to the future by one dotted line like a path through a courtyard. The task was to get there somehow from here. They called it management by objective and it seemed simple.

It was simple. Because there was only one future, the one we could extrapolate from what we knew was true.

Then we realized (a) we didn't know what was true and (b) we could not extrapolate bull-dippy.

So we invented scenario planning. Actually we borrowed it. It was used in military circles for a long time. It was a methodology the time of which had come.

It works like this: we may not know where we are, but we know we're here. What are the likely theres out there? We fanned hands of possible futures like playing cards. Three or four hands were plenty. Pick one, any one.

We asked ourselves, what has to happen for this or that to happen?

As futures emerged faster and faster from rapidly receding presents, we had to ask that question again and again, faster and faster.

Yep, you're ahead of me: feedback loops. That's correct.

We needed more and more frequent feedback loops to map what was happening now compared to what had just happened. That helped us guess which futures were likely to emerge.

It did not go unnoticed that we were manipulating information a lot like computers. There were lots of "if-this-then-that's" with logic gates AND OR and NOT between them.

The way we were thinking was how our machines were thinking. We built the machines but then the machines built simulated worlds in our minds to match.

Now there's so much feedback it's too big to manage. No, that's not quite right. There are too many feedback loops for the old machinery to manage. We needed new machinery.

And we got it. Or should I said we'll get it? Both. We got it.

And... we'll get it.

See, the problem is obvious, isn't it? As fast as we can dream or, more accurately, as fast as the human-machine symbiosis can dream, the thing is realized, if not in actual fact at least in a simulation. But the machine doesn't know the difference. And because we live inside the mind space made by the machine, we don't know the difference either. The symbiot dreams and the dream becomes real. Immediately.

It can even become a thing of the past before it is manifest in the present.

By the time *The Matrix* was made, everybody understood. It wasn't science fiction, just a metaphorical adventure. *Blade Runner* screened like history. It had already happened. The symbiot invents memories at all levels from perception to conception. The symbiot dreams and immediately believes the dream. The dream is reality before we wake up. Or say that the dream takes place at a slower pace than the implications of the dream, fed into a faster part of the symbiot brain before the dream has ended. Like a spell-checker finishing words for us. We're still typing "spellche –" but "spell-checker" is already on the monitor.

Some of our best dreams like getting lost and finding our way home are over.

We used to be able to get lost. It was exciting. Will it get dark before we get home? Will they find us? Will some animal eat us?

GPS killed that dream. Dreams predicated on being lost from Homer's *Odyssey* to Joyce's *Ulysses* are dreams of the past. The space into which we are all looking now is inside the sphere. Everybody can see anything they want.

This is why the soft stuff – humanities, history, theology – has broken down.

Deconstruction took apart the humanities and keeps on reducing whatever we find in any text to a lower level. It never ends. There is nothing more fundamental to find that is also more real. Whatever "real" means.

History ended when we began inventing myths and narratives to contain them. Need to know and compartmentalization finished the job. Humans live in different niches, swimming in narrative streams that do or don't connect with one another. We look at painted images on the gerbil tubes of our lives, thinking they're mirrors.

Anyway, how would anyone know? And who might that person be?

Theology? Don't make me laugh! Once we shake ourselves free of Greek or medieval models, it turns into modular fluid constructions that fly by like fractals animated by a fast processor. God is interactive, morphing like us.

OK, go back to that paragraph you just read beginning with GPS about being lost. "Lost" was a metaphor. For everything I am talking about. See? Shadows have vanished. Nighttime is over. There is bright light everywhere and those of us who have lived at the poles know that makes us giddy.

Think of the moon without a terminator. Night meets bright with no liminal zone, no borderland or portal. The magic of twilight has vanished.

I could go on, but what's the point? You get it, right? The flat earth fills with streams of feedback overflowing their banks. As soon as we dream of the future, trying to write science fiction, feedback loops capture our dreams and deliver them to the recent past. By the time we finish, the future is past. The symbiot anticipates the ending and fills in the blanks, getting there before the author.

Reality, that is, the information we call "reality," happens so fast from so many directions, so many flows, that it factors back into the mindstream and makes reality one more dream. By the time we wake up to that fact, it's already morning.

Real dreams, the ones that happen out there beyond our ability to sense or know, come after the fact, not before, like before.

Throw in non-local consciousness, using event horizons of black holes to move around the galaxy, listen to our designer progeny laughing at those who were merely born – what is there to write about? As fast as we put finger to keyboard or voice to conversion program, our visions are obsolete. Think up an original story, and guess what? You can find it in some anthology a decade or three ago. Or covert operations have already produced the miraculous shape-changing metals, remote viewers and Psi spies, multi-Manchurian candidates, anti-grav, you name it, they already made it and keep it hidden. Aliens have come and gone, everybody who looks at the evidence knows that, but so what? Contact is an empty set, a null set, as boring as UFOs on Mars, a couple of big orange beach balls bouncing down and delivering two little robots that crawl out and drill and transmit, squeaking like R2D2.

See what I mean? R2D2 in fact was squeaking like *them*. We just didn't know it yet.

Vanity of vanities, saith this writer. All is vanity. I am a silverback, ancient of days, and I know: in my entire life, every idea I have had, including the five or six that were terrific, had already been thought. Every single one. Some were in books, some in blogs. Some were footnotes, some mentioned casually over coffee. Originality no longer exists. Creativity might be real but it's an action in a collective and nobody can claim credit for anything any more.

Including this so-called work of science fiction. That "by-line" is a joke. As if all this came from an "individual" with a boundary around its brain!

Besides, there's not one original idea in this entire story.

Some of you will insist this isn't a story. It's not fiction. It's real, you will say. In fact, of course, you already said it. This dream, you said, is a string of obvious facts.

But then, that's the point, isn't it? When I began this story, short as it is, it was fiction. Now, just short of the end, it is not only fact, it is fact of the past. I can hear you saying, I know that. Everybody knows that.

That's how fast it happens.

Others, of course, think this *is* a fictional narrative but like most fiction, it's a dust devil on Mars whirling past fast. Now you think it, now you don't. I mean, think it through. What have I actually said? Nothing. Everything I mention – hard science like physics and biology, soft science like soc and psych, social roles, what it means to be human, alien visitation, time dilation – all of the themes of twenty-first century science fiction have already come and gone. This is the first century in history that lasted only five years. I don't think it's fair even to call it a century anymore.

So let's agree on one thing: Everything is over. The feedback machine is faster than we are. Individuals don't exist. Dreams come after reality, now, not before.

A left brain civilization has gone so far to the left we're right. The circle is complete. The fractal is self-similar at all levels. Goedel said it best: we can't even say we're here, doing this, except from some other place. But when we go there, there we are, all over again. There we all are, stuck once more. Inside a circle turned into a moebius strip.

There's just no escaping the bad news.

So do whatever you like with the rest of the story. Take the narrative anywhere you want. I don't care. Take the "I" or "we" or whatever it is, take it away or take it apart. The "I" telling this story is as insubstantial as smoke. So is the "we." So, dear reader, are "you."

It's all mist or haze or vapor or fog – they're all words from the built-in thesaurus anyhow, we all build with the same bricks –so watch the smoke that we were once upon a time drift out of the window and disperse in the wind, a colloidal mist that seems to vanish in the empty air but is there forever.

That's what happened to science fiction.

This is where or should I say when you found out.

And that, I'm afraid, is the end of the story.

Introduction to "SETI Triumphant"

This collection (almost) ends on a note of unmitigated joy. My son Aaron Ximm, noted technologist and sound artist, suggested the idea for this story when I was regaling him with tales of the dozens and dozens of rejections that come before a story is accepted.

OK, I said, I'll write it, you review it, and we'll submit it as a collaborative story.

So we did. It was accepted by *Analog Science Fiction Magazine* and published in real print.

Now, here's the funny bit. I published my very first story, "Pleasant Journey," which concludes this anthology, in *Analog* in 1963. I received $64 for it.

When this one was accepted, Aaron and I divided a check for $64 too.

Some things really don't change much, do they? Including the thrill of being published in partnership with your son.

That first story, "Pleasant Journey," is about a man immersed in virtual reality who doesn't want to leave his escape-space, written long before we called it that. I discovered the story in the Gutenberg Project online which said there was no longer any copyright on the tale. So I guess I can include my own story from 47 years ago (I was 18 when I wrote it) as a forecast... of the past.

SETI Triumphant

By Richard Thieme and Aaron Ximm

We have been sending signals, one way or another, for centuries, and listening for a reply, thanks to the creaking machinery of that ancient looking-for-a-message-in-a-bottle process we affectionately call SETI.

Never mind that earth cultures long ago abandoned radio waves and adopted lower-register gravity waves for near-instantaneous transmissions to near-star systems.

And never mind that only a few hobbyists know how to build radios.

And never mind that our tidily-wink style of exploring neighboring systems has turned up nothing but rudimentary life forms.

Never mind all that. Religious rituals die hard even in our enlightened times and radio-band SETI searches are definitely a religious ritual. Custodians of the project, spending the accrued interest from an endowment that has grown bloated, are dug in and locked down.

So radio signal sending has continued for centuries because we had the means, the method, and the opportunity.

I don't think anyone really expected to hear anything back. Even diehard SETIsts greeted the announcement with disbelief.

One can announce the second coming only so many times before true believers stop selling their furniture and heading for the hilltops. Yes, maybe the Prophet is right, one learns to say, but... let's wait and see.

This time, however, it happened. The design of dashes and dots was undeniable. Not in clouds of glory had the extraterrestrial message come but as coherent digital signals enclosed in code wrappers.

Those wrappers were tough to detach. They consisted of braided twists of alien symbols, hundreds of them, interlocking in complex patterns, and it took a massive cracking consortium using Monolith Links in four systems to distinguish the meaningless (to us) hieroglyphics of the alien race from the lucid Chingleese that remained when the wrappers were removed.

The message was distressingly clear.

So we now have a bona fide response to all those messages in all those bottles. But which one did they receive? To which of our many communications do they refer?

Hence this broadcast to all human-cyborg-kind-and-kin in near systems. If any of you has so much as a clue how we might respond, please transmit to Central Station immediately.

The problem is not trivial. Our forebears transmitted millions of ancient and modern messages from "Hello, Rainey," to weekly installments of WormHole Runners of HyperSpace. We have transmitted on all frequencies, broadcasting in all directions around the spherical bandwidth shell. We have sent the silliest giggles and the most profound insights.

We have sent, alas, everything.

The received message was clearly a response to one of those transmissions. But which one?

WHICH ONE?

We must redress the aliens' error in judgment. We are a diverse multi-talented species with many variations. We are a bell-curve of modified life-forms, not a simple species that was merely born. Yet we can't just transmit,

Dear Allegedly Superior Species,

Thank you for your reply. However, to which transmission do you refer?

Perhaps another might be more suitable? Something funnier, perhaps? Or shorter?

Sincerely,
Human-Cyborg-Kind (and kin)

No, that won't work. It would take forever to get an answer back, if they answer at all. I can imagine the blue-tipped tentacle of some clueless intern wiping out our message, oblivious to the implications.

So SETI may be nothing but a monument to the foolish optimism of human-cyborg-kind. At least the sentient life in our little neighborhood can have a good laugh before shooting itself in its collective head with a gun that flaps *BANG!* on a drop-stick.

Enough preamble. Here, dear kind and kin, is the unanticipated climax of SETI:

Dear Human-cyborg-kind,

Thank you very much for your transmission. A majority of systems in the universe have now had time to review it and we believe that you show promise. Even the Blander-gsst-thupfft!

agreed, and they seldom respond positively to any unsolicited transmission (they stamp "we have heard this before" on every one; given their age, maybe they have.)

While your transmission does suggest a certain quirky creativity, unfortunately you do not meet our current needs. There is, in addition, a backlog of species of your type in the universe, so we will not be reviewing transmissions from your sort for an indefinite period. Please listen to this frequency to learn if this policy changes. Policies are reviewed once every galeemp.

This negative response is in no way a comment on your planetary systems or the life-forms they have produced.

Although we would like to reply to each and every transmission, please understand that with millions of systems broadcasting in thousands of media 4889999955677000-seven, an individual response is impossible.

Perhaps a (very young) parallel universe would find your transmission suitable. I believe the Dirnsa are looking for a pet so you might try the umpteenth bubble in the thirieth froth. If you do transmit to a universe less than six billion years old, however, remember to include return-energy-bands to ensure a response.

Sincerely,
Lem-Lem-Three-bang)!, (designated receiver of unsolicited Flotsam, Jetsam, Detritus and Fluff)

On behalf of HelllenWuline and Associates, (nested at the seventeenth level of the HoHo Reception Group and interim assistant to the seventh sub-Intern's fourteenth aide)

Pleasant Journey

It's nice to go on a pleasant journey. There is, however, a very difficult question concerning the other half of the ticket....

"What do you call it?" the buyer asked Jenkins.

"I named it 'Journey Home' but you can think up a better name for it if you want. I'll guarantee that it sells, though. There's nothing like it on any midway."

"I'd like to try it out first, of course," Allenby said. "Star-Time uses only the very best, you know."

"Yes, I know," Jenkins said. He had heard the line before, from almost every carnival buyer to whom he had sold. He did not do much business with the carnivals; there weren't enough to keep him busy with large or worthwhile rides and features. The amusement parks of the big cities were usually the best markets.

Allenby warily eyed the entrance, a room fashioned from a side-show booth. A rough red curtain concealed the inside. Over the doorway, in crude dark blue paint, was lettered, "Journey Home." Behind the doorway was a large barn-like structure, newly painted white, where Jenkins did his planning, his building, and his finishing. When he sold a new ride it was either transported from inside the building through the large, pull-away doors in back or taken apart piece by piece and shipped to the park or carny that bought it.

"Six thousand's a lot of money," the buyer said.

"Just try it," Jenkins told him.

The buyer shrugged. "O.K.," he said. "Let's go in."

They walked through the red curtain. Inside the booth-entrance was a soft-cushioned easy-chair, also red, secured firmly in place. It was a piece of salvage from a two-engine commercial airplane. A helmet looking like a Flash Gordon accessory-hair drier combination was set over it. Jenkins flipped a switch and the room became bright with light. "I thought you said this wasn't a thrill ride," Allenby said, looking at the helmet-like structure ominously hanging over the chair.

"It isn't," Jenkins said, smiling. "Sit down." He strapped the buyer into place in the chair.

"Hey, wait a minute," Allenby protested. "Why the straps?"

"Leave everything to me and don't worry," Jenkins said, fitting the headgear into place over the buyer's head. The back of it fitted easily over the entire rear of the skull, down to his neck. The front came just below the eyes. After turning the light off, Jenkins pulled the curtain closed. It was completely black inside.

"Have a nice trip," Jenkins said, pulling a switch on the wall and pushing a button on the back of the chair at the same time.

Currents shifted and repatterned themselves inside the helmet and were fed into Allenby at the base of his skull, at the medulla. The currents of alternating ions mixed with the currents of his varied and random brain waves, and the impulses of one became the impulses of the other.

Allenby jerked once with the initial shock and was then still, his mind and body fused with the pulsating currents of the chair.

Suddenly, Roger Allenby was almost blinded by bright, naked light.

Allenby's first impression was one of disappointment at the failure of the device. Jenkins was reliable, usually, and hadn't come up with a fluke yet.

Allenby got out of the chair and called for Jenkins, holding on to the arm of the chair to keep his bearings. "Hey! Where are you? Jenkins!" He tried to look around him but the bright, intense light revealed nothing. He swore to himself, extending his arms in front of him for something to grasp. As he groped for a solid, the light became more subdued and shifted from white into a light, pleasant blue.

Shapes and forms rearranged themselves in front of him and gradually became distinguishable. He was in a city, or on top of a city. A panoramic view was before him and he saw the creations of human beings, obviously, but a culture far removed from his. A slight path of white began at his feet and expanded as it fell slightly, ramp-like, over and into the city. The buildings were whiter than the gate of false dreams that Penelope sung of and the streets and avenues were blue, not gray.

The people wore white and milled about in the streets below him. They shouted as one; their voices were not cries but songs and they sang his name.

He started walking on the white strip. It was flexible and supported his weight easily. Then he was running, finding his breath coming in sharp gasps and he was among the crowds. They smiled at him as he passed by and held out their hands to him. Their faces shone with a brilliance of awareness and he knew that they loved him. Troubled, frightened, he kept running, blindly, and, abruptly, there were no people, no buildings.

He was walking now, at the left side of a modern super-highway, against the traffic. Autos sped by him, too quickly for him to determine the year of model. Across the divider the traffic was heavier, autos speeding crazily ahead in the direction he was walking; none stopped. He halted for a moment and looked around him. There was nothing on the sides of the road: no people, no fields, no farms, no cities, no blackness. There was nothing. But far ahead there was green etched around the horizon as the road dipped and the cars sped over it. He walked more quickly, catching his breath, and came closer and closer to the green.

Allenby stopped momentarily and turned around, looking at the highway that was behind him. It was gone. Only bleak, black and gray hills of rock and rubble were there, no cars, no life. He shuddered and continued on toward the end of the highway. The green blended in with the blue of the sky now. Closer he came, until just over the next rise in the road the green was bright. Not knowing or caring why, he was filled with expectation and he ran again and was in the meadow.

All around him were the greens of the grasses and leaves and the yellows and blues of the field flowers. It was warm, a spring day, with none of the discomfort of summer heat. Jubilant, Roger spun around in circles, inhaling the fragrance of the field, listening to the hum of insect life stirring back to awareness after a season of inactivity. Then he was running and tumbling, barefoot, his shirt open, feeling the soft grass give way underfoot and the soil was good and rich beneath him.

He saw a stream ahead, with clear water melodiously flowing

by him. He went to it and drank, the cold, good water quenching all his thirst, clearing all the stickiness of his throat and mind. He dashed the water on his face and was happy and felt the coolness of it as the breeze picked up and swept his hair over his forehead. With a shake of his head he tossed it back in place and ran again, feeling the air rush into his lungs with coolness and vibrance unknown since adolescence. No nicotine spasms choked him and the air was refreshing.

Then up the hill he sped, pushing hard, as the marigolds and dandelions parted before him. At the top he stopped and looked and smiled ecstatically as he saw the green rolling land and the stream, curving around from behind the house, his house, the oaks forming a secret lair behind it, and he felt the youth of the world in his lungs and under his feet. He heard the voice calling from that house, his house, calling him to Saturday lunch.

"I'm coming!" he cried happily and was tumbling down the hill, rolling over and over, the hill and ground and sky blending blues and greens and nothing had perspective. The world was spinning and everything was black again. He shook his head to clear the dizziness.

"Well?" Jenkins said. "How was it?"

Allenby looked up at him as Jenkins swung the helmet back and unhooked the seatbelt. He squinted as Jenkins flipped the light switch and the brightness hit him.

His surroundings became distinguishable again very slowly and he knew he was back in the room. "Where was I?" he asked.

Jenkins shrugged. "I don't know. It was all yours. You went wherever you wanted to go, wherever home is." Jenkins smiled down at him. "Did you visit more than one place?" he asked. The buyer nodded. "I thought so. It seems that a person tries a few before finally deciding where to go."

The buyer stood up and stretched. "Could I please see the barn?" he asked, meaning the huge workshop where Jenkins did the construction work.

"Sure," Jenkins said and opened the door opposite the red curtain into the workshop. It was empty.

"You mean it was all up here? I didn't move at all?" He tapped his cranium with his index finger.

"That's right," Jenkins said anxiously. "Do you want it or not?"

Allenby stood looking into the empty room. "Yes... yes, of course," he said. "How long did the whole thing last?"

"About ten seconds," Jenkins said, looking at his watch. "It seems much longer to the traveler. I'm not sure, but I think the imagined time varies with each person. It's always around ten seconds of actual time, though, so you can make a lot of money on it, even if you only have one machine."

"Money?" Allenby said. "Money, yes, of course." He took a checkbook from his inside pocket and hurriedly wrote a check for six thousand dollars. "When can we have it delivered?" he asked.

"You want it shipped the usual way?"

"No," Allenby said, staring at the red-cushioned chair. "Send it air freight. Then bill us for the expense."

"Whatever you say," Jenkins said, smiling, taking the check. "You'll have it by the first of the week, probably. I'll put a complete parts and assembly manual inside the crate."

"Good, good. But maybe I should test it again, you know. Star-Time can't really afford to make a mistake as expensive as this."

"No," Jenkins said quickly. Then, "I'll guarantee it, of course. If it doesn't work out, I'll give you a full refund. But don't try it again, today. Don't let anyone have it more than once in one day. Stamp them on the hand or something when they take the trip."

"Why?"

Jenkins looked troubled. "I'm not sure, but people might not want to come back. Too many times in a row and they might be able to stay there... in their minds of course."

"Of course, of course. Well, it's been a pleasure doing business with you, Mr. Jenkins. I hope to see you again soon." They walked back to Allenby's car and shook hands. Allenby drove away.

On the way back to the hotel, and as he lay for a long time in the bathtub, letting the warmth drift away from the water, the thought ran over and over in his mind. *They might be able to stay there,* Allenby said to himself. They might be able to stay there. He smiled warmly at a crack in the plaster as he thought of the first of the week and the fragrant meadow.

About the Author

Richard Thieme has used his skills as a writer and speaker his whole life. Born in Chicago, Illinois, Richard taught literature and writing at the University of Illinois, was an Episcopal priest for sixteen years, and has traveled the world as a professional speaker, thrilling and enlightening audiences from Berlin to Brisbane, Amsterdam to Auckland, on the impact of technology on human identity, spirituality/religion, security and intelligence; on creativity and managing change; and further afield, on biohacking, "UFOlogy 101," and likely but disquieting futures.

His pre-blog column, "Islands in the Clickstream," was published internationally and distributed to thousands of subscribers in sixty countries before collection as a book by Syngress Publishing, a division of Elsevier, in 2004. His work has been taught at universities in Europe, Australia, Canada, and the United States. He lives with his wife, Shirley, in Fox Point, Wisconsin and can be reached at www.thiemeworks.com.

About the Illustrator

Over the last two decades, Duncan Long has created over a thousand illustrations for *Asimov's Science Fiction Magazine,* HarperCollins, PS Publishing, Pocket Books, Solomon Press, Paladin Press, American Media, Fort Ross, Lyons Press, and many small publishers.

Long often does graphic design/layout work, sometimes even producing a new typeface for a publication. He has also written four science fiction novels published by HarperCollins (the *Spider Worlds* trilogy) and Avon Books (*Antigrav Unlimited*).

View Long's artwork at www.duncanlong.com.